To John Jill

God bless you all + thanks for the support

Cheers!

THE
BORDER

[signature]
June '07

This is dedicated to my wife Brenda, my daughter Vicky and my son Guy.
Thank you for your continued patience and devotion.

Published in 2007 by 30° South Publishers (Pty) Ltd.
28, 9th Street, Newlands,
Johannesburg, South Africa 2092
www.30degreessouth.co.za

Copyright © AJ Brooks, 2007

Design and origination by 30° South Publishers (Pty) Ltd.
Butterfly image on cover by pdphoto.org

Printed and bound by Pinetown Printers (Pty) Ltd.

All rights reserved. No part of this publication may be reproduced, stored, manipulated in any retrieval system, or transmitted in any mechanical, electronic form or by any other means, without the prior written authority of the publishers. Any person who engages in any unauthorized activity in relation to this publication shall be liable to criminal prosecution and claims for civil and criminal damages.

Set in Aldine401 9.5/15

ISBN 978-1-920143-10-7

THE BORDER

AJ Brooks

PROLOGUE

"Ondangwa tower, Hotel Five Two Quebec, request taxi clearance."

"Cleared to runway zero eight for take-off."

Two Puma helicopters rolled down the runway and lifted off into the starlit sky, their cargo a motley crew of soldiers, each armed with an AK-47 assault rifle. No rank or insignia identified them as they sat around the ferry tank fitted to the centre of the load bay. They leant back, nonchalant, their *mochila* backpacks full and heavy. The wind and jet noise engulfed them through the open cargo doors and forbade any conversation.

The heat of day still lingered but the buffeting from the disc above and the passing wind cooled them as they sat, each with his thoughts. Their blacked-up faces exaggerated the size of their eyes, some of whom blinked owl-like in the darkness. It hid the hardness of their faces and their determined look, for these were soldiers of the most elite and secretive One Reconnaissance Commando. The pilot set a heading for the helipad at Rundu and they settled down for the flight.

The commander took long hurried strides back to the waiting helicopters, pursed his lips and waved a leaflet of paper at his colleague.

"Jamba," he said.

The co-pilot nodded. It was as expected.

Jamba. The name left the pilot feeling cold and he shivered. It was the Unita headquarters and Jonas Savimbi's stronghold in southern Angola. From there Savimbi directed one of the most nefarious civil wars in Africa. Comrades in arms with the South Africans he may be, but he was no saint and the two regimes tolerated each other purely out of mutual benefit.

"Same as usual?" asked the pilot and he cringed at the sight before him. The Unita soldier's hair was thick and matted, his uniform tattered and threadbare and he smelt like an old dog's breath.

"Yes." His face was deadpan and he smiled suddenly, a rotten-toothed smile, but his eyes remained evil and suspicious. He handed a piece of paper to the pilot. Surprisingly, the co-ordinates were written in a neat hand.

The helicopters buffeted the bush headquarters and disappeared into the blackness as the pilot guided the machine onto the new heading. Soon the first dull glow alerted them.

Flying at about one hundred and fifty feet and to the right of the signal, the pilot looked down from his seat of command at the roaring fire below and flipped his intercom switch.

"Jesus! Do you think they'll ever learn ...?"

His co-pilot adjusted his microphone so that it touched his lips and spoke. "Damn right! That's hardly a signal fire, it's a ruddy bonfire?"

They continued on their given heading, passing the fires one by one until the co-pilot pointed. They had reached the sixth fire.

"How's that for bush telegraph, eh boyo?"

The pilot shook his head in wonder as he noticed the little pencil flare shoot up and pop brightly in the night sky. He banked left, pulled up on the collective, touched left rudder, adjusted the cyclic slightly and executed a perfect night landing.

"Shit, we're in the middle of the Angolan nowhere. I certainly don't envy these bastards."

Lieutenant 'Jakes' Jacobs ran lithely through the bush until his group was well away from the landing site and the clatter of the Puma blades had faded completely. Of the seven Unita troops waiting near the signal fire, two ran over and joined the South Africans. The small group squatted around Jakes' map, illuminated by the mini Mag-Light held between his teeth. All of them wore Fapla fatigues, the adopted uniform of Swapo's army.

Jakes stood at last and pointed. "That way gents, let's get on with it."

They moved fast that night. As the outline of the thickening bush became visible, Jakes held up a clenched fist and the soldiers disappeared. They rested for the day and when the setting sun painted the diaphanous clouds a light sanguine, Jakes lead his men to the objective.

In the pale dawn of the second morning Jakes held up a fist and the stick of men froze.

"We're here," he whispered.

"Already?"

Jakes nodded and retrieved the map from his breast pocket.

"We need to get here, here and ... here." Jakes pointed a blackened finger at the map. "Chummy, you with me, the rest, form ground defence—let's go."

The men spread out and disappeared into the grass as Jakes shimmied up the rough bark. Achingly slowly he parted the branches in front of him, lifted the binoculars and scanned the area. Somewhere ahead a twig snapped. Jakes froze. Above the screech of the cicadas he could hear the blood thumping in his ears. A Swapo cadre ambled into the clearing before Jakes' tree. The terrorist yawned widely, came to a halt directly below Jakes, unbuttoned his fly and began to urinate. He hefted his AK higher up his shoulder, farted loudly and looked up. Jakes could feel the sweat run down his back. The man's eyes seemed to bore into his and Jakes felt every fibre of his being stiffen in readiness to explode into action. The terrorist suddenly turned away and mumbled something. A second man stepped into the clearing and laughed. Together the khaki-clad figures strolled back into the bush. Jakes exhaled slowly, raised the binoculars and continued his reconnaissance.

At dusk they hid their *mochilas* and waited for the darkness to envelope them. Jakes peered at the sentry for over a minute until he was completely satisfied. Almost imperceptibly the man's shoulders rose and fell in a steady rhythm. It was one of the fundamentals of his business; the Recces counted on the enemy's amorphous structure.

Don't be too bloody cocksure Jacobs, he thought as he slithered past the sleeping form. A few metres further Jakes flattened as the half moon delivered the mottled shape of a gun placement. He took a notebook from his trouser pocket, screwed up his eyes and began to sketch—14.5mm he scribbled and circled the figures. Material brushed against grass and Jakes stopped breathing. The sound came from his rear and a figure passed within a metre of him. The soldier sniffed, turned towards Jakes and spat. Jakes closed his eyes and waited. Silence. He looked up and the man was gone! Impossible! Where was he? Jakes groped his way towards the gun. He was about to drag his way past the placement when the ground beneath him disappeared. Jakes lunged for the corner of the hole, latched on to a handful of grass and roots. Clods of earth rained down into the gaping black maw and a dampened voice floated up out of the hole. Jakes quickly rolled to his side and stood. With heart pounding he fought the urge to run. He strolled through the darkness to a large tree past the gun emplacement and flattened himself against the bark on the far side. He swallowed hard and felt sweat soak his shirt. *They've dug bunkers next to the gun*, he thought. *That's new! A gun crew on tap!* He clutched his AK and waited. A murmur of voices emanated from the bunker and someone laughed. He exhaled, wiped his brow on his sleeve and continued.

Before dawn, Jakes sat in a thicket at the RV and waited for the others. In total silence and like wraiths they returned and Jakes scribbled their findings into his little black book. The tension had been draining and sleep came easily to the infiltrators.

That night they set off for the second objective. Using the Southern Cross constellation to steer them, Jakes walked his men hard.

For days the clouds had been building. They massed for a final assault upon the thirsty earth before the autumn and the long dry season, only to dissipate again at night. Jakes set a gruelling pace and with alarming suddenness the guiding light from the firmament was cut off. The wind howled through the trees, throwing up a barrage of dust and leaves while the clouds blotted out the light. Jakes lifted his arm in front of his face to protect his eyes, called a halt and prepared for the storm as the lightning danced about overhead, illuminating their black faces to ghostly silver. The thunder crashed and boomed in reply.

Without warning and with amazing violence, the wind drove the rain in sheets around them. For over an hour the storm assaulted the baked earth. At first the soil drank greedily but eventually the water began to pond and then flow past their feet. The storm finally subsided to a steady downpour and then to a light drizzle. The clouds lifted, the rain abated and a fine mist shrouded them in the gentle grey light of dawn. Jakes took the opportunity to put some distance behind them and they walked on into the dripping, thickly misted bush.

Time passed and the line-of-sight distance lengthened as the mist lifted. Suddenly, all about them were eerie shapes of people floating around like ghostly apparitions, their sound muted by the wetness and mist. Jakes stopped, windmilling his arms at the lip of a trench guarded by a young boy dressed in faded khaki and armed with an AK. The boy looked up at what he thought was a drenched Swapo officer and, remembering his discipline, quickly stood to attention, looked straight ahead and said something in Portuguese. Jakes seized the opportunity and dropped into the trench behind the boy.

The boy opened his mouth to speak and Jakes' arm slid around his throat. The boy began to struggle and stiffened as a blade slid between his ribs. He issued a stifled grunt and slumped to the floor. The ghosts faded quickly into the lifting mist.

They hurriedly retraced their steps, bypassing other shadows, weapons held ready for fire a fight ... for survival. They walked south until the last of the mist burned off and the sun baked the wet earth to a sauna. Once well away from the enemy camp, Jakes found a small forest of acacias partially surrounded by thick bush. He removed his heavy pack, sat down and opened a can of food.

"Shit, that was too close," he said. "We walked right into a bloody hornet's nest and walked right out again."

"What the hell was that?" asked Chummy.

"A third bloody camp, that's what that was," said Jakes around a mouthful of beans. "Plumb between Mulemba and Chifufua."

"But there wasn't even a hint ..."

"Exactly," said Jakes as he scooped the last mouthful of beans into his mouth. "That's why we're here."

The sun set red on the horizon. The evening was clear from the morning rains and the smell of damp earth still strong as the evening star brightened with the onset of night. As the last smudge of purple disappeared from the rim of the cloud base, Jakes and his ghosts floated through the bush towards the enemy position. The camp was huge and well spread out, making any form of surprise attack almost impossible. Its position was easy to mark on the map as it lay concealed in the thick bush adjacent to a large *shona*.

"I don't see any water. It must be open at one end." Jakes tried again with the binoculars. "Anyone see any water?" he murmured as he peered through the lenses in the fading light.

Chummy shook his head, "One good thing about it Jakes …"

"Yeah?"

"This *shona* is so bloody big you can hardly miss it."

"True …" Jakes nodded and spun around as the crackle of AK fire shattered the still night air. The Recces dropped to the ground, weapons held ready. Raised voices. A shout. Two more shouts and an urgent riposte much closer. Something tugged at Jakes' sleeve and he leapt to his left, brought his weapon to bear and exhaled as he recognised one of the Unita soldiers.

"You shouldn't do that," he whispered, his finger white on the trigger.

The Unita soldier held up his hand, his eyes wide. "We must go. They have found the boy and our spoor."

Jakes stood slowly and scrutinised the darkness. "Are you sure?"

"I heard them. That was the shout, they have our spoor, and they are coming."

Jakes looked around at his men and frowned. He was incredulous. "It's pitch black. How the hell are they going to follow our spoor in the middle of the bloody night? They don't have any goddamned dogs do they?"

The Unita soldier held the malevolent stare of the South African. "This is the camp of Grootvoet. He has powers and can see in the darkness. He will follow us with ease."

"Bullshit!" exploded Jakes. "That's utter bullshit! Grootvoet is just another bloody Swapo terrorist whose reputation has been blown out of all proportion! Frankly I don't think he even exists!"

"We have been looking for his camp for a long time. He exists and he is coming. We must go now!" The Unita soldier was clearly agitated.

"Oh, we're going alright, but purely because this operation has been compromised by the discovery of the boy, no other reason." Jakes shook his head. "Grootvoet!" he spat. "Chummy, we're going to have to leave our recce on Chifufua for a rainy day."

"Probably a good thing," said the commando. "Look."

Jakes followed Chummy's gaze. In the furthest reaches of the night a glow of fiery torches bobbed and they were heading directly along the route Jakes and his men had travelled earlier.

"Okay, we have a head start; they still have to find where we doubled back." Jakes turned to Chummy. "Call the giant. Tell them RV 2, dawn two days." For the first time a tendril of anxiety weaved its way through the pit of his stomach. *How the hell could they follow us at night-time*, he thought.

All night they ran and into the oppressive heat of day, resting only briefly to take in some water and to confuse the trail with anti-tracking, but all the time Jakes knew the enemy were near. At last they reached the river. The men were exhausted, but still Jakes chivvied them on.

"About ten clicks up there should be a bend in the river. Our RV is just beyond that," he said.

The soldiers walked up the shallow river and in the dim light of dawn the river turned north. Some way to the west a small rock outcrop marked the RV. It was one of the very few features in an otherwise featureless flat land. It was too obvious, but there was no other option. The men melted into the bush and formed an all-round defence. All they could do now was wait and all the time the enemy closed in.

Sweat trickled down Jakes' blackened face and clung to his beard. The tension was a physical thing and Chummy cocked his head. Jakes frowned and Chummy nodded.

"Choppers. I'll have to give them some smoke."

"Just do it. If it's gonna start it'll be now."

Jakes peered through the bush to where he thought the attack would come. Two Pumas banked hard overhead and put down in a grassy clearing beyond the outcrop. The leaves above Jakes' head flipped and danced as if being pelted by a hailstorm. Jakes saw the movement out the corner of his eye and realised that the terrorists had waited for Pumas. Even with the noise of the helicopters he heard the whips and cracks above his head. Jakes was incredulous. *Jesus! They stayed right with us*, he thought.

"Swaps three o'clock! Fire and movement! Let's get the hell out of here!" The soldiers used the leapfrog tactic, covering each other as they moved to the helicopters. One of the Unita soldiers went down and Chummy reached for him. As if buffeted by a violent storm Chummy danced back, staggered and fell as the bullets thumped into him.

"No! Oh no!" Jakes wailed. "Cover me! Cover me you bastards!" He launched his *mochila* and rifle toward the helicopter and hauled Chummy up by his arm. Chummy was bleeding from half a dozen wounds and Jakes used every ounce of his strength to lift his large colleague and friend onto his shoulders. He ran awkwardly under the burden, with bullets kicking up sand about his feet, hunting him. Steadfast hands hauled Chummy aboard. The AKs around him chattered in response. A Swapo soldier went down and another. The pilots wasted no time and the big machines lifted into the hazy sky. Tracer fire whipped up at them and the Recces fired back, their superior training coming to the fore as the terrorists dropped. Finally the terrorists broke and ran, diving to the most meagre of cover. All of them—all but one who seemed unfazed by the volume of fire being directed at him. He was a tall, athletic man; very black, very powerful and, even over the ever-increasing distance between them, Jakes was sure he could feel an aura of evil about the man. He felt a tug on his sleeve and turned. The surviving Unita soldier pointed to the figure.

"Grootvoet," he said and smiled.

CHAPTER 1

There was an odd combination of anxiety and reluctant anticipation prevalent among the new troops as they made final preparations. Their dismay was evident as the section leader discarded most of the food-carrying compartments and altered the webbing to carry at least seven water bottles and as many magazines. The harsh reality of Ovamboland thwarted the infantry school's textbook for this was war ... war in a thirsty land.

Corporal Geoffrey Kent pursed his lips. His nostrils flared white at the edges and he tossed the webbing to his troops. "Come now. You girls are big enough to sort out a gippo webbing yourselves." Geoff bent and peered into the next tent. The muscles in his jaw worked. "Rudi, where the hell is Dawid?" Geoff was blessed with height and width. Sporting a number two haircut—his blond hair, penetrating grey-blue eyes and granite face betrayed the youth the war had partially robbed him of.

"I think he's in the mess," answered Rudi vaguely. He was bent over his radios. Geoff walked out of the double-roofed tent into the blazing, late-afternoon sunlight and jogged lightly through the lines of tents to the troops' mess. He stopped immediately as he entered. Lance-Corporal Dawid Gouws stood at the far end with his head thrown back, a beer can to his lips and his Adam's apple bobbing up and down. The troops at his table encouraged him in a raucous chorus of 'down-down'.

Geoff felt anger displace irritability and his voice boomed across the smoky mess. "Gouws, to your tent now! You and I have something to discuss!"

To this day Geoff questioned his decision to choose Dawid as his MAG gunner. Dawid was as tall as Geoff, powerfully built and a ruthless soldier who had rescued the section more than once through sheer guts, stamina and his acute hatred of his black enemy. But he also hated the English-speaking South Africans, especially if they out-ranked him as Geoff did. He slammed the empty tin down on the aluminium table, making as big a show of his annoyance as he could and leered bleary-eyed at Geoff who had already turned for the showers ... Simply, though, Geoff needed him.

After showering, Geoff pulled on a clean pair of issue black PT shorts, a clean vest, slipped on his sandals and walked from the ablution block to the line of tents where the veterans lived. Most of the chaps greeted him with a smile as Geoff walked in to Dawid's tent. Geoff was born with the gift of leadership, but at that moment this attribute let him down. He grabbed Dawid by the front of his faded brown shirt, hauled him off the bed until their faces nearly touched and spoke through clenched teeth.

"Dawid, throw that beer away and start your preparations right now and that's an order. Final order group is at oh-four-hundred tomorrow and we leave at oh-four-thirty and if you run out of water because of your hangover I'll leave you to Swapo, do you understand me?" Geoff's voice was a fervent whisper and his finely muscled arms trembled with a mixture of effort and anger. Dawid's arms windmilled as his boots scraped across the ground. Although most of his section were veterans with dozens of contacts behind them, Geoff had lost no man and didn't need Dawid to spoil that record now, especially with unblooded raw troops marching with them tomorrow.

Tomorrow, he thought ... *Tomorrow*. The nerves in his stomach tightened at the thought and he realised that he desperately needed complete rest from the constant edginess he felt from so many patrols. Sickened by all the violence he'd endured and this pathetic and emotional conflict between him and Dawid, Geoff let go suddenly and walked out the tent. His mind raced. There was still so much to do.

A shout from someone, somewhere, warned him.

Almost too late Geoff spun around to the rush of army boot on unforgiving sand behind him and felt the sting of cold metal grazing his ribs. The wind was driven from him as Dawid ran into him with the force of an enraged bull, his face a mask of contorted hatred. Both men crashed to the ground and instinctively Geoff lashed out with a powerful right and caught Dawid in the throat. The blow knocked him off balance. They were on their feet in an instant and it was only then, as they circled each other, the crowd gathering, that Geoff noticed the bayonet held low in Dawid's fist. Geoff lifted his hand to his ribs and felt it come away sticky with blood.

He lost his temper. He ran forward, grabbed Dawid's right wrist in a vice grip with his left hand and lifted his knee into Dawid's crotch, head-butting him squarely on the nose. Dawid's head shot back leaving an arc of blood in its path. He fell against the cabled guy rope, which served to steady him, and launched himself into a counter-attack. Geoff knew he had to act fast. Dawid was bigger and stronger and this ebullition was his nature. Dawid wiped the tears from his eyes and bulldozed forward. Geoff took the opportunity to dive to the ground and scoop up Dawid's ankles. His momentum carried him over Geoff, who lifted his attacker's booted feet high in the tackle causing Dawid to flail the air for balance. Dawid landed hard on the side of his face and shoulder, losing the bayonet in the process. They wrestled, each trying desperately to gain control. Just as Dawid's superior size, strength and weight started to give him the advantage, they were roughly dragged apart. A few of the troops stood back panting and watched intently, ready to dive in should the sparks, fanned by the winds of hatred, glow and ignite once more. The adversaries dusted themselves off and eyed each other like pit bulls in the ring.

Standing stiffly to attention in front of the Regimental Sergeant-Major, Geoff felt uncomfortable as he had to make an important decision and quickly. Either he had to report the bayonet stabbing and see Dawid taken off to detention barracks, which every fibre of Geoff's being urged him to do, or not mention it and keep Dawid in his team and on his side.

The RSM looked up and let them stand like that for a moment. "Okay, at ease, *manne*. Tell me the story." Both men started talking and gesticulating together. The RSM leant back slowly, held up his hands and shook his head. "*Kom manne*, one at a time. Let's hear your side first Kent."

"Why him first?" demanded Dawid.

The RSM straightened up suddenly, leant forward on his knuckles and glared at Dawid. At that range Dawid couldn't help notice how scarred the sergeant-major's face was and he paled as he realised that the bar-brawling reputation of the RSM was probably never embellished.

"Because if you had any brains, Gouws, you would be the section leader here, not this bleddy *Engelsman*, but you are too bleddy big for your boots so shut up!" he roared. "Carry on Kent!"

"Well, sergeant-major, it's simple. Gouws is drunk, we are going on patrol tomorrow and I need his help, especially with the new troops. I told him as much and he attacked me in the lines in front of the troops."

"Without provocation?" RSM Joubert's eyebrow lifted slightly.

"No, I suppose I lost it with him and grabbed his browns but I feel that he overreacted," replied Geoff.

"Okay, how did you get such a deep gash on your side?"

Geoff hesitated. "Um, during the scuffle I fell against a tent peg … I don't know." Dawid looked at Geoff and his eyes widened. The RSM seemed not to notice as the colour returned to Dawid's face.

"Get out 'til I call you; I want a word with this idiot."

Geoff left and headed for the ablutions to clean up. He found Rudi there.

"You'll need a stitch or two in that," Rudi observed. "You're lucky that the bastard didn't kill you. I bet you didn't even tell Joubert about the bayonet."

Geoff looked down at the bloody wound on the side of his abdomen and shrugged. "Shit, Rudi, I'm worried about these new troops. It's unheard of to take a patrol of fourteen men ... as you know we can hardly see each other in the thicker bush with ten of us ..." He looked around as if for an escape and shook his head. "I need him to cover our arses." He shrugged, "Anyway it's my turn for a grilling."

"So you'll eat shit for Gouws?"

Geoff sighed, "Look Rudi, we need him." Geoff was becoming irritated. "After I've seen the medic, I'll catch you at your tent. Don't forget to take some of those new disposable aerials with."

"Okay, but mark my word, that madman is going to kill or maim someone in his own bloody section soon. That guy has way too many demons and one day he's going to go over the edge."

Two stitches and an anti-tetanus injection was all it took and now Geoff felt pleased with his actions as the RSM spoke to him.

"You've saved us a whole heap of shit, Kent. Your buddies told me about the bayonet. Just hold onto Gouws long enough to give me a chance to transfer him." The RSM looked about and blurted out, "You're the best goddamned section leader I've got. Keep up the good work and I'll sign you up for the Permanent Force and promote you to sergeant."

Geoff grinned sheepishly, "Thank you sergeant-major." *The day I join PF is the day Good Friday falls on a Saturday. This place drives me to the edge of my sanity already,* he thought and grimaced.

"He would have gone to detention barracks you know," added the RSM. He lifted his pen and attacked the pile of papers in front of him. "Oh yes, by the way, good luck for tomorrow, you know, with your new troops. You may go," he said without looking up.

Geoff shuddered when he thought about DB, the terrible stories, the brutality and bullying. That was a place to avoid! Immediately he allowed himself to think about home in Johannesburg and ... Kathy. *I need a break,* he thought. *After this one ...*

Geoff strode towards the tent of Corporal Mike Theunissen. He had much to discuss with his new charge. *I suppose corporals or not, they have to cut their teeth sometime,* he thought. The slap and drag of a loose boot lace caused him to glance down and outside the tent he squatted to attend to the lace. Rudi's voice was clear and Geoff's ears pricked up as he heard his name.

"... of course I was disappointed," Rudi sighed. "When Geoff and I met, we took an instant liking to one another." Rudi hesitated as if to confirm a thought. "It was quite daunting as an English speaker to be thrown into a sea of Afrikaners, so when I clobbered that bastard who jumped the food queue, Geoff came over immediately and introduced himself. I think he was less impressed with the punch, but could hardly contain his excitement at hearing his mother tongue. First impressions mean a lot and we hit it off straight away. We shared the opinion that the only way to rise above the unwashed herd, so to speak, was to get some rank and we set our sights on JLs …"

"So you both went on as Junior Leaders?"

Rudi smiled. "I'm going at it like a bull in a china shop, hey?"

"No, no," said Mike, "I'm going to run my own section soon. I need to know as much as possible. You're doing just fine. Please continue."

"Yeah well, we both cruised selection and then the course began. It wasn't as tough as we'd expected and we pretty much excelled. In fact I was actually enjoying it."

"You sound surprised by that."

Rudi nodded. "I never expected to enjoy anything in the army, you know, seeing as it is compulsory …"

"But you made the best of it?"

"Oh yes," Rudi's smile faded. "That was until I fell from the rope bridge … I broke my ankle," he shrugged. "Instant RTU," he added.

"Returned to Unit?" Mike shook his head. "Nasty."

"Yep." Rudi became sombre. "The worst is that of course I never received any rank. And even worse, I could see how it changed Geoff's life." Rudi shook his head. "He rose above the rest of us and became a damn fine leader. Now I will never begrudge him that, but what rankles the most is the fact that I know I would have been a good leader too. I would have done the job as well as Geoff."

"Surely you would have been separated then?"

Rudi's frown deepened and he smiled suddenly, a radiant smile. "Yeah, perhaps that fall was my fate and I'm glad it turned out like this because I have his friendship."

Mike nodded. "He's a hard act to follow but I have to try … I have to try and emulate him."

"No you don't. There's only one Geoffrey Kent like there's only one Mike Theunissen. Just be yourself." Rudi pursed his lips and stood. "You'll see in the next couple of days."

❈

Geoff looked up at the lead Buffel and watched Dawid place the MAG onto its bracket on the front right side. He snapped the cover shut and adjusted the belt of shiny cartridges.

Geoff's ambivalence towards Dawid was confusing and he shook his head as he climbed over the thick armoured side of the Buffel and took his position of command behind the driver. Without asking, he noticed everybody strapping into their seats. Too many of these guys had seen the effects of a Buffel hitting a landmine. The weight of the Unimog chassis with thick armoured sides rolling on a man hanging over the edge would cut him in half like a sharp knife through raw biltong and some of the vets had seen it … and worse.

Geoff turned to Rudi. "How're the comms?" Without communication they might as well not go at all.

"Reading five-five Geoff."

Geoff turned and spoke over his shoulder. "Patmore and bombs in the dog box, um, Martin?" he asked, cursing himself for being so remiss. Martin was so popular. How could he forget the little mortar man's name?

"Hey, corporal, stop worrying man, we've all done this before, plenty," Martin's voice emanated from below Geoff somewhere as he struggled with a stubborn bootlace. He sat up suddenly and Geoff smiled. His face alone was cause for mirth. "We've got enough ammo here to scare Swapo to death by just showing them!" The laughter rippled around. Martin's humour seemed boundless. Geoff noticed the four blowies. Their faces were set in nervous grins.

Geoff took a last look around for obvious faults and, finding none, nodded to the driver. "Okay boys, let's get the flock out of here!" he shouted.

"Wait for me!"

What now? thought Geoff as Sergeant Gerrie Niemant appeared like an excited wraith out of the pre-dawn darkness.

"I want to be in on this one boys. *Ek kom saam!*" said the sergeant throwing his kit into the second Buffel. *Damn it!!* thought Geoff, this is all I need now, a bloody PF coming along to shit on my parade.

The sarge stood up on the back wheel and handed a note to Martin. "Pass this on to Corporal Kent," he looked at Geoff and winked. "A new destination Kent," he raised his voice an octave, "and if any of you wanted to see a bit of action you gonna get it!"

"The engineers haven't swept for mines yet. We gonna spook the road?" asked Rudi above the wind and engine noise. Geoff pursed his lips and nodded. He opened the note and squinted through the pale light of pre-dawn at the scrawl on the page. There was a radio frequency and a name next to it.

"Here Rudi, turn to this frequency and call a …" Geoff studied the page again, "Corporal Hunt."

Rudi placed the handset to his ear, spoke, listened and spoke again, pulled a pen out of his brown shirt pocket and scribbled something in his little notebook.

"Okay, what's the beat?" asked Geoff.

"We need to RV with some tracker team lead by your Corporal Hunt. Apparently they've cut fresh spoor somewhere in the Oshikoto area down the Ondangwa-Tsumeb road."

"Shit, that's miles from here!" exclaimed Geoff. He shook his head and screwed up his eyes.

"Yeah, some forty clicks before Oshivelo, where the Etosha National Park fence moves west, away from the road!"

"I wonder what the hell Swapo are doing so far south?" mused Geoff to no one in particular as the wind whipped through his hair. He turned to the driver, who sat separately in his own little mine-proofed box. "Ondangwa please, my good man!" he shouted and received the thumbs-up. Geoff flopped back into his seat and Rudi shrugged.

"Well, to answer your question, according to Hunt, they hit a farmhouse outside Tsumeb, killing all the people there—or something like that."

"And then they have the balls to saunter past Oshivelo as if they own the place!" exclaimed Geoff. He was incredulous. "It's crawling with soldiers and police, even some special forces are based there at SWA Spes!"

"Not to mention Koevoet!"

"Oh shit yes! Jeez, they're either bloody brave or bloody stupid!"

Koevoet was the crack police anti-terrorist unit, credited with as many kills or more than any other unit in the defence force.

"I think 'clever' is the word!"

"Clever? You think so?" Geoff challenged.

"Sure do."

"Why?"

"Because wherever they go they end up getting their arses shot off, so they're looking for softer targets." Rudi shrugged and dropped his head, "I dunno."

"Shit, Rudi, you should tell the intelligence boys about your theory. I bet you it'll confuse the shit out of them too." Geoff smiled and changed tack, "I wonder why the adj. didn't tell us that we were going after hot spoor!"

"I don't know. You should ask him when we get back! It could be important … like maybe some pending cross-border op?"

"Anyway, this is great!" sighed Geoff. "We all love chasing hot spoor at some ungodly hour in the morning, especially of some smart-arsed gooks!"

"That's not all. Let me really make your day—they think that this is Grootvoet and his band of merry men." Rudi noticed his concern reflected in Geoff's face, "At least twelve of them!" he added without humour.

CHAPTER 2

John Mulemba was pleased that he had a reputation. It suited him that his enemy feared him. He smiled to himself as he imagined how the South African forces at the border spoke of him. As far as he knew he was one of the few Plan soldiers that had lasted long enough to gain this dubious honour. He had lasted this long for a couple of reasons. The main one being that he was part of a clever strategy dreamed up by his leaders at the South West African People's Organisation headquarters in Lusaka.

If, at some of the fiercest contacts, a man could leave a mark of sorts that would be easily recognised and would be seen again and again, would it not begin spreading a degree of negativity among his hated enemy, the South African soldier? Maybe an error of judgement by some inexperienced commander might lead to some South African deaths.

It was at one of the many small temporary bases in southern Angola, some years ago, that John, freshly returned from his second stint of intensive training in the Soviet Union was noticed by one of the Swapo leaders. Despite the excellent report by his Russian instructors, his sharp mind and his natural leadership, it was something physical that led the Swapo captain to call John.

"Come, sit." The captain's outstretched hand proffered the well-used carved wooden stools beneath the ivory palm. John did as he was bid and when they were seated the captain dug into his top pocket and produced a crumpled packet of cigarettes. The captain lit both of them a smoke and handed one to John.

"It has been a while since I have last laid eyes on you, comrade, and judging by the reports we received, time away was well spent. I congratulate you."

"Thank you, captain. I have learned much to help us overcome the southern racist regime and regain what is rightfully ours." John's teeth were particularly white against his very dark Ovambo skin. The captain's mouth turned up at the corners in an involuntary smile as he looked at this man's incredible physique and at his feet. In particular his feet.

Although John was taller than the typical Ovambo and finely muscled, his feet were huge, out of all proportion to his height.

"We at Plan have a very special assignment for you, comrade."

Plan, the People's Liberation Army of Namibia, was the military wing of Swapo. By fighting this war they were learning, and fast, but they had mostly suffered losses to date. They had not had one decisive victory over the security forces and new tactics were urgently sought.

"You are a man well respected by the members of Plan. I have seen how they react to your command."

John nodded seriously, "Thank you."

The captain stood. "I see too you are extremely fit and …," he looked John up and down like a conquistador inspecting the finest slave, "you are larger than any Ovambo I have ever seen."

Again John nodded.

"Your feet are extremely large," said the captain, "And probably in keeping with your manhood," he added quickly should he invoke the wrath of this fearsome warrior. "And therein lies our plan."

"Tell me about your plan, captain." The reference to his feet stung and his anger simmered below the surface. The reference to his manhood gave John no vindication. From his teens onwards people who knew him also knew not to mention his feet. It only took one violent scuffle at a local tavern and the death of a bombastic headman at the hands of John Mulemba for him to secure the respect of the people and for no one to mention his feet again.

"You will be given two askaris. The men have been chosen already. They will die for your survival."

John frowned, "What purpose will that serve?"

"You are to build up a team that can strike anywhere, anytime, but never to engage the enemy head on." The captain paused. "You are to attack the soft underbelly of the white racists—the farmers."

John hesitated and frowned. Attack the farmers?"

The captain smiled, "And their women and children. Their livestock, domestic workers, even their dogs." He held up a finger. "The most important part of the plan is that they must know it is you!"

John's head snapped up and he glared at the man before him, "They have commandos and are in radio contact with the police. The territorial force. It is madness …"

"You will have a well-trained platoon and the askaris …"

"That is not enough. The white soldiers; they have powers, they are well trained and their hatred for the black man equals our hatred of them. It makes them eternally suspicious."

The captain's eyes narrowed. "And the vow to your grandfather. The vow you made to him over your father's dead body! Does that now count for nothing?"

John leapt to his feet. "How do you know about that?" He lunged forward and pointed an accusing finger at the captain. "How do you …?" John froze. The unmistakeable metallic 'shlack' of a dozen AKs being cocked held him in check. Slowly John looked to his left and then right. The Swapo soldiers who previously seemed to be going about their business in the lethargic heat now aimed their rifles at him. "So it has to be like this?" John looked at the captain.

The captain lifted his hand and the men stood back, "No. It is simpler; you carry out our bidding or disappear."

John exhaled, his head hanging. He looked up after a while. "I vowed," he said. "I will fulfil that vow. What are my orders?"

The captain smiled and placed a reassuring hand on John's broad shoulder. "You will be given a basic plan, but really it is up to you." John frowned and the captain continued, "Yes comrade, that is the beauty. You can do as you please. You can go anywhere and attack our enemies anytime. It is up to you."

"I am still uncertain of the revelation my presence will bring."

"Ah," the captain nodded, "that is the question I was waiting for. At every contact, wherever it may be you are to make sure that your bootprint is visible. And you should always wear these …" The captain nodded to one of the Swapo soldiers. The man walked over and offered John a massive pair of boots, easily size fifteen or sixteen, Soviet-made with their familiar chevron soles. "At every massacre you leave these prints and soon enough you will become very well known."

John drew in a deep breath, "They will hunt me."

"Yes," said the captain, "yes they will."

John nodded. He had vowed to die for the cause. He turned a boot over and studied the sole. "How did you know of my father?"

The captain pulled his combat shirt from his pants and lifted it. There was an ugly shiny scar on the black velvet of his stomach next to his navel. "I took the bullet before the one that killed your father."

John's eyes flew wide. "You were there?" he whispered.

"Right next to him."

That was some years ago now and John smiled to himself with grim humour at the thought of how successful the ploy had been. All around Ovamboland people and soldiers spoke about 'Grootvoet', Bigfoot. He had become legendary.

First-time blowies spoke about him with a sort of superstitious awe. The more seasoned veterans wanted to catch him, the intelligence people wanted him dead, soldiers who had come into contact with him all swore that they had seen him but their description of him always seemed to differ. And now he was embarking on a mission that would increase the tempo of the war. The band of insurgents that ran with John had grown to eighteen and all the time more Plan guerrillas wanted to join him. At first this worried John for an armed gang this size was easy to spot and engage but on their own volition, his soldiers learned to move in small groups, rendezvousing at night to move onto their target together. Despite that, it began to suit John as, in the event of a contact, he had a much better chance of survival. Whenever soldiers of his were killed, there were always others to take their place. This was fortuitous as the amount of casualties John's guerrillas suffered was alarmingly high.

John shook his head as if to force himself to concentrate. Despite his askaris, his constant alertness aided by an uncanny sixth sense was the main reason for his survival. He trudged through the sparse bush with his troops spread out so that he could only see two askaris on either side of him in the darkness. They were walking in an area well south of the operational area—a white farming area near Tsumeb.

Their objective was one that they had watched for the last few nights and finally selected as a target. John had seen the farm he wanted. It was a big solid house with gables, built in the old fancy Cape Dutch style. It had a freshly painted green roof and glaring whitewashed walls. Surrounding the house was a large colourful garden, with purple bougainvillaea creeping up the veranda columns, rhododendrons in the beds against the walls, white and red standard roses tied to fencing posts lining the paths and wide, well-watered lawns. The place displayed a subtle colonial opulence.

During the day John and his men split up to hide out. They waited for the heat to subside and the sun to set. Then at night small groups of insurgents met at the fork of the riverbed, appearing out of the darkness like ghostly apparitions. They wore more or less the same khaki shirts and shorts, an innocuous sort of uniform. As each group arrived, they set to digging up their buried AK-47s and Tokarev pistols.

"Enoch Shongwe, my old comrade," John placed a hand on the wizened old man's shoulder and smiled. It was the closest any of them had seen as a show of affection from their leader. "Stay here and set up your ambush. Lay your mines carefully. Should anyone inquisitive enough want poke their heads into our lair, instead of finding a lynx I want them to feel the wrath of the leopard."

Enoch smiled back, "You can count on me, comrade."

John nodded and turned. "You," he pointed, "when we get to the house you are to neutralise the servants. Go to their kraal behind the farm house and threaten them with their lives. Leave a man to guard them. Come in from the back when the shooting starts."

John briefed each group personally and at his signal they moved in for the kill. John crawled as close to the house as he dared without being spotted. The fine dust from the dry earth covered him and made his skin seem almost translucent. He waited and watched while the old woman walked out onto the dimly lit veranda. She brought a silver tray loaded with drinks and placed it on the table. The old man came out holding a stick of well-dried biltong. There was other food cooking and when the aroma reached John, the saliva poured into his mouth from under his tongue.

The insurgents had eaten little for the last three nights and John found himself licking his lips. *Soon I shall eat my fill*, he thought and concentrated on the veranda. Sweat cut dark paths through the dust on his face and John wiped it out of his eyes—the evening was not too hot, but the air was still and his nerves tight. Lightning flashed somewhere far off and lit a bank of clouds pearly white as the young woman came out. She settled the two small children on their stools and began to pour the drinks. Still John lay motionless. At last the farmer drove his white Toyota bakkie around the island at the back of the house and into the carport. The headlights momentarily flashed past John and he closed his eyes. *I hope those other idiots have hidden themselves well*, he thought as he waited for the farmer to appear. The minutes dragged by but finally the farmer appeared. John heard the low murmur of his voice and the family laughing. The children were off their stools. They jumped about his legs and their tiny arms reached up to him. Their faces glowed with delight as they sought his attention.

A very agitated servant appeared. He was desperate and he grabbed the farmer by his arm. John pushed the selector on his AK from safe, down one click, to automatic. He took vague aim in the darkness and fired.

CHAPTER 3

It was mid-afternoon when Gabi Wolbrand returned from the small trading store. She parked the Land Cruiser in the garage, stood on tiptoes and hauled the bags of groceries from the load bay. The heat was oppressive and made her irritable. She walked across the paved driveway, up the stairs into the kitchen and placed the brown paper bags on the table. She looked out the window. Her four-year-old son struggled along with the big packet of sugar. Her fine features softened as she watched him toddle across the wide veranda. He made it to the kitchen and, with a huge effort, lifted the sugar onto the step.

Gabi lifted him and squeezed his hard little body. "You're such a fine strong lad, thank you for helping *mutti*," she said in German. As she put him down a thought struck her. Where the hell were the servants? This was their job and her irritation returned as she watched her daughter lug the last shopping bag. Gabi looked up. Big anvil-shaped clouds, starkly white against the indigo sky, piled up in the distance and with the heat and slight humidity she was sure that welcome rain was on its way. The thought cheered her and she sent the twins to their room to play. She strode through the kitchen, across the veranda and out onto the driveway with its island of lala palms and pretty rockery of plumbago and strelitzia. Gabi hardly noticed the brave show of colour as she headed off down the path towards the servants' kraal, her hasty step betraying her agitation.

Even in the late afternoon the heat lingered. She entered the crude log palisade kraal and walked briskly past the first two huts belonging to the chiefs who worked for her husband. Chickens dashed in all directions, clucking as she approached the third hut belonging to her nanny. Gabi was suddenly aware of the silence. She stood—her long shapely brown legs thrust into dusty old canvas takkies, her short pants partially hidden by one of her husband's large khaki shirts—and looked about. Usually there was a lazy hum of voices around the kraal at this time of the afternoon and certainly, one or two of the babies, tightly strapped to their mothers' back would be squawking out some protest or other.

A tendril of long blond hair fell across her face and her pale blue eyes widened. She had a sudden premonition of impending disaster. She felt as if someone was watching her. Her thick ponytail whipped about her shoulders as she glanced around. She shivered and she turned and fled back to the house. As she ran her feeling of disaster was replaced by genuine fear as she noticed that the usually ubiquitous dogs were also missing and she reached the study in record time. She snatched up the handset of the two-way radio, depressed the button and spoke breathlessly into the mouthpiece.

"Hein, Hein, come in, over," she called. The radio remained obstinately silent. "Hein, Hein, please answer me!" she called frantically. Her fine skin was lined with fear and worry. Gabi reached out to change to the police frequency but her husband's voice suddenly crackled back happily and Gabi flinched.

"*Ja, meine schoene medchien*, what must I do for you this time? Over." The reply a mixture of German and English.

"There are no servants anywhere, Hein and the dogs are missing, where are you?" Gabi asked with tremulous voice.

There was a pause as if Hein controlled his annoyance. "Relax, my darling. Sit down and listen to me. I told Jacob to take all the staff to the store today because they have not been for over a month now, over."

Gabi hesitated, "Well not even the nanny is here and you never told me! Over."

"She probably felt that she also needed a trip to the store and seeing that the little ones were with you—no? Over."

"But, *liebling*, not even the dogs are here. Are they with you? Over."

"Ja, ja, the boxers but not the little ones, they never come with us. Maybe they went with Jacob in the other bakkie, over."

"Okay, when will you be back? Where are you? Over."

"Quite a bit later. I am fixing the fence along the western boundary and it looks as if it might rain so I must finish tonight." There was a drawn-out silence. "Look, I'm sorry I forgot to tell you about the servants, over," replied Hein. The annoyance was unmasked in his tone.

Just because the security forces had warned them that the insurgents could operate this far south was no reason to be fearful. The operational area began far to the north of them, starting at the Oshivelo gate and stretched from there all the way over the border well into Angola where all the fiercest fighting took place. To the northwest and west of them was the Etosha National Park, over two million hectares of harsh, wild bushveld with a half a million hectares of impassable pan in the middle. And more or less north was the Oshivelo training area, full of armed troops. What terrorist had the guts to come into the white farming areas this far south and still think that he could get away with it?

"Please don't forget that Johan and Valerie are coming for dinner tonight, my darling, over," said Gabi in a half-hearted attempt to change the subject for now she was convinced her husband must believe her to be childish in her fear.

"If you are feeling insecure, get the R1 rifles out the safe and put them in the lounge for now. I have to clean them later anyway and, yes, I remember we have guests tonight, over and out."

She replaced the handset and felt foolish. How could she worry her husband like that? After all, the war was miles away. She took the bloody topside out of the fridge where it had been thawing for the last two days and smeared lard over it. She hesitated, sniffed the air, hoping that it had not started to turn. The aroma was strong, clean and meaty, and home-grown, for theirs was some of the finest beef in the district. Gabi thought for a second and smiled. Her smile radiated youthful beauty and love—love for her family and for her life. If she added a bit of garlic to the meat and wine to the gravy, it would make a perfect roast. She finished larding the meat, placed it in a roasting pan, wiped her hands and headed for the cellar to look for a suitable wine. *One bottle for the gravy and one to drink*, she thought happily as she approached the cellar.

The cellar door was in the middle of the yellowwood passage floor, its pull-ring cunningly laid into the timber so that it was barely visible. She grasped the ring and pulled with all her might and, slowly, the heavy door lifted and opened. She pushed the door back against its stop action and walked down the steep wooden staircase into the cellar. She ducked under the thick, rough support beams and groped for the switch above her head. A thick layer of dust shrouded everything in the cellar and puffed up in small clouds around her ankles. She walked past the old stinkwood bookcase containing the archived farm journals and the smell of dust and mould coated the back of her throat and invaded her nostrils. She stopped in front of the rows of bottles in the wine rack. She squatted, pushed a loose lock of hair behind her ear, reached forward and brushed away the spider's web and dust obscuring the labels. One by one she carefully pulled the bottles from the rack, read the labels and returned them, until she found what she was looking for. She turned the bottle around and read. Nederburg Selected Cabernet, 1974, it said and boasted a gold label. It was a fine South African wine and perfectly aged in her opinion. *Yes, eight years old*, she thought, happy with her find and laid it aside. She searched on for a less extravagant wine, one suitable for the gravy, being careful how she handled the bottles, as this was her husband's prized wine collection.

Back in the kitchen, she placed the topside into the preheated oven and set the timer. She turned to the vegetable rack, selected half a dozen large potatoes, placed them on the kitchen sink and began to peel. A flurry of movement alerted her and she looked up and smiled as the white Land Cruiser of her in-laws arrived. Gabi wiped her hands on the dishtowel, threw it aside and walked across the veranda out into the twilight to meet them. Hein's mother was short and stood on tiptoes to fling her arms around Gabi's shoulders.

"How are you my beautiful daughter?" she asked smiling broadly.

"Always better to see you, *mutti*," answered Gabi, moved by the affection she felt for these two old people.

"It's my turn you old busybody. Move aside so I can also see her," said the old man and held her at arm's length. He looked her up and down for a moment then pulled her closer and kissed her on both cheeks. "Erm is right; you are the most beautiful girl in the land."

"How can you call her a girl, you decrepit old man? She's twenty-two already," admonished Ermgart in a jovial manner. An embarrassing silence followed. Four years previously Hein had introduced Gabi to them as his bride-to-be and went on to announce that she was pregnant. At eighteen, a mere child. The marriage had flourished. It was these two old people to whom she turned when things became too much or when she and Hein had gone through the usual marital tiffs, for she was still very young to run such a huge farmstead. And they, in turn, loved her as if she was their own. They were never far away and lived in the cottage on the northern boundary of the farm.

A whirlwind of children burst into the kitchen, shrieking and grabbing at their beloved grandparents' legs. After a flurry of hugs and kisses, young Sven struggled free of his grandmother's embrace and piped up, "Where are the sweets, grandpa?"

"Sven!" exclaimed the astounded Gabi. "Where are your manners?"

"Never mind the children, they are just excited," cooed their protective grandmother.

"Still, he can say please, can't you my boy?"

"Please, grandpa."

"And since when do you ask for gifts?" Gabi was more embarrassed than angry.

"Just as well you asked, my boy," said Heinrich, squatting in front of Sven. "I had forgotten. They are in the Land Cruiser and if you don't fetch them quickly, they might melt."

Sven took no more prompting and tore out of the door followed by his more sedate sister. Being the first born Ermie held herself somewhat aloof. It was beneath her to gallop after her 'younger' brother.

"You two spoil them, you know. It's not good for them."

"Grandparents have a licence to spoil. Come, let us give you a hand."

"I'll finish those potatoes," said Ermgart.

"What other vegetables shall I prepare?" she asked, taking up where Gabi left off.

"I'll get the other goodies out of the four by four," said Heinrich and hurried out the door, his bandy legs of sinew comical as he ran.

"Okay, we've got roast potatoes so let's do baby peas, diced carrots with mint—um and, oh yes, cauliflower in cheese sauce, and Hein's favourite—brussel sprouts … yuck!" exclaimed Gabi. They smiled at one another and Gabi placed her fingers lightly on Ermgart's bony shoulder. "That's great. Thanks, *mutti*. I can get on with the snacks."

Heinrich return to the kitchen. "Look what I've got," he said and held up a huge stick of biltong.

"Fantastic! Hein always said that you make the best kudu biltong. It is kudu, isn't it oupa?" asked Gabi. She looked up and brushed a lock of hair off her forehead.

Heinrich nodded absentmindedly as he placed the beers in the fridge. "Shall I open the champagne?"

"Why don't we wait for the guests, old man?" asked Ermgart.

"Who else is coming? I thought it was only us getting spoilt tonight," he frowned. Heinrich's nose was out of joint. He didn't like sharing his most precious people with anyone.

"No," replied Gabi smiling, "our good friends, Johan and Valerie Erasmus should be here around six thirty."

"Ah yes, old Nick's son."

"A little less of the 'Old Nick'; he's younger than you." They laughed.

"Alright, I'll go and take a look at the borehole pump that's been giving Hein a problem," said Heinrich contritely and he strode from the kitchen. "Come with me young man!" he bellowed over his shoulder at Sven. "There's man's work to be done!"

CHAPTER 4

Hein drove fast along the dust road through the land that he had inherited from his father. Lucas sat quietly in the front and the dogs on the back leant forward into the wind, their mouths open. Disproportionately long tongues lolled out the corner of their mouths and they seemed to smile. Hein's mind wandered back to the story that his dad had told him as a youth. A tale of brave men and heroes on both sides, of conquering a vast, wild land and the spoils of victory was the land itself. The tale was one of romance and bloodshed and probably hugely embellished after years of telling.

Hein's great-great-grandfather had arrived with the German colonialists who landed at Luderitz in 1884. Being hardworking and energetic, the Germans quickly developed the country, building roads, railways and health services and called it German South West Africa.

They spread out into the vast country and with them went Günter Wolbrand. This land was huge, mostly dry but possessed an inherent beauty. A country of many contrasts and when Günter had ridden his horse up the slight rise, he looked across the vast shallow depression before him and declared that all the land he could see from that rise, was his.

Years later Tsumeb was built some kilometres to the southwest of his farm. During this time the local and indigenous inhabitants began to resist the German encroachment on their land and after more than thirty years of German rule, rose up against them. Eighty thousand Hereros took up arms under their chief Samuel Maherero. They were joined by the later famous bushveld general Jakob Morenga of Damara ancestry and attacked the Germans all over the country. A bitter war raged, led by the ruthless German General von Trotha. In 1907 the rebels were crushed, including the Nama rebel chief Hendrik Witbooi. Günter also perished in the hostilities during this time but left a son and heir to take over his land.

Then in 1915 the South Africans invaded German South West Africa on behalf of Britain and conquered the Germans. Despite the country flourishing under South African rule it left Hein's great-grandfather a bitter man—a bitterness that lingered and festered for many years. After World War One the League of Nations gave South Africa a mandate to govern South West Africa as a virtual extra province for the betterment of all its inhabitants. At last everyone was happy ... for the time being.

So too was Hein. He looked forward to seeing his wife whom he loved; she surely was a catch. And a long time ago Hein had made up his mind that his children were the meaning of life. They filled his heart with joy and he looked forward to seeing them each day as he returned from the lands. His loving parents and his good friends were coming for supper—what more could a successful cattle rancher ask for? He drove up to the kraal and stopped hard, producing a cloud of dust that billowed over them.

Lucas, the farm gang boss, opened the door, stepped out and smiled as he turned to Hein and spoke in Afrikaans, *"Môre vroeg,* tomorrow we must finish the fence in the south quarter."

Hein smiled back and replied, "Ja, you are right, we will do it," and as an afterthought added, "Margaret was not helping the madam with the children today and Sissie was not in the kitchen either. Please ask them to see me tomorrow before we leave."

Lucas gave Hein a thumbs-up, smiled again and turned and strode into the unusually dark kraal. Hein drove the bakkie into the carport, extracted his lanky frame and stretched his weary muscles. A massive lightning bolt lit up the sky to the northeast and the deep rumble of the thunder reached him some time later making him shiver slightly as he strode towards the kitchen.

Gabi stepped out of the shower and dried herself vigorously. She hung up the towel, walked through to the capacious bedroom, sat down at the edge of the bed and began to apply moisturiser to her legs. She caught the movements in the full-length mirror at the end of the room and she stood and studied her naked reflection critically. She turned sideways, slid her creamy hands up her flat belly and after a while, nodded with grudging approval. Despite her pregnancy and the birth of the twins, her body had returned to normal. Her hands continued moving up slowly past her rib cage, over her breasts, her fingers slowly caressing her already erect nipples and her breathing quickened. Her right hand slid slowly back down to the trimmed bush at the base of her stomach, her head tilted back slowly and she closed her eyes as her fingers began to explore. Her skin prickled with excitement, she shuddered, opened her eyes, sighed deeply and strolled through to the walk-in cupboard.

Smiling wickedly to herself and slightly embarrassed she flipped through the hangers and chose a simple black mini dress with spaghetti straps and a tight body fit—Hein's favourite. She closed her eyes once again and frowned. She could see the wide-shouldered silhouette of Hein but his face was a blur. Gabi quickly turned to the dresser and stared at their wedding photo. Hein's face smiled back at her and she sighed deeply as she sat. Just a little make-up to enhance the lovely lines of her face and she strode through to join them on the front veranda. Tonight, her husband wouldn't be able to resist. She stopped in the lounge and shook her head. Try as she might, the face of her husband in the photograph eluded her. She could never picture his face and it vexed her.

Hein strode into the lounge, called a greeting through the windows, which opened onto the front veranda. "I'm just going to have a quick shower everyone!" he shouted and noticed the two rifles lying on the couch. *Damn!* he thought, *I must speak to Gabi about leaving loaded rifles lying about. She knows better than that, how many times …?* The kids were too small to even lift the rifles but it was the whole principle. He showered and changed into clean shorts and pulled on a casual golf shirt, combed his hair and walked to the front veranda.

"A quick triple rum on the rocks?" he asked his mother who, everyone knew, only drank beer and champagne and they laughed. Suddenly, the dogs started to bark loudly and Lucas, clearly agitated, ran in and grabbed Hein's arm.

"They are here! You must go! I must go back!" he stuttered and stumbled over the words. Hein controlled his annoyance at the effrontery of this disturbance and reached out to steady the near hysterical gang boss.

"Lucas!" he demanded, "Lucas!"

Lucas was slammed against Hein. Both men tumbled back through the door. Only then did Hein hear the report of the rifle. Still Hein was uncomprehending. He stood up and looked down at the blood spreading on Lucas's back. Then the bullets started to buzz and crack past his head and slam into the wall behind him. The huge plate-glass window exploded, sending shards of glass flying. A large piece of glass dropped vertically and sliced into Ermgart's forearm cutting it to the bone. She leapt to her feet. Instinct and adrenaline took over and she grabbed the children. Thick arterial blood pumped out of her arm and she staggered wildly for the front door. As Ermgart ran past the threshold, a burst of bullets thumped into her back. The force threw her forwards onto her stomach. The twins, flung from her arms, fell into the passageway.

Hein grabbed one of the rifles and set the selector to rapid fire. He dived behind the main wall of the lounge and fired at the muzzle flashes in the darkness.

"I'm going to fire and you must get in here!" he shouted above the din of flying bullets and breaking glass. "Now!" he shouted and stood up. Hein fired bursts of automatic at the flashes. Gabi and Heinrich dashed inside, miraculously unscathed. Heinrich snatched up the second R1 and immediately fired into the darkness.

Gabi ran to her children. She scooped them up and skirted the mutilated body of her mother-in-law. She glanced back and tears welled up at the sight of the untidy heap that was her darling Ermgart. She sprinted down the passage towards the study, ducking instinctively as bullets ricocheted off the walls. She ran into the study and punched the emergency button linked to the police station. Immediately the house alarm howled its ugly tune. Frantically she searched for the key to the safe. She remembered that she had left it in the kitchen after removing the rifles.

"Stay here!" she commanded the children sternly. Tears of dread and confusion plastered their faces. Gabi shook them gently to get through to them. "Do you hear me?" she asked frantically. Tenuous nods were all the confirmation she needed and she ran to the kitchen. Thinking that the attack was restricted to the front of the house, Gabi didn't hesitate to launch herself into the brightly lit kitchen. She saw the key on the worktop next to the sink. She dashed across and grabbed it but a movement out in the yard caught her attention.

The backyard was full of armed black men clad in dirty khaki. She screamed involuntary and they saw her. Bullets crashed through the windows and slapped the walls about her. Fear-driven, Gabi disappeared around the corner and sprinted down the passage to the safe in the study. Her fingers were clumsy with fear and she fumbled and dropped the key, once then a second time before it slid it into the slot. She turned twice and the door opened. Expecting at any second a powerful black arm to close around her throat, she grabbed the .357 magnum and a spare box of cartridges, kicked off her shoes and ran to the cellar door.

She heaved on the pull-ring and the heavy door lifted. "Sven, Ermie, come here now!" They ran frantically to their mother who shepherded them down the steps into the darkness and she slammed the door behind them.

Gabi reached above her head, flipped the light switch, looked about and dashed for the old wooden bookcase. She threw the magnum aside, placed her shoulder against the ancient timber and heaved. Inch by inch it slid across the dusty floor and came to rest in front of the steep cellar steps. She stood for a second, panting as she looked around desperately. She bent, forced an opening between two wooden crates and toppled a pile of National Geographic magazines in the process. She peered through the gap to the darkness beyond.

Gabi squatted and pointed through the gap. "Ermie, take Sven to that darkest spot at the corner there." Sweat poured down her face and she took Sven by his shoulders and looked at both of them. "There are some very bad men in our house and you have to be very quiet now. Do you understand?" she said forcefully and they nodded, slowly. Big wet eyes looked pleadingly at her. "Ermie is going to take you to that dark place and you must sit so still and stop crying. Do not move until mommy comes to fetch you no matter what happens." She looked from one pale face to the other searching for confirmation. "I'm going to turn off the light now and it will be very dark but I will be near," she said peering through the gap in the boxes. She hugged them both, crushing them to her body and quickly turned to the light before they could see the tears sliding down her dusty, sweat-streaked face.

CHAPTER 5

Hein realised that he had to watch his ammo and pick each shot in an effort to inflict the most casualties. If he could just repel this first wave it might buy him enough time to get to the safe and bring back the spare magazines. A while longer and the police would arrive. The moment the first terrorist ran into the outer extremities of the big mercury vapour security lights, Hein fired. The man went down and Hein sought the next target. He fired again as they vaulted the veranda wall and entered the house. He slid down, his back against the wall and killed the first terrorist through the front door. He looked up in time to see the first of them run through the lounge entrance. Unbelievably the terrorist danced a macabre puppet dance in front of him as AK bullets ripped into his body. Hein saw the big terrorist kill his own man then he dived to the floor. The terrorist skidded along its polished surface, turned and looked straight at Hein. Both hesitated. Then together they brought up their rifles, aimed and pulled the trigger.

At that range Hein couldn't miss. The pin clicked on an empty chamber. The blood drained from Hein's face as he realised that his magazine was empty and he looked at John. The hopelessness turned to surprise as he realised that his enemy was in exactly the same situation. John pushed the magazine release button on his AK and began to flip it around to insert the full spare taped on the other side and Hein hit him. John's head exploded with a brilliant flash and then darkness invaded and he fell. The big white farmer bore down on him and John struggled to focus as his adversary stood over him triumphantly.

Hein stood over John and rifle fire chattered from all sides. Bullets thumped into Hein and knocked him around like a rag doll. Slowly, as if to resist the inevitable, Hein slumped on top of John. He bled from multiple wounds. John sat up, shook his head and pushed Hein off him. Hein's blood flowed and a dark pool of it spread across the floor. John shook his head and peered at the body of the old man slumped over the arm of the high-backed chair. The antimacassar soaked up his blood. There was no doubt that he was dead.

"Find the woman and the children; we need to use her, all of us," said John rubbing the lump on the side of his head. "Look for the safe, there is bound to be money there, perhaps even Kruger Rands. Take only the food you need now for there is a long and dangerous road ahead of us," he commanded in a hoarse voice. They quickly searched through the house firing precautionary rounds into each room. A shout echoed down the passage as one of John's men discovered the open safe. There was money, lots of it, but no Kruger Rands. It was a pity! Kruger Rands were excellent exchange for arms in the eastern bloc countries.

John's askari reported back. "She is not here, comrade, we have searched the house and she is just not here," he said sheepishly, fearing retribution.

"Is it possible that she grew wings and flew out of here?" asked John in a quiet, menacing voice. The askari shuffled his feet and looked at the ground. "You idiot!" he ranted. "She must be here somewhere. Now find her!" he shouted more out of desperation than anger. John knew that with every minute they remained at the house the chance of their discovery increased. John felt cold sweat run down his back.

"She and the children are paramount to the success of this mission. They must be found, the children killed and she must be used!" he ranted, spittle flying from his lips. John shuddered to think of the consequences if the security forces caught them after this atrocity. Surely they would receive no mercy and die badly.

"You!" he pointed at one of his men. "Find the wires to the siren and cut them. I need silence. You!" he pointed to another. "Search for the telephone wire and cut it." John delegated and set his men to work.

A movement off to his left caused him to duck. John swung his barrel onto the target. The servant lying on the floor next to the body of the white farmer tried to lift himself but his hands skidded and slid through the sticky pools of blood. John straightened, walked up and kicked the man over with his big boot. He was still alive.

John's eyes lit up with an evil glint. "It was you I saw. It was you trying to warn your master," he said in a menacing tone. "And I sent my men to tell you to flee your kraal before the fighting started." John paused. "You did not heed me therefore you are a traitor. It is difficult to know what to do with traitors but perhaps if you have no lips with which to speak, you cannot betray anyone ever again." John turned to the man who had cut the telephone wires. "Give me those pliers," he ordered. Lucas's face was grey with pain and now fear. He had heard about this vile torture from people living in the operational area and he tried desperately to move, but his legs would not respond. John stooped over Lucas, grabbed his top lip with the pliers and at the same time drew his hunting knife from its sheath. Lucas struggled feebly and cried out as John yanked up his lip and sliced it off at the gum. John tossed the lump of flesh aside then repeated the process to the bottom lip. A wet patch formed at the front of Lucas's pants and the stink of urine invaded the room. It mixed with the blood, creating swirls of colour that moved together on the floor. His cry gurgled as blood ran down the back of his throat.

Inevitably, one of the insurgents found the pull-ring to the cellar and he shouted for support. John and some of his men crowded around as the terrorist yanked the door up. As it was only the white bitch and her young, he confidently jumped down the stairs into the darkness. John heard the dull crack of the magnum directly below him, the thump of bullet striking flesh and the death moan of his man.

"They're in the cellar!" he shouted.

❈

Gabi moved another wooden crate in front of her, opened the box of cartridges and tipped the contents out onto the crate. The bright brass casings rolled around as she unclipped the cylinder of the pistol, checked the load and satisfied, snapped it closed. She crept over to the main support beam, reached out with tremulous hand and switched the light off. The darkness was a physical thing, but gave the arcane effect of comfort and she stood like that for a while. At last she felt her way back to the box and crouched behind it, facing the trap door. The tumult above was appalling and she shut her eyes tightly trying to block out the sound of breaking glass and gunfire hammering away above the wail of the alarm. Suddenly all was quiet and she listened, wondering … hoping … There was some shouting and then a loud scream and Gabi's heart sank as she feared the worst. Footsteps all around. Shuffling movements. Muffled voices and a bang as the safe door was slammed—and then, at last, tugging at the pull-ring. Her heart skipped a beat. She lifted the magnum with both hands and aimed over the top of the bookcase. Light poured in as the door was lifted. A silhouette appeared and Gabi fired at the widest part of it. The man grunted and fell into the cellar. There was a long silence and nothing moved. A slight shuffle behind her alerted her and Gabi spun around. Sven was moving about, coming towards her. She put her finger to her lips and shook her head vehemently.

Another shout and a head poked quickly through the opening and disappeared again. Gabi aimed at the space where the head had been. The head came back and she fired. She nicked the edge of the opening, sending splinters of wood flying but the bullet's shape and direction was altered. Its copper head deformed and it smashed into the side of the terrorist's head. It was as if someone had grabbed a handful of the man's tight black curls and yanked him out of the hole.

John watched the man's head snap back out of the opening as he rolled sideways. Blood sprayed from the massive hole, his legs kicked and convulsed and then finally he lay still. Everyone froze. They were shocked at what they had just witnessed.

"We'll burn her out," said John. "Fetch me the paraffin from the store!" he shouted, his anger evident. Eager men rushed to John's bidding and they produced the familiar silver twenty-litre can with its green paint label. The men poured the paraffin over the floor and around the edge of the of the cellar entrance. They poured it on the curtains and carpets and threw the tin with the last of the paraffin down into the gaping hole in the floorboards. John herded his men into the kitchen, pulled a packet of crumpled cigarettes from his top pocket and drew one out. He patted his other pockets and found his matches. He lit the cigarette and let the burning match fall to the floor. The blue flame spread quickly across the yellowwood floors, through the rooms, up the curtains and down into the cellar where the last of the paraffin had been poured out onto the ground.

John was angry with the number of men he had lost. It wasn't supposed to be like that but it was too late for recriminations. When he finally captured the white woman, he would make her pay—dearly. He sent two sentries out to patrol the house and let the rest of the men help themselves to the roast in the oven. He hoped the fire would drive the woman out quickly as time was running out fast. When the house really started to burn, its glow would be seen for miles around. John turned to the sink and washed the blood off his hands as he heard an explosion in the distance. He stared out at the two boxer dogs lying dead in the yard without seeing them. Time had run out.

CHAPTER 6

Valerie Erasmus sat at her dressing table and regarded her face and then her dress before selecting the eyeshadow. She was attractive; her long dark hair had natural reddish tints, which enhanced her olive skin and slender neck. She sat forward, dabbed the applicator into the light green compressed powder and closed her left eye.

"My treasure, did Hein tell you who else would be there tonight?" she asked in Afrikaans and sat back, flicking her hair over her shoulder.

"Ja, just us and his parents," replied Johan as he walked in from the shower. He breathed in deeply and buttoned his shorts.

"You're getting fat you know." She lifted an eyebrow at his reflection in the dresser mirror.

"Ja, ja, when do I get time to exercise? All I do around here is work and more work and by the time I get home, I'm too tired to go jogging. You know that?" he answered lamely. He knew he was letting it slip.

"Hein doesn't carry any weight," she countered and smiled at his reaction.

"You didn't marry Hein, you married me and this is as good as it gets, even though I know you've got a soft spot for him."

Her eyes widened. "Soft spot for Hein? Since when?" she exclaimed and placed her hands on her hips. "And how about you? I've seen your face when you look at Gabi."

"Same story. I married you, not Gabi and although she's sexy, I love you," he taunted back, a big smile on his face.

"Oooh! You're treading in thin ice, Erasmus," she fumed with mock annoyance.

"You started."

Valerie shook her head, "I'm glad we're the only friends going tonight; it makes me feel kind of special. Besides, you and Hein are best friends, aren't you?"

Johan hesitated, "Oh, I don't know. I think so. He's got lots of friends." It was a tough question. These hardy farmers of South West Africa found such talk difficult. He picked up the deodorant can from the dresser and sprayed copiously all over his shirt.

"You'll ruin that shirt!" she admonished.

"Then I'll buy another. The shirt doesn't feel it, my skin does," said Johan defensively. "Come on, how much longer are you going to be? We have to be there between six thirty and seven." He stood behind her and massaged her slender shoulders.

"Don't rush me. Why don't you try some other deodorant? Simple huh? I'll buy you a different brand for your next birthday … ahhh, don't stop," she said, closing her eyes in delight as he rubbed his thumbs down either side of her spine through the silk of her blouse. He looked over her shoulder at her lightly freckled cleavage and ample breasts. She wore no bra and the sheer silk of the blouse enhanced the roundness of them.

Her tanned legs protruded past her lacy skirt and Johan announced huskily, "Let's go or we'll be very late."

"Oh la la, thank you, darling man," she beamed at him. Her face shone and she stood up and slipped the little black purse strap over her shoulder.

"Okay, okay, don't get soppy on me now," he smiled at her as they walked out the back door. He placed a big calloused hand on the small of her back and ushered her ahead to the white Toyota light delivery van parked on the red brick driveway.

"Oh no, do we have to go in the bakkie, can't we go in the BMW?"

"The Bee Em," said Johan reproachfully, "was washed today and it'll just get dusty going down that shitty road to Hein's place. Stop being such a snob."

The farmers in the area prospered and the young ones who had inherited the farms worked hard and played harder; their 'toys' were expensive and life was good to them. Tsumeb was a growing mining town and the farmers grew with it.

"Oh no, it's not that. It's the plastic seats. They make my legs all sweaty and sticky and don't you give me a hard time about my car."

"Your car? Now it's your car is it?" He smiled and opened the bakkie door for her. Valerie slid in and winked at him through the open window. He walked around to his door and looked up quickly as the flash of lightning in the distance lit the horizon.

Johan lowered his bulk behind the steering wheel and pointed, "There, taking the bakkie is justified now, isn't it?"

"Maybe we should take the four by four," she suggested looking up, wide-eyed.

"Nah, we'll be fine." he said turning the key in the ignition. Johan accelerated down the rose-lined driveway without bothering to look for oncoming traffic.

It was hardly necessary in the remote farming community. He spun the wheel left and accelerated the LDV through the fancy curved front entrance. They slid sideways onto the corrugated dirt road and sped up the rise to the next-door farm.

"Shit Johan!" exclaimed Valerie. "We're not that late, are we?"

"No, but the faster you go across these bloody corrugations, the less they bump. Anyway, I'm thirsty and Hein's beers are always cold." He smiled devilishly. That was the last thing she saw before the ground below them erupted.

The TMA-3 and TMA-4 Russian-made landmines were commonly known as the 'cheese mine' probably because of its khaki colour and three protruding detonators. The soft-skinned Toyota LDV was no match for the nefarious blast. The vehicle catapulted into the air. The explosion occurred between the front right wheel and the driver, sending shrapnel flying right through it. The shattered vehicle landed at the side of the road and the door on the driver's side was thrown thirty metres. Flames poured from the chassis and Johan slid out onto the road, his nether regions shredded. His first concern was for his beloved wife. Where was she? What had happened? Why couldn't he move? He just needed to hold her hand and tell her that everything was going to be fine and of course he loved her. Why did he feel so terribly sad?

Through the heat waves of the burning vehicle a distorted silhouette of a man approached with a pistol held in his hand. Good, perhaps the officer would explain this outrage. Yes, he was certainly going to give this man a piece of his mind and he had better apologise to Valerie. The edges of his vision blurred, not only because of the tears that filled his eyes but more because he was suddenly desperately tired. He needed Valerie now because he loved her so much and something was wrong with him—he could tell. Val! Val! He shouted but no sound escaped his lips. Massive trauma and haemorrhaging drained the life out of Johan. Thick, dark arterial blood flowed from his mangled flesh onto the white sand, where it pooled.

Enoch Shongwe bent over Johan, placed the Tokarev pistol to his forehead and pulled the trigger. The execution was for the benefit of the police and security forces as Johan was already dead and Enoch turned to his men. "Find the woman," he commanded. "Carry out Comrade Mulemba's bidding and hurry." They found her at the furthermost reaches of light from the burning vehicle.

❦

For Valerie the blast had been shockingly loud, the whole world spun about her in a maelstrom and pain racked her body. She landed awkwardly, the wind driven from her lungs and she gasped for breath as darkness closed around her.

She tried to imagine what had happened and lay for a while as the confusion robbed her of reason. A stabbing pain in her side took her breath away as she tried to move, so she lay back a while to try and piece things together.

Okay, her ankle was sore, her ribs too, probably broken and a stinging pain in her back might be a torn muscle but that was all. Surely she could get up, despite these little injuries? She needed to get to Johan and help him. Why did he have to drive so fast? They were bound to have an accident at that speed. She looked up and noticed the men. It was only then that Valerie realised her blue lacy skirt had been burned away. Her tanned legs and silky white pants were exposed and reflected the orange glow of the fire. She sat up, despite the stabbing pain in her side. Her green eyes flared wide as she realised their intentions. She tried to back away but the bones in her broken wrist grated and she collapsed. The first terrorist stopped in front of her and deliberately unbuttoned his khaki shorts. Valerie screamed. The man grabbed her and slapped her face. Valerie tasted blood. It spilled over her lip and dripped onto her blouse.

"*Bly stil, jou teef*... shut up you bitch or I will cut your miserable white throat! If you be quiet we won't kill you," said number one in Afrikaans. He held his hunting knife in front of her face and the blade reflected the flames of the LDV. Frozen with disbelief, fear and humiliation, Valerie shook her head slowly from side to side. The man stooped and violently ripped her panties off. He forced his knees between her legs and spread her thighs apart with muscled arms. A searing pain filled her lower abdomen and her eyes flared wide as his huge blackness penetrated her dryness.

She tugged and pushed ineffectually at his khaki shirt and the tears poured down, stinging the burns on her face. "Please don't do this to me," she begged him. "I've got money for you at the house ... Just come with me and you can have it all ... I'll even give you a lift to where you want to go if want." The pain was incredible and the pounding incessant. "You can even take the new car. It's a BMW," she tried. Her body rocked with the man on top of her. The sobs racked through her. It was as if time stood still. He went on and on rutting and bucking and the sweat dripped off him and splashed onto her. The sour smell of unwashed body and stale tobacco assaulted her nostrils and he breathed his rotten-toothed breath into her face. Eventually number one stood back and looked down at her. He grinned as he buttoned his fly. Valerie glanced up and her heart sank as number two stepped up and pulled down his pants. He was massive and fully erect and very black. He gave her a truculent look. She tried feebly to cover herself with her hands and crossed her legs ineffectually. He roughly brushed her efforts aside and forced himself into her. They went on ... number three? Her mind could not conceive the horror and mercifully she started to fade from reality. How many more? It did not matter; she just wanted to die now. *Please God let me die*, she prayed silently. Number five stepped forward and regarded the bloody mess between the white woman's spread legs with some distaste. Suddenly and violently he rolled her onto her stomach and took her from behind. Mercifully Valerie passed out.

Vaguely she heard someone speaking to her in English. "I am sorry. I want you to know that I did not take any part in this … I am so sorry," the voice said simply. It was a kind voice, a voice of a well-spoken man. Then there was nothing.

❁

Enoch Shongwe stood some distance away out of the light of the burning wreck and waited until it was all over. He didn't have the stomach for this sort of thing and was somewhat appalled by his freedom fighters. This was neither the glorious war of liberty he had been told about nor the one he came to fight and that woman writhing on the ground, being totally abused by his men, was not the enemy. She wasn't even a soldier. He walked over to her when they were finished, squatted and whispered his feeble apology, suddenly feeling very sorry for her.

"We had better move." He stood and loped off into the darkness. Enoch looked up as the lightning flashed. It momentarily lit the pale form of the woman as the clouds above released their first few drops.

CHAPTER 7

John ran out of the kitchen to the front lawn and listened for a long time before turning back. He whistled shrilly above the banter of his men.

"That was Enoch and our comrades I just heard and surely that was the police that detonated their mine. We must leave now! We cannot wait for the woman any longer," he said urgently.

"Do not despair comrade. Look!" his askari pointed at the flames. "They grow big and she will perish in the heat and smoke when this house burns," he said.

"Come, we must run. There is a long and dangerous road ahead," John called to his men over his shoulder. He led them off the property and turned north to the operational area. The first big drops of rain slapped down on them. Lightning flashed its tentacles about the night sky and thunder crashed and boomed out in response. Seconds later the wind whipped about them and the heavens opened. John was glad about the rain. It would be impossible to follow their spoor and they would lose less energy running all night in the cool rain.

John's mind wandered back to the day his father was killed in front of him—he was only ten.

The year was 1959 and John, his family and friends and in fact all the residents of the 'Old Location' were forced to move from their homes to a new township, built further away, named Katatura. The inhabitants of the Old Location became very disgruntled and refused to co-operate with the authorities on this matter. The more the authorities pushed them, the more disgruntled the inhabitants became until they finally embarked on a mass civil disobedience campaign. They boycotted all municipal- and government-supplied services and amenities and on the tenth of December marched to confront the authorities.

"Where are you going, pa?" The excitement was infectious and John tugged on his father's arm. His eyes sparkled with anticipation and his father squatted.

"We are going to the white man's town to tell them that we don't want to move away from here, boy."

"But why, pa? They have built us a new town haven't they?"

"Yes, but it is further away, into the desert and the transport will be a problem, despite their reassurances to the contrary."

"But it's new ..."

"Hush, boy. They are doing to us what they do to the black people of South Africa and we must fight it ..."

"With guns?" John's eyes widened.

"No. We fight peacefully. We will march as one to show our discontentment. The more we do this the more they will have to concede."

John squeezed his father's arm. "Please let me come. Oh please, pa."

His first reaction was to deny his son and then he looked at the boy's shining eyes and beaming face. "I suppose it will be okay ..., " he said and lifted a pink-palmed hand to forestall his wife's protestations. "It is a peaceful march; nothing will go wrong."

Human tributaries trickled down the narrow lanes and alleys and flowed into the seething mass that was the river of people in the main street. It started quietly and then someone began to sing. The song was taken up and soon a swaying, chanting hoard of black faces bore down on the waiting line of police.

The loudhailer was all but drowned out by the singing and the police in the cordon shuffled about uncomfortably. One of the young ones lifted his rifle and aimed at the crowd.

"Shoot!" they taunted. "Shoot, white pigs!"

The police commissioner turned the loudhailer to his men. "*Staan!*" he commanded. "Do not fire!"

The young policeman only heard the last word. He squeezed the trigger. A volley of shots echoed about the street. People fell. The rest turned and fled, leaving a litter of bodies lying bleeding.

Among the dead and wounded a youth knelt next to a dying man and vented his grief. He remained like that until his grandfather found him.

That was twenty-three years ago and John had never forgotten his grandfather's words. The old man had placed a big hand on each of the youth's narrow shoulders, looked down into his big brown eyes and spoke quietly but forcefully. "You must avenge your father. You must take up arms, boy, and with the support of the masses, you will drive the white racist authorities into the sea, even if you die doing it! This is our Namibia. We must fight for it. One day you will be a great leader and lead us to freedom," he said with a fervent certainty. "And it all depends on you."

These were strong words for one so young and difficult to comprehend but John understood and, later, proved time and time again that he was equal to the task. Now this new war that he had started was going to sow the seeds of defeat within the enemy camp and bring them to their knees.

It was a pity about the woman. She would have made his mission complete and victorious. *I must return*, he thought and he concentrated on running through the rain with the wind starting to chill him.

CHAPTER 8

Sergeant Carel Brits sat in his office in the Tsumeb police station, his booted feet on the desk, one hand behind his head and the other supporting a Coke bottle covered with fine droplets of moisture. He peered suspiciously at the man opposite him. The complainant on the other side of the desk looked longingly at the cold drink as the overhead fan battled tenuously to move the dank air. The early evening still carried the heat of day and the office was unbearably stuffy.

"Just run through the whole story again," said the sergeant sounding bored. He suddenly stood up and adjusted the rheostat of the fan to full as the powerful body odour of the man in front of him filled the room. He flopped into his chair once more and took up his position of comfort.

"Sir, I recognised the one man in town two days ago. My brother made him known to me. He pointed him out on my last visit to Oshakati. There, they are too scared to report him to the security forces as he is a member of the gang of Grootvoet," said the local man. He wrung his hat nervously in his hands.

"Okay, so you too are after the reward offered for the capture of Grootvoet or any of his gang, aren't you?" Carel shot back at the man, his anger rising. "Do you know how many people come in here every day telling me that they have seen these bleddy *skabengas*—this bleddy rubbish and ask for the reward, huh? Hundreds I tell you!" he bellowed and stood. He leant over his desk and eyed the man ferociously.

"*Nee, meneer,*" answered the man stepping back out of range should this angry white policeman elect to beat him. "I want no reward. I want only peace. These Swapo in Tsumeb will make more war in this area," he continued nervously. "I have settled here to get away from the war up north, you see, sir."

Carel sat down and carefully considered the man's words. If he did not want the money and he had asked for Carel by name, knowing how fearful the locals were of him, then maybe he was telling the truth or … was there some ulterior motive.

"Philemon!" shouted Carel and leant back. "You sit there," he said, indicating the chair in the corner. The door opened and a blue uniformed policeman marched in.

"*Ja sersant?*" answered Philemon, standing smartly to attention just inside the doorway.

"Take down this man's statement, word for word, while I question him again. Leave nothing out. This might be something very important ... or this bastard is lying for some reason that I don't know about ... yet."

Sergeant Brits prided himself in the fact that he could sniff out a liar as well as a dog finding its long-buried bone and he was usually remarkably accurate but this man had him confused ... there was no war in Tsumeb.

The drafting of the statement got underway with Carel rephrasing the questions as much as possible. A knock at the door interrupted them.

"*Kom!*" he shouted, clearly irritated by this disturbance. A camouflage uniform filled the doorway.

A white constable leant casually against the door. "The lieutenant wants to see you right away, sarge," he said and disappeared. The door remained open and Carel stood up.

"Carry on with this man, constable, I'll be right back."

"An emergency signal has come through from the Wolbrand's farm, Carel," said the lieutenant before the sergeant was even fully through the door. "Take whoever and check it out. I'm a bit worried about this one. There was no reply by phone and we couldn't raise them on the radio."

"Was the signal from the old folks or the main house, lieutenant?"

"Good question, sarge," answered the lieutenant as he rubbed his jaw thoughtfully. "Check the main house first and then the cottage. It's probably just the kids playing around. I'm a bit worried that there is just no contact with them at all and the phone at the old folks just rings and rings too. Better take a fully armed section and a Casspir. Oh, and call for back-up should there be a problem," he added.

"A Casspir, sir? Why not just a couple of Land Rovers ... I'll see you at the mess a bit later for some darts and a few beers?" asked Carel, his familiarity bred out of the mutual respect both held for each other.

The lieutenant hesitated. "No," he said at last, "just do as I say, I've got a feeling about this one. I don't know if it's good or bad yet."

"Okay sir, I'm on my way. Philemon!" he yelled. "Get me the reaction police. Now!" he bellowed down the passage. "Tell them: full kit, possibly for a few nights and get them to meet me at the vehicle park!"

The Casspir roared out of the gates and onto the road heading out of town. The men—both black and white—dressed in faded camouflage uniforms, sat forward attentively, their rifles between their legs as they listened to the sergeant. The heavy vehicle bounced off the tar road on the outskirts of town and bumped onto the gravel.

"Same as usual. If there's any shit, we drive right into the middle and fire from the top," he shouted above the vehicle noise. "And you two," he pointed at the men at the back, "open the back doors and start firing should we need to debus!" The noise of the heavy-duty tyres moaned through the sand and the wind whipped about the open-topped armour plate. "Okay, buckle up and load, there's about twenty minutes until we get there! Any questions?"

"Where are we headed, sarge?" asked one of his men eagerly.

"The Wolbrand farm!"

"What's the buzz?" shouted another above the added noise of the cocking levers of half a dozen R1 rifles.

"Emergency signal. No response by radio or phone!"

"Isn't that farmer your buddy, sarge?"

"Ja ... and his wife!" The wind buffeted their hair as they drove into the night. "But it's probably a false alarm," whispered Carel and he made the sign of the cross on his chest. People wanted to be friends with Hein and Gabi. They were like royalty in Tsumeb and she was the most adored woman in the entire territory—followed closely by her friend Valerie.

They sat in silence, not wanting to have to strain their voices above the noise of the vehicle and the wind. The headlights caught the solid wall of water ahead and suddenly they were into the downpour. Sheets of water obscured the driver's vision and a fine mist swirled about them. The driver slowed until he could see more than just a blur. He peered ahead and squinted through the sheets of water which obscured the thick armour-glass screen and he tapped Carel on his knee. A bakkie burned furiously on the side of the road despite the rain.

Carel shouted. "Stop! Dammit!" Too late the driver reacted and a brilliant flash of light followed by an earth-shattering roar threw them against their harnesses and they ground to a halt.

"Mine! Ambush! All-round defensive arc of fire! Two magazines! Find muzzle flashes and return fire!" Carel's instinct took over as he shouted the commands. He ducked down below the shattered two-inch-thick armoured glass windows and grabbed the radio. "Zero, Zero, Zero, this is One Zero, message, over!" he shouted above the crackling of R1 fire.

"Zero, send, over," came the almost instant reply.

"One Zero, we have hit a mine and possible ambush, no casualties yet, send back-up, recovery unit and ambulance to position Romeo Zero Seven, five clicks from Wolbrand south entrance—over!" Carel barked out his message, grateful for the quick response from the signaller on duty.

"Zero, roger, understood, out." The handset went dead. Empty brass shells pinged off the armour of the Casspir body and fell on the wet gravel road, hissing as they cooled. As quickly as it started, it was over.

"There's no return fire, sarge," someone whispered in the buzzing silence.

The rain poured into the vehicle and thunder rumbled overhead. "Okay, then … let's get out and assess the damage … ," began Carel. "Wait! You fool!" Carel reprimanded one of his more eager constables. "Altogether man! We jump from all sides and RV at that thick bush on the side of the road there," Carel pointed. "And wait for my signal." He looked back in the direction from which they had come. "They might be smart and start shooting as we get out. On my signal," he whispered fiercely.

"Now!" shouted Carel and they moved as one. Over the edge, out the back, adrenaline pumping. Dive, a long fall, smack onto the wet surface, leopard-crawl through water, mud and finally, thankfully, into dense bush. There they waited. Raindrops pelted their backs. Two men faced outward, the rest scrutinised the area ahead, the burning LDV, the centre of attraction and they waited. The wind drove the rain in sheets about them and the large earth drain at the roadside began a turbid flow and still, they waited. The storm burgeoned as if to thwart the entire approaching dry season and Carel drew in a deep breath. He stood up and indicated one man to follow.

The two men crept through the bush. Duck for a branch, climb over a log and leopard-crawl under a thicket. Achingly slowly, they made their way until they were opposite the burning wreck. The rain drenched them and Carel wiped the rain off his face and out of his eyes. His hair was plastered to his head and he surveyed the scene before him. The flames drummed and hissed in the rain. He could see the mangled silhouettes of wreckage around the burning vehicle. Lightning cracked overhead as if to remind them that the onslaught of the storm was not yet over and the thunder reverberated against their wet clothes. In the instant the lightning lit the skies, a horrific sight flashed before Carel. He thought he was imagining things and rubbed his fingers into his eyes as if to clear them. But the image of what he had seen in that instant remained imprinted at the back of his vision— the grizzly mess out there had the face of his good friend on it, the face of Johan Erasmus. Carel shook his head slowly from side to side not wanting the nightmare to be real but believing the worst. His mouth dropped open, his eyes filled with horror and slowly he rose. He walked trancelike through the bush towards the body of his friend.

A bone-jarring blow felled him as the constable following him tackled him to the ground. He climbed over Carel and held him to the ground.

"*Wat die fok…!*" exclaimed Carel. The tackle and the profanity served to steady him. "What are you doing, have you gone mad, you blithering idiot!"

"Look here, sarge!" whispered the constable with vehemence. "Look at this! You could have got us both killed." The constable's face shone white in the dim light. "How can you just stroll up to a scene like this without even checking?" The constable whispered with such force that the veins in his neck bulged and he pointed a tremulous finger at the ankle-high trip wire. It was carelessly strung in the grass and quite visible despite the dark night and heavy rain. Had a little more care been taken the men would surely have missed it.

"I … I … um, I wasn't thinking. *Ek is jammer*, I'm sorry … ," stammered Carel. "I think that's Johan lying there … um, we better check for booby traps." Together and very carefully they followed the trip wire to its origin. There, with grass hastily pulled over it, pegged into the ground and strapped to the base of the bush was a POM-Z anti-personnel mine.

Carel placed his hands on his hips and looked around. "Go back to the others and tell them to search the area for more of these while I sort this one out then meet me at the wreck. Tell Ambrose to get on the radio and find out where the hell the back-up is." Carel glanced at his constable. "Thanks, *boet*, I owe you one."

"Okay sarge. Are you sure you're alright now?"

Carel nodded slowly. He didn't look back as he bent to the mine and released the trip wire. Using his rifle as a balance he leapt over the brimming side drain and walked up onto the road. As if an incorporeal being nudged him on, Carel approached the wreck. Every fibre of his being tried to resist going there but his legs carried him as if remote-controlled. He couldn't stop himself and finally he arrived at the edge of the wreck. The lambent flames flicked and danced, trying desperately to survive the onslaught of the rain. They broached the darkness and Carel gasped. His chest began heaving as if he had run a marathon and he stood holding back the waves of nausea.

"Oh no," he whispered. "Oh dear God, no!" He sunk down on his knees next to Johan. The blood still flowed onto the dirt road where it mixed with the rainwater, diluted and ran in rivulets. Carel reached out to hold his friend but it was impossible as Johan's body was covered in wounds. There was nothing to hold. Despite his iron resolve, tears flowed down his cheeks, mixed with rain and dripped off his nose and chin. One by one his constables joined him as he knelt in the mud, rocking slowly back and forth, his friend's head in his lap.

Two Casspirs roared onto the scene followed by a small convoy of vehicles. They stopped well short of Carel's Casspir and immediately a section of minesweepers began sweeping the road. The second Casspir disgorged a section of constables in camouflage uniform. They spread out into the bush on either side of the road. The rain pelted down obliquely in the beams of light from the lead Casspir and the lieutenant followed the minesweepers. They swept past Carel and his men and carried on down the road, linking up with the section that had scoured the bushes.

"Don't just stand there, man! Get that body into a bag and search the area for spoor. We're going to catch these bastards if it's the last thing we do!" shouted Carel as he stood to meet his lieutenant.

"Jeez man, I'm really sorry, Carel, I know you two were close," the lieutenant tried in his clumsy way to comfort.

"Ja, thanks, but there's no time for that; we still haven't finished our job. We haven't been to the Wolbrand house yet and I think we should get there as soon as possible." Carel looked about and then at his lieutenant. "I'm scared of what we are going to find there after this."

The lieutenant nodded. "Okay, let's take that Casspir and go. We'll take your men, Carel, and half the ..."

A constable ran up to the two men and slid to a halt in front of them, his face a study of concern. "Come, sir! You gotta come!"

His urgency had the desired effect and they followed the constable off the road, through the sparse, low bush to where the medics bent over a semi-naked body lying on the ground. She lay on her back and the medics were busy lifting her onto a stretcher. Carel caught a glimpse of her abused body before they wrapped a damp blanket around her. He walked closer and his eyes flared in shock. "Oh, Jesus, It's Valerie! Oh shit no! Oh please no! Is she ...?"

"No, Carel" the medic interrupted. "But she might as well be; I'm afraid those savages raped her," he said. "And I'm fairly certain that there is some internal bleeding. If we move now, we can get her to the hospital and maybe Doc Watson can save her ... but we must go now."

"Yes, yes, of course. Go and we'll radio ahead to the ICU. But as soon as you get her settled and in good hands, I want you to come back to the Wolbrand house and make it snappy. I'll guarantee you this is only the beginning. I'll bet there'll be a few more surprises in store for us."

Even from a distance they could see the glow. Part of the roof over the kitchen had collapsed and the fire still raged in a few of the rooms. The rest of the house smouldered and steam and smoke rose off the big, blackened timbers of the main roof trusses that lay on the kitchen floor. The rain had almost doused the fire.

Carel ran and flattened himself against the wall at the kitchen door. A quick look around the corner showed no life. One by one they entered and spread out through the house, checking all the rooms. Carel moved to the lounge and, by the glow of the fire in the first room, could see bodies lying there.

"Can anyone hear me!" he shouted but there was no answer as the wind blew a fine mist around the dark room. Carel took another look and summoned the others. "You and Piet bring the garden hose in here and you two go to the generator out back and bring back a lead light." The rain had saved most of the house. The roof over the passage and kitchen had collapsed, allowing the rain and water in.

Carel took the light. "Cover me," he said as he crept along the passage in search of the distribution board. He clambered over broken smouldering roof trusses, twisted corrugated-iron sheets and other debris in an effort to get to the board. Once there he opened it, found the power transfer switch and snapped it across. He was relieved when they heard the generator fire up and parts of the house lit up. There was a sudden lull in activity and Carel climbed back over the wreckage to find most of the police crowded into the now brightly lit lounge. He too came to a standstill when he saw what the Swapo insurgents had done. Somehow he was not as shocked as when they had found Johan. Perhaps he had expected it.

Carel squatted and rolled Hein onto his back. "God go with you my friend," he whispered and lifted Hein's bullet-riddled body in his arms. He held him to his chest and let the tears roll unashamedly down his face. He looked up and noticed a movement from the badly mutilated servant. "Somebody see to this man; he is still alive! The rest of you look for the remainder of the bodies," he said, knowing there was little chance of finding any survivors.

"Carel," the lieutenant squatted next to him and spoke with as much compassion as he could muster. "That is just the shell, the man has gone," he said softly. Carel nodded and the lieutenant stood up. "I need you to come and speak to the servant we found at the kraal. He says you know each other." Carel nodded and carefully placed the body back on the bloodstained floor. He pushed Hein's body away from the pools of blood and the lieutenant frowned as Carel jolted. "*Wat is dit?* What's the problem, Carel?"

"Grootvoet!" Carel pointed at the huge bloody bootprint next to Hein's body.

"What's that?"

"That is the most wanted terrorist bastard in the whole country. Surely you've heard of him, Jack?" asked Carel, momentarily forgetting his station.

The lieutenant frowned thoughtfully. "Vaguely, but that was from one of the security force chaps up at the border. He can't be here, can he? I mean, are you sure that's his bootprint? How can you be so sure ...?"

Carel looked up sharply. "Absolutely. No doubt," he said. "Let's go and talk to the servant. Maybe he can shed some light." Carel smiled humourlessly and he stood.

Carel recognised the man immediately. "*Is dit jy?* Is it you, Jacob?" and the man smiled with relief as he recognised the policeman friend of his dead boss. He fell to the ground, his legs unable to support his fear-racked body any longer. The police who had found him would surely have killed him had it not been for the fact that he mentioned Carel by name and now rough hands lifted him.

"*Ja, my baas,* it is I, Jacob and I praise God that you are here as these people think I am involved!"

"Well, are you?"

"No, no!" Jacob said quickly. "But they did come to the kraal. They told us to leave for good as there would be nothing left for us here."

"Who is 'they', Jacob?"

"The Ovambos ... and lots of them, *baas.*"

"Why didn't you come straight to us at the police station?"

"My cousin knew of these people before me. When I saw him in town, he told me that he was on his way to see you."

Carel slapped his forehead. "Lieutenant, do you remember when you summoned me to your office in connection with the emergency signal?" His eyes had a haunted look. Lieutenant Jack Botha nodded. "Well, I was busy taking a statement from a man who said that he had seen these bastards two days previously." Carel turned back to Jacob. "Is your cousin's name Henry Makoena?"

"*Ja baas.*" Jacob had regained some of his strength and stood unsupported.

Carel turned back to the lieutenant. "I was just thinking that had that signal been five minutes later I would have known Jacob's story and all of this might have been different. Completely different!"

Lieutenant Botha pursed his lips and shook his head. "Don't go down that road Carel ... please let's stick to the facts. Even if you had Henry's story, how quickly would you have reacted ... if at all?

"I don't know but for the first time in many months I had a man giving me feasible information without wanting a reward. All he wanted was peace for him and his family. I think I would have acted on his information immediately, sir." The irritation in Carel's voice was clear.

"Carry on now, Carel," ordered the lieutenant.

Of course! Jacob is from the Herero people, thought Carel as he acknowledged his superior officer stiffly, and turned to Jacob. He might know a little more, if prompted.

"Was there one taller than the lieutenant with feet double the size of mine and skin as black as coal?"

Jacob contemplated his answer carefully. "He did not come to our kraal with the others but when I drove back to the farm, the bakkie got stuck in the mud on the lands and as I walked, they ran past me in the rain and darkness. I saw him in the flash of lightning and he is this man that you now describe."

"Why did you come back all the way to the kraal then?"

"To fetch the block and tackle in order to pull the bakkie from the mud. When I got here the house was burning and the fear of the coward entered my stomach and I lay on the floor of my hut until these people found me. I am so sorry, my boss," said Jacob now blubbering as he watched the policemen bring out the bodies. They laid them out on the veranda. Five terrorists together and Hein, his mother and father on the other side where it was still dry. Carel gawked at the bodies and paled as he realised that some were missing.

"My God, lieutenant, where the hell are Gabi and the twins?" He didn't wait for an answer as he summoned a few idle policemen. "We are missing a woman and two children! Spread out and search the house, the grounds and the servants' area. Hurry, man, hurry!" The men dashed off in all directions.

One by one, his men returned empty-handed. Carel began to despair as he searched the workshop area and shed without success. He was about to commandeer one of the Casspirs when it suddenly dawned on him. He'd been down there only once before to look at Hein's wine collection, and he ran.

He sprinted into the house, through the kitchen and halfway down the passage to where one of the terrorist bodies had lain and began to tear debris out of the way. He shouted for help and minutes later, assisted by two of his men, he ripped at the pull-ring in the partially burned floor. Carel lifted the door and peered down into the pitch dark. He coughed as the smoke billowed out from the cellar. Cautiously Carel climbed into the smoky hole and felt for the light. He found the switch at the back of the timber beam and flicked it on. Covering his mouth with his damp shirt, he carefully skirted the bookshelf, dropped to his knees and drew his side-arm. A khaki-clad bundle lay on the floor at the bottom of the stairs. Slowly, carefully he approached the prostrate man and felt his neck for any signs of life.

"Are you okay, sarge?" called a loud voice.

Carel jumped back with fright. "Ja, man. Don't shout so loud. You nearly scared the crap out of me. Come down here and remove this dead gook."

"Okay, sarge!" came the booming reply. Carel shook his head, coughed and stepped over the body as he continued his search. At last he found them at one of the vents at the back of the cellar. He lifted Gabi easily over his shoulders and removed her from the smoking pit.

Quickly, the medic took over. Maybe because of the crisp, post-storm night air or because God meant her to, Gabi coughed and sat up. Tears from her smoke-reddened eyes rolled down her cheeks. She coughed and coughed, doubled over and started retching. The medic laid her back and placed the oxygen mask over her face.

"Water. Water please," she croaked through the mask.

"Water!" shouted the medic and two constables arrived seconds later holding a glass each. Gradually Gabi regained control and sat up slowly, removed the mask and gulped the water. In her haste she breathed some in and immediately coughed again. Water shot from her mouth and nose.

"Slowly please ma'am," soothed the medic.

"My children! Where are my children?" she croaked and looked about frantically. She saw them then and watched helplessly as the medics tried to work their magic.

Carel walked over with a blanket. He wrapped her up, squatted and smiled at her. "Thank God you're alive. At least we've got you," he whispered and immediately regretted his words. Gabi was anxious and disoriented. She seemed not to have heard as she watched the medics.

Then she turned to face Carel. "What's going on? What do you mean?" The curtains of doubt and confusion peeled back. She shook her head slowly, then faster and her face dissolved. She began to struggle wildly as the medic slipped the needle into her arm.

CHAPTER 9

It was still dark when the Buffels pulled up next to the palm. They rocked on their big suspension springs and the soldiers immediately disembarked.

They formed an all-round defence and Geoff jogged up to the doggie corporal. "Howzit," he said and offered his hand, "I'm Geoff Kent, Three South African Infantry—Potchefstroom currently based at Eenhana, at your service." He smiled his irresistible smile.

"Hello Geoff. Allan Hunt, Four South African Infantry—Middleburg, B—Special Forces Dog Squad and Tracking, Pretoria, currently based at SWA Spes, Oshivelo, Legion of the Damned and in cahoots with Attila the Hun, thanking you for your services," he replied and grinned. Allan was as wide as Geoff but half his height. His powerful forearms supported a mat of thick, steely white hair and his green eyes shone with mischief. The two young men took an instant liking to each other. Corporal Mike Theunissen trotted over and joined them.

Geoff introduced him. The men squatted and Allan began the briefing. "Okay, this is definitely Grootvoet and twelve, although I only get eleven but I don't argue with my Bushie over there," he nodded towards a wizened little Bushman who squatted at the periphery of the vehicle lights. Allan stroked his Alsatian and the dog's pink tongue lolled out the corner of its mouth. "I don't know if you guys have heard about their colourful little sojourn into Tsumeb and environs just lately?"

"Only that they attacked some farm near Tsumeb and there were casualties," replied Geoff.

"Well then, allow me to fill you in." He popped a glucose sweet into his mouth and spoke around it. "They breezed in from up north, probably from the border area and split up into two groups …" Allan told the torrid tale. None of his audience uttered a sound, so appalling the story, so eloquent the narrator.

" … meanwhile mom held off the gooks with her 357 magnum—stop me if you find me too boring," said Allan in attempt to keep the story light-hearted.

"To end my tale, old shot-up farmer's wife is apparently even more beautiful than old blown-to-pieces farmer's wife but both ladies are pretty screwed up by all this." Allan crunched his sweet. "So now … here we are," he spread his hands, "and off we go to fix, without prejudice. I reckon it'll be quite fun chasing after Grootvoet."

They were silent for a while as the horror of the story sank in. Geoff stood up, pushed his bush hat back and scratched his forehead. "Thanks for a tale well told, Allan. I've just got one or two questions."

"Go ahead," he invited and stood. He adjusted his faded webbing and slung it over his shoulder.

"Didn't the police find and follow spoor?"

"Rain stopped play that night, so no external spoor was found. Apparently there is a police sergeant who was personal friends of the murdered people and he's hell-bent on revenge. He's champing at the bit to join our patrol, if and when contact is inevitable."

"Isn't that typical! We'll do the hard work and he joins us when we've found them," Geoff shook his head.

"Well, he is the investigating officer and he did find them first," Allan pointed out. "Maybe he'll be of some help."

"Rain? You said rain … then how do we know it is Grootvoet?"

"Beautiful bloody bootprint of his size fifteen found in the house and positive ID on some of the other dead gooks."

"No heelio search?"

"Oh yes. Hundreds of PBs, locals, were spotted from an Alouette in the morning. It could even have been one or two of our boys. You know how they mingle with the tribesmen. You can't tell who's who in the fucking zoo."

"How the hell did you find his spoor then?"

"On occasion this 'hearts and minds' shit seems to work. Some PB reported seeing him near Oshivelo and we picked up the spoor the other side of the Oshivelo Gate." Allan shrugged. "But the cop you are so ready to defame had a hunch they'd come this way."

"I don't want to defame him," protested Geoff, "but this isn't a police matter …"

"You thinking Parabat then?"

"Yeah," Geoff nodded.

"Glory boys aside, I believe he has a personal interest, so …," Allan spat. "Anyway, I called for a patrol and ended up with you lot. But don't get me wrong, the pleasure's all mine," he said, smiling broadly.

"You said that they identified some of the dead gooks, so I take it that these farmers managed some sort of resistance?" asked Geoff. "How many did they kill?"

"I don't know ... but they managed to kill several and as I told you the wife killed a couple, which is good news for us otherwise we would be chasing seventeen or eighteen of them."

"Eighteen in one gang!" exclaimed Rudi. "That's unheard of. I wonder what they're up to?"

"Yep, pretty unusual hey?"

Again there was an ephemeral silence as they contemplated the task ahead. "Alright, listen up, men. This how we play it," said Geoff to the soldiers around him. "Rudi, firstly, contact base, tell them we're on our way ..." Geoff snapped out a string of orders.

Geoff shifted his webbing, draped his arms over his rifle and settled in for a long, arduous walk. Thick sand muffled their footfalls as they trudged after the dogs with the early morning chill upon them. The silence was heavy on the nerves and Geoff shivered slightly as a light breeze caressed him, lifting the hair on his forearms.

The sky was pearly pink, but the bush was still dim and hazy ... a particularly dangerous time. With dawn rapidly approaching, everything at ground level was a silhouette. The sun soon broke the horizon and the land, with its green scrub and acacias, came alive with colour.

Red in the morning ..., thought Geoff as he jogged to the front of the line and spoke quietly to Allan. "Any sign that fun and games might begin soon?"

"I'm not sure yet. We still have the scent alright but we slowed for the light. I don't feel like an ambush right now." Allan seemed a bit frayed.

"I was just wondering when we could stop for a bit of tea. It's chilly enough," whispered Geoff and rubbed his arms.

Allan peered at Geoff. "I could do with a cuppa myself right now but let's go on until Bushie can see the spoor," he smiled. "Anyway, give it a few hours and you'll be cursing the heat."

Allan was right; the sun rose and the air warmed—then it became hot. Their tea stop was brief but welcome. The Bushman tracker took the spoor and led them along at a pace just short of a trot. Resisting the urge to drink from their water bottles too often became a mammoth task for the new troops. It was a consuming thought.

The sun beat down as it reached its zenith. The white sand dragged at their boots and reflected the sun's rays into their faces. Like standing before a furnace, the heat engulfed them. The gentle breeze was hot and sucked the moisture from their bodies. It was a battle against the elements.

Geoff called a halt and he and Allan scrounged a meagre piece of shade in which to sit and assess their position. Sergeant Gerrie Niemant, Corporal Mike

Theunissen and Rudi joined them while the section formed a defensive ring around them. The men sat in pairs and faced outwards. They sat mostly wherever the shade was greatest and although hungry, few ate, electing rather to mix an energy drink or chew a glucose tablet. Allan took a map from one of his pouches and spread it before them.

"Well, at this stage the Swaps seem to be holding due north according to my map," he observed.

"All I've seen is low bush and flat land with a tree here or there. What landmarks were you using?" inquired Geoff. He wiped the sweat on his already grease-blackened sleeve.

"Oh, nothing really, just the path of the sun," answered Allan casually

"What? Only the sun? By just looking at the sun you could be walking northeast and not know it! Surely you need some sort of reference to orient our position?"

"I know this area fairly well and I think that they're heading straight for the border ... somewhere between Okongo and Eenhana, I'd say," Allan stabbed at the map with a grubby finger. "We should cross this riverbed before nightfall if the Swaps hold this route."

"Hell, if we cross that riverbed before sunset, then we're really moving," commented Geoff. "I doubt it though. Look how far to the north that river is," he observed and smiled mischievously. "Not only that, with your navigation methods we might stumble upon the ocean."

Allan smiled at the jibe. "Why pray, are you so eager to find our exact position? It doesn't really matter, does it? I mean as long as we follow them, who cares where the hell they go as long as we catch them?"

"Sure, but we weren't expecting to make your acquaintance and we've only packed enough rats for three days," said Geoff raising his eyebrows. "If and when we need to call for more, we need to know where we are."

"Okay," said Allan pensively. "We had better find a distinguishable landmark before the rations run out or we'll lose our friends up ahead.

As the sun slid below the horizon, Geoff felt the ground dip steeply away and they ambled down through the thick sand into the dry riverbed. Geoff was surprised and in the slightly cooler evening called a halt—it was getting too dark for Bushie to follow the spoor. The Alsatian took the scent and Allan increased the pace. Some hours later Geoff jogged to the tracker group up ahead in the darkness and found Allan.

"You've proved your point and I'm sure we've broken some sort of world walking record, so let's call it a night. I bet we've walked about forty clicks since morning."

They set up a temporary base and Geoff walked round to the men on the defensive ring and judged the mood. He asked a question of one of the blowies and shared a joke with Martin. All seemed fine but tired. It was a well-timed stop. The gutsy rookie le Roux had black rings of exhaustion under his eyes.

Fully clothed—boots and all—Geoff slid into his sleeping bag. He placed his rifle next to him and pulled his webbing up behind him. The firmament was beautiful and endless. It had a calming effect and Geoff placed his arms behind his head, sighed deeply and looked across at Allan.

"Do you see the Southern Cross rising over that palm tree?"

"Oh boy, here it comes," said Allan not without humour. "Yes I do. Why, do you ask?"

"Well, take a good look and remember, so at least you know where south is," he said with light-hearted sarcasm. "Amazingly you can work out all the other points of the compass from that." Others in the leader group chuckled. They were following the friendly debate of exactly where they were with a degree of interest.

"So what time do you want to move tomorrow …?" Allan yawned.

The low murmur of voices subsided and a hush descended upon the soldiers. Somewhere a jackal broke the silence with its eerie howl. Sometime later, the same tenuous night breeze sprang up, whispered through the grass and rustled the palm fronds. Geoff succumbed to sleep at last.

No dog barked. No sentry alerted him and the black man stood over him. His look was one of savage delight. His AK was slung over his shoulder. He held a machete firmly in his right hand. Geoff looked up, horrified. He realised that he had no chance to swing up his rifle. Where the hell was his bayonet? This terrifying man was going to hack the life out of him. He was huge with shiny ebony skin. He had well-defined, wiry arms and big feet. He had the biggest feet that Geoff had ever seen. Slowly and jubilantly he lifted the machete above his head. Geoff lapsed into cataleptic fear. Incredibly he could not move a single muscle. He opened his mouth to scream and he looked up. The huge black warrior had a white man's face. He had Dawid's face! He screamed again but no sound issued forth. Suddenly he was looking at Allan who crouched next to him.

"Jesus!" Geoff gasped.

No, just Allan, now get up sleepy head, you're the one who is supposed to do the waking-up around here."

"I had the most awful dream," croaked Geoff. "It was Grootvoet. He was standing over me with a huge bloody panga …"

"Well, let me be the bearer of good news; it's only me and the time now …," Allan lifted the leather flap on his watch and peered down, "is oh four hundred oh one and I'm sorry that there's no tea in bed but we've got some terrs to catch, so lets go."

"Ja, ja, give me a break and a chance to pack my kit, funny boy."

Geoff dabbed at the sweat on his brow. "Shit, this bastard is working on my nerves. Is Rudi up?"

"Yep, here I am and I have radioed in already. We're just waiting for you to finish your beauty sleep."

Bushie squatted out in the open at the edge of the *shona*. It was late in the season for the shallow depression to hold so much water.

"If there were any Swapo out there they would have shot the stupid little bugger by now. Let's go and see what he's found for us." They walked to where Bushie scratched in the sand. "Bushie, you like living dangerously hey?" asked Allan, irritated by the negligence of his tracker.

"*Nee, korperaal*. This spoor is not as fresh as that." Bushie's teeth were stained yellow by years of plain cigarettes but his wrinkled grin was incorrigible.

"How old?" asked Allan.

"Less than a day."

"How can you tell that?" Geoff was sceptical.

"Don't worry, we'll know when we get close because this little bugger suddenly looses the spoor and he feels like a rest or he feels sick. Am I correct, hey Bushie?"

"*Nee korperaal!*" protested the little man, "it's not like that man!"

"Don't argue, you little blighter," said Allan rubbing his head jokingly. "You always slow down as soon as we get too close for your liking."

"Do you suppose we'll pick up the spoor on the other side of the *shona*?" asked Geoff.

Allan pursed his lips, "Good question. Let's get across and see."

The section formed up in single file again and followed the tracker team across the *shona's* grey shallows. The openness left them feeling vulnerable and uneasy. The tension was tangible as each man waded slowly through the water. They tried desperately not to splash too much, but the noise still seemed so loud in the early morning. Surely the enemy could hear them? Dawid waited until the man in front of him was about halfway into the *shona* before he too followed. He could see the sanctuary of the bush on the other side but it seemed miles away. He gritted his teeth and took a deep breath.

Last in the queue! If Swapo decided to attack, he'd have no chance. That was a tactic of theirs; take out the last two or three in the line and bombshell. The sun began its assault on the soldiers as it climbed inexorably skyward. Dawid felt the sweat bead and collect and trickle down his back—a cold sweat.

His chest heaved as he stepped out of the water on the far side. He walked up the shallow bank and suppressed the urge to run. Beyond the *shona*, through the first line of bushes a movement to his left startled him. Instinct took over and he dived to the ground. In a flash he brought the MAG to bear. Geoff stepped out of the bush and froze. Their eyes locked. The corners of Dawid's mouth lifted in an evil grimace.

The MAG pointed at Geoff's stomach. "You have no idea how tempting this is, you bleddy Engelsman." Dawid's voice was low and menacing.

"I actually stayed back here to cover the tail in case of ambush. I surely wasted my time watching your arse." Geoff deliberately turned away from Dawid and the MAG. He jogged to catch up to the tracker group. Geoff held out his hand as he reached Rudi. It shook like a dead leaf in an August wind and his back was in spasm. *Would he really shoot a fellow soldier in cold blood? The section leader? So close to contact too? Does he hate me that much? He would need to be bloody mad,* thought Geoff. Maybe he was and Geoff shivered despite the climbing temperature.

"Jesus, Geoff, you're as white as a sheet. Are you alright, man?" whispered Rudi.

"Just a bit of nausea; gripes maybe. I'll be okay. I must have put too much condensed milk in my tea," said Geoff. He frowned and rubbed his stomach. It was a poor attempt at hiding adrenaline reaction.

"Don't bullshit me, I know you too well by now," said Rudi. "It was that bloody Neanderthal again, wasn't it? What did he do this time?"

"Nah, forget it Rudi. I've got it under control, thanks."

"You know what really irks me is when you try to lie about that bastard because he's a good soldier. It's an insult to me. Why can't you just tell me? Share it with me," Rudi appealed. "Let him be a good soldier but when he fucks with you, he fucks with me."

Geoff's forehead creased into a deep frown. "Not so loud Rudi. Do you want the whole of Swapo to share our problems too?"

Allan hardly disguised his irritation. "Anything I should know about?"

"No," said Geoff quickly, "I'll sort it out."

Allan raised his eyebrows and nodded, "Okay. It looks as if the bush is thinning. I'll bet they're heading straight for the '*Yati*'. Allan glanced over his shoulder. "I'm going up that anthill. I need to have a look around. " Allan pointed to the massive grey-white mound. He took out one of his water bottles and offered it to Geoff who shook his head.

He took out one of his own bottles, unscrewed the cap, and saluted Allan as if he held a glass of champagne. "Cheers," he said and lifted the bottle to his lips. Geoff, like Allan, used the first mouthful of the warm liquid to rinse his dry, sticky mouth. He spat onto the hot sand. The second mouthful was swallowed ... and the third and Geoff, with his head thrown back, his eyes tightly closed, had to tear the bottle from his lips.

The steadily rising temperature was not the only cause of Geoff's thirst.

CHAPTER 10

Allan glanced at the road and then scrutinised his map. "Okay, this is where we are ... what do you say, Geoff ... and there's a village marked here?" Allan pointed a square-tipped finger with a crescent moon of dirt beneath the nail.

"No doubt ...," began Geoff and he looked up in utter astonishment as Dawid sauntered down the track as if he were on his way to the corner café. They stood, frozen, waiting for a hail of AK bullets to cut him down. "Take cover you idiot!"

Dawid stopped nonchalantly in the middle of the track, turned to face them, his legs astride, hands crossed over, holding the MAG low in front of him. "There's a kaffir kraal over to the east there," he pointed with his chin, "so you won't find the Swaps here. They would have gone there for food and water."

"Thank you Corporal Gouws! That's exactly what we needed ...," began Allan. "Just stay exactly where you are, Gouws. You and I need another little chat ..."

"What is the matter with the two of you?" No one had noticed the sergeant stride over. "Can't you see how much time we're wasting here? Hurry up and get this show on the road, otherwise I'll take command. If you need a chopper, Kent, then call for one now before it's too dark. You, Gouws, take a few men and find out what you can from the civilians at that kraal ... Just remember that you're not RSM Joubert's favourites at the moment so just behave. Both of you need to leave your personal differences for base camp or any other time but now." The sergeant glared at Geoff then directed his scowl at Dawid, "Just watch your step Gouws, these bleddy PBs, *plaaslike bevolking*, local population or whatever you want to call them are bleddy jumpy in these remote areas."

It was Dawid's turn to be angry. His eyes blazed and the deep frown between thick black eyebrows enhanced his murderous scowl. He turned and strode to the nearest pair of soldiers on the perimeter of the defensive position and shouted. *"Wat die vok!* Who are you staring at, you should be looking for Swapo, not at us, you bunch of clowns! Hey Martin, come with me."

Geoff cringed at the booming voice and shook his head incredulously. "This is crazy; we are acting like a bunch of fucking amateurs ..."

"Your helicopter is going to make more noise than you care for anyway, so get on with it, man," snapped the sergeant.

As Geoff turned to Rudi the sergeant caught his arm. "You need to sort your little problem out soon or else you'll have a mutiny on your hands, Kent."

"With all respect, I was doing quite well until you butted in, sarge." Geoff shrugged off the sergeant's hand and walked to where Rudi and the others waited under the big acacia. It was cool under the tree and a faint breeze whispered through the mass of tiny leaves. Geoff dropped his webbing beside the trunk, removed his bush hat, wiped the sweat on his sleeve and took a deep breath. "Okay, we've got a lot to do so let me start with you, Allan ..."

A burst of automatic fire shattered the lazy mid-afternoon silence and the leader group was catapulted into a frenzy of action. Geoff grabbed his webbing and rifle and ran in the direction of the gunfire.

He shouted over his shoulder, "Mike, stay here and guard this position for the chopper, we'll call if we need you—the rest of you come with me, spread out! You two and you with the rifle grenade, come with us now!" Geoff took the lead as the sergeant, Rudi and the others fanned out in a V formation next to him. They ran through the bush and Geoff held up a clenched fist as they reached the clearing.

The area around the kraal was trampled bare and dry from overgrazing. The group of soldiers took cover on the perimeter. Eyes darted and they sat like that for a full minute.

Geoff made a decision and spoke quietly but urgently to Rudi, "Take Pieter and cover the kraal so there can be no escape out the back ..." A terrible moaning sound interrupted them. They looked at each other as the moaning increased in volume. Geoff had never heard anything like it before; it was a cry of pain ... or anguish, he couldn't be sure. The sound was haunting and distressing and he willed it to stop. As if his wish were granted, a bellow and another burst of automatic fire drummed against their ears. The wail ceased abruptly. The silence sang loud after the hammering of the MAG.

Another bark and Geoff recognised Dawid's voice. "Are you alright, what's going on, Gouws?" Geoff scrutinised the wooden palisade fence through the sights of his R1.

"Is that you, Kent—sorry, I mean, corporal. Everything is just fine; you'll find the entrance at the north side of the log fence if you want to come in, that's if you can find it." Dawid sounded drunk or high, his speech slow and deliberate.

"Are you okay? Are the enemy in there? Do we need to surround the place?" Geoff was suspicious. Perhaps the insurgents hiding in the kraal had captured the South Africans and held them hostage.

"*Nee, man*! Just get your arse in here. I've found out all we need to know. I've done your job for you."

Geoff beckoned the others and he stopped opposite the cleverly disguised entrance. There they waited again. Then Geoff ran to the entrance. Two men followed and the others covered. Geoff hesitated, dodged through the maze-like opening in the pales and dived onto the bare earth floor.

At first all seemed normal. Dawid leant against the fence and smoked. Martin herded the inhabitants of the kraal like a sheepdog about the flock. The Ovambos sat, frozen in a cataleptic state against the fence with their hands upon their heads. A bowl of maize beer lay overturned, its contents splashed across the swept dung floor and a large bundle of rags lay in the middle of the kraal.

Geoff stood slowly, dusted himself off and peered at the bundle of rags. A tenuous trickle of blood emanated from the rags and slithered across the dung floor where it pooled against the fence. Then the horror dawned as Geoff realised the rags were the twisted forms of two ancient people with massive holes draining their life blood. The top of the old man's head was missing and his eyes stared dull and unseeing into the blue sky. Their threadbare clothing could not soak up any more blood and it pooled. Geoff gagged and turned away as he realised that it was not spilt maize beer.

Horrified, he faced Dawid and whispered slowly. "What the fuck have you done?"

"I told you. I've done your job for you," said Dawid and he drew on his cigarette. "They told us that our friends were here earlier but have since moved on. They couldn't tell me the exact time that they left but they did tell me, after some persuasion, that they fed them and gave them water. Two of those whores over there even satisfied a few of them." Dawid pointed his MAG at the terrified group sitting on the floor. The smoke trickled from his lips as he spoke. "At first they wouldn't talk to us and then that old fart lying there started shouting something and attacked Martin, so I shot him and *then* they told us everything. They even tried to bullshit me that the gooks raped those two cows. Next thing, that old bitch fell on her knees next to him and started making a godawful noise. I reckoned she was trying to warn someone so I shot her too."

"But they are innocent civilians and you've just murdered them!" Geoff felt an uncontrollable rage overwhelm him. "Now you've really screwed up, Gouws and I'm going to have your balls for this!" Geoff made as if to turn, spun around and lashed out with the butt of his rifle. He caught Dawid on the side of his head, a glancing blow. Dawid fell back against the fence, slid down and brought the barrel of the MAG up in one fluid movement. The intention on his face was clear. His eyes were dark pools and his mouth twisted with hatred. Dawid snatched at the trigger.

The ground between Geoff's legs exploded. Clods of earth and sand flew into his face. He lifted his left arm to protect his eyes and fired. He dived sideways and rolled over as the fusillade of bullets smashed and splintered the timber pales of the fence on the far side of the kraal. More shots were fired, someone shouted and Geoff lifted his head in time to see Rudi kick the MAG out of Dawid's hands.

Geoff lunged, aimed his rifle at Dawid's torso, knowing that a stomach wound was one of the most painful ways to die. White lights burst in his head before the final resistance on the trigger. He fell sideways, losing his rifle and lay stunned on the ground trying to work out what had happened as the bright afternoon light faded into darkness around him.

Rough hands lifted him to his feet and slowly his vision cleared. It had taken mere seconds and Geoff looked around groggily at the scene before him. It was as before—the two old people lay dead on the floor and the rest of the Ovambos sat against the fence, their hands on their heads, staring, wide-eyed at the madness of war. So it was true then; he wasn't dreaming.

Sergeant Niemant handed Geoff a water bottle. He poured some over his head then put it to his lips and finished the contents. "You are going to have to explain very carefully what went on here, Corporal Kent," said the sergeant menacingly. "There are two dead PBs lying here. I saw Corporal Gouws try to shoot you and you tried to shoot him."

"Firstly, what the hell hit me?" asked Geoff rubbing the side of his head.

"I did, but don't worry about that now. Just tell me what the fuck happened!"

Geoff sighed and began. The distant but familiar sound of a Puma helicopter caught their attention and all conversation ceased. Heads turned skywards and searched. "Rudi, run, man, run!"

Rudi reacted and sprinted to the position where he had thrown the net antenna over an acacia. He plugged it into the radio, just in time to hear their call sign through the hissing static. "One Five Charlie, this is Giant, message over."

"Giant! Giant! This is One Five Charlie. Send over!" panted Rudi, relieved that they had clear communication.

"Giant, throw smoke, over."

Rudi unclipped a beer-can-sized canister from his webbing, pulled the pin and threw it as far into the centre of the landing zone as he could. The handle flew off, the canister bounced once as they heard the 'pop' and deep crimson smoke billowed from the ground where the canister came to rest. The camouflaged Puma roared low overhead, slightly to the west of them.

"One Five Charlie, throw your smoke!" The pilot sounded anxious.

"Giant, I have you visual; you were just too quick for me. Turn through one eighty and you should see our smoke." Immediately the graceful craft bunted up, banked hard and dropped back to tree level. Rudi watched as the undercarriage lowered. Some turned their backs while others covered their eyes as wind and dust buffeted them while the helicopter lowered like a contented petrel settling upon her nest.

Allan looked towards the kraal and watched the group of soldiers walking towards the chopper. Geoff was talking heatedly to his sergeant. His shoulders were hunched up in a shrug and a frown of concentration creased the sergeant's forehead as he listened. Dawid followed and behind them, Pieter carried Dawid's MAG, his R1 pointed at Dawid's back. What Allan saw distressed him.

Sergeant Niemant jogged to the Puma and spoke to the commander. "*Gooie middag, kaptein*. Good afternoon captain, thank you for the rats. We've got a bit of a situation here and I need a few minutes to sort it out. Is this your last rat run of the day?"

"Actually, yes," replied the captain.

"Did you collect our rations at Eenhana or Oshivelo?"

"Eenhana, why?"

"We need to send a troopie back. Heat exhaustion you know and maybe one or two others. We'd be very appreciative if we can just have five minutes to get something sorted out."

"Okay fine, just get someone to offload please. We've got a briefing back at Ondangwa, so make it snappy."

"Sorry. Of course. You and you," the sergeant pointed, "and don't forget the water."

Sergeant Gerrie Niemant walked back to the acacia tree where Geoff and Allan were talking. Mike and Rudi stood off to one side and watched Dawid.

"Van der Merwe! Come here." Martin walked apprehensively over to the group, his concern evident.

"Tell us the way you saw things in the kraal."

"It's just as Dawid said. That old man attacked me. We genuinely thought that the old woman was trying to warn someone. We didn't know that the area was clear. How could we? The gooks could easily have waited for us in those bushes." Martin pointed to a thicket near the kraal, "I mean what …?"

"Okay, what about you, Barker. You shot at Gouws. What's your story? You could have wounded or even killed him."

"I stopped him from killing Corporal Kent." Rudi's nostrils flared white. "There's more though, back at the shona …" Geoff frowned and shot Rudi a venomous glance. Rudi pursed his lips and lapsed into silence.

The sergeant seemed not to hear and faced Dawid. "Right, when you get back to Eenhana you can go and explain to the RSM why we sent you back, Gouws! The rest of us can distribute the rats and then move out—agreed?"

Geoff shook his head. "I'm afraid it's not that simple, sarge. Gouws forms an integral part of the section and without him …" Geoff shrugged, "I hate to say it, but he's good at his job."

Sergeant Niemant placed his hands on his hips and looked about. His head dropped in resignation and he spoke softly. "I told you before, I'm just here for the ride, so it's your call, Kent. But we can't carry on like this. Just make up your mind and let's get going. I don't know what we are going to do about those dead Ovambos though," he said looking back at the kraal. "I think that we're going to have to take Gouws's word and with van der Merwe as witness put in a report as soon as we return to base." The sergeant scowled suddenly, "Because I have no doubt that the villagers are going to report a murder. I want to tell you that if I'm asked I'll tell them murder. As for you …," the sergeant pointed at Geoff, "I'd say attempted murder! And you too Barker."

Geoff pursed his lips and nodded. "Would you give Dawid and me a few minutes?" As soon as everyone was out of earshot, Geoff looked Dawid in the eyes. "That was close. Too goddamned close and I know that it's not over but it has to be for the rest of this hunt. We need to concentrate on the job, not on our backs or on each other. If we're not fully alert we could get taken out. Let's shake and get on with it." Geoff held out his hand. Dawid hesitated then grabbed Geoff's hand with his powerful right and shook.

"Would you have shot me back there?" Geoff asked roughly.

"Just as surely as you tried to shoot me."

They stared at one another, seeing for the first time the killers behind their young faces.

The difference was that Dawid enjoyed it and Geoff didn't. They turned and walked away with a new, grudging respect for each other.

Cirrus clouds skidded across the pale sky for a couple of days and finally the intense heat led to a build-up of cumulus clouds. They piled up on the horizon like massive snowy mountains. Then they heaved upwards into the atmosphere only to have their heads guillotined by the jet streams, forming great anvil-shaped monsters that inexorably bore down upon the soldiers below. The corporals lay in the bush on the bank of the Nipele River and studied the spoor crossing the flat, dry bed. The gang had done little if anything to hide their tracks.

It was a hot wind that dried their sweat before it cooled them and the flies sat thick and black on their shirts. Allan's ambivalence irritated Geoff. He found himself praying that the storm would bucket down and drench them and at the same time he hoped it would blow over. It sickened him when he thought that he was praying for better conditions in which to kill other human beings.

On the fifth morning Allan peered over his shoulder as he tightened his bootlace and he rubbed the thick stubble on his chin. "It's close, hey?"

Geoff raised his eyebrows and looked up. "One storm and we'll be toasting failure back in Eenhana." Allan nodded pensively and together they led the section into another day.

Close to the lunchtime siesta, Geoff pointed ahead and almost casually announced to Allan, "Look, another road. Maybe we should stop and have a break." Geoff's eyes were slits against the glare. "Where's that map of yours?" he asked holding out a filthy hand.

Allan foraged in his webbing. "Break sounds fine to me."

Geoff flipped the map open. "Oshakati is further away than I thought." He looked up. "We'll make sure the spoor continues …," he began and realised that Allan wasn't listening. Instead he stared across the road. He lay like that for a while and Geoff interrupted his thoughts. "Are you alright? What are you staring at?"

"What's that on the other side of the road? What do you make of it?"

"Where?" asked Geoff and screwed up his eyes against the glare.

"Look man, there, just next to the slightly greener bush on the edge of the road. On the ground next to that sort of windrow." Allan pointed his finger and sighted down his arm.

For a few seconds they stared across the road and at last Geoff smiled. "Those are the pretty little white butterflies with the orange on their wings. You know, we always see them at the edge of the shonas, man. They stop in … flocks or whatever you call a crowd of butterflies and they drink."

Allan frowned, "I thought so, but what the hell are they drinking? Jesus, the only liquid around here is in my water bottle." Geoff paled. The pretty little insects hovered above their drinking patch where they settled from time to time, unfurling their coiled tongues and dabbing at the moisture. Some of the bubbles still stubbornly survived and Allan instantly knew why Geoff seemed agitated. In the stillness and the heat of the day, the smell dispelled any doubt as they looked at the drying puddle of urine.

"These are our boys," whispered Allan. He frowned and shook his head.

Geoff nodded, his eyes wide, his heart pumping. He drew in a huge draught of air and slowly breathed out. The knot in his stomach was back. "Mike, this is it. Please brief everyone."

"Shouldn't we move forward in V formation from here?"

"Yes, yes of course, the bush is pretty thin under the trees so let's get well spread out, and, Mike, get back to the point as soon as possible." Geoff stood up where all his men could see him, spread his arms horizontally with his R1 in his right hand; the signal to form up in V formation with the MAG gunner on his right. They were well drilled in the action of fire and movement and moved quickly into familiar positions.

Geoff walked at the point and followed the tracker group. Rudi, Mike and the sergeant walked with Geoff and the rest of the section spread out on each side of them like the swept-back wings of a fighter jet. In the heat of the day little Bushie stalked ahead like a bloodhound, his face a study of concentration. Allan, with the trackers and dogs, walked along with the little Bushman. Their eyes relentlessly searched and watched the dogs for reaction. The ubiquitous cicadas hissed their sibilant song and it buzzed in their ears as Bushie drew level with a palm tree and stopped suddenly.

His yellow-brown skin turned grey and his eyes bulged as he peered at the ground. Allan held up his fist then extended his arm horizontally. He waved his hand slowly up and down and the section disappeared. He squatted as Geoff crawled to their position.

"Give us the gears," whispered Geoff.

"Do you see that Russian bootprint, *korperaal*—do you see how it covers this lizard spoor over here?" Bushie pointed at the picture on the ground.

"Clearly. So what?" whispered Allan.

"Well, there's the lizard under that bush." Allan and Geoff looked at the reptile; its beady eyes stared back, unblinkingly. "We're so close that they can probably smell us already." The veins in Bushie's neck stood out; he was plainly terrified. Allan's dog lunged at a movement ahead through the bush to their left. The ground shook with the blast of the RPG as it hit the trunk of the palm tree above them and the air was filled with the buzz and whine of deadly shrapnel.

CHAPTER 11

The white staff car sped over the saddle between the two hills, wound its way down towards the end of the Ben Schoeman highway past the prison and into Pretoria. The car took the first slipway left, turned left again and right where it stopped at the security check boom. A guard marched smartly to the driver's side, bent slightly and peered into the vehicle. He stood back and saluted as he recognised the rank.

"You're expected, colonel. Please go to the parking reserved for you at the front of the building and someone will escort you from there." He saluted again, marched around the car and lifted the boom.

The driver nodded his thanks and accelerated down the paved ramp. He drove to the front of the building where he found the designated parking spot and switched off the engine. He opened his door and had every intention of opening the passenger door for the colonel but was too late. He was out and halfway across the car park to the front entrance. The driver cocked a salute at the colonel's back, shrugged his shoulders, leant against the car and pulled a pack of cigarettes from his pocket.

Colonel Schalk Lombard marched around the neatly tended lawns of the traffic island where the orange, white and blue South African flag, along with the Defence Force flags hung limply at the top of their poles. It was a typically warm Pretoria afternoon. Clear blue skies above and not a breath of wind inspired movement from the flags. The colonel hesitated for a minute. He placed his hands on his hips and looked up at the grand old Victorian building with its carved granite plinth blocks and redface bricks. Granite arched openings supported large wooden window frames and tall columns supported an ochre-clay tiled roof. This was Defence Headquarters. The building where the top brass sat and controlled the military machine that was the South African Defence Force.

Wearing his short-sleeved step-out uniform with the seams of his pants ironed to a knife-edge and an impressive array of colourful bar medal ribbons on the left of his chest, the colonel had to restrain himself from bounding up the stairs. A bright brass name-tag on the right announced 'Lombard' and his shoes shone like mirrors. The silver castle accompanied by two stars on each shoulder glinted in the sun and the colonel drew in a deep breath, composed himself and deliberately took the stairs one by one.

He was a tall, slender man with a beaky nose that spoiled what would have been a handsome face but his intelligent eyes were as hard and grey as the granite steps beneath him. He held a brown leather briefcase in his hand and looked up as he reached the top of the stairs. A pretty young lieutenant stood rigidly to attention and saluted him.

He returned the salute and she smiled at him. "Please follow me, colonel. You're a little early but the general will see you in ten minutes." She turned and walked through the large wooden doors and the colonel followed.

What was bothering him? He frowned and wracked his brain. Was it something he'd forgotten or had the general … suddenly Schalk realised that he was actually mesmerised by the sway of the lieutenant's neat, round bottom, her shapely legs and well-defined calf muscles. She was short with a tidy bun of jet-black hair beneath her regulation head-dress yet she somehow made the drab standard woman's uniform look like it was tailormade to fit her various curves … all of them equally tantalising.

As the colonel followed her down the wide passage with its gleaming floors and high pressed-metal ceilings, he relished seeing her face again. His mind had been preoccupied with the urgency of the meeting when they had first met and he hadn't noticed her other womanly assets. They branched off left down a similar passage and the lieutenant looked back as they rounded the corner and smiled brightly at the colonel. He caught the flash of her green eyes, the curve of her pert, ample breasts and her ivory skin. His heart skipped a beat as he realised that she was really attractive, very sexy. The time would come in the future when she might find herself becoming a little plump if she did not take care of herself, but right now, as far as the colonel was concerned, she was perfect.

Just as quickly as this bright, young woman aroused him, he was swamped with guilt at the thought of his own vigilant, ever-faithful wife, sitting at home entertaining his fellow officers' wives. She did her duty and she never complained. He clenched his jaw and determinedly, angrily thrust such pernicious thoughts aside. The lieutenant stopped suddenly in front of a huge, stained meranti door at the end of the passage. The colonel almost bowled her over and in his effort to stop a collision, dropped his briefcase. It burst open and the papers took off in all directions.

"I am sorry. How stupid of me … I wasn't concentrating … actually thought we might go down to the left here …"

"Oh no, please colonel, it's no problem, just a small accident. Here, let me help you with those." They bent together, their heads almost touched, their eyes met. Her deep green eyes bored into him. He stood up quickly, straightened his shirt and tried desperately to maintain his countenance.

"I'm sorry again," he mumbled and caught a glimpse of her inner thigh as she stretched for a sheet of paper just beyond her reach. She noticed the direction of his fleeting glance and collected the rest of the papers. With a Mona Lisa smile she handed them to the now red-faced colonel.

"Please don't apologise, colonel. How about some tea or coffee?" she asked over her shoulder as she opened the large door to the general's waiting room.

"Rooibos tea with two sugars and no milk would be excellent, thank you. You do have rooibos tea don't you?"

"I think the SADF runs on rooibos tea, colonel." She smiled again, turned and left the room. The colonel swallowed hard and placed his briefcase on one of the deep armchairs. He clasped his hands behind his back and strolled around the waiting room. Abstract wildlife paintings adorned the walls. He decided that the general's taste in art left a lot to be desired. The other door opened and a captain escorted the general's civilian guest out. "I'll be with you in a minute, colonel."

The general stood up smartly from behind his desk, walked around, grabbed the colonel's hand and shook it vigorously. He looked up at the taller man and smiled a warm friendly smile.

"*Dit is goed om jou weer te sien*, Schalk. How long has it been? Two years? Man, you haven't changed a bit," the general enthused. "Still so fit, I see. Look at my body, out of shape, stuck behind this desk all day. Man, what I would give to get back into the bush with you and show that bloody Nujoma and his henchmen what us *Boertjies* are made of. Sit, man, sit." His comments about his physical condition were unfounded. The general was a short man but large in stature with penetrating, steel-blue eyes and a hard, sun-tempered face. It was the face of a professional soldier and a farmer. The wings on his chest showed him to be a parabat. To pass selection into the parachute battalion itself was no mean feat and his stomach hidden behind a long-sleeved issue shirt was as flat and hard as the armour of a Buffel. The man commanded respect wherever he went and was given it, unequivocally.

"*Ja generaal*. Operation Sceptic was two years ago now," answered the colonel, beaming at the welcome as he settled into the comfortable chair, his previous discomfort all but forgotten.

"How is your lovely wife Ansie, and the kids … three of them, not so?"

"Yes, always well and wonderful thank you general. The children grow so quickly. My oldest is going to high school already and the younger ones are in standard three and four."

"That's fantastic, eh?"

"Well, not always. My daughter is now a young lady and I have a continuous stream of boyfriends traipsing through my house after her attention. She's also at the age where her parents are old fashioned and a little bit stupid. She knows it all. So it's no bed of roses but we cope."

"With all the military discipline you've dished out over the years you should be a past master at dealing with her," the general winked at him.

"That's just it; I've only ever had to deal with boys or men, never a spoiled young woman."

"She's never too old to get a spank when necessary, you know. Spare the rod and spoil the child is what the Good Book teaches us."

"You're right general, but I can't bring myself to spank her … the boys yes, but not my little girl."

"Ah yes, girls, they always bring out the soft side to their pa don't they? So anyway, let's get down to business. I suppose you're wondering why I summoned you here today?"

"It did cross my mind, general." The colonel smiled and sat forward, attentively.

"Cast your mind back to the winter of '80. Operation Sceptic, as you said—objective 'Smokeshell' and how well you boys did. What a major defeat for Swapo, hey?" They lapsed into silence. The general gathered his thoughts and suddenly the colonel was back there.

Colonel Schalk Lombard remembered how they had driven across the border into Angola at sunset. Long columns of Ratel personnel carriers had driven all through the bitterly cold winter night, stopping only for the occasional flat tyre, to reach the objective at Chifufua. Code-name 'Smokeshell' was to be reached by lunchtime the following day.

They waited for the South African bombers to streak overhead and drop their deadly cargo of thousand-pound bombs. The enemy's V-shaped trenches were clearly visible from the air and the battle group instinctively ducked as the jets shot soundlessly over, followed seconds later by the thunderous rumble of their powerful turbojet engines. The battle group watched as the Impala Mk IIs climbed away and the ground shook as the bombs exploded. A short silence followed and the ground began to shake again as the artillery batteries, several kilometres away, pounded the target with their usual incredible accuracy.

The Ratel engines growled, and the infantry, commanded by then Commandant Schalk Lombard, began their attack. It was South Africa's largest mechanised infantry assault since World War Two and the attackers relished the surprise advantage they had over the enemy.

The advantage was short-lived and Swapo put up a surprisingly aggressive retaliation, pounding away at the Ratels, helicopters and ground forces with their 14.5mm anti-aircraft guns. Soon the first Ratel was hit directly and along with it, the first South African casualties. In the dust, oily smoke and enemy gunfire Commandant Lombard rallied his men to hunt out the 14.5mm guns and destroy them with single-minded aggression.

The battle was originally planned to last a week with the aim of destroying the Swapo command-and-control centre for the entire operational area, based at Chifufua. It lasted twenty days.

Commandant Lombard excelled as the ground commander of the operation. He moved the artillery to new positions, softened the target and attacked with a focused ruthlessness, repeating the process over and over. He earned himself the reputation of a brilliant strategist, leader and soldier, which did not pass unnoticed by the visiting general.

Finally the main battle was won. You regroup with your platoon, sit on top of your Ratel and relax a little. You pull out a well-earned cigarette, light up and drag deeply to sooth your war-torn, adrenaline-pumped nerves. Suddenly a young boy with an AK runs from cover. He fires wildly in all directions. Everyone stares at the utter stupidity and futility of this youngster. The Ratel commander swings the turret of the 20mm gun. He fires a single round. The bullet hits the boy. He lies at an impossible angle. A few R1 rounds thump into the dead boy. The body twitches. A macabre break-dance. A soldier walks closer. He inspects the body and his head drops. It was a girl. Maybe in her early teens. Damn this war. Damn it to hell.

"Schalk! *Schalk, ek praat met jou*! I'm talking to you." The general sat forward and frowned.

"I'm sorry general, I was thinking about Smokeshell." The colonel's mind had raced over the events of the operation but stuck on the one point that haunted him the most. "I lost seventeen troops on that op you know, general."

"We counted four hundred of their dead. That equates to more than twenty to one; a resounding victory I would say. You can't go through every op and come out fatality free. It's impossible. I would put that behind me if I were you and concentrate on what I've got to tell you."

"I'm sorry. Let's continue general."

"Good. Now the reason that I reminded you of Smokeshell will be made clear by looking at these." The general pushed a brown manila envelope towards the colonel.

Schalk lifted the flap of the envelope with the red ink stamps that announced

'Top Secret—Confidential' and 'Eyes Only' and retrieved the contents. He spread the satellite photos out in front of him and studied them carefully. He looked up at the general who held up his hand and shook his head.

"Take your time please Schalk, I want you to tell me what you are looking at."

"But I know what I'm looking at. How could I possibly not? It's all Smokeshell. The whole op on a series of satellite photographs with the exception of these two and they look like the MAOT and main echelon back near Mulemba."

The general produced a second envelope. "Okay. Now, look at these."

The colonel spread the second pile of photos like a pack of large playing cards. "They're the same ... only much closer. There is more detail on this lot but ..." He scrutinised one of the photographs as if he were attempting to look deeper than the surface of the picture. "This one looks like one of the thirteen sub-bases of Chifufua and obviously before we attacked. There are no vehicle tracks ... the trenches look well maintained ... there are plenty of personnel walking about and here is one of the gun emplacements. I would have to study the rest of these in my own time to make a definite conclusion but yes, Chifufua, before the attack. Where did you get such excellent photos; who would take satellite photos for us?"

"It's amazing what a little trade with the United States of America will get you, especially if the product is South African uranium. The second lot were from one of our very own Mirage reconnaissance jets. Pretty good stuff, huh?" The general had no time to gloat. "Look at the date the Mirage photos were taken ...," he pointed, "there, at the bottom." He sat back in his chair, placed his hands behind his head and a slight frown creased his brow.

The colonel's eyes widened. "These are only a week old but ...?"

"Exactly, I thought you might be interested."

"How? What's going on here?"

"That's what we'd like to know and this is going to be your baby. What do you think?"

The general smiled and the colonel was confused. "Fantastic, but I can't figure out what it is you want me to do. I would like to know what Swapo are doing reviving a previously destroyed base. They've never done this sort of thing before."

"Correct. You are going to have to find out for us. Once we know we'll have to destroy the base again. Another Smokeshell so to speak."

"But I can't do that from Potchefstroom."

"Right again, so here comes the catch." The general paused and savoured the moment. "You're going to have to move, lock, stock and barrel to Sector One Zero, Oshakati, South West Africa. There you'll have all the resources right at your fingertips."

"To work under the current Officer Commanding Sector Ten, I take it?"

"No, to replace him."

"Replace him ... that means ...?"

The general broke into a huge grin, stood and reached across the desk, his hand extended. "Congratulations, Brigadier Lombard."

"This is ... words fail me!"

The newly promoted brigadier stood up, grabbed and pumped the general's hand.

"It gives me great pleasure to see you so happy. I take it you accept the position?" The general sat.

"Oh yes, general. I thank you from the ...," the brigadier cleared his throat. "You don't know how much this means to me," he added in a controlled voice.

"Actually, I think I do, I was in a similar situation once. Do you realise that this makes you the youngest brigadier in the Defence Force?"

"I didn't know that but what is important is that I succeed."

"Ansie will be okay with this? She'd have to move with you and the kids you know?"

"I'll have to give that some thought because as I said earlier, it's high school for my daughter, but never mind we'll make a plan."

"I'm sorry there's nothing more formal to offer you by way of a promotion party but I want you to go up to Oshakati this weekend. They're bound to give you a formal dinner there, you know, a sort of an incoming—outgoing party. You need to get cracking on this little problem ASAP."

"I'd better get going then. One thing about climbing the ladder is that the work always increases proportional to the rank and now I'm really going to have to move my arse."

"You've got that right." The general's smile faded. "There is one other item. The little lieutenant who saw you in ...?" The brigadier nodded. "She is going to be your right-hand man. She must do all the dog work for you. You must work her ruthlessly in order to lighten your burden and hence concentrate on the task at hand." The brigadier paled, opened his mouth, closed it again and stood up. "Do you have a problem with her Schalk? You seem uncomfortable."

"No, no, she's fine. It's just that I've very little experience with lady soldiers and it'll take some getting used to."

"The Prime Minister, the Minister of Defence, you and I are the only ones who know about this operation at present. I cannot stress enough the importance of discretion. Swapo are up to something new and we know the Russians are behind it so we need to cauterise it now." The general stood, "God go with you, Schalk."

The two men looked into each other's eyes and shook hands. The brigadier stood back, placed his beret on his head, saluted, collected his briefcase and left the room.

CHAPTER 12

"Swapo!" shouted Geoff and felt the adrenaline surge through his body. "Eleven o'clock, seventy-five metres! All mortars to Martin! Strims fire! Fire for fuck's sake!" Geoff aimed in the general direction of the enemy fire and emptied his first magazine. He pushed the catch, released the empty clip and snapped a full one into place, flipping his firing selector from automatic to rapid. He fired again. Deliberate, concentrated fire.

"Fire that mortar, Martin! What's the fucking hold-up?" Geoff steeled himself. He was about to run from behind the stump of the palm when he felt the rubbery give of flesh beneath his boots. He realised he was standing on someone. He looked down and saw the sergeant.

At a glance Sergeant Gerrie Niemant looked unscathed but lay still—too still. Geoff stepped off the lifeless body and looked around guiltily. It had been a terrible feeling and he shuddered slightly. "Medic to my position! Check the sarge!" he shouted above the crackle of rifle fire. He saw the dust as the first mortar exploded up ahead. "Ten metres further, Martin!"

Geoff sprinted to join his steadily advancing line of troops. Several men fired a volley of bullets at the enemy while others advanced. One of the blowies crouched, estimated the distance and fired his rifle grenade. Geoff followed the arc of the grenade and watched it explode in a clump of bushes. He cursed the futility of a badly aimed shot. *Waste of ammo,* he thought. A body blasted out of the bush into the air. It performed a macabre, single-armed cartwheel before it landed in a heap of unmoving humanity.

"Yesss! You beauty! Hit them boys! Hit them hard!" he laughed and fired blindly toward the enemy as he ran. Still smiling, Geoff pushed the magazine release catch and watched the empty clip bounce away. He snapped the next magazine in place, looked up and the adrenaline flowing through his veins turned to ice. A Swapo soldier stood in the open, aiming his AK at him. Geoff dived forward and watched in horror as the mouth of the barrel followed him to ground. *This is how it all ends*, he thought. Geoff's fear turned to fascination as the man suddenly stumbled backwards. Little clouds of red mist bloomed from his chest. Incredulously he shook his head and watched the blur that was Dawid Gouws. He was running in from the right flank firing his MAG with uncanny accuracy. Nearly every time the MAG spat out a load, a man died. Geoff took a second to observe the spectacle. Once again he was awed.

Dawid's mouth was twisted in a rictus of hatred and his shoulders jumped and shook in rhythm with the MAG. Two of the insurgents broke and ran but Geoff saw them. From his position on the ground they ran directly away from him. He took a dead-rest aim with his elbows firmly planted in the dirt. He squeezed the trigger. A man went down in the grass and Geoff swivelled slightly to his left and picked up the second target. He aimed and fired again. He felt the recoil kick into his shoulder and sensed the gas piston slide back into the butt and slam the next round home. This time Geoff saw a spurt of dust about fifty metres ahead of the diminishing figure. *Damn!* he thought and took aim again. The terrorist leapt forward and performed an untidy sort of pirouette. He hit the ground hard, head first and ended up in an awkward pile of humanity, his leg kicking. Geoff looked to his left and watched Rudi sprint to the next acacia, take a dead rest on one of the lower branches and fire three, four, five shots at an unseen target.

Geoff glanced around, jumped to his feet, darted off on adrenaline-pumped legs and came to a sliding halt behind one of the huge white anthills that dotted the area. A movement to his right. One of his blowies ran out into the open. It was le Roux—his favourite.

"No! No! Bloody crazy!"

Too late. The lad's legs pumped like connecting rods on a crankshaft and Geoff urged him on with all the will he could muster for it was a brave but foolish endeavour. Suddenly his mad dash faltered. His strides became uncertain and he hesitated. He stopped. He looked around frantic, desperate.

"Le Roux!" Geoff bellowed.

"Le Roux! Get down you idiot!"

The lad looked at Geoff and his confidence returned. There! There was his mentor. His leader. And he moved. Le Roux smiled and headed towards Geoff. Even over the distance and above the noise of the contact, Geoff heard the sickly thump of bullet striking flesh and le Roux sat down. Still he smiled and the blood welled up and spilled over his lips. He reached out to Geoff, his fingers spread. A second RPG whined overhead and exploded harmlessly behind them. Geoff used the distraction. He slung his rifle over his shoulder, sprinted across the open ground, grabbed le Roux by the strap of his webbing and dragged him towards the bowl of a large tree.

Geoff was fervently aware of the dust leaping about as the enemy bullets sought him and the fear numbed his legs and sapped his strength. He let go of his burden and covered the last few metres to the tree in seconds. He squatted with his back against the rough bark and gulped in draughts of air. He stood up after a moment and glanced at the youngster lying out there.

Anger spread through his body like venom. It crushed his fear and he bellowed, "Cover me you bastards!" He hesitated a few seconds, grunted and dashed from cover. He dragged the lad behind the trunk, sank down with his back to the bark and pulled the wounded man up next to him.

Geoff hefted the lad up against the tree. He tried to make him more comfortable and knelt next to him. There were two wounds; one a flesh wound through the meat of the lad's thigh, not too much trouble there but the second bullet had struck him in the middle of his chest, a lung wound. The little hole hissed as red froth bubbled with each laboured breath.

Le Roux's expression changed. His eyes were wide with shock and fear ... fear of the inevitable. Somewhere behind him Geoff heard the familiar popping sound of Martin's Patmore and he looked up, waiting, watching trying to blot out the picture of the terrified youth lying on the ground before him.

The mortar exploded neatly among the fleeing enemy. Paths of dust jumped as deadly shrapnel skidded across the earth but still they ran. Suddenly the lad grabbed feebly at Geoff's hand. His eyes implored. His fingers clutched. His expression was of a desperate plea. He tried to speak and the blood gushed from his mouth and nose. Geoff noticed how the lad's eyes glazed over and slowly his head sagged sideways.

Geoff felt reckless fury boil to the surface. Le Roux was one, maybe two years younger than Geoff but his face was that of a youth, so innocent—and now he was dead. Some mother's son was dead and Geoff felt responsible. He ran from cover and began firing at the retreating terrorists.

The last of the mortar bombs exploded among them. A fusillade of bullets whipped past and with the rapid advance of the obsessed South Africans, the insurgents broke and ran for their lives. Dawid's MAG barked and another man fell. By now the counter-attack had reached the terrorists' original ambuscade and Geoff slowed to snap on a full magazine as he passed the first of the enemy dead.

He looked up and Allan released Dart. The Alsatian flew after a retreating insurgent, legs pumping, mouth open and saliva streaking his flanks. The dog caught the fleeing man by the arm and man and dog bowled over in a cloud of dust. Dart yelped once as the nine-millimetre bullet crashed through his rib cage forming a massive exit wound. The force of the bullet lifted the dog clean into the air and he fell to the ground in a blood-smeared furry heap. Desperately the terrorist struggled for purchase on the sandy ground as Allan caught up with him. He shot the man through the head at close range. It burst like an overripe melon.

It dawned on Geoff that he was using his last magazine and he took cover.

"Rudi! Rudi!" he shouted. "Where the fuck are you!"

"Coming!" A distant reply and Geoff went down on one knee. He aimed, squeezed the trigger and the man went down but in a flash was up again. The terrorist bounded off on one leg almost as fast as he had run. Geoff lifted his rifle and fired again, saw the sand jump up next to the man and he fired again and again until the trigger stopped responding, the magazine empty.

"You called?" Rudi puffed and slid to a halt next to Geoff. It was then that Rudi saw his friend's face. "Jesus, Geoff, it's me man! Calm down!" Slowly the murderous scowl that twisted Geoff's face eased and returned to normal.

Geoff wiped the sweat and dust from his face on a grease-blackened sleeve. "Call in the contact. I've run out of ammo."

"What about Allan?"

"Fuck Allan. Call in the contact. We should have done it straight away then those other black bastards wouldn't have got away." Geoff took a water bottle from his webbing.

"But Allan's gone after them!" explained Rudi.

"Oh Jesus! Tell me you're kidding!" Alarm replaced Geoff's anger.

Rudi shook his head, "No shit, man, he's gone after them."

Geoff reacted quickly. "Call in the contact and you and Mike sweep the area with the rest of the troops. Find our wounded and call in a casevac too. Watch out for trigger-happy wounded gooks and set up a TB."

"What are you going to do?"

Geoff took a mouthful of warm water and rinsed the thick saliva out of his mouth. He spat and drank again. "Go after him and give support." He coughed as he breathed in and he coughed again, the water spurting from his nose.

"Take it easy, buddy."

"I'll be okay," said Geoff, hoarsely.

"Don't go on your own ..."

"No. I'll take Dawid and Martin with me ... Oh yes, have you got a spare magazine for me?"

"I've got two," Rudi foraged in his webbing. "Here, take both."

"Thanks buddy. Please task someone to pick up the empty magazines and don't forget to tell the incoming troops that we are in pursuit and *not* to shoot us." Rudi nodded and smiled. He watched Geoff turn. Salt bordered the dark patches of sweat on his shirt.

Geoff trotted over to Dawid. The big Afrikaner was busy loading a fresh belt of cartridges into the MAG. Geoff lifted the cover on his watch. It had been a long contact, probably the longest any of them had endured … at least seven minutes—maybe longer.

CHAPTER 13

"Come with me and bring Martin. Let's go finish this."
Dawid stood up, placed the MAG belt over his shoulder and adjusted the ammunition. He spoke around the cigarette dangling from his lips. "Now that's the best bleddy suggestion you've made all day, corporal."

Geoff ignored the comment. "Did you see which way they went?"

"Of course. I had every intention of following them myself anyway."

"Okay. Stop wasting time and lead on then."

Dawid's eyes were slits against the brightness. He glared at Geoff before taking the stub from his mouth. He exhaled a cloud of smoke, flicked the stub away, turned and jogged ahead.

Allan and his quarry had left a clear spoor. Geoff ran with single-minded concentration. He ignored the heat, but feared the worst. Grootvoet and his askaris against Allan. Geoff clenched his teeth and quickened the pace.

Not far through the high acacias and open ground they heard the first exchange of fire—the automatic hammer of an AK-47 and the return of single cracks from an R1. To hear the return fire gave Geoff added strength. Running at three-quarter pace, Geoff passed Dawid who immediately took up the challenge and they ran side by side.

"Watch out, Dawid!" shouted Geoff as he pulled up sharply behind a tree and Dawid hit the ground. Geoff fired four times and waited.

"What the hell are you shooting at?"

"A fucking gook lying out there but I think he's dead …"

Dawid stood up and glanced around. He found the target and fired a volley into the body and ran on.

"Now you *know* he's dead!" he shouted over his shoulder and Geoff ran after him, cursing. They passed the bullet-riddled body of the Swapo soldier. The fleeting glance was for any sign of life. There was none, so on they ran. Martin followed some way back. He was exhausted.

Geoff glanced at Dawid with grudging admiration. He seemed tireless. His breathing was deep but easy and his legs pumped. His boots kicked back a spurt of sand with each powerful stride. Geoff's legs felt like they were about to seize. He gasped in air that seemed to scorch the back of his throat and the sweat ran down his face and dripped off his nose and chin. Geoff looked ahead. A termite mound about a hundred metres away shimmered in the heat. *I'll run to that anthill and then I'm going to have to stop*, he thought. He was disappointed at the thought of losing to his adversary and Dawid stopped suddenly.

Geoff ran on a few paces, stopped and turned. "What's wrong?" he gasped.

"*Nee, fok dit*! I'm bleddy tired now. I must rest," Dawid gasped. He placed his hands on his knees in an effort to control his breathing.

"Can't take it hey?" said Geoff and smiled more from relief than anything else.

"Fuck you Kent. You're just as tired as me."

Geoff was enjoying his lucky little victory. "I don't think so, Gouws. I reckon I'm just fitter than you?"

"Okay. Here, why don't you take the MAG for a while and then we'll see, hey?" Dawid lifted the heavy machine gun from his shoulders.

"Don't bother, I was only kidding. Let's wait for Martin."

"No. We can't wait. That other corporal friend of yours up ahead is all alone to face Grootvoet."

"How do you know it's Grootvoet? How do you know that he isn't lying back there with the other dead gooks?"

"Because I didn't shoot any big kaffirs, only small ones."

Geoff smiled again and shook his head at the callousness, the confidence, and the indifference of Dawid's reply. To him it wasn't killing people, whatever derogatory name he might call them. It was as if they'd gone fishing. "… didn't catch any big ones today, ma, only little ones. We'll try again tomorrow, ma."

"What's your problem now, Engelsman?"

"Nothing. Just that you're a classic, my boy," said Geoff and patted Dawid's shoulder.

"What's that mean?" Dawid looked suspiciously at Geoff.

"Nothing bad I promise. Don't worry about it. C'mon lets go." Geoff glanced back. Martin was way behind them.

Dawid grabbed Geoff's webbing and pulled him back. "What now, you …?"

"Shhh. Listen man." They cocked their heads. The faraway but unmistakable whine of the Alouette turbine grew louder and then it was over them at tree-top level. A Puma followed. Geoff and Dawid ran into the open and waved frantically as the second Alouette helicopter roared over.

"One Six Charlie—Giant!" The radio strapped on the front of Geoff's webbing crackled. Geoff grabbed the handset and depressed the lever. "One Six Charlie send, over!"

"We've been past your TB and spoke to your One Five Charlie. We gather that you are in pursuit of a few unfriendlies?"

"One Six Charlie—that's correct, over."

"What's the situation, over?"

"We've been in an extended contact with a group of insurgents and are in pursuit of the last two, over."

"Confirm this is Grootvoet and his gang, over."

"We've been led to believe so but haven't identified him so this could be incorrect information, over."

"Whom am I speaking to?" barked the voice on the other side, obviously irritated. Geoff took a deep breath. He had expected this might happen once he called in the contact but he could not guess that it would anger him so. This was their contact. It was their opportunity for some praise, some acknowledgement, and some honour in this filthy war. They had done all the hard work. Were others now going to snatch the trophy from them at the finish line and with it the battle honours?

"Corporal Geoffrey Kent, over," answered Geoff in a controlled voice, deliberately using his rank and first name against standard radio procedure.

"Well, *person* Kent, I've got twelve Parabats in the back here all champing at the bit to get at this Grootvoet so a simple answer will suffice." The pilot's deadpan reply dripped with sarcasm.

Geoff looked at Dawid and shook his head despairingly. "Parabats, bloody Parabats. Same shit hey? We chase them for days, soften them up and the glory boys fly in, shoot one or two and fly out again, needless to say, claiming the victory! Fuck them!" Geoff spat and the big MAG gunner simply shrugged his shoulders and started off after the spoor.

Geoff walked after Dawid and, after a while, depressed the lever of the handset so hard that the bakelite plastic creaked and his knuckles turned white. "We've been after this gang for a week now and we've finally caught them and killed most. Two of them are somewhere ahead of us with one of the dog handlers chasing them. We're going in support of this man so please caution your precious Parabats on who to shoot and who not to shoot. As for who we're chasing I can't really say and I don't really care. I only want them caught because I have some dead and some wounded back at the TB—over!" Dawid looked back and smiled at Geoff's spitfire answer, his teeth white against his filthy face. Geoff waited in vain for a sharp reprimand from the pilot. The radio remained stubbornly quiet and Geoff swore again.

Up ahead Dawid caught a glimpse of movement and brought the MAG up parallel to the ground as he ducked to his left behind a small bush. Geoff followed and in heat and silence they waited and watched. Geoff was uncomfortable and still agitated from the conversation with the pilot.

A second movement and a picture jumped into focus. It was a dirty, sun-darkened, hairy arm swatting listlessly at a pesky mopani fly. The arm lifted slowly, waved back and forth next to the barely visible ear and sank lazily down again landing palm up, somewhat reminiscent of a chimpanzee. Geoff smiled. He was relieved to see Allan's shoulder and outstretched leg protruding past the base of the acacia tree against which he leant. Allan faced away from them and from their position they couldn't see if he was wounded or not but he sat very still.

"Howdy boys," said Allen, his Afrikaans accent amplified through his attempt at an American affirmation. Geoff and Dawid looked at him then back at the tree. Allan stood. He stretched and his shirt pulled out of his pants. His hairy stomach shone white—a strong contrast to his filthy, sweat-streaked face.

"Doctor Livingstone I presume?" announced Geoff uncertainly and he stood.

"Oh, hello Stan. I've been expecting you," Allan's mouth twisted in a half-smile.

"Stan?"

"Stanley?" Allan widened his eyes and spread his hands.

"Of course. Sorry. We were just a bit worried. We heard an exchange of fire and then nothing 'til now. Couldn't be sure if you were still with us, old boy." The situation seemed tense and Geoff was confused. "Are you okay?"

Allan lacked his usual mercurial demeanour. He slung his rifle over his shoulder. His expression remained blank and he shook his head. "The bastards killed my dog."

"Yes. I know, I saw it happen … I'm sorry."

"Don't be. They meant to kill our troops, us … that's worse. It's just that Dart saved my life a few times and it was hard seeing him shot up like that."

Geoff could see Allan's hurt and was unsure how to console him so he tried some amateur reverse psychology.

"They shot my one young blowie too."

"Oh, Jesus Geoff! Who?"

"Le Roux."

"Is he dead?"

"Yes." Geoff was surprised at how it hurt.

Allan looked at him sympathetically, "Now I'm sorry …"

"Don't be." His psychology had worked … too well.

Allan stopped at the fence and pointed. A limp piece of plastic hung over the last rung of the low, rusty, barbed-wire fence and flapped lethargically in the hot breeze. Another lay half-buried in the Ovambo sand. Close by, also semi-buried was a plastic hypodermic syringe. Its bent needle glinted in the sun.

Dawid uttered one word and then they knew the reason for the hopelessness in Allan's tone. "Adrenaline. The bastards took adrenaline and now they're gone, for sure." Dawid pulled a crumpled packet of Texan plain out of his side pocket and retrieved a bent cigarette. He lit up. "Sorry boet," he said and exhaled a cloud of smoke. They were all sorry then. They knew too well that a man pumped full of adrenaline would run like the wind until he dropped dead from exhaustion.

"Please gimme one of those, Dawid," Allan pointed at Dawid's cigarettes.

Geoff looked surprised. "You don't normally …?" he quizzed. A deep furrow creased his brow.

"I don't normally kill people either … got a light?" Dawid lit the cigarette. Allan puffed, inhaled, coughed once and spat loose tobacco from his parched lips. "Come. Take a look at this too." They followed Allan along the fence. "Okay, look here, " he indicated the area ahead with the palm of his hand down, fingers outstretched. There was a collage of Soviet bootprints. One smallish and the other unmistakably that of the legendary Grootvoet. It was as if they had been carefully arranged to draw attention.

"Watch it, Dawid. Don't stand there or you'll spoil the spoor. Just step back here and look. Mind your shadow there, Geoff. Okay, now, kneel down and look up the line of the spoor here." They obeyed and Allan looked at them. "Well. What do you see?"

"I see GV's spoor disappearing into the distance, albeit a bit wobbly," offered Geoff.

"Exactly!" Allan beamed.

"Show me," pleaded Martin.

"Come here and look up the line there." Allan pointed and they craned to see past his shoulder. "Do you see the spoor moving away from us?" They nodded. "Well apart from the fact that they are widely spaced because the man is sprinting like a springbok, look at how the bootprints fall."

Then they saw it. One print would point out to the left, the next out to the right at such an angle that any intelligent man would believe they were following a cripple.

Geoff pushed his bush hat to the back of his head and scratched his temple. "I'm sorry but, so what?"

"Jesus! Can't you see it man." Allan was incredulous.

"No to both."

"What both?"

"I'm not Jesus and I still don't see it."

Allan dropped his head in defeat. He looked up slowly and laughed. He laughed and coughed and laughed again, so impulsively, so contagiously that soon they were all at it. Dawid threw down his webbing, dropped the MAG onto the sand and sank down laughing. Overcome with mirth, the others fell to the sand. Geoff wiped a tear from his cheek.

The sound of a heavy 20mm machine gun hammering away in the distance startled them. Allan's eyes were sunken and there were dark rings of exhaustion beneath them. "Your Parabats have nailed our boy but not Grootvoet."

"Fuck off Allan. They're not my Parabats. You know I had to call in the contact and, in any case, that sounded like a gunship to me—not goddamned Parabats. I want GV as much as you do!"

"Okay, okay." Allan shrugged into his webbing and walked back to the fence. Geoff caught up and put his hand on Allan's shoulder.

"What do you mean they haven't nailed Grootvoet?"

"That's what I've been trying to tell you." Allan stopped and looked at Geoff, his eyes brighter. "That Askari has taken GV's boots to deliberately mislead us. That's why the spoor was so wobbly. He's got that huge pair of boots on his small feet and they're flopping around like a week-old baby's head. He's gone!"

"Who?"

"Grootvoet"

"How? Where?"

"That's the mystery man! Just think, if the askari has taken GV's boots then where's the other spoor, the second spoor. Where is Grootvoet's spoor? Bare feet ... anything?"

"Maybe the askari carried GV on his back," offered Geoff as he climbed back over the fence.

"Yeah, I also thought of that, especially after they took the adrenaline but the spoor isn't deep enough for two people."

"There has to be a logical explanation."

"Sure. Just tell me the first one that pops into your head then."

Geoff scratched his head and scrutinised the ground around the fencing standard. Allan had to have missed something. There was nothing. It was as if Grootvoet had grown wings and flown.

"This is a load of shit, man! Let's get back to the TB and we'll find the bastard there all black and dead!" Dawid's eyes were wide, his awe of the supernatural threatening to unnerve him. Geoff smiled. A merciless killer who was scared of ghosts.

CHAPTER 14

Relief flooded Rudi's entire being as the four soldiers strolled into the temporary base. Tired, dirty and bedraggled but smiling at a witticism from Allan.

"Howzit okes!" Rudi walked over and shook each of their hands in turn.

Mike jogged up and grinned. "Okay boys. Where is it?"

"Where's what?" Allan frowned.

"Grootvoet's head." Laughter rippled and Dawid glared at them.

"He's gone you know … like he vanished. Like a spook, man!" Dawid's eyes were big again. "What the fuck are you laughing at, Kent. Why don't you show us where he is then, hey?"

"Calm down, Gouws. Ghosts don't fly around during the day. Just tonight you had better not go to sleep." Geoff lifted his hands and hooked his fingers like claws. He squinted, bent his head and stumbled toward Dawid like the ghost of Quasimodo. "Woooo. Wooo!" Dawid lifted a water bottle to his lips and waited for the laughter to subside.

"Piss off, all of you," he said and wiped his mouth on a sweat-blackened sleeve. "None of you can tell me where he went, can you?"

"He's right about that," said Martin.

The helicopters roared overhead, temporarily blocking out conversation and Rudi watched for a second before grabbing his radio. "Giant, Giant. This is One Five Charlie, message, over."

"Send, over."

"We have wounded, one critical. Request immediate casevac, over."

"You called for casevac when you called in the contact. Bravo Four One Delta has been dispatched. ETA five minutes, over."

"Five minutes might be too late, over." But for the dwindling sound of the choppers, all was quiet and the group of soldiers waited. "Giant, this is One Five Charlie, do you read me, over," Rudi sounded desperate.

"Okay, we're coming back. We'll swop missions, out."

"Who's critical, Rudi?" Geoff was concerned.

"The sarge, but I don't know what's wrong with him. Come and take a look." The ops medic knelt beneath a large shady tree tending the sergeant. He wiped the sergeant's forehead with a cool damp cloth and adjusted the flow of the saline drip hanging from a low branch. His expression was a mixture of puzzlement and worry. "We need to get him to a doctor, now corporal. This is the only drip I have!"

"Look there," Geoff pointed towards the waning sun. The sound of the returning helicopters filled the sky. The undercarriage of the Puma lowered and the aircraft descended, flanked by her gunships.

Geoff examined the tiny rivulet of blood that snaked its way down the sergeant's forehead. The blood hesitated at his brow, worked its way around and slid down his cheek. Geoff took the cloth and wiped the blood away. He peered at the minute hole just below the sergeant's hairline. No sooner had Geoff wiped the wound when the blood welled up again.

"What do you think it is?" asked Geoff. He stood back and studied the sergeant's face.

"I'm not sure, corporal. It looks like a huge big acacia thorn stabbed him right there but that wouldn't put him out unless he's suffering from anaphylactic shock. I don't know what to do."

They stared at the sergeant. His breathing was low and shallow. Beneath the streaked dirt his face was as white as marble and tiny beads of sweat formed as the blood flowed thick and slow, like treacle.

"Have we got any other wounded?"

"Two others slightly wounded and one dead, corporal." The medic pointed to the groundsheet partially covering the body of le Roux. A blood-stained arm protruded from beneath the groundsheet. The blood had dried black in the sun.

"I know we've got one dead, you moron!" Geoff realised that maybe he was human after all. There was a lump in his throat and his chest hurt deep inside.

"I'm sorry, corporal ..."

"No, I'm sorry. Get them into the Puma," Geoff ordered as he turned and strode towards the aircraft.

He ducked instinctively as he passed under the spinning blades. He leapt into the load-bay area and immediately noticed the wounded terrorist lying at the back of the chopper. Geoff studied the man for a while. He suppressed the urge to drag him out and blow his head off.

The flight sergeant and the pilot interrupted his thoughts. "Are you person Geoffrey Kent by any chance?" asked the pilot. His eyes sparkled with humour.

"Yes, Captain ...," Geoff shot a glance at the pilot's name tag, "Wessels. I'm sorry about that." Geoff shouted above the noise of the jet engines

"Don't worry about that. I understand the resentment you *pongoes* have for the Bats. They're always butting in when least needed, hey? Well it looks like you boys are clear winners today though. How many dead gooks are laying there, corporal?" Captain Wessels pointed at the line of black bodies lying in the open ground beyond the landing zone where clouds of flies were already busy.

"Oh, nine and one on the way captain but we missed Grootvoet I'm afraid."

"Don't be, corporal. This is impressive stuff for one section. How many of you nailed this lot?"

"There were twelve of us, three doggies and one tracker." The first of the wounded arrived. Willing hands assisted them into the helicopter.

"You said 'were' twelve. Did you lose some?"

"Yes captain. One dead, one in a coma of sorts—he's the critical we told you about—and these two wounded ... oh yes, and we sent one back with heat exhaustion."

Geoff and the pilot conversed a moment longer as le Roux's body was loaded. Geoff leapt from the load-bay and strode back to the others.

"What did you and the happy captain chat about?" asked Rudi.

"Oh, just this and that, you know. How many did we kill etcetera, etcetera."

"What's the story with the gook in the back?" asked Allan.

"Apparently he's the Swapo they shot at earlier," Geoff shrugged. "He surrendered—threw down his weapon and just stood there. I reckon that the Alouette gunner would have taken the bastard out, but there were too many witnesses. Anyway, he spilled the beans. He confirmed it was them in Tsumeb—with Grootvoet." Geoff shook his head. "Now he wants to change sides because of what happened there."

"Who the hell is he then?" asked Allan

"They said his name is Enoch Shongwe or something, but who the hell cares?" answered Geoff vaguely. The sun was a shimmering red ball melting into the horizon and the silhouettes of three aircraft dwindled into the distance. Geoff watched them for a long while. "Go with God, le Roux," he whispered.

CHAPTER 15

Ansie Lombard literally pined for her children, her appetite was almost non-existent and the will to hide her misery waned with each day. She missed her neat, modern home with its splendid little garden of well-tended lawns with splashes of colour radiating from every corner. Between the dedicated gardener and herself, Ansie's garden was the envy of the neighbourhood in the plush suburb of Baillie Park in Potchefstroom. But despite that, her children were well mannered, well dressed and well educated and now she missed them dearly.

When Schalk Lombard had been promoted and transferred back to Potchefstroom from Walvis Bay some years earlier, Ansie had pleaded with him to rent in the suburbs rather than accept one of the military houses in the military village with it's military neatness and military pecking order where any rank senior to your husband gave that man's wife charge over you.

Schalk had agreed. Not merely to please Ansie but more because his closest friend lived in Baillie Park and the Lombards had managed to rent a house right next-door to him. Ansie was at her happiest then; her husband had been promoted from battery commander in Walvis Bay, where he held the rank of major, to second-in-command at Fourteenth Field Regiment, Potchefstroom and later to colonel as the Officer Commanding the School of Artillery, Potchefstroom. Colonel Schalk Lombard was good at his job, a natural leader of men, a splendid gunner and mostly he was happy.

As a youth Schalk had decided upon a career in the military. The choice was easy. His father was a military man, an officer in the artillery. Schalk had been schooled in Potchefstroom, a town he grew up in and loved. He had signed up as a gunner and as soon as the opportunity presented itself, he applied for and was accepted into the School of Artillery where he went on to win the coveted prize—the sword for the best student in the junior leaders.

The many war games played out on the gun ranges of Potchefstroom and Lohatla honed Schalk into one of the best artillery officers in the country. This was made plainly evident in Operation Savannah when as a captain, he captured a town of strategic importance in Angola using a BP road map and firing only smoke projectiles as the ammunition re-supply had not yet reached them. This effort had earned him the Honoris Crux—South Africa's highest medal of honour.

There were formal functions when Schalk wore his mess dress or undress blues as the occasion warranted. Ansie was so proud of her husband then. He looked so smart, so dashing, with all his medals and other finery. Ansie dressed to match his splendour. Long evening gowns with trains that slid noiselessly over the gleaming, highly polished floor of the officers' club.

They were the admiration of all; pausing at the entrance, hand in the crook of her man's arm, waiting to be announced and noticing the reaction of the other women. Some were envious and others purely respectful.

There were Sunday braais when the men wore shorts on the hot summer days and drank icy beers as they tended the meat. The smell and the smoke of slowly grilling boerewors wafted around the garden and the kids played rugby on the long stretch of lawn down the side of the house.

There were holidays. Not many, for his work was seldom done but she had wonderful memories of lying on Durban's North Beach, soaking up the sun or of crayfishing off Robberg in Plettenburg Bay. They would take the ferry out of Hout Bay to Seal Island and of course the visits to the Kruger National Park—the family's unmatched favourite. There was never quite enough money for these holidays but the children never noticed and the memories were simply wonderful.

There were also the lonely times when Schalk and the men went into the bush, sometimes overnight but sometimes for months. At first Ansie never knew what 'the bush' was or meant but over the years Schalk confided in her and explained in some detail what he was up to. Whether it was a training camp somewhere in South Africa or a cross-border operation into Angola—never the details but certainly enough to know where he was and more or less what he was doing. During these times friends and other officers' wives gathered together in support. And she would reciprocate, always putting on the air of the soldier's strong and dutiful wife. Ansie *was* strong and dutiful but she had her children and her friends.

Now, for some reason, her vitality had deserted her and many seemingly small problems led to a kind of misery she had never known—the misery of depression. The house of the Officer Commanding Sector One Zero, Oshakati was big and old, slightly run down but solid. The garden was well established with wide lawns and palm trees that towered over the silver-painted corrugated-iron roof. The shrubs added a much-needed greenery to the dry town. The veranda, like most of the houses in those hot, dry climes, ran all the way around the house, keeping the direct sunlight out to reduce the temperature.

There was an air-conditioner but Schalk insisted that it wasn't used as he said too much change in temperature led to sickness. Gauze netting enclosed the veranda, giving it a stifling feeling although it was necessary to keep the swarms of flies out by day and the swarms of mosquitoes out at night. The stove was old and the fridge never seemed to get things really cold. The flex leads that hung from the old pressed metal ceilings culminated in a shadeless light globe and were spotted with fly droppings. The passage ran right through the middle of the house, door to door, old fashioned and somewhat eerie. As far as the garden was concerned, all one had to do was water the plants and they grew but only plants that could stand the extreme temperatures—unbearable summer heat and freezing winter nights.

Ansie had a gardener. He worked for a few of the houses in the area, all belonging to officers of the SADF. He tended their gardens, touched up the paintwork when necessary and performed other minor handyman tasks. He had a favourite in Ansie. She was kind to him and spoke to him like a real person unlike some of the others who almost treated him like the enemy.

Ansie looked at him and noticed the breadth of his shoulders beneath one of Schalk's cast-off, knitted shirts. She noticed how the muscles of his forearms and legs moved and writhed beneath his shiny, ebony skin as he thrust the garden fork into the seemingly lifeless soil and turned it over. He was tall and although a little thin, his body was well defined and his skin very black—typically Ovambo. There was something else. He had about him an air of dignity, perhaps even aloofness and Ansie smiled as she approached him with a glass mug full of orange juice. The ice jingled against the glass. A plate was piled high with thick slices of fresh bread and apricot jam.

"Here, Victor. Have a break. Eat some sandwiches and wait out the heat of midday," she commanded.

"Thank you ma'am. You are very kind to this old man," said Victor. He stood and wiped the sweat from his brow with the back of his hand. He took the plate and mug and bowed slightly in thanks.

The typically western statement of a thirty-something person who has toiled at physical labour amused Ansie. "You're not old, Victor! In fact I know many men half your age who would not be able to keep up with you in your work." She noticed the silver glint in the tightly curled, woolly cap of hair as he stooped to wash his hands and her face dropped. The dull pain returned to spoil the light-hearted moment for suddenly the misery was upon her again. She knew what had sparked it off this time.

Ansie sighed. She knew why the love-making between her and her husband had diminished to a sporadic monthly ordeal … She had aged while he had maintained his youth, her body had changed shape while he remained fit and slim. Her stomach had never returned to normal after the children and she often found him looking at her with a sort of loathing.

Too many days spent tanning in the harsh South African sun had wrinkled her face and freckles covered her shoulders and legs like a rash.

And then there was that privilege that came with the position held by her husband—a personal aide de camp. It took a great physical effort on Ansie's part to hide her dislike for Lieutenant Elsa Botha. Ansie knew that her feelings were mostly of unfounded jealousy as Elsa's work was very important to her husband and, more importantly, to his success, but the woman was just too sexy. Her fair skin had hardly seen the sun and it complemented her jet black hair. Her face was unwrinkled and her green cattish eyes seemed to bore into Ansie, unnerving her. Ansie knew, too, that Schalk trusted Elsa with some secrets of the war that he had not confided to her. The fact that he seemed to trust Elsa more than her was insufferable.

There was more. The way they looked at each other was overly familiar and when she was present in their company, Schalk always looked guilty.

Ansie spread her hands and studied them. Were those liver spots already? The tight silver curls in Victor's dusty black hair reminded her of the first few grey hairs that had appeared in her own glossy, auburn mane. At first she had aggressively pulled them out but now there were just too many.

She walked slowly up the stairs through to her bedroom and lay down. Two Puma helicopters flew over, probably on their way to Ondangwa, judging by the sound and she smiled humourlessly to herself—she'd recognised the sounds of the helicopters as those belonging to a Puma and she knew where they were going. What did that tell her? That she was part of this bloody war? It wasn't long before she drifted off to sleep.

She awoke with a start. The sun was well down in the sky. She slid her slim legs gracefully over the edge of the bed, stood and walked listlessly out to the garden to inspect Victor's work. She tried to force it away but her mind automatically returned to where it had left off.

"Is the madam sick?" Ansie was so lost in her thoughts that she winced visibly as Victor approached her. It was uncanny how he seemed to … stalk. "Maybe you should sit down." Victor held out his hand.

"I … I'm so sorry Victor, I just wasn't …"

Victor nodded to his hand and Ansie hesitated for a second before she took it as he led her to the veranda. Victor's hand was hard and calloused but gentle and surprisingly comforting. She took the stoep chair he offered, sat down and suddenly she was weeping. Her head sank slowly to her hands. Victor squatted in front of her and waited for the sobs to subside. He cleared his throat and she looked up.

Her eyes were wet and red and her misery was painted in lines on her face. "I'm sorry, Victor. I don't know what's wrong with me. I ... I don't think I'm sick but I am embarrassed to be like this in front of you. Please go away." Her head sank into her hands and sobs racked her body.

"You are sick. You are sick in your heart. I can see it. If you talk to me perhaps I can help you."

Ansie quietened but her head remained in her hands for a while. Then she looked up. "You are a kind man, Victor but how could you possibly help me?" Ansie's tone was flat as she wiped the tears away with the palms of her hands.

"You don't like this place. It is too hot. There is too much war. It is always dangerous and your children are far away."

Ansie sat up, her eyes wide and her surprise total. "How do you know about my children and how …?"

"Your husband is the big army boss and must stay here but you don't have to."

"Victor ..."

"There are many flights to South Africa from Ondangwa."

"Victor! Answer me!"

"I have seen the pictures when I painted the lounge. They are very handsome—like their mother."

"But ... the rest ... I mean how ...?"

"There have been others before you. Some like it here but most are like you; they need to go home. This is not your home. It is not your country. It is not your war."

"Victor, are you involved in this ugly war?"

"South Africa is a big and beautiful land, much bigger than ours. You have much gold and many other riches there. I wonder why you fight for this land." Victor swung his arm in an arc. "Go to your man, the big army chief, and tell him you need to go home." He looked at the woman for a while and saw something in her eyes. Hope? Relief? And he turned, walked down the steps, picked up his garden fork and thrust it into the ground.

Ansie stared at him, but no longer saw him. Instead, she heard the laughter of her younger children. She spun around, half-expecting to see them standing in the cool, dull passage with their sister behind, smiling, gently herding them forward. Ansie stared into the gloom and sighed.

She made a concerted effort to straighten her shoulders. She lifted her head and walked inside, her stride determined. Two more Puma helicopters roared over so low that she lurched and missed her step. Minutes later she strode out with a handbag slung over her shoulder. Her face was washed, her hair brushed and she had touched up her make-up. The determined set of her features allowed a smile as she passed Victor. "*Dankie*," she whispered, "thank you." She passed through the pedestrian gate, turned and headed to the office of the Officer Commanding Sector One Zero, Oshakati.

The sentry's greeting was warm and friendly and Ansie's heart sang as she walked briskly up the stairs and passed through the empty office of the adjutant. She hesitated, smiled and quietly opened the door to her husband's office lest she disturb his important work. But for the light above the operations board the room was dark. Ansie pushed the door wider and looked about. The room seemed deserted but a groan emanating from the far corner caught her attention. Ansie smiled as she recognised the back of her husband but the smile vanished as she realised he was in the arms of another woman.

Ansie froze. Thoughts raced through her mind, one of them being the answer to the strange perfume that she had smelled on Schalk's soiled shirts in the wash basket. Like a hailstone smashing on the paved macadam, Ansie's newfound resolve shattered and she gasped as if dealt a blow to her stomach. The woman was Lieutenant Elsa Botha.

CHAPTER 16

The Buffel roared past Ansie as she ran from her husband's office. Doctor Arthur Thompson frowned. Ansie had been to see him on occasion at the hospital in Oshakati with an unrelenting sore throat or a deep bladder pain and, her favourite, a recurring migraine headache. These conditions seemed to vanish miraculously as the good doctor inquired about her family and friends back in Potchefstroom and her old life there. She was attractive, intelligent and outgoing and seemed to glow with each consultation.

Doctor Thompson enjoyed her company, for her light-heartedness and quick, intelligent mind spanned further than the war and the weather. But there was no doubt that she was depressed. He would like to help her, to be there for her, but there were other patients to attend to. Perhaps he should mention it to her husband at an opportune moment, but then again, the brigadier seemed to have enough on his plate already.

The Buffel barrelled through the winding streets of Oshakati, canting dangerously on every corner, as its huge suspension springs compressed to compensate for the load of men and armour. Once through the boom, the gunners high on the Bofors tower watched the Buffel speed off into the distance.

Gaining experience as a surgeon on the border was, without doubt, about the best training Arthur could ever have hoped for and many times put his medical knowledge and skills to the test, but this case was different … he was no neurosurgeon.

The wind blew through the Buffel, blustering his thinning, sandy hair. He sat back and tried to relax on the long straight road to rescue a dying man. As the sun began to set, they passed a few scattered buildings, brightly painted. 'Mississippi Satisfaction' boasted the first and 'California Girls' competed the second—but they were strictly out of bounds to all members of the SADF.

Arthur looked up and noticed a yellow-billed kite gliding effortlessly ahead. He scrutinised its shape, especially its characteristic V-shaped tail, its yellow beak and its colours as they passed beneath it. He was starting to take a keen interest in birding and recognised this species easily as they seemed to be ubiquitous along the border areas, mostly solitary and always scavenging. The kite turned and dropped from the sky, aiming at some unseen prey and the feathers above its wings lifted and fluttered like a pianist's fingers and then it was gone. Gone, too, was his anxiety—he felt relaxed, confident and ready as the Buffel ground to a halt at the medical centre behind the huge airfield at Ondangwa.

"Hello, Jannie. I believe we have a challenge on our hands, eh?"

"Arthur, ja, this bloke sure looks sick to me, man," replied the lieutenant as Arthur scrubbed up.

"What's his name?"

"Sergeant Gerrie Niemant. We believe that he might have some shrapnel in his head ..."

"Let's take a look then. By the way, good evening, gentlemen." The team answered the greeting and followed Arthur into theatre. Their respect and liking of the man was made obvious by the way they eagerly responded to Arthur's easy manner. He wiggled his fingers into the latex gloves, scrutinised the sergeant and then bent to take a closer look at the wound. "Okay, firstly let's intubate." A calm flurry of activity and the tube was in place. "Heart-lung." More activity and the lung machine concertinaed up and down in its Perspex sleeve. It made a slight scraping sound that irritated Arthur. "Music!" he demanded. "What are the details, Jannie?"

"Well, we aren't too certain, doc. Apparently these blokes were chasing Grootvoet and were lucky to escape an ambush. The bastards shot an RPG at our boys and the corporal in charge said that it hit a palm tree. No one saw the sergeant until the contact was over."

"Okay, but who said he's got metal in his head? Did someone see him go down or get hit," asked Arthur. He lifted first the left eyelid and shone his light into it and then the right.

"The corporal. He said that only after the contact did someone go back for the sergeant and he was already unconscious. He said that the sarge went down immediately after the RPG hit the palm. From that and only that the corporal deduced that shrapnel was the cause of the trauma."

Arthur smiled under his mask as the senior assistant proudly displayed his command of the English language as best he could with the heavy guttural accent of an Afrikaner. Arthur looked up at the X-ray board. He walked around the operating table, stood with arms folded and scrutinised the images. "Damn!" he whispered under his breath.

"What was that, captain?"

"I can't see much from these," Arthur nodded at the X-rays. "First prize would be a bit of computed tomography." The voice of Stevie Nicks filled the room. "Ah, Fleetwood Mac, that's better."

"CT imaging. CT scan?"

"Yes. Rumours isn't it?"

Jannie shook his head at the turn of conversation, "Ja, Rumours."

"Even cerebral angiography would be nice but we ain't got either, so we're going to have to make some assumptions. I really need to know what hit him and how far he was from the blast." Arthur put his fists on his hips and sighed deeply. "In case you're wondering why I hesitate, it is because I remember reading some literature about missile injuries to the head. One of the more important pieces of information I need to know is whether the missile was high or low velocity. That will determine the procedure we need to follow. Right now let's dress the wound with gauze and Betadine." Arthur turned and busied himself with his own instructions. "Okay, now I need to apply a heavy sterile dressing." He worked carefully over the shaved, shiny dome. "Wheel him through there, Jannie. I need some plain roentgenograms of the skull," Arthur pointed to the X-ray room.

Once inside, positioning was the most important factor. Arthur needed three projections and aided by the medics battled a bit with the floppy dead weight of the sergeant.

Arthur pointed at the Towne projection. "This looks like bone that's been driven intra-cranially … and this," Arthur hesitated, " … this could be the needle in the haystack." He pushed hard just below a larger irregular shape and his index finger turned white. "What we're looking for is solid evidence that our patient has metal in his head and not to kill him unnecessarily by opening him up for nothing." Arthur looked at the damning translucent blot on the plate for a second longer and he murmured, "But now we have all the evidence we need, so let's get started."

Arthur removed the dressings, draped and positioned the scalp to facilitate the entry wound. There was no exit wound. He took up the scalpel and cut the flesh away from the skull and exposed the bone.

"Betadine," he said quietly. "Right. We'll have to excise and then debride the wound. Hand me the Z extensions." He enlarged the wound. "And now the bony defect. Now you're going to see why we're all so clever." There was a murmur of light heartedness and Arthur opened the dura with a cruciate incision and immediately hemorrhagic necrotic brain began oozing out of the incision. A sharp gasp from one of the medics and the tension was palpable.

"Jesus! What's that?"

"That's a bit of dead brain, Jannie. Just relax everyone, I was half-expecting this. Now will someone please wipe my forehead." An eager hand reached forward and dabbed at the dampness on Arthur's brow. "Turn the tape over please. Right, now I'm going to tell you what I'm doing for my sake and if you hear me say anything crazy, let me know." A low giggle emanated as the team eagerly shuffled forward to watch Arthur begin. "The cortical wound should be smaller than the track of the missile in the cerebral white matter, so we are going to explore the track for debris and haematoma. Asepto syringe." Arthur took the blunt-tipped needle and slid it carefully into the wound.

"Okay, as I irrigate the track, I slowly withdraw the needle ... like ... that! Fine! I must make sure I don't block the cerebral entry wound ... we don't need water to dissect into the brain." Arthur stood back. "Thorough debridement of the track is necessary to float out any foreign matter ... let's do it again."

Arthur had hardly hoped things would run this smoothly. "Fine, I'm quite happy with all the debris we're retrieving ... so far so good."

He smiled and continued the delicate process. "By the way, did our boys get that Groot whatever his name is?"

"Afraid not, doc."

Arthur nodded and scrutinised the wound. "I see some larger fragments of bone. Pass the fine forceps.

"After a little more debridement we can start to think of patching the dural defect with a pericranial graft ..." He was interrupted by an irritatingly loud alarm. "What's ...?" Arthur exclaimed and heads lifted as one. The screen showed a flat line where the peaks and troughs of the sergeant's weak, erratically pumping heart beat should have been. "Jesus! That was too sudden! What the hell happened?"

"He's gone into cardiac arrest!" Jannie's eyes were wide with surprise and he spoke as if it were a question.

"Quick, the defibrillator!" cried Arthur. He grabbed the electrodes, rubbed them together and placed them on the sergeant's chest. "Hit it, Jannie!" The body jumped as the electricity surged through. They looked up expectantly at the screen. It remained stubbornly unchanged.

"Increase and hit it again!" Once again the body did a gruesome jig and lay still. The screen seemed to fill Arthur's whole field of vision and the straight line mocked him. "Again, damn it!" Wump! Still nothing. Arthur changed the position of the electrodes. "Again!" Wump! No change. "Again, Jannie and this time give him the max!" Wump! "Again!"

"We can't keep this up, Arthur. If he isn't dead already then we're busy killing him!"

"I know, damn it! We were so close to saving him. Once more." The veins around Arthur's temples stood out. It was as if he was willing the stubbornly flat line to start its regular hiccup. It didn't happen. Arthur shoved the operating trolley out the way, sending it crashing into the far wall. He placed the heels of his hands over the sergeant's heart and began pumping ... one-two ... one-two ... he continued and counted and pumped. The sweat changed the colour of his cap to its original dark green and a wet patch spread out over his chest.

"He's dead, Arthur." Jannie's voice was soft and compassionate.

Arthur seemed not to hear and continued. He stopped suddenly, ripped the surgical mask from his face and glared at them for a moment. He turned and punched his fist onto the wall behind him. The alarm continued, the lung machine scraped up and down and the music played. "Turn it off please, all of it." Arthur turned, placed his hands behind his back and leaned against the wall. "Record time of death as twenty-one forty-two. Jannie would you be so kind as to close him up and then meet me at the officers' pub for a beer."

"Sure, Arthur. How's your hand?"

"Bloody sore, thank you." He strode towards the door.

Jannie grabbed his sleeve. "You did all you could, you know," Jannie spoke frankly. Their faces were close and they looked into each other's eyes.

"Not a happy tale though ... he dies in the end."

Jannie nodded, "Chopper's corner for that beer?"

"Chopper's corner it is," said Arthur and closed the door behind him.

CHAPTER 17

"Strewth, look at that!" exclaimed Allan quietly and Geoff followed his gaze. Standing close to the passenger entrance near the front of the huge Hercules C-130 was the brigadier's party, chatting congenially to one another.

"Yep, you're looking at the Officer Commanding Sector One Zero and his wife ..."

"I couldn't give a shit about them, look at that woman. The lieutenant." Allan stood mesmerised. Geoff noticed her for the first time. She had on one of those stupid little gnome-like hats issued to all women soldiers but, strangely it seemed to suit her. Her uniform seemed to suit her. Everything seemed to suit her, in fact, in Allan's eyes, she was a veritable goddess. He felt his loins tighten and squeeze until they hurt. Her severely tied, jet-black hair was iridescent below the stupid hat and her shirt was tight enough to emphasise her generous breasts. Her bra straps were very visible and her short legs with athletic calves and slim ankles protruding below her knee-length skirt suited her small, curvy frame. Her arms were sun-browned and toned as she handled the two official-looking briefcases.

This was a woman. Not a classic beauty but extremely appealing and very sexy and Allan had to physically clench his teeth to stop his jaw hitting the runway. They ogled her with pained expression. The siren noticed the direction of their stares, immediately stood straighter, thrust her chest out and stood back a pace behind the brigadier so as to deny them scrutiny of her womanly assets.

"Sweet Jesus, would you look at that," whispered Geoff. "She's absolutely gorgeous." He took a step forward to get a better view.

"Down boy. Don't bullshit yourself. To her we're just smelly *pongoes*—brown jobs, we don't even exist, so have a good stare and save it for your piece of fluff back home," said Allan, smiling broadly at the lieutenant.

"My piece of fluff back home doesn't do that yet," answered Geoff despondently. He stared longingly at the lieutenant.

Allan turned his head slowly. "Surely you jest!"

"Nope. Holier than thou, I'm afraid. 'Saving it for marriage' and all that."

"Ditch the bitch now before it's too late!" Allan was incredulous.

"Look, I've got a piece on the side, so don't think there's a drought but …," Geoff blurted out.

"Ha ha, shit kid, you're a marvel. I learn more about you every time we speak and I'm impressed."

Geoff's sanguine hue and forcible laughter confirmed that his mouth had been faster than his mind. He led the way into the hot, gloomy hold and sat below one of the small portal windows towards the front of the plane. There was a whine and the aeroplane shook as one by one the four Allison T56-A-7A turboprops fired up and the strong but not unpleasant smell of avgas invaded the cargo hold. The plane rocked once and moved off the apron towards the runway.

The faces of the men were set nervously as the most dangerous part of the flight was about to begin. There was no danger in the take-off for the most successful cargo plane in the world—unless a well-aimed SAM-7 rocket hit it. Minutes before any aircraft departed or landed, two Alouette gunships took to the sky and flew an aerial patrol to secure take-off.

The C-130 hurtled down the runway and seemed to leap into the sky. It banked sharply and began the characteristic tight spiral climb above the airfield, gaining height with each turn. Only when out of range from missiles and when the big camouflaged aircraft had straightened and set course for Pretoria did the men inside sit back and visibly relax.

The excitement was tangible as the men shouted and gesticulated above the noise of the aircraft. Seven days! Seven glorious days of leave. The men were still being entertained by storyteller Allan Hunt when the peals of laughter were drowned out by the heavy bang of the lowering undercarriage. The aeroplane flew low over the highway, across the double security fence and dropped gracefully onto the runway at Waterkloof Air Force Base outside Pretoria.

Hasty handshakes and farewells saw the men disperse into the car park, searching for friends and family. Geoff strode through the gate into the car park and saw Mark. *Now life's about to begin again*, he thought as the excitement surged through his body.

Mark was hard to miss in a crowd. Although he leant against his Ford Escort Sport, he still towered above the few other people in the car park. Even though Geoff stood a good six feet two, Mark was taller by a fair way, standing at least six feet five. Mark caught the swift movement out the corner of his eye and steadied himself for the onslaught as Geoff dropped his duffle bag and charged. The two thudded together in a great bear hug, driving the wind from each other, squeezing hard and released, laughing, beaming with happiness.

"So the fucking gooks haven't slaughtered you yet you crazy bastard?" shouted Mark as Geoff retrieved his duffle bag.

"They'll never get me. You look slim and armyish—tough course huh?" Mark had grown a thick bushy black moustache and wore a white T-shirt that hung out over a pair of Levi's. His jet-black hair was shorn, typically military and he looked like a hardened athlete.

"Nah. Just never ending, but it's over now and you'll have to salute me from now on old cock."

Geoff looked up at Mark. "You made it *and* became an officer to boot!" he hooted, grabbing his friend's hand, pumping.

"Yep. Thanks," Mark beamed at the acknowledgement, "I've been a loot since the passing-out parade in November but you've been on the border all this time so I guess it slipped my mind to tell you." Mark folded his large frame into the Escort and slapped the steering wheel. "C'mon, let's go. I promised to get you home in one piece. Your mom commanded me to bring you straight home without starting a pub crawl *and* Kathy's there."

"You could've told me in one of your letters; it's a bloody great achievement man!"

"What, the fact that Kathy's there?"

"No, you arsehole. That you're a lieu … oh! Piss off!" They hooted with glee.

"I don't know; sometimes I think it would have been better to be an NCO like you rather than live with the pretence of this officer-gentleman crap. The Dutchmen love it. You take one off his dad's farm where one minute he's slapping the workers, the next humping them. You place a pip on his shoulder and all of a sudden his knuckles don't drag on the ground anymore."

"Wow, you've got it in for them, I see. Surely they're not all bad?"

"No. You're right. Only the ones I've met so far." They burst out laughing as Mark turned onto the N1 South and headed for Johannesburg.

"Despite dear mum, I hope we'll stop for a little moisture. It was a long, dry flight with no air hosties and not a cold drink in sight."

"I'm afraid I cannot let your mother down. I gave her my word as an officer and a gentleman but fear not, dear boy, if you care to reach behind you, you might just find a little box of fun behind the seat." Geoff looked over his shoulder, reached back and wrestled the small Coleman out of its hiding place.

"You bloody marvel!" He lifted the lid, plunged his hand into the ice and produced two cans of Castle Lager. He opened the cans and passed one to Mark. "Cheers, buddy! Good to see you and good to be home."

"Likewise dear fellow." They clanked their cans together. Geoff put the can to his lips, tilted it back and downed the beer in six big gulps. He wiped his mouth with the back of his hand, burped loudly and dug around in the ice for a second. "Thirsty boy, huh?" said Mark. He raised an eyebrow theatrically and followed suite. "While you're at it you may as well pass me another."

Homecoming was a little overwhelming for Geoff as his mother hugged him, his father shook his hand, Kathy tried to squeeze in somewhere, the dogs jumped around while his brother waited patiently for all of them to finish so he could shake hands with his hero. The whole bunch moved inside via the kitchen door followed by Mark who smiled as everyone fired questions at Geoff all at once.

Geoff's nostrils flared at the aroma coming from the kitchen. "Oh man, roast chicken! That smells great. Let's eat."

"Its not quite ready, my son. You'll just have to wait a little longer." Gill Kent couldn't help showing her pride. Her son was so big and handsome and so dashing in his brown, ironed-to-perfection uniform with his clean corporal chevrons on his arms and green beret upon his head. "Come, let's sit a while and hear some of your news. Who taught you to iron like that?" she asked leading her son by his arm.

"One guess, mom. Let me just change into some civvies and I'll be right back. Come Mark, bring us a couple of beers."

Geoff returned wearing a pair of shorts, a T-shirt and bare feet for it was a warm evening. He flopped down on the couch and Kathy was quick to take her place at his side. She sat close, as close as she could and her lightly tanned legs distended her not quite mini, denim skirt. She placed her hand on Geoff's leg and gently raked her fingers though the thick hairs.

Geoff swallowed the last mouthful of beer. "Chuck us another please Mark." Geoff cracked open his fifth, or was it his sixth beer and realised that he was becoming mellow, very mellow indeed and he enjoyed the feeling. Something else was making an impression. Like the germination of a flower it emerged from the depth of his subconscious. The gentle attention his nubile, young girlfriend was administering to his leg was arousing him, so much so that he suddenly sat up and leant forward.

He listened vaguely to his mother " ... you know that nearly every day on the TV now they announce the death of a soldier killed in action on the border ..."

"I'm sure Geoff doesn't need to hear about that sort of thing at this point, my dear," said Byron Kent. Deftly he poured a measured tot of Johnny Walker Black Label. There was silence as he sat and Geoff realised that his mother was embarrassed.

"No, it's okay dad," he said holding up his hand. "You don't have to worry, mom. Where we are at Eenhana it's like a holiday camp, not much action there.

We spend more time tanning than anything else." The lie came easily.

"The problem is that it's spreading further south. Just a couple of months ago we saw the dreadful story on the TV news of a farmer and his wife who were killed in a landmine explosion outside … where dear?" Gill turned to her husband, lines of concern showing on her face.

"Tsumeb."

"But that's miles from here, isn't it Geoff?" asked Steve, Geoff's brother.

"Sure is and we nailed all but one of that gang anyway, so there's no chance of the war reaching here." Geoff suddenly realised what he had said and hurriedly continued, "This war won't ever get to the South African borders."

"You said 'we' nailed them. Were you involved?" Kathy sat forward and faced Geoff. Her eyes seemed to grow with the horror her pretty face conveyed.

Damn! thought Geoff. She sure latched onto that. "I'm sorry. That just slipped out …" Suddenly Geoff's mind painted a vivid picture of a young man with a pale, pleading face—pleading to live as he lay in Geoff's arms, his life's blood pouring from his mouth and Geoff shuddered, shook his head and stood up suddenly. "Who's for another drink?"

"You can fill me up, son," said Byron recognising his son's pain. "How's the grub, wench?"

"Oh, you!" said Gill and she hurried out to the kitchen. Geoff handed Mark a beer and followed his mother. He found her sitting at the breakfast nook, her head in her hands and she was crying softly. Geoff sat next to her and put his arm around her. She leant over and buried her face in his shoulder.

"I'm sorry," she whispered, "I didn't want you to see me like this but I worry so much. I love you so much and can't bare the thought of you being in any danger."

"You know mom, it's like I said, it's a low-key war and we are far superior soldiers to those Swapo guys, so you've got to stop worrying …."

Gill stood and inspected the roast. "How do you expect me to stop worrying when civilians are getting murdered and you have to go and find their killers. You could get killed you know?"

Geoff smiled lovingly at his mother. "Thank you for caring so much, it means a lot to me but I'm a big boy now and I've got a lot of living to do, so I don't intend to get myself killed." He stood and cradled his mother's face in his hands. "Stop worrying about me," he commanded.

Gill hugged her son, wiped her eyes and announced. "Dinner's ready!" Geoff turned to call the others and found Kathy leaning against the door, her cheeks shiny with tears.

"Oh no! What now?" asked Geoff. He took her gently in his arms and squeezed.

"You're so sweet to your mom and I love you so much," she whispered in a tremulous voice, nuzzling against him.

Her body was warm and soft and she smelt of roses and spring freshness. Her pale brown hair shone in the light of the kitchen and Geoff could feel the thrust of her pert young breasts against his stomach and once again he was aroused. He'd been on the border for months and the feel of a pretty young female—his woman—in his arms was too much. The stirrings in his groin were uncontrollable and startling in their suddenness. Instead of letting go and walking away from this same situation he'd been in with Kathy a hundred times before he decided to let it happen. He needed her more than just emotionally, damn it, he needed her physically—and now more than ever.

Kathy felt it too and pushed herself away gently so as not to attract Gill's attention. She blushed and looked up at Geoff with a confused, angry expression. She deliberately turned away and walked through to the lounge. "Dinner's ready, everyone! Come and sit down!" she announced indignantly. Immediately Allan's words echoed in Geoff's mind. "Dump the bitch." He too was angry, really angry. The woman was a first-year university student for God's sake. Surely her mother had taught her about the birds and bees—bugger the birds and bees! How about just plain sex? And if not in conversation with her own mom, then with her hundreds of radical student colleagues. They probably discussed the subject ad nauseam.

Once seated, the easygoing conversation bounced back and forth to the clank and scrape of expensive cutlery on fine china. Inevitably politics and the situation in South Africa raised its ugly head.

"... and I've just read about some munt, Tambo I think, who has just addressed—wait for it ... The United Nations Special Committee against Apartheid. So they have this special committee and decree this year, 1982, as the International Year of Mobilisation for Sanctions against South Africa. I mean can you credit it? They want to impose sanctions against us and it will hurt the blacks the most ..." Beneath his tan Mark's face was red, more from mild inebriation than annoyance.

"What else can they do though, Mark? What recourse do they have?" Kathy had been attentive but quiet, but this was an area she understood as she was exposed to it all day at the University of the Witwatersrand.

"They've got the best bloody life in Africa and should be grateful for what they *do* have. Anyway, what do you know about it?" Mark spat, and cracked another beer.

"That 'munt' Tambo you happen to be defaming is actually Oliver Tambo, the leader of the ANC—quite an important man, don't you think?" Kathy's cheeks were slightly flushed. "And you don't even know his name."

"Quite important ... he's an ignorant munt like the rest of them," Mark hissed.

Geoff tried to dismiss the argument airily, "Ah c'mon guys, let's not get into this now, shall we? Pass the fucking sal ... oh shit ... damn. Oh boy, I'm sorry everyone ..." Gill bent her head to hide her mirth and mild shock while Mark, Byron and Steve exploded with laughter. "I'm afraid the saying 'swearing like a trooper' is quite pertinent. Every second word is a swear word and I need to remind myself that I'm in polite company. I apologise." Geoff blushed scarlet beneath his tanned skin. The laughter continued for a while and even Kathy seemed to relax.

"Do you have the same problem where you are, Mark?" Gill's face was still flushed.

Mark nodded and swallowed a mouthful of roast chicken. "Oh yes, I'm afraid so, but Geoff and I manage to rise above the unwashed herd and maintain a high standard of the Queen's English."

"Yes, well Geoff just proved that admirably a moment ago. By the way, do you still need the offending salt, son?" asked Byron

"Yep. Please pass it on." Geoff blushed and the humour prevailed.

"Mark, do you think you'll be going to the border too?" Steve spoke around a mouthful of roast potato.

Byron looked fondly at his younger son and then said to Mark, "Yes, what are your chances of going north?"

Mark shrugged. "That's a fair question. I'd say pretty good mainly because I was sent back to the hellhole, Fourteen Field and not to Fourth Field, which has just taken in new recruits." Mark rotated his knife as he spoke. "Artillery School might call me back too. We'll just have to wait and see."

"There's also the Cuban question and their Russian buddies," said Geoff grimly. "That'll get you to the border quickly enough if they continue to flock into Angola like they are."

"Oh, son, don't tell me that," pleaded Gill.

"Well, I'm afraid that's the reality of it ma and if it continues, the whole of southern Angola could break out into conventional war—us against the bloody Commies."

"Ja, while these arseholes call for sanctions against us. They're so stupid," Steve added his opinion and missed the warning flash of anger from Kathy. "They must go ahead and impose their sanctions. This country is virtually self-sufficient and we don't need the rest of the world ..."

"You can be so thick sometimes, Steve. What about foreign currency just for starters. What about exports and imports. What about tourism ... and what about human rights?" Kathy was annoyed but calm.

"I thought it was a BA you were studying—you know, a Bugger All, not economics and human rights," barked Steve. How dare she call him stupid.

Kathy was stunned by the retort but managed to maintain her composure and went on calmly, "That's why I think you're so naïve. We wouldn't have any sanctions against us if we abolished apartheid and held democratic elections for all South Africans including the 'munts' as you and Mark so open-mindedly put it."

"Perish the thought. Imagine if the munts came to power—they couldn't run a piss-up in a brewery let alone a country," sneered Mark, avoiding eye contact with Kathy lest she see the bitter dislike he held for her.

"But they *will* come to power, and before that happens, you guys will find yourself fighting a far more powerful enemy than you are now …" Kathy felt as though they were ganging up on her and had to attack to survive. At least Geoff was quiet although he wasn't exactly supporting her. "You wait until you come up against the might of the ANC's military wing."

"This sounds interesting. The banned ANC has a military wing that's going to take on the might of the South African Defence Force where Swapo is trying and failing." Mark sat forward; the knuckles of his fists were white. "They fail even though they've employed the services of MPLA who are also taking a beating. So they've invited the Cubans and Russians who are also taking a beating. If you happen to be referring to the cowards who kill innocent women and children by planting bombs in shopping malls then you have my attention. I'm looking forward to meeting them."

"That was an isolated incident. Umkhonto we Sizwe is an organised army and are poised to fight for freedom if they can't get it by peaceful negotiations."

"The only negotiating they'll get is a bullet from my R1."

"Ah, yes, the mature attitude we were all waiting for."

"Look, whose side are you on anyway, Kathy?" Mark leant forward, placed his elbows on the table, his tanned forearms huge and intimidating as he pointed at her with a well-chewed drumstick. "By the sounds of it I had better watch my back in case I get sold out for the proverbial thirty pieces of silver …"

"I would be obliged if the three of you would stop this useless bickering and help me clean away the dishes so we can bring on the pudding," said Gill petulantly.

"Hey, ma, where's Happybum?" asked Geoff.

"It's Thursday night son, maid's night off."

"One forgets so quickly," commented Geoff.

"Happybum?" Mark shook his head.

"You know, our maid …"

"Yes, yes, I know your maid Gladys, oh …"

"Boy, you're slow tonight," said Steve and they laughed.

Geoff smiled, "Good old Gladarse."

Dessert was a quiet affair with most lost in their thoughts. Where undercurrents of anger and resentment had prevailed, short polite conversation again began and slowly the atmosphere lightened, much to Gill's relief. A favourite topic was sport and, of course, rugby.

The excitement was building for the upcoming Springbok tour of New Zealand. The two greatest rugby-playing nations in the world expected nothing less than a win from their teams and the build-up held hours of debate on every possible statistic from the condition of the pitch to the length of studs that should be used for the wet, soft-underfoot conditions in New Zealand.

The discussion on the game continued through coffee and adjournment as the men headed for Byron's oak-panelled bar. "Mark, who is this Umzinto wee whatever Kathy's talking about?" asked Geoff when he was certain the ladies were out of earshot.

"Umkhonto we Sizwe? I'm not too sure, but I've heard of them on one or two occasions before and I think it's as Kathy says—they are the African National Congress's military wing, you know, sort of the same as Plan is to Swapo."

"What's Plan?" asked Stephen.

"People's Liberation Army of Namibia," said Geoff. "What does Umkhonto wee whatever stand for?"

Mark downed his beer and shrugged, "Who the hell knows?"

"Well, either they haven't started anything yet or they're bloody useless," added Byron. "Which reminds me, did I ever tell you the story of … ?"

The ladies returned to raucous laughter. Byron spoke around a huge Willem II cigar. The night was warm and the wooden sash windows were open. A cool breeze dissipated the pleasant-smelling smoke and Geoff pulled up a bar stool for Kathy. She sat carefully and crossed her legs. Geoff placed his hand on her knee and she looked at him adoringly.

Gill Kent noticed the little exchange and a feeling of such joy boiled up within her that she could practically hear the patter of little feet coming down the passage.

The night drew on and finally Mark stood, "I must go. Thank you Kents for everything tonight. I love you all and had better go before I can't speak properly anymore."

"You can't speak properly now!" laughed Geoff.

"Yes, you're right but neither can you. Just you remember tomorrow night we're meeting the others at the Sunnyside."

"Oh shit yes ... sorry." Geoff looked at his mother and smiled sheepishly. "You'll pick me up Mark?"

"Of course. Welcome home again."

"Thanks buddy. Good to be here, good to see you." The men walked together.

"Are you alright to drive, Mark?" asked Gill with growing concern as she watched them stagger down to the hallway.

"Yep! Fine thanks." Mark hiccupped once, turned and waved as Geoff closed the door behind him.

"Don't worry so much ma, he'll be alright."

"Well, I'm bushed and I've got school tomorrow, so I'll see you all in the morning. G'night all." A chorus of 'good nights' followed and Steve left, followed closely by Byron. Gill Kent hesitated a minute and resisted the temptation to fling her arms around her son. She was well rewarded for her restraint as Geoff stood, drew his mother to him and hugged the breath out of her.

"Thank you for such a wonderful welcome home, ma," he said.

Alone at last Geoff stood up from his stool and held Kathy's hands. "Would you like some more wine or an Irish coffee?"

"Nothing for me thanks and you've had enough too."

"So now you're telling me what to do ..." Geoff's eyes flared with annoyance.

"No Geoff, I'm sorry." Kathy looked up, she seemed helpless. "I just want you to myself for a little while."

Geoff suddenly felt the urge to hold and protect her. "Let's go and sit in the lounge then." Geoff took her hand and led her to the couch. The lounge was dim with only a hint of soft light shining up from behind the oak pelmets. Kathy sat on the couch and lay back. Her short skirt rucked up and displayed her graceful legs. Geoff slid a cassette tape into the hi-fi.

The romantic piano of Richard Clayderman caressed them and Geoff turned to Kathy. He stood for a moment, admiring her shapely legs, her clean shiny hair, her pretty face and her petite breasts. In the dull light he could see her nipples thrusting against the cotton and wondered if she was excited or perhaps even aroused. She lifted her hand to him and he walked slowly toward her, not wanting to rush the moment. Not wanting to put her off or scare her. Not wanting it to go wrong as it had so often in the past.

He took her hand, lowered himself next to her and gently slid his arm under her shoulders. Slowly, achingly slowly, the gap between them closed and their lips touched. Warm, full and inviting, her lips parted slightly. They stayed like that for a second before their tongues, hesitantly at first, began to explore. In ecstasy her eyes closed. Geoff slid his hand down her arm onto her bare leg.

Down her thigh across her calf to her ankle and started slowly back up, feeling the smoothness and warmth of her skin. The tension mounted as his hand slid up over her cotton top and encompassed a small round breast. Her nipples were erect and hard and she gasped and moaned softly as he rolled the nipple gently between thumb and forefinger. Her breathing became deeper, harder and she turned her head and gasped for breath as he kissed her chin and neck. Slowly Geoff manoeuvred her until she lay on her back. Her legs hung over the edge of the couch and her arms circled his neck.

Geoff slid his fingers between the buttons on her cotton shirt and released them one by one. She wore no bra and he lowered his head to her breasts. Kathy moaned softly and Geoff felt a different movement. Almost imperceptible at first, Kathy began gyrating her pelvis. Geoff caught the movement out the corner of his eye. He noticed that Kathy's denim skirt had rucked up her legs, far enough to expose a pair of black lace panties and from that angle Geoff could see the mound rising up and disappearing between her inner thighs. He worked his way up to her mouth again and took her lower lip gently between his teeth and at the same time let his free hand work its way down to the lace. His hand slid gently up over the mound and her legs fell open to accommodate him. Her thigh pushed hard against his groin and she massaged back and forth over the bulge in his pants.

Geoff slid his hand under the lace, over the trimmed bush and his finger slid into her. It was hot and slippery and Kathy gasped as he massaged the hard little pea at the top of her moist vagina. Their mouths met again as she groaned and gyrated her pelvis wildly to the attentions of his hand and Geoff could stand it no longer. His skin tingled with anticipation as he pulled his arm from beneath her. He slipped off the couch onto his knees in front of her and whipped down his shorts. He moved between her parted legs, pulled the flimsy panties to one side and thrust.

Kathy squealed, sat up suddenly and smiled at him. Her chest still heaved. "Geoffrey Kent! You are such a naughty devil! What am I going to do with you?" she laughed breathlessly. "You so nearly caught me off guard and we can't have that, now can we?" Geoff's mouth fell open in horror. He was so bloody close. How could she stop now?

Kathy slid off the couch onto her knees in front of Geoff, straightened her denim skirt and flung her arms around him. Geoff couldn't respond for a second as he knelt with his shorts around his knees, a slowly receding erection and the very reason for the sexual tension, hanging around his neck.

"Jesus Christ, woman! What the hell do you think you're doing to me, hey? You can't spend the whole bloody night arousing me just to snub me at the death!"

"Oh, stop being so pedantic. You know that we aren't going to do *that* until we get married, silly. And if you continue to shout like that, you'll wake your parents."

"I don't give a damn if I wake the whole bloody world! Having sex is a basic human need; a man's got to have it and if you don't give it to me, I'll find it elsewhere!" His eyes blazed and her tenuous smile dissolved. Geoff sighed and dropped his head, "Why don't you just leave. Just go home!"

For a moment Kathy was dumbstruck and she stared up at him in disbelief. "I … I'm sorry," she whispered and shook her head slowly. The hurt showed and the tears welled up. "I … I didn't know it was so important to you. I thought I was doing the right thing for us … for you. I'm so sorry." She quickly buttoned her top, sank back and sobbed. Geoff pulled his pants up and looked down at her. She turned and buried her face in a cushion and her shoulders heaved as she sobbed. He scratched his forehead and looked around; he was a sucker for other people's misery especially if he were the cause. He bent and lifted her gently to her feet. She turned in the circle of his arms and hugged him so tightly that he was surprised at her strength.

"Look I'm … I'm … I don't know Kathy." Geoff felt like a bully. "Okay, let's talk about this …"

She rounded on him, "You asked me to leave, so that's what I'm doing."

"Look, don't …"

"Shut up Geoff."

He followed her to her car. Geoff opened the door and she recoiled as he attempted to usher her in. She slid into the car, closed the door with frosty dignity, turned the ignition and drove off without a backward glance.

Who the hell does she think she is? Damn it! Damn it to hell, Geoff thought as he pulled the motorbike helmet over his head. On his bike and out in the street, he rode slowly, giving the engine time to warm up but at the next stop street he took off like a dragster. *Sister bloody Theresa? Does she really even love me? Do I really love her? Surely we should try sex before marriage?* He changed to second gear and then once in third pulled hard and accelerated onto his back wheel.

Stop street! Down boy!

Maybe it's wrong for us. After a few short years we find we're incompatible? I think we're much too bloody young. We shouldn't even be thinking of marriage.

God, I'm horny! Damn her pretentious views of celibacy before marriage. Such a farce!

He took off again, the wind pushing tears along his cheeks and he controlled the urge to race the whole way to the flat land of Windsor Park.

I show her! Damn me if I'll be celibate!

Geoff turned off the well-lit side street onto the dark, pot-holed asphalt drive of the townhouse complex.

Steady boy. You can do this. A light breeze sprung up and ruffled his cropped hair, sending tingles down his spine.

This is not revenge and guilt has no place here.

The hair on his forearms rose up in goose flesh at the prospect of a violent highveld thunderstorm. He realised that he should have phoned first. He ran around to the front and rang the doorbell.

Courage brother! At least here you should get lucky. Guilt oozed between the lust.

Damn her! I wouldn't be here if…

A light went on, the door opened against the latch and the worn, haggard face of Mrs van Zyl peered through the opening.

This is a bodily need. Months away from civilisation with no women about. It's only natural. Reward yourself!

"You want Lorna?"

"Yes please Mrs van Zyl." *You don't know how much.* The door closed, reopened with vigour.

"Geoff!" Lorna squealed and flung her arms around him. "It's been so long! Where have you been?" She drew back and looked at him, her eyelids drooping. "God how I want you," she whispered in his ear.

Damn you! Look what you've made me do!

"Sorry I'm so late, Mrs van Zyl," said Geoff sheepishly. He knew it was late and she could probably guess why he was visiting. "I've just got back from the border. Perhaps next time I can visit a little earlier and we can do some catching up."

Mrs van Zyl stopped at the top of the stairs and peered down for a moment before smiling. "You're kind. Thank you." She turned and disappeared.

"Do you always lie so smoothly?" Lorna said craftily. Geoff studied her. She was tall and too slim, her hair cascaded onto her bony shoulders in tight blond curls but now, without her glasses, her hazel-green eyes transformed her into an appealing young woman, very different from the gangly, bespectacled schoolgirl he had once known. They fairly flew at each other, lips crushed together, tongues wrestled, bodies writhed and she made little high-pitched pleading noises in the back of her throat as she felt his manhood press hard and big against her belly. She tasted of cigarettes and wine but Geoff didn't mind as he slid his hand inside her tracksuit pants and grabbed her small firm buttock.

"Not here," she whispered breathlessly, "my room." Geoff followed her up the stairs to the room furthest from her mother's. "Kathy let you down again or have you left her for me?" For a moment she was frightened by what she saw in his eyes but suddenly he smiled.

"Yes and no, how's that?"

"Okay, we'll talk later," she said and closed the door behind him. She removed her T-shirt, exposing her small perfect breasts. Geoff pulled his shirt over his head, threw it in the corner and grabbed her. They kissed, she unbuttoned his fly, loosened his belt and kissed his nipples.

"Help me get these off," she breathed and tugged at his jeans. Geoff stood back out of his jeans, looked down and Lorna was, as if by some magic, stark naked. She rose, walked over to the bed and stood next to it. She swivelled on the ball of her foot, raised her index finger and invited him. Geoff reacted like the first hound to sight the fox and flew at her only to have her step nimbly out of the way which sent him crashing onto the bed. Lightning fast he flipped over but seconds too late as she was upon him, kissing, holding, feeling and suddenly she sat up, impaling herself upon him and they gasped together. *God, he's so big*, she thought as the tendrils of ecstasy spread rapidly from the base of her belly. Geoff gasped for it was happening at long last and it was beautiful.

"Just tell me who they are so I'm not caught off guard," he demanded as they walked slowly arm in arm down the back passage towards the thumping music at the end of the corridor. The distant thunder drew nearer, the wind blew her hair into her face and Lorna was in her element. The boy that the girls loved most at school had just been inside her—again and again and as many times since their school days at Roosevelt High. Furthermore he was going out with the belle of the school who had already won a beauty competition at the university, but it was she, Lorna van Zyl, making him feel good about himself because little Miss Kathy goody two shoes didn't fuck. What a bloody pity.

She smiled to herself and shuddered slightly as the recent memory of him rutting on top of her was so vivid in her mind that she wanted him all over again. Despite their move to Bryanston, Geoff remained the same and swore that his dad had only moved there to give his family a bigger property, bigger rooms, more space. That was despite the fact that Geoff's sister had long since left the country for greener pastures due to her lack of belief and confidence in the present government—what a bitch! Maybe she would freeze her tits off in Canada and good riddance.

"Hey, I'm talking to you," Geoff squeezed Lorna.

"Oh, yes, umm ... they told me that they go to Wits too."

"Too? As well as who?" Geoff looked down at her.

"Oh, just a figure of speech, I don't know," she dismissed his question irritably, hiding the near error. If he could read her mind now, how shocked would he be?

"Well, be prepared for trouble if any of those radicals are there because I won't take any of their shit."

"Jesus Geoffrey, lighten up. Don't be so bloody defensive!"

"I can't help it, I just had a whole evening of it at home ..."

"Kathy still won't open her legs, huh?"

"Shit you've become crude and hard in a very short time, hey?"

"Well check it out buster," she rounded on him and her eyes sparkled with anger. "You never even bothered to look at me at school and since you've been in the army, you come to me. You come here, come in me and go to her and I don't see you till next pass and the whole process starts again. Foolish me!" Lorna curtly flipped the hair out of her face.

"It's not like that Lorna; you know I've got a real soft spot for you ..."

"Yep, like the one between my legs."

Geoff packed up laughing—she was so accurate that trying to convince her otherwise was futile.

Lorna opened the door and Toto's 'Hold the Line' blared from the nearby speakers. For Lorna it was a perfect entrance; these guys knew her well, maybe too well for Geoff to know anything about it. But Lorna looked up in admiration of her tall, beautiful god as they walked in. Heads turned and all present saw Lonely Loose Lorna with a big, broad-shouldered, handsome soldier boy. The music banged on as Lorna paraded her man around for all to see, introducing him to a long-haired hippy here or a Rastafarian black dude there and lastly, the tenants of the duplex. Nervously, albeit enthusiastically they welcomed Geoff to their humble abode. Geoff, for the first time in his life, found himself in the centre of a crowd of truly cosmopolitan people—some black, some coloured, the rest white and their common interest was simply the pure enjoyment of life together—amazing.

Outside the first large drops of rain smacked down on the broken asphalt.

CHAPTER 18

All night they slogged through the bush on thick sand. They paused only to take a mouthful of water. John knew the pace was tough but if they were to reach their destination before dawn, they must hurry. He had chosen his askaris not only for their ruthlessness and fighting ability but also for their stamina.

At some stage John looked up and could distinguish the earth from the sky on the horizon—dawn was very close and with every second the danger of discovery increased. John was agonising over the decision whether to stop now and bury their weapons or to push a little harder and deny dawn the chance of exposing them when, to his relief, he saw the sharp, uneven points of the log palisade.

He brought his askaris to a halt. They crouched and observed their first destination. The kraal was dead quiet, nothing moved and John felt anxious as a small breeze caressed his sweaty skin in the chill of dawn. Change of season was imminent and the mornings were getting colder.

John needed a sign. He had to be sure that the South Africans hadn't discovered this hideout and were waiting in ambuscade. John peered at the kraal in the growing light and one of his askaris jumped as a cock crowed. John gave the man a withering stare. A dog barked and someone called his name.

"John. John Mulemba."

"It is I."

"Come in, it is safe."

"I have men with me." John was still not sure.

"Bring them with." It was the answer John had hoped for. Had the voice asked how many they were he would have been suspicious. Still, he was taking no chances and sent forward the nervous askari. The sound of whispering reached him.

The askari turned and spoke. "The man says he is your brother."

"If you are my brother then show yourself and tell me you name," John spoke to the tall silhouette next to his askari.

The man stepped forward. "It is me, Victor." John smiled. His teeth shone white in the dawn twilight. The two men embraced, one slightly taller and slimmer wearing a Fapla uniform and giant-sized Russian Army boots.

"I see the life working for the Boere in Oshakati has treated you well," said John patting his brother's stomach.

Victor didn't miss the sarcastic jibe. "As you can see they like me and treat me well and soon, very soon they will give me the information for which you so hunger, my brother. Even now I have something to whet your appetite."

"Let us go and sit in your hut lest the Boere see us in these clothes. We might have a hard time explaining." The laughter was as hushed as the conversation.

John and his men stripped and washed from the buckets at the far corner of the kraal while Victor lit a fire beneath the old, blackened pot.

John observed the many full containers around the kraal. "Where do you get all your water from?"

"The Boere like us so they bring it," Victor's answer was deadpan and the others laughed delightedly at the brazen cheek.

"If only they knew!" laughed one of the askaris.

Later, donning cast-off civilian clothes and seated with the sun warming them, the conversation became more serious. Each man had a bowl of steaming mielie meal porridge as they sat in a circle outside Victor's hut.

"What you tell me is of the greatest importance," said John around a mouthful of porridge. "We will take this information back with us and prepare for it."

"I hope it does not waste your time, my brother."

"No, it will ensure readiness at all times and can be treated as an exercise."

"So, do you still wish me to join with you or should I continue as I am?" asked Victor with a twinkle in his eye.

"No. Your security clearance into Oshakati is invaluable to us. You must stay and learn all you can."

"Ah, so, you don't begrudge me my easy life working for the Boere then?" Victor was eager to avenge his brother's earlier remark.

"On the contrary, I could never do your work. It would be too difficult for me to call any white man 'baas' or any white woman 'madam'."

"Let us hope then that the great warrior Grootvoet is not caught and made to suffer the same fate as his best friend Enoch Shongwe in the Mariental gaol while his brother continues to grow fat and lazy at the expense of the Boere."

"Best friends don't get caught as he was. He is no longer a friend but an enemy," said John calmly. "The only reason that I risk my life and travel back to Tsumeb is because he failed, causing me to fail. That white bitch is still paramount to the success of the New War!"

"Then take me with you!" Victor pleaded. He leant over and grabbed his brother's muscled forearm.

"You don't realise how important your job is. You must stay there and gather as much information as you can. Who knows," John spread his hands and shrugged, "you might end up as one of the country's greatest heroes."

"Come," Victor stood, "we need to hide your clothes and weapons and you need to rest." Victor entered his hut, lifted the basket-weave rug and squatted. In the gloomy interior he inspected the dung floor minutely. Victor lifted the cork plug, which concealed the string. He pulled on the sisal. Under his bed a false floor slid open exposing a dark hole in the soft earth.

Victor lit a paraffin lamp, placed it next to the opening, threw his legs over the side and slid into the hole. He called up to John who passed the lamp down into the dank, sour-smelling pit. John looked about as the lamp lit up the blackness below, exposing an underground chamber. The walls were lined with trimmed mopani logs for prevention against collapse in the soft ground. But that was not the focus of John's attention—rather it was the arms cache.

AK-47s lined the walls, magazines of ammunition filled one corner, round shiny Chinese hand grenades spilled out of a box in another corner and mines, dozens of mines of all sorts, lay scattered around the floor.

"By day I am a servant to the Boere, a servant who is constantly alert to the loose tongues of the leaders, and by night I am a freedom fighter like you."

John reached down and placed a hand on Victor's shoulder. "I am proud of you," he squeezed affectionately. "Be sure that our commanders will hear of your efforts."

The brothers stood, brushed the dust off and stared at each other—the one proud, the other with newly acquired admiration for his sibling.

Dawn the next day saw the rusty, beige Toyota Land Cruiser leaving a dust cloud down the dirt track as John and his askaris travelled south. They wore cast-off clothing in varying degrees of ruin in keeping with the average Ovambo civilian. The road was long, hot and dusty and for every kilometre they journeyed the tension mounted as the Oshivelo Gate beckoned.

The Oshivelo Gate was the gateway to the Red Area. Anywhere north of the gate was declared a war zone and people travelling either way through the gate were subjected to rigorous searches—unless of course you were white, then you were waved through by a friendly smiling sentry of the SADF.

The farmers appreciated the effort made by these men and on travelling through the gate would hand out such gifts as cartons of cigarettes, sweets, cold drinks and even biltong, the dried strips of seasoned beef so sought after by the troops.

Leniency, if any, was accorded the Ovambo people who carried coffins containing the dead. But it was a folly to carry anything other than dead bodies in these coffins for these too were searched.

Finally, dancing in the heat waves loomed the gate. The driver of the Land Cruiser slowed and rolled to a stop well short of the boom.

A mean-looking sentry marched over. A big frown creased his brow. He was clearly very angry. "Why do you park so far away, you bloody kaffir!?" he shouted.

The driver shrugged and smiled sheepishly. "I'm sorry my boss. It won't happen again, boss."

"It had better not! Where are you lot going?" asked the sentry. He jotted the registration number into the guard book.

"We must fetch the body of my uncle to bury him in Oshakati."

"Are you brothers?" The sentry looked up from his book and peered menacingly at them. But for the driver, the others wore the deadpan mask of Black Africa—the look of a simpleton and it worked, nearly every time.

"Yes, we are brothers." Brothers could mean that they were cousins or even distant relatives and the sentry glanced at each in turn. Then he turned his attention to John. The sentry made to turn away, stopped suddenly and peered at John.

"You," he pointed at John with his rifle barrel. "Get out." John obeyed immediately and stood next to the Land Cruiser. "Haven't I seen your face somewhere before, boy?"

John did not answer and stared into the distance. Outwardly he remained unaffected and totally neutral but inside he seethed. This young rookie was deliberately baiting him. Calling an older black man 'boy' was as insulting as one could get. The sentry looked down and noticed John's feet. He wore no shoes and his big toenails were the size of sliced potato medallions. To the sentry, they were a sight to behold. "What the hell do you call those?" he exclaimed pointing at the huge pair of feet. "Makoros?" A makoro is a dugout canoe made of the trunk of a jackal berry or mashatu tree and used by the fishermen of the Caprivi and the Okavango Delta. "You people are just like baboons. Get in your Cruiser and bugger off!" he said, smiling at John's huge feet.

"Thank you boss," the driver smiled broadly. He ducked into the cabin and drove slowly away.

The sentry returned to the sand-bagged guardhouse, flung his bush hat onto the table, brushed away a pesky mopani fly and flopped into the chair.

"Shit, it's hot!"

"What took you so long?" asked his colleague lazily, hardly glancing up from his *Scope* magazine.

"Nothing really. They looked like a bunch of gooks and I wanted them to sweat a little."

"And did they?"

"Nah. That's why I let them go, but, hey … you should have seen the size of the one kaffir's feet! Shit they must have been at least a size fifteen or even sixteen!" The sentry held up his hands to indicate the size as if measuring a fish, "I've never seen anything like it!"

The second sentry's eyes widened. He sat forward and placed his fingers on his cheeks in horror, "You know what?"

"What?" The first sentry was alarmed.

"It was probably Grootvoet!"

They erupted with laughter.

❋

"I really liked that young Boer," said John with a contorted grin as they continued on their journey.

The driver was horrified. "How is that possible, comrade?"

"He is the fuel that feeds the fire in my soul. And my soul burns hotly for the death of these Boere. He makes me remember why we are fighting so hard for the freedom of our people," John looked at the driver, his eyes ablaze. "Now, is there any chance that you could drive this heap of scrap iron a little faster?" The driver nodded and the vehicle surged ahead. "By the way, I hope you have a coffin and a body for our return trip. That Boer is not stupid; he wrote down all our details."

"But comrade, my uncle really is dead."

It was late afternoon before the old Cruiser drove through the streets of Tsumeb, paused at the stop street, turned and drove off the macadam onto the gravel and headed out of town. The setting sun lit the way ahead in a collage of orange and yellow, exaggerating the green hues of the scattered acacias. The huge clouds on the eastern horizon formed a backdrop of exquisite colour to the otherwise stunted and gnarled trees. The Land Cruiser left a long dust trail which hung, unmoving, in the still early evening. With headlights lighting up the road, John peered ahead before instructing the driver to pull off into one of the mitre drains cut by the graders.

Whenever rain did fall in these parts, it mostly came down in sheets as if the heavens had literally opened and in a very short time the roads could be transformed into torrents. The mitre drains helped remove the excess as soon as possible. When this happened, the run-off water would form vast pools around the mitre drains and the vegetation in these areas flourished.

John knew this and it served him well for as the Land Cruiser drove off into the sandy drain, it disappeared in the thick bush. From here the men disembarked and began preparing. John took two askaris with him and set off into the darkness.

Armed with a flat size seventeen and a shifting spanner the driver wriggled beneath the Cruiser. With much grunting and cursing he battled with the rounded nuts distributed about the fuel tank. The use of the incorrect size spanner and the shifter had worn the once-hexagonal nuts round. Sweating, the driver extricated himself from beneath the Cruiser, dug about in the tool kit, smiled triumphantly and produced the tool of Africa. One could completely strip a motor vehicle and rebuild it with this, a vice-grip spanner. He then groped around under the seat of the Cruiser and found the old Eveready torch. An askari wriggled beneath the Cruiser with him and aimed the weak, flickering beam as the driver attacked each one of the nuts with his shiny vice-grip.

The tank came away. It proved to be a container fitted around a purpose-made tank of much smaller dimension, creating a void into which almost anything could be placed and still escape the scrutiny of the security forces.

"There!" whispered John fiercely. Once convinced he was in the right place, John ordered his askaris to dig while he kept vigil. Soon enough they uncovered the Hessian sacking and dragged it out onto the sand. John thrust one of his askaris aside and struggled with the knot.

Five AK-47s and one rocket propelled grenade launcher with grenade. John had no doubt that the AKs would be in working order, despite the sand in the breech and the rust from being buried for such a long time. It was the RPG that worried him, but there was no time for that now. They hastily changed into the camouflage fatigues and boots retrieved from the false tank. They took up their weapons, clambered onto the Land Cruiser and pulled out onto the sandy road to the farm.

John finished lacing his extra-large boots, sat back and looked at them indifferently. He had to wear them; it was all part of the bigger plan. It was a long time since his last visit but John recognised the entrance immediately and was pleased that they were not on foot this time for it would only hinder his plans. He leaned close to the driver and snarled, "The minute you hear the firing, you speed up to us. Do you understand me?" The man was irritating him.

"Yes, comrade, of course."

"Up this drive is a big, old farmhouse. We will be there." John grabbed his AK, closed the door and trotted towards the old house.

Soon the dark outline of the house became visible in the starry night sky and John stopped. He crouched and the others followed. For a long time he stared at the darkened building—something was wrong. The house seemed too quiet. Not a single light, no dogs barked and even the generator was silent. John indicated for the others to follow. They crawled on their stomachs until they were at the steps of the front veranda and John stood up suddenly. The others looked at him quizzically.

"They have gone," he lamented. The house stood as he had last left it, ruined. One half of the house was completely burned away with large roof timbers hanging precariously over the support walls.

Hot earth mixed with cool night air and a light breeze sprang up. It raised the hairs on John's forearms and he shivered. But with the breeze came a smell that was so faint at first he did not recognise it. A light gust carried a stronger whiff of the aroma and John smiled. It was the familiar smell of mielie meal cooked in an old black pot on an open fire. The thought of the stodgy maize porridge bubbling lethargically in the pot over the mopani wood coals sent the saliva pouring into John's mouth. *I'll have some of that a little later*, he thought to himself.

When the gang of insurgents was still a way off they could see the distant light of the cottage through the sparse vegetation. *I should have known that the old goats would have lived with their offspring on the land they stole from our forefathers.*

They crawled closer. John stopped again and this time he shook with rage. The operation had not been well-enough researched. The intelligence report made no mention of the fact that the white woman had moved to the cottage. Neither did it mention the three-metre-high surrounding security fence adorned with great big security lights.

John crawled as close as he dared, stood up behind the nearest acacia and scrutinised the entire area. Lights burned in the cottage, which was a scaled-down replica of the grand old house. John could hear music playing faintly. He knew that he and his men had killed the farmer and the old goats, so surely the only ones living here now would be the white bitch and her kids. The best thing would be to wait and see. But if one of the askaris could go around the back and check ...

John called one of the most intelligent of his gang. "Go to the back and check for motor vehicles. Count them. Check for people in the kitchen. Count them. And lastly check for servants. We do not know if they are loyal to our cause or not so if we see any on our way out, they must be shot. Do you understand me?"

The man nodded, "You can count on me comrade."

The askari spent much time rounding the house, not because he was cautious but because he was terrified. They were so far south of the border he thought he might as well be in South Africa and on a white man's farm and the consequences, should they be caught, were too terrifying to contemplate.

The most important thing was not to let the commander down, for then he would be shot anyway. In the relative safety of their camp in Angola, this all seemed like such an adventure—now it was reality, and terrifying. Suddenly he was at the back of the house next to the security fence. A white woman with long blonde hair glided into the kitchen, moved around a bit and glided out again. The askari looked around for motor vehicles and found two parked in the open carport off to his right beneath a huge tree.

He looked back. The white woman came to the door and whistled a high-pitched note. A sudden movement near the askari had him leap clear of the ground. A small golden dog stood from its sandy bed in the corner of the fence not ten metres from him. It dashed along and stumbled over paws too big for its little body. The woman smiled and the puppy licked at her face. A second puppy loped into the light from the shadows and wagged its tail at the presence of its owner. She took two huge bones off a plate and dropped them in front of each dog. The animals ceased panting, closed their mouths and looked up expectantly.

But for the slight quivering of their tails, the dogs sat dead still. At the clap of her hands they leapt forward and retrieved the treat and she laughed delightedly. Just then a young white boy ran out and flew at the woman who scooped him up and hugged him and the smile on her face brightened. The askari smiled at the union of mother and child and he suddenly longed to see his children again. He knew though, that so long as the war lasted he could not see them. The South Africans watched all suspected insurgent families day and night not to mention the informers who lurked in the villages these days. He had seen enough and returned to his commander. His fear had been replaced by melancholy.

John had waited enough. There was only one plan he could think of but it carried the risk of killing all the occupants in the house. Did it really matter? It was quite simple. He must shoot the house with the RPG. He had to be careful to fire through the fence. In the ensuing pandemonium, enter the house and abduct the woman and her child. They must kill the remaining servants or visitors and flee. Should all the occupants die in the initial blast, then so be it. He would not be burdened with hostages and the results would still be good for Swapo.

The askari crawled to the fence. When John arrived he was pleased to see the huge hole the man had made and he signalled for the RPG. He positioned himself along the fence with the RPG at right angles so as to be out of the way of the back blast. The others moved away and John took a deep breath, aimed and squeezed the trigger. It was one of the last things that could go wrong and it did—nothing happened. John quickly checked the weapon, aimed and pulled the trigger again ... still nothing! What now? He flung the weapon aside and crawled back to his men.

"There is only one way now, comrades ..." The sound of the Land Cruiser alerted them. It drove slowly up the road towards the cottage. John was livid.

"Go and tell that moron to stop his car immediately and tell him to join us in the attack. I'll deal with his stupidity later." The askari dashed off but returned shortly, wide-eyed and breathless.

"Hurry! You must all hurry! Two vehicles are coming and one is the police! We must flee!" Back at the house the puppies deserted their bones and barked. In an instant the whole area was flooded with light.

CHAPTER 19

For Gabi the healing process was less devastating than she cared to think about. Her abjection should have been deeper. Perhaps it was because there was a farm to run and *that* was a big enough undertaking for anyone, or maybe it was because if she let it, the loss of her beloved husband and child would swamp her with an all-consuming grief.

She mourned Hein so. She looked at the wedding photograph on her dresser and felt the tug of pain in her throat and the sting of tears. She thrust the emotion aside. *I must be strong for Sven*, she told herself—but she knew that wasn't the main reason. A huge part of it was the pang of guilt she felt, for when she closed her eyes she could see her Hein standing there, tall and broad-shouldered but his face was a blur and no matter what she tried she could not see his fine features.

She dashed to the bedroom and snatched up a photograph of him, gazing at it intently as if to burn the image of his face into her mind. After a while she held the picture to her breast and let the tears come.

But, without doubt, the loss of her daughter caused her the greatest pain. She wished with every fibre of her being that by some dint of incredible magic she could turn back the hands of time and see her cheerful face, her beautiful smile. To see her shiny cheeks beam up at her with so much love and dependence.

The thought of Ermie's limp body with her long blond hair in disarray about her pale face as her head lolled on the medic's shoulder and then being bundled into the ambulance was too much for Gabi. The thoughts of her dead daughter were so vivid and the feelings of loss—such aching loss—overwhelmed her. Gabi felt so utterly miserable that thoughts of suicide were frequent and strong. And with these thoughts she felt she would go completely insane. *Wasn't that right anyway? People who seriously contemplated suicide are insane? Have I come to that line? Can I cross it?* she thought as she sobbed quietly, desperate to feel anything but the pain that consumed her.

At times like this, Gabi would run from the confining walls of the cottage.

Run. Run out to the stables, vault onto her horse's bare back and gallop out into the vast lands until the froth sprayed from the animal's mouth and its flanks were wet with sweat.

As the horse slowed, Gabi would fling one leg over the shiny rump and slide to the ground. She would veer away from the animal and sprint. She ran until she too was panting and the wisps of loose blond hair stuck to her sweaty forehead. There, in the vast openness of the dry land and in complete solitude, she would scream her madness away. She would scream and scream until her voice would no longer obey and no more sound would issue.

Then she would sink to the ground and vent her grief. She cried until her body's natural preserve took over and she would fall into a troubled. trance-like state. Once before it had happened that Gabi fell into a deep enough sleep that the horse had returned rider-less to the stable.

How fortuitous it was that one of the grooms had been busy in the stable at the time and had seen her ride out. Hours later when the horse returned without its rider, he ran up to the cottage and alerted the servants. They made an extraordinary din and were still vacillating on what to do next when Valerie, who was staying there at the time, snapped out of her virtual coma-like existence and took over.

For Valerie, one could only guess the torment that her tortured soul had endured after that fateful night. Like someone awaiting the gallows, she had withdrawn into herself and waited to die. She might have done just that but for the love Sergeant Carel Brits held for her. He had kept his love for her a secret when Johan was still alive.

Carel had considered Johan his best friend and did nothing to jeopardise that friendship. But with Johan's tragic death, Carel could help her. And maybe, just maybe, with the right amount of tenderness, care and a lot of time, she might even begin to tolerate him. Mostly, in the past, Valerie had never given Carel the time of day and greeted him only because her husband had seen her ignoring him and he had seen the hurt in Carel's eyes.

"If you do not show him the courtesy he deserves at the dance tonight, I will make a point of embarrassing you as you do him," Johan once promised her.

"But he's so coarse, my love."

"Because he's a policeman?"

"No, noo. Because … you know …"

"Ja. Because he earns a meagre salary."

"Oh no …! Valerie protested.

"You've become a snob. Let's not forget where I found you, dear wifey."

And she had blushed at the thought of her own pauper family.

Carel gave it a few days before he plucked up the courage to visit the Erasmus farm and was surprised to find the house in total darkness in the early evening. Surely the house should have been lit up? Even if the generator was out of diesel, the lanterns would have been ablaze, everywhere. Valerie had developed a phobia; she was intensely afraid of the dark.

Carel drew his service pistol and cursed. If he had gone straight to the farmstead from the station, he would have travelled in the police Land Rover with its radio and the standard-issue pump-action shotgun clipped to the dashboard. He had opted to go home and shower, administer a touch of Aramis and travel in his own Mazda. Now he would have to go in cold and hope for the best.

The back door was slightly ajar and goose flesh covered his body in a rash as he slipped into the darkened farmhouse. The warm, light breeze that carried the high-pitched screech of crickets was snuffed out and replaced by a stuffy, humming silence. Carel took a long time to move through the cavernous homestead. Quietly and deliberately he placed each step and searched the rooms. He was about to give up and try the lights when he noticed an irregular shape on the bed in the guestroom.

He froze and watched the form for a long time. It did not move and he waited. He aimed his 9mm at the shape until his eyesight blurred and finally the faint light from the lingering rays of the sunset disappeared. The house was plunged into total darkness.

Slowly, very slowly he slid his hand up the wall. Carel felt the old-fashioned type of Bakelite switch between his fingers. He flipped the switch. Behind the toolshed the generator kicked into life, revved up and settled down to a steady throb.

In an instant the passage was bathed in light which radiated through to the darkest corners of the house and Carel gasped. He ran into the room and slid to a halt on his haunches next to the bed. Valerie lay in the bed as if in death.

Her usually dark, pure complexion was sallow, her lips cracked and dry, her shiny black hair was greasy and lifeless and her pale green eyes stared wide and unseeing at the ceiling.

He placed the back of his big hand gently on her forehead and he breathed out sharply as he felt the warmth. As gently as he could he lifted her body, carried her out to the car and slid her into the front seat. She slumped forward and moaned in protest. Carel held her shoulder and tilted the seat back. As an automatic gesture he clipped her seat belt into place. All the time he spoke softly to her, reassuring her as the little sedan sped off to casualty at Tsumeb hospital.

Under constant nursing and care Valerie's physical recovery was nothing short of miraculous but it was her mind that worried the doctor.

He took Carel aside and told him, "Valerie lay down on that bed to die and you have deprived her of that. She is very angry with you but I think that that is a good thing. It will give her something to live for even if it is at your expense for the moment. Now I say 'for the moment' because she could soon tire of being angry and she could make another attempt on her life. You have saved her once and you need to continue to do so ..."

"Tell me what to do, doc. Anything. Anything you want me to do, I'll do it!" Carel grabbed the doctor's arm and squeezed.

The doctor looked up at the big policeman hovering impatiently in front of him and raised his eyebrow. "It seems to me you are more than just worried about her survival ..."

Carel made to interrupt and the doctor held up his hand and smiled. "No no. There is nothing wrong with that. On the contrary, it can only help, but you can't do it alone. You have work to do. Gabi has also had a time of it and the two of them must get together and share in their grief. It might add another dimension to Valerie's state of mind. Find her father and any other friends you can think of. Get them all to visit."

Carel did. He did so to the detriment of his job, which did nothing to enhance his relationship with his commanding officer. Lieutenant Jack Botha wasn't stupid though. As much as he would have liked to discipline the sergeant he could not do so as Carel had become the sort of town hero and everyone was talking about how he had not only given the army enough information to enable them to hunt down and kill the terrorists, but he had also saved Valerie.

Carel persuaded Gabi to take Valerie into her cottage and give her various tasks that were important to the running of the farm. Not that it took much persuasion but Carel planted the seed. He awakened Gabi to the fact that the two women staying together would comfort each other.

It was slow at first and Gabi rued the day she offered her home to this miserable, speechless, anorexic shell of her former friend. But there was work to be done and Gabi couldn't spend too much time trying to reach Valerie through her shield of despair. Anyway, it wasn't good for the bright light that shone for both of them in the form of young Sven.

In the wonderful way of the world, the boy seemed able to recover from such a tragedy far faster than the adults. Of course there were nightmares of bad men sent by the devil and Sven would scream himself awake. Gabi would run through, snatch him up and squeez his tense, shaking little body to her bosom. She would hold him and rock him, singing lullabies until she felt him relax. Slowly he'd become heavier and finally his deep breathing told Gabi that sleep had come again at last.

Other than the nightmares he was a source of constant delight and amusement to his mother and he asked less and less for his sister and father. Finally, with some scepticism he accepted the fact that they had gone off to be with Gentle Jesus because his father and his sister were the only ones who could do the work He wanted done in that part of Heaven.

Sven wandered into the lounge to look for his mother. Valerie sat cross-legged on the couch and stared at the TV.

Sven stood next to her, placed his hand gently on her arm and asked sweetly, "Have you seen my mom, Auntie Val?" It was quite scary for Sven. Valerie turned her head slowly and stared at him for some time. Sven let go of her arm and took a pace back and Valerie shook her head once, so slightly that anything other than young bright eyes might have missed it. Sven turned and ran through to the kitchen and found Gabi preparing the evening meal. He stood there a while until his mother looked at him and smiled.

A frown creased his little brow. "Mom, what's wrong with Auntie Val?" he asked quietly as if he knew he had to whisper around her.

Gabi sighed deeply, turned, pushed a loose tendril of blond hair behind her ear and began scooping the pips out of the boiled gem squash halves. It was no use lying. It was no use trying to run away from the reality of what had happened. After all, just a few kilometres to the north raged a war where men were dying. Now the war was coming to them and it terrified her. "Uncle Johan was killed by the same bad men that came to our house and she just misses him so much, my boy. She misses him so much that she can't do much and she can't say much."

"But why?"

"Because she loved him so."

"But why?"

"That's enough young man. Now run along and get into your pyjamas," she admonished and tapped him gently on the bottom as he turned to leave.

After supper Gabi settled into the high-backed chair and took up her knitting. Sven played with his Dinky Massey Ferguson tractor on the rug as Gabi heard the toilet flush. Valerie stalked back into the room and settled into old Heinrich's La-Z Boy recliner.

The evening dragged on and Gabi asked, "Anyone for a cup of coffee?" As expected, she received no answer. She walked through to the kitchen and waited for the coffee to filter before returning to the lounge. She placed her mug on the oak side table, sat down and looked around for Sven. She found him curled up on Valerie's lap, his head upon her chest as he stared wide-eyed at the TV. Gabi smiled and took up her knitting. The eight o'clock news came on and ended.

With a start Gabi remembered the time. It was way past Sven's bedtime. She dropped the knitting into the hand-woven reed basket and turned to Sven. He was still curled up on Valerie's lap but he was fast asleep and she smiled. The love she felt for the child was obvious and maybe it was so great as to be a physical thing for when she looked at Valerie her face was without expression but her cheeks were wet with tears. At last the healing had begun.

The day Gabi had gone missing, the commotion made by the panicking servants sent Sven into a frenzy of fear for his mother. He ran into the house and buried his head in Valerie's lap and sobbed hysterically. The desperation in young Sven's voice must have struck some chord deep within her tortured soul and she lifted the child and ran outside.

The servants became very quiet at her presence. They had seen how she sat in the cottage and never spoke, never did much at all.

"What is the matter? Where is the madam?" There was a stunned silence for a while and one of the nannies piped up.

"Her horse has retuned to the stable without her."

"Take blankets and water and place them in the bakkie," Valerie pointed to the Land Cruiser, "and follow the spoor on foot and I will follow you." She ordered the man she recognised as one of the farm foremen. "You two climb on the back, you're coming with us." Valerie's tone was quiet but forceful. Soon they were on their way with Valerie driving the four by four over the sandy terrain after the big black foreman following the well-defined spoor of the horse.

After jogging for a couple of hours in the blazing heat, his body shiny with sweat, the foreman stopped, squatted and pointed to the figure in the distance. Walking towards them, her legs obscured by the shimmering heat waves, was Gabi. Valerie leapt into the Land Cruiser and sped off to meet the forlorn figure. The Cruiser skidded to a halt in a cloud of dust, the doors flew open and Sven and Valerie engulfed an astonished Gabi.

Her skin was burned from the sun and her eyes were red and swollen from grief. But now she laughed and cried and Valerie laughed and cried with her and together they hugged Sven. They cried tears of relief. Relief not so much for finding Gabi but for being alive and for surviving and for the purpose of life and for each other. Beneath the big sky in that vast, dry, beautiful land, they were healing.

Valerie moved back to her farm during the day and threw herself at the task of running a cattle ranch with such vigour that often Carel would find her working in the office near the farmhouse well into the night.

"You're working too hard and I worry for your health," he told her gently.

"It's the only time I get to do the paperwork. The transport rigs are arriving next week for the beef and I want everything to be perfect for this first sale." Valerie was pleased to have Carel near when night came. She was always afraid in the dark, even more so than before.

Carel stood quietly and admired her beauty while he waited for her to finish up. She had almost regained her former beauty. Her skin was pure and smooth, her hair shone and her shoulders were straight and square once more. She was still too thin though and her self-esteem remained shattered but Carel was working on that. It was her family that amazed him. Not one of them had contacted her since the attack and for Valerie it cut her deep down.

They walked in silence to their vehicles and Carel followed her to the Wolbrand cottage. En route they passed the burned-out old farmhouse and Carel wondered if Gabi would ever have it restored. It was such a grand old homestead but what memories did that building hold for her now?

He stared ahead at the tail lights of Valerie's car, which rose and fell as she drove over the erosion-control humps. Carel was lost in thought over the woman he loved and grappled with the dilemma of how to get through to her, to accept his attentions, when suddenly a tenuous movement in the periphery of his vision alerted him. It was so fleeting that he wondered if he was imagining things but when he closed his eyes briefly a picture of a farm labourer running out of the extremity of the light flashed in his eye.

He stopped the Land Rover briefly and shrugged uneasily. It was more important that he saw Valerie safely in and he accelerated after her. Light flooded the area and Carel lifted his arm to shield his eyes. He braked hard and scrutinised the area. The puppies barked half-heartedly at the far end of the security fence. Nothing moved. He scanned the area once more, shook his head and drove through the gate around to the back of the cottage and parked. He sat for a while before opening the door. Again he hesitated but this time he frowned and reached for the radio—perhaps he should call in. But what for? Carel had always learned to trust his instincts but he didn't want to alarm Valerie and the others unnecessarily. He stood up out of the police van and placed his elbow on the roof.

"What's the matter, Carel?" He spun around to face Valerie. "What did you stop for back there?" She was agitated.

Carel smiled reassuringly, "Well, the security lights came on and I just wondered why ..."

"You stopped before they came on. Did you see something?"

"I don't know. Let's just go in and I'll have a look around on my way out." Carel was concerned. If there were some undesirable out there, then he and Val, bathed in the security lights, were excellent targets. He ushered her through the kitchen door and smiled at Gabi.

"How are things with you?" she asked.

"Fine thanks ..." Carel cut her short.

Although he smiled the muscles in his jaw were working and Gabi felt the tension. "Why did you turn on the security lights?"

"Sven thought he saw a movement or heard a noise or something, I don't know. He was scared so I turned on the lights ..."

Sven charged in and launched himself at Carel. "Yaaa!" he shouted and Carel fielded the human rugby ball, lifted him upside down and gently shook him from his feet. Sven giggled with delight and Carel flipped the boy over and hugged him.

"How are you, little general?"

"Fine, do it again!" he demanded. "Turn me upside down again!"

"Fine *thank you*, Uncle Carel," admonished Gabi.

"I can't my boy, I must go now," said Carel and lowered the boy to the ground.

"You can't just leave, Carel. It's a long way back to town. Stay and have some home-made butternut soup." Valerie wasn't the only one who felt comfortable with his presence. He was so big and unafraid and yet gentle and he played so well with Sven.

At times Gabi would find Carel staring at Valerie with such love and affection that she felt slightly jealous. She was glad for Val as it seemed to help her cope and she realised why he was around so much.

"Come Uncle Carel. Come and see my tractor." Sven grabbed Carel's big hand and tugged. Valerie managed a smile and followed them through to the lounge.

Gabi flipped the dishcloth over her shoulder, sighed deeply and stared out into the darkness. How she missed male company ... no ... Hein. How she missed his big hands on her shoulders and the warmth of his breath on her neck. The way he made her feel so secure. Hein was always there for her and she felt safe. She shivered suddenly—why was Carel so agitated about the lights? Had Sven seen anything or was it just his overactive imagination? She strode through to the lounge, afraid.

Her voice shook, her fingers clutched her daughter's favourite little Teddy bear to her bosom and she blurted out, "Carel, did you see something out there? When I turned on the lights ..."

"Whoa there!" Carel held up his hands, "I was just being cautious. I'm sure there's nothing. Maybe a buck alerted the pups?" He stared at the button-eyed bear and frowned.

"I'm scared too, Carel," said Valerie. Her eyes were wide and she seemed frail and vulnerable. Carel wanted to take her in his arms and hold her, protect her.

"Okay, I'll go and take a look around but I want you all to stay in here. Just lock the door behind me."

Carel opened the police van door, pulled the Mossburg pump-action from its clips and checked the load—eight rounds of LG shot, large game. At short range, one shot would cut a man in half. Carel pumped a round into the chamber, slipped the safety catch, retrieved the Mag-Lite and walked out the gates of the security fence. The puppies ran ahead, periodically sniffing the air but mostly they kept their noses to the ground and Carel jogged after them.

At the far corner of the fence the larger Boxer whined with excitement. Immediately Carel noticed the hole in the fence. The cut edges of the wire shone. The hole was recently made. He felt the blood drain from his face. He took another look around and wished he had an R1 rifle rather than the shotgun. Still nothing. As far as the security lights shone into the bush nothing moved. He switched on the Mag-Lite. The security light did not shine straight down to where he stood. He peered at the tracks around the hole. For a moment his mind did not want to register. His eyes saw but the message went no further. Gingerly Carel squatted and shone the torch at the one well-defined spoor in the harder ground next to the tree.

"Jesus Christ Almighty," he breathed to himself—*Grootvoet*! So absorbed was he that only at the last second did he hear the crunch and squeak of the footstep in the sand behind him. Carel spun around and fell on his back. He aimed the shotgun at the midriff of Gabi.

"Christ woman!" he shouted and leapt to his feet. "I nearly blasted you away. Don't ever, ever do that ...!" The look of utter anguish and raw fear on Gabi's face served to steady him. Carel watched the little bear fall from her grasp and she lifted her hands slowly to her face. She sunk to her knees and began to rock back and forth.

"No. Dear God, no," she prayed as the huge, dusty spoor melted and swam before her eyes. It changed into a terrible, bloody print on the wooden floorboards of the old house. A footprint she could never forget.

CHAPTER 20

Outwardly, Regimental Sergeant-Major Joubert maintained his exemplary decorum and entertained every translation with utmost concern, pausing to write a note here or query a statement there but below the surface he seethed. He had been summoned to Oshakati by the Sector One Zero adjutant and now his huge moustache twitched as in front of him sat the representatives of the village where one of his patrols had allegedly, without provocation, murdered the elders.

At this stage all he could do was to take notes and give his assurance of a thorough investigation and, on finding out the truth, act on it. He was hoping to trip them up with a bit of cross-questioning and then he could dismiss them as liars, forget the whole affair and send them rudely on their way, but this was a vague hope as he marvelled at their persistence in reaching the right person to tell their shattering tale.

Why would they go through all that just to tell a story? There were many in the local rural population who despised the presence of the SADF soldiers but they were generally too petrified to make up stories in order to discredit them. Others had tried and failed to the detriment of their village as the 'hearts and minds' programme suddenly stopped supporting them. The weekly visit by the doctors ceased, the water carts were withdrawn and with it the supply of precious water and many such aids that made their lives in the kraals, *cucas* and villages more bearable.

No, you did not have to like the white soldier dressed in brown carrying an assault rifle but it sure helped your quality of life, so woe betide anyone caught jeopardising the fragile relationship. RSM Joubert knew this all too well, but that was not the only reason he believed this motley crew of Ovambos. It consisted of the incumbent elders, the children of the slain couple and two young, nubile women who carried the goatskin water containers—seven of them. Seven of them who had trekked across the burning Ovamboland veld. They had followed the cattle and goat paths and the white sand burned their bare feet. The old lady walked unaided in the high heat of the day and every now and again she offered an encouraging hand to the old man when he complained. Seven of them who slept huddled together beneath their meagre skins as the first evening chills of the coming winter began. They walked until they found the vague ruts of the vehicle track leading to their first food stop at the tiny village of Okankolo.

At first light the seven travellers set off. The early morning chill soon gave way to the onslaught from the sun and into the oppressive heat they walked. They walked on relentlessly without a break, pausing only to slake their thirst with a few mouthfuls of precious water and shortly before the setting of the sun they stumbled off the track into the side drain of the main road. There they camped for the night, eating a little of the food given them by the old chief from Okankolo.

The old man slept fitfully, worrying if they were doing the right thing only to feel the reassuring hand of his wife. What strength, what endurance that little gesture gave him—of course this was right. Of course they must complete what they had set out to do. With his wife at his side it would be alright. The last leg to their destination seemed endless but at last the party walked into Ondangwa.

The old man was tired. A fine sheen of dust covered his wrinkled skin and enhanced his age. He took leave of the others at the road and alone he walked to the entrance of the military base. It was an overwhelming sight. The base was surrounded by high double fences of barbed wire; a well-guarded boom blocked the entrance and brown vehicles moved about behind them. And finally he saw the feared white soldier. They seemed to be everywhere. The old man stood in the middle of the road, awed by all he witnessed. How could Nujoma compete with this? There were so many soldiers, all armed, so many vehicles and so many buildings.

A loud noise behind him alerted the old man. He spun around and witnessed the most fearsome sight. A monstrous vehicle bore down on him. The sun reflected off the armoured glass, its engine growled at him and thick dust flew off the black wheels. It had a brown, odd-shaped, bulging body not unlike a giant, metal hippopotamus and many soldiers sat on the back beneath a large steel handle.

The old man froze. He closed his eyes and waited for the inevitable. Surely this monster would trample him like an enraged elephant. A loud voice steadied him and he opened one of his eyes. The vehicle had come to a halt in a cloud of dust barely a track width in front of him and a man stood above the reflecting glass. The old man shook his head. He could not move.

The man shouted. *"Skyf uit die vokken pad uit anders gaan ek jou dood ry jou dom kaffir!"*

Once again the old man shook his head for he did not understand Afrikaans and remained where he was. There was some laughter from the soldiers in the back and the man climbed out from behind the glass and dropped to the ground. He walked over to the old man who, by this time, had squatted as he was sure that if he continued to stand, his legs would no longer support him. He lifted his arms to shield the blow as the soldier stooped towards him. To his surprise the soldier lifted the old man bodily off the ground and moved him to the side of the road where he was unceremoniously dumped to the hoots of glee from the soldiers. The soldier then climbed back into the vehicle and roared past the dumbstruck old man. To add to his confusion the old man caught a glimpse of the soldier behind the glass as he passed; he was smiling broadly and he waved. Fear swamped the old man and for a moment his resolve deserted him as he watched the vehicle enter the camp. He was about to turn back when he felt an arm slide in next to his and a hand grabbed his fingers.

"Come, my man," said his wife. "Let us do this thing together." Arm in arm, they walked to the boom.

That was only the beginning. On hearing their confusing story the sentry asked them to leave; he had no interest in their problem. In typical African fashion their faces became deadpan, a trait that served to frustrate the white man. Even when he threatened to shoot them they would not budge despite their obvious fear.

The sentry called his commander who informed the old couple that if they did not leave he was entitled to shoot them. Of course this did not work. The guard commander found that he could not bring himself to shoot them so he tried assault. He walked over and knocked the old man to the ground with his rifle. The old man stood up, dusted himself off and stood resolutely.

The guard commander looked into the old man's eyes. He saw no offending expression. He backed off and shook his head. Maybe he'd better report the matter to the adjutant.

From there things began to happen until finally they found themselves sitting in an office in Oshakati repeating their story to a translator for the benefit of a big moustached Boer soldier. The main thing was that this big, scary, angry-looking man seemed to believe them.

CHAPTER 21

Rudi looked worried. "We've been summoned. The SM wants to see us!" he announced.

"Who's 'us'?" enquired Geoff without looking up as he packed clean fatigues into his cupboard.

"The 'Grootvoet Section' I guess you could say."

Geoff spun around and looked at Rudi. "Murder at Ovambo Kraal has come home to roost then, has it?" he suggested sarcastically but not without a hint of concern in his voice. "Took longer than I thought," he murmured and slid the cupboard door closed.

"I dunno, maybe. The SM looks hugely pissed off." Rudi's eyes were wide.

"We had better ..." Geoff never finished. Dawid stormed into his tent and sat rigidly on the bed. He held his bush hat in his hands and wrung it nervously through his fists. His face was fixed with a sneer.

"So whacha gonna tell Joubert hey, Kent?"

Geoff stood, glared at his hands until they were still and then frowned at Dawid. He realised that if there were anybody in the world that he truly hated, it was this man. "Listen to me, you piece of Ovambo dog shit—you're the one who shot those defenceless old people and now they've come back to haunt you. What makes you think I'm going to tell anything but the truth, especially when you waltz in here with that attitude?" Geoff spoke quietly through clenched teeth.

"You wouldn't drop a fellow soldier?" Dawid's face changed. He paled visibly, his fear real. His hands wrung the bush hat again.

Geoff was amazed. It was the first time he'd seen it. "You tried to shoot me, or have you forgotten?" Geoff pressed his advantage. He would love to see Dawid grovel. "You tried to kill a fellow soldier ..."

In a flash Dawid flew off the bed and grabbed Geoff by the throat but he was ready this time and he simply lifted his knee into Dawid's groin and he dropped like a sack of potatoes.

Geoff stepped over the writhing body, stooped out of his tent and spoke to Rudi. "Get the boys formed up in a squad on the parade ground between the mortar emplacements ... well out of earshot. I'll go call Joubert." Geoff carefully placed his faded bush hat on his head, making sure the 'virgin' was at the back of his head, took a deep breath and marched off.

Rudi called after him, "What you going to say?"

Geoff looked back and winked. "Who's the only witness to this heinous crime?"

"... so what you are basically telling me is that Sergeant Niemant saw it all and holds all the answers?" Sergeant-Major Joubert sat back, regarded them suspiciously and gave a twist to one of the handlebars of his moustache. He had moved the section out of the heat into the mess tent and questioned them one by one, just the way Geoff wanted it. That way no one had the opportunity to back Dawid and what was beyond doubt was that he had shot the two old people. Now Sergeant-Major Joubert had them together and questioned them as a group.

"Yes sergeant-major," replied Geoff.

"And fortunately for all of you he's conveniently very bleddy dead, eh?"

There were slow nods from innocent faces. "Yes sergeant-major," repeated Geoff.

The RSM turned and aggressively aimed an index finger as thick and brown as a well-grilled pork sausage at Geoff. "You! Corporal Kent! Why didn't you file a report on this incident?"

Up to now Geoff had believed he was exempt from the proceedings and filled an informative role only. Mostly his interest was to see Dawid squirm under the spotlight. Now he had been dragged in. Geoff was prepared though. "With the tragic death of Sergeant Niemant I was distracted and clean forgot sergeant-major. It's been months ..."

The RSM cut him off. "Martins. You say the old man tried to attack you and that's why Gouws shot him?"

"It's Martin van der Merwe, sergeant-major ..."

"Shaddup and answer the question."

"Well, yes," replied Martin, his pride dashed.

"Could it not be that the old man was trying to protect his family and was perhaps pleading with you and in so doing grabbed your arm to attract your attention? Could it not be that he was begging for mercy because in his kraal stood some very tired, nervous South African soldiers with a killing rage upon them?" The RSM spread his hands, his eyes bored into Martin and he smiled. The smile was unnerving and Martin dropped his eyes.

"Well, I suppose ..."

"Sergeant-major could I perhaps be of assistance here …?" tried Corporal Mike Theunissen.

"No you can't. You, my boy, are going to lead a bleddy long patrol soon. Save your energy." The RSM didn't even glance at Mike. "How about the old woman, Gouws?" Sergeant-Major Joubert smiled that dreadful grimace. "Tell me how you shot a defenceless old granny."

"She was shouting a warning to Swapo out there, sergeant-major! She was trying to warn them!" Dawid was almost hysterical. "I had to shoot her to save the section." Dawid looked around. "I did it for them—I did it for you okes," he pointed at the men of his section. "Do you think I had a choice? Do you think I enjoyed it, sergeant-major?"

The RSM regarded him for a good few seconds and raised a bushy eyebrow. "Yes … to both," he said quietly and smiled again. The RSM sat back, tweaked his other handlebar and sighed. "Is it not possible she was engaged in a typical Ovambo dirge?" The RSM shook his head. It was clear he knew far more than any of them expected. Dawid looked around, held out his hands and sat forward to explain. "Don't even try and answer that, Gouws. Now let me tell you what my problem is. A group of very scared but courageous old Ovambos sat at the gate at Ondangwa and took the abuse of the sentries without flinching for two full days. I was told that they were nearly shot as a threat to security, but they persevered and finally their story was told. It was told to many people. Fortunately they were held up just short of the brigadier himself and I was called in to speak to these people because it was you lot who were patrolling that area when they say their elders were shot. In cold blood. Murdered."

There was shuffle of amazement. The men glanced about. A few hands lifted in protest and Martin cleared his throat. The RSM held up his huge hand and glared at them. "Don't you dare interrupt me. Here's what I do know. To them, you lot murdered their people. To you, they tried to attack you and tried to warn the enemy who had just recently passed though that kraal. The man to corroborate these stories is dead. Their story checks out under cross-examination … but so does yours. You all seem to have the same story and I hope this was not orchestrated before I spoke to you …" Sergeant-Major Joubert eyed them one by one before continuing.

"Further, all of you were under extreme duress, knowing who you were following, and might have acted as expected under the circumstances. Later you caught up with your quarry and killed all but the patriarch himself, making you all a pretty heroic bunch." There was a murmur of astonishment and one or two smiles. A compliment from the sergeant-major? It might still snow in the desert. "However …," the RSM wagged his finger, "there is now a cloud hanging over said heroics and I have been tasked to settle the matter. So, this is what I'm going to do with you lot. Kent, get out your notebook and take this down." One or two of the men cleared their throats, others shuffled in their seats and the RSM took out his pipe. He made a show of lighting up, sat back in a cloud of his own smoke and gathered his thoughts.

"Grootvoet is alive and well ...," he began. That statement caught their attention as the RSM continued. "So much so he's been back to the origin of his misdemeanour ... well, that is to say his spoor was picked up on the same farm outside Tsumeb, if it really is him," the RSM added with some scepticism. "The survivors of that ordeal all live on that farm and are understandably terrified. The local police sergeant seems to think that Grootvoet has targeted this miserable bunch for some reason or other and is hell bent on wiping them out." He paused. "So, this is where you lot come in. With Corporal Kent in charge of all of you, including you Gouws, you are going on a special guard assignment. You are going to look after those people, by one," the RSM held up a finger, "walking patrols on the farm. "Two," he held up a second finger, "twenty-four-hour, round-the-clock guard duty and three, personal guards for the owners. This will serve two purposes. Firstly we protect the soft and innocent and secondly it gets you out of my hair so I can put this whole bleddy shooting story to bed. With you lot out of sight you'll be out of mind." The RSM puffed on his pipe and sat forward in his chair. "Are there any questions?"

Inside Geoff was celebrating. What an absolute peach of a task. It seemed too good to be true and he cringed when Mike put up his hand. *Don't ask any questions lest the RSM change his mind!* Geoff thought and glared at Mike.

"What is it, Corporal Theunissen?"

"Tsumeb is other side the Oshivelo Gate. It's south of the danger zone. Will we still be paid our danger money, sergeant-major?"

"Yes, yes! If what the police say is true and Grootvoet is trying to kill those people then you are also in danger, not so?" He smiled that humourless smile again. "Anything else, girls?" Geoff looked around and willed no more questions. They were silent and the sergeant-major nodded. "Okay then. You had better go and pack because you leave at first light tomorrow. You may go, except you Kent. Stay here, I want to talk to you." Geoff's heart sank. Here came the catch.

The RSM waited until the others had shuffled out of the tent before he spoke. "I noticed the post arrived. Did um ... did your mother send more crunchies?"

Geoff smiled. "Yes she did, sergeant-major."

"Is it possible that I may partake or am I a little late?" Why couldn't he just ask normally? Why did he have to go the high-falutin route and make it sound like a statement? Were all sergeant-majors so goddamned pragmatic?

"Yes of course, sergeant-major, I'll bring you some after supper."

Fortunately the sappers were very experienced and could tell when the alarm from the headphones had picked up a rusty old tin buried in the road or if it were more than that. On this occasion sapper number four on the right came to an abrupt halt. The other engineers crouched. The section in the bush formed an all-round defence and went to ground. The men on the Buffels pointed their rifles in all directions, the barrels protruding like lethal porcupine quills.

This was the perfect setting for an ambush. The tension mounted and Geoff leapt from the Buffel. He ordered the Buffels and men to pull back a safe distance from the suspected mine. Geoff jogged to sapper number four. The man had placed his mine detector to one side and carefully scraped the loose sand off the area immediately in front of him. In the cool morning with the rising sun shining red through the palms, Geoff felt the sweat run down his back. "Do you think we've got a ripe one?" he asked and squatted.

The sapper nodded and continued to scrape at the sand. "*Ja korperaal*," he answered in Afrikaans, "this is the real thing." Geoff noticed how the sweat ran down his face in rivulets. With wiry, sunburned arms the sapper scooped the sand away, a handful at a time. Finally his fingers scraped across something hard. Carefully he enlarged the hole, removed more sand and blew into the depression. Dust billowed out around his head. "It's a TMA-4," he announced finally. "We'll have to blow her in situ."

"Can't you just lift it? We might attract Swapo for miles around."

The sapper considered Geoff's request for a moment, looked down at the beast in the hole and shook his head. "It might be linked to another mine and I don't know if it's got any light sensor equipment rigged to it. Also that mine wasn't here yesterday, so Swapo must have planted it last night. They might even be watching us right now."

Geoff looked around nervously. "Yeah, you're right," he said. "Okay, then blow her but make it snappy. We need to get the hell out of here. If Swapo is watching then the attack will come as you blow the bitch."

He wiped the sweat out of his eyes and watched as the sapper unravelled a reel of cord fastened to the mine. The engineer moved off to one side of the road, lay on his back with his feet towards the mine and looked back over his shoulder at Geoff. Geoff nodded and lifted his thumb. The sapper yanked the cord and the ground ahead erupted. A massive fireball billowed up and evaporated in the morning sky, followed by a thick cloud of black smoke. Sand and clods of earth rained down around the sapper who jumped to his feet, spat on the ground and ran back to join the others.

With every nerve on edge they waited. The eerie silence hummed in Geoff's ears after the explosion as he peered ahead into the bush. It was dead quiet and nothing moved. Geoff counted slowly to a hundred before rising cautiously to his feet. He looked around and saw nervous faces looking expectantly at him.

Geoff nodded and spoke. "Okay, *manne*," he said evenly, "let's get out of here."

The number one sapper waved at Geoff. He turned and walked off at the same quick tempo. Geoff felt a little easier as the sappers skirted the crater in the road. Their destination was a point of rendezvous with the sappers heading towards them from Ondangwa. Once the parties met, the road was declared safe for the rest of that day. The whole process would have to be repeated the following day and the day after that—in fact every day until the government found the money to paste asphalt on all the roads in the operational area.

Out the corner of his eye Geoff caught a flash of light and simultaneously a deafening crash as something slammed into the side of the Buffel. Instantly Geoff knew it was a rocket-propelled grenade and knew too their time was up—an RPG would rip a massive hole in the side of a Buffel, spraying the interior with deadly shrapnel.

It took Geoff that long to react and instinctively duck. He knew it was futile but his mind was frozen as he peered over the top of the Buffel's armour. A second flash and the same instant the crash-slam as the RPG found its target once more. In the absolute terror of the moment Geoff found time to question why they were all still alive and why both RPGs had ricocheted off the side of the Buffel only to whine off into the heavens.

Geoff witnessed the third flash and felt the grenade slam into the Buffel once more. This time his reactions were lighting fast as he marked the source of the attack. They were close, too close, off the side of the road at the base of a jesse bush thicket. Geoff shouted, "Swapo! Nine o'clock, twenty metres!" He slipped the selector of his R1 to automatic and emptied the first magazine into the bush. He saw the bullets kick up columns of sand around the target. Geoff released the empty magazine and slammed the next one home. This time he flipped the selector to rapid and aimed each shot at the base of the bush. By this time all rifles were pouring deadly fire at the target.

Not to miss out on the action, Dawid lifted the MAG from its bracket, scrambled over the central back rests, aimed and guided the belt of bullets into the mouth of the machine gun.

The din was appalling and soon the air was filled with the strong smell of burnt cordite. With no return fire from the enemy the firing tempo slowed and finally stopped. Once again silence descended. Geoff looked about and noticed that from their elevated position on the back of the vehicles, they had been firing over the heads of Corporal Mike Theunissen's section.

Geoff sat, scratched in his webbing, retrieved a hand grenade and held it aloft. Mike nodded. He turned and pointed at two of his men. The men took a grenade each from their webbing. Together they pulled the pins, looked at each other, nodded and lobbed the grenades. Everyone ducked and Geoff watched the curved trajectory. Its handle glinted in the sun as the spring mechanism flicked it away and the pin slammed home, priming the bomb. It lifted into the blue sky, arced down, hit the ground, skidded across the sand and disappeared from sight.

Geoff whispered to Rudi. "They've dug bloody trenches ..." A dull double whump! reached them, followed by a scream. A cloud of dust emanated from a cleverly disguised trench at the base of the jesse bush. Immediately the rifles opened up and bullets flailed the area. Geoff waved his arms frantically and shouted, "Hold your fire! *Staak fuur*! Cease fire!" The rifle fire died away barring one or two nervous shots and then all was quiet. "They're in a trench for fuck's sake! Stop wasting ammunition man! Mike! Take a few men and clear that trench! The rest of you cover them!"

Two men followed Mike as he dashed to the edge of the trench. They pumped rounds into the hole, edged closer and peered cautiously over the lip. Three terrorists lay there, two of them obviously dead judging by their massive wounds. A third sat wedged in the corner cradling his arm. He rocked back and forth in an attempt to ride the pain.

Mike aimed his rifle at the man and shouted, "*Klim uit, jou fokken moer*! Get out the hole, you black bastard!"

The man begged. "Please ..." He held up his arm. His hand was missing and the blood pumped from the severed wrist. Apart from the hand he was unscathed.

Mike took a little time to marvel at his survival after such an intense fire fight. "Guard him well," Mike instructed the others. "I'll go get the medic. This bastard might hold some valuable info that could interest the intelligence people."

Geoff climbed down off the Buffel and watched Mike talk to his men. He slung his rifle over his shoulder and walked to meet his rookie corporal. Geoff looked up and smiled. The action was over. The tension eased.

A dull explosion shattered the quiet. Mike disappeared in a cloud of dust. The smile died on Geoff's lips and he hit the ground. When the dust drifted away on the light breeze Mike lay on his side and held his knee. From where he lay Geoff could see Mike's leg had been severely lacerated by an anti-personnel mine. His boot had been blasted clean off and his leg below the shin was a pulpy, bloody mess. The blood pumped thick and black and Mike groaned. Geoff looked around in desperation as he realised that the enemy had set AP mines as a grisly twist should their ambush attempt fail.

"Rudi!" he shouted, "Get those sappers over here and get us out of this fucking mess!" Geoff's voice had an edge of hysteria. "Call in a casevac too! Mike's down!" Geoff lay there for a few seconds and steeled himself. He couldn't leave Mike like that. He drew the bayonet from the scabbard on his webbing and slid the blade into the ground ahead of him. This was no practised drill; he had merely seen it in the movies and decided it was all he could do to get to Mike without being blown up in the process.

Two of the sappers swept a path towards Geoff as he dug the ground ahead of him. Geoff reached Mike, bumped foreheads, curled his arm around Mike's neck and cradled his head. "What the fuck are you doing buddy?" Geoff whispered as he desperately tried to distract his young charge. "Who said you could go doing flick flacks in the bush without my permission?"

Mike tried a smile and groaned, "Is it bad, Geoff? I ... I mean is this it ...?"

"No!" Geoff whispered harshly and then gently, "No, you'll be okay, I promise."

"God it hurts, Geoff."

"I know. I know. I'm here with you. I won't leave you. The chopper will be here soon." Geoff squeezed Mike and restrained him as he tried to sit up. "Don't ... just lie here, Mike. The casevac Puma is nearly here."

"I want to see it, Geoff."

"No. Let the medic look. You just talk to me. Tell me what happened in the camp while we were on leave. You were number one corporal hey? Did you take the parades?"

"Geoff help me. It hurts so much, man. I'm so thirsty," Mike groaned.

Geoff peered over his shoulder. He was about to scream at the sappers but they were already near. The first sapper swept past and carried on to the trench where Mike's men still guarded the wounded terrorist. The second swept a circle around Mike and Geoff, stopped and removed his headset.

"Jesus!" he exclaimed as he noticed Mike's leg.

"Shut up you idiot. Where's the medic?"

"Here, corporal," said Martin breathlessly. "Help me get this drip in."

"You!" Geoff pointed at the sapper. "Help the medic and give Corporal Theunissen some water." The man nodded and placed his minesweeper on the ground. Geoff waited until the first sapper had reached the men at the trench before galloping after them.

He peered down into the trench. The wounded terrorist held his wrist. The man's face was ashen with pain and loss of blood. His eyes flared wide as Geoff lifted his rifle. He fired three quick shots.

"That's what I was going to do," said the first soldier.

"That's bloody murder!" exclaimed the second.

"That's war," said Geoff flatly and he turned back to Mike.

The Puma faded into the distance and Geoff stared after it until it was a dot on the horizon. He felt a tap on his shoulder and he looked around. Rudi held out a water bottle.

"Thanks." Geoff took the bottle, put it to his lips and drank. He had not realised how thirsty he was. With all the action, the adrenaline, the fear and with the sun at its zenith, Geoff finished the water. "God, that was excellent. I feel half human again." Geoff's hand shook as he handed back the empty bottle. "You can help yourself to one of mine, Rudi."

"This is yours."

"Ah, I might have known."

"Well you can drink as much water as you like when we get to the farm, eh?"

"Shit, yes. I'm looking forward to that."

"Do you think they'll save it, Geoff?"

"Save what?"

"His foot."

"Nah. I bet they'll have to amputate," said Geoff, shaking his head. "At least he won't be coming back here, though. For him the war's over." He looked down at his hand and spread his fingers. They shook like a madman's.

"This lot were clever, hey?" said Rudi, purposely changing the subject. "Planting AP mines like that. And the way they waited 'til we were right opposite them before firing. Come to think of it, why didn't those RPGs blow us to shit?"

"You know, I've been thinking about that. I think they were too close and the grenades didn't have time to arm."

"Ja, or they didn't take off the det caps."

"Shit, that could be it too. They might be stupid enough to leave one on, but three?" Geoff smiled, "Three fucking RPGs and not one exploded!" They laughed.

"Three RPGs; it must be brewer's angel, hey?" said Rudi and the laughter increased. Dawid and Martin strolled over and soon all of them were laughing.

"Three fucking RPGs!" blurted Dawid and the men fell about. Eventually Geoff stopped his manic laughter and wiped the tears from his eyes.

"Okay boys, let's go farming."

At Ondangwa the Buffels turned onto the tar road and headed south for Tsumeb. With every kilometre they travelled south Geoff relaxed and he saw it on the faces of his men. They smiled and chatted above the wind and noise of the

Buffel. One or two opened rat packs and began swopping contents. Somehow in the wind Martin managed to light a cigarette.

Soon they arrived in Tsumeb and headed for the police station where they waited while Geoff ran in to look for their contact person.

Geoff walked to the desk and spoke to the black constable. "Hi, I'm Corporal Kent and I'd like to speak to a Sergeant Brits please."

"Yes, just hold on sir, I'll call him for you." The constable disappeared through the door.

A large, ruddy-faced man with wavy, jet-black hair appeared. *"Ek is Sersant Brits,"* he began in Afrikaans and looked at Geoff's faded name tag. "You English?" he asked seemingly surprised.

"Yes sarge, I am. Are you the man responsible for showing us the way to the ..." Geoff retrieved the notebook from his top pocket, "Wolbrand Farm."

"Dis ek, ja." The sergeant shook his head. "Sorry, ja, I'll show you the way. I'll bring my Land Rover to the front and you can follow me. Are you the ones to look after the farm?" His accent was strong and guttural and Geoff liked him.

"Yes. I have a whole bunch of soldiers out there all ready for action," said Geoff reassuringly

"Good, thank you. I called for you lot because that bleddy kaffir wants to kill them and I can't be there all the time."

"But why?" asked Geoff. "Why does he want to come so far south out of the operational area and kill innocent women and children?"

"I don't know. *Miskien is hy net fokken mal.* Sorry ... I think he's bleddy mad, *jong!*"

Geoff smiled and shook his head, "I'm a corporal in the SADF. I understand and speak Afrikaans fluently, sarge."

Geoff drove in the Land Rover with the sergeant.

"So it's no coincidence that you're here. They sent you because you know this man and how he works." Carel was adamant despite Geoff's best attempts to play down the contact and the reason why they had been chosen for this task. Carel turned and drove through the open gateway over the cattle grid and onto the Wolbrand farm.

They brought with them a cloud of dust and Geoff jumped out. He was deep in thought. The mission might just be more serious than he had first perceived.

Carel interrupted his train of thought. "Geoff, let me introduce you to Gabi."

He had not seen her walk out the kitchen and he looked up and smiled broadly. The smile froze on his lips.

"Hi, I'm Gabi," she held out her hand. There was a definite German accent but it was very subtle and extremely appealing. Geoff stood riveted and stared. Gabi looked at Carel and then back at Geoff. Carel cleared his throat.

"Oh shit ... I mean, sorry ... I didn't mean to ... er, wow, when they said farmer's wife I expected ... well I didn't ..."

Geoff cleared his throat, took her hand and shook it. "Hi, I'm Corporal Geoffrey Kent but you can call me Geoff. I'm very pleased to make your acquaintance." A red hue crept up his neck and covered his face. *What a clumsy, blithering idiot I am,* he thought. *Especially in the presence of such beauty.* Geoff recovered quickly enough to see the red patches high on her tanned cheeks and for a moment their eyes locked. "Let me introduce you to my band of merry men."

CHAPTER 22

"Let's go away now, Schalk my love. How about right now?" she smiled and placed her hand on his. Schalk smiled his boyish smile and squeezed her hand. He was affected by her excitement and enthusiasm. "We could even stop at Lake Otjikoto. You've told me about it before. Stunning. Beautiful, you said," she said expectantly.

"I'd love to go right now but we are fighting a war and I am the boss."

"But why? There's nothing happening to demand every minute of your time. Let's pack and go now," she implored.

"I'm afraid that's where you're wrong, Ansie. Quite a lot is on the go actually. In fact we are going to undertake a few cross-border operations very soon."

"How soon?" she asked, her disappointment evident.

He looked at her and raised his eyebrow.

"Oh come on, Schalk. You've always briefed me in the past."

"Well ... this is very delicate and highly secret."

"You're just saying that because you don't want to go away with me."

Schalk frowned, looked down into his coffee mug and then up at her lovely face. It was true. He had never kept anything from her, not even secret matters. Sure, in the past, he had spared her the intimate and intricate details and only told her enough to quell her curiosity. None of the secret material previously discussed with Ansie was ever really a matter of national security. This was different.

There was also another reason for his hesitance. One that was new to Schalk. A reason born out of his own infidelity. He had betrayed his wife as easily and callously as drowning a kitten and there was guilt to deal with now. But it was a funny thing—just because he had cheated and abused the trust they had built up over the years, it had had a reverse effect on him. For some reason he no longer trusted her. Schalk drew a deep breath.

"This is not as before, Ansie. These are issues that, if they fell into the wrong hands, could mean the lives of our soldiers. Before, if the contents of the meeting involving my promotion with the general got out or if I told you who the new adjutant for Walvis Bay was before I informed him, it would harm no one. My credibility could have taken a beating but the situation would harm no one. This is different …"

"So you don't trust me anymore," there was a hint of venom in her tone and she grimaced.

Schalk's face hardened and his eyes narrowed. "What's the matter with you?"

"All I want to do is get away with you for a while and you won't because you say you have some or other secret agenda to maintain. How the hell do I come to terms with that when you can't even give me the most basic information to convince me that you are not avoiding me? You've been working very closely with Elsa lately. Am I supposed to be okay with that?"

Schalk looked at her for a second before answering. "Is that what this is all about then? I'm glad I know now because I was beginning to think I had a real problem on my hands." Schalk was angry and his face reddened at the mention of Elsa and how close to the truth Ansie was. "If you really need to know why we are working so closely together then I'll tell you. We are working on a double cross-border operation. The first will take place in about a month's time when we will send in a hundred Parabats to take out the newly revamped Chifufua base. Some time later we will send in a mechanised-infantry assault to tackle the 'New Chifufua' south at Mulemba. It is a huge operation and needs incredible attention to detail. That's what we do so closely together. Now, I would appreciate it if you would show me a little more respect and remember your station." There was a drawn-out silence and finally Schalk wiped his mouth with his serviette, dropped it on the table and stood up abruptly.

"I'm sorry, my man. You are quite right and I apologise for any disrespect." Ansie looked up at him and tugged gently at his arm, "Come, it's time for you to go to work." Schalk pushed his chair in and made for the door. Ansie followed him out, caught up and slid her arm around his waist. He reciprocated and placed his arm around her shoulders. They walked arm in arm down the short path and kissed briefly at the gate.

"I should have known I was letting myself in for a challenge when I married an older, educated, beautiful woman."

Ansie was taken by surprise and for a moment she wanted to drop to her knees and beg his forgiveness for her driving him into the arms of another woman. Just for a moment she felt hope. Hope that the mess could be salvaged. She knew in this world of men she was almost a second-class citizen; the laws of South Africa certainly made her feel that way. Most other women accepted this as the norm—Ansie often questioned it, making her unpopular in various social circles. The fact she had no power of attorney and could make no decisions without her husband's consent; at times treated like a queen and others, scolded like a child—she could live with all that. But his total betrayal of their mutual trust was too painful to bear. Dear God how it hurt. The worst part was how he lived the lie, sure and confident that his wife was keeping everything neat and orderly back home while he went off to his lover at work. Of course there was no hope.

The adj. was waiting in the Land Rover. Schalk returned his salute and together they drove the short distance to the office. Ansie watched as the vehicle disappeared down the road. She stood for a moment then turned from the gate. A movement from the beneath the fig tree at the corner of the house startled her and she gasped. Then a smile creased the corners of her mouth—the same humourless smile she had flashed at Schalk earlier.

"Hello Victor."

"Hello madam."

"Are you in good health?"

"Yes madam. And you?"

"I'm fine thanks," she nodded and continued after a short pause, "but I worry for your people."

"What people madam."

"Your Swapo people."

Victor's face went deadpan and he shook his head, "I don't understand madam."

"Well, my husband is going to send one hundred soldiers into Angola to a place called Chifufua, to murder all the Swapo at the old base there. That's why I worry for your people."

"But what has that got to do with me, madam?" Victor spread his hands, looking mightily confused.

"Probably nothing," said Ansie as she climbed the stairs to the porch. At the top she turned and looked at him, "It's going to happen in a month from now." Then she turned and disappeared through the door.

Victor stood riveted, his mouth hanging open. How could she know? How could she possibly know about his activities with Swapo? She must be a witch. He quickly picked up the garden spade and began trimming the edges of the flowerbeds. He had to act as normally as possible but inside he was in turmoil. If she knew by some magic then he was doomed and he should get the hell out right now!

He realised how stupid he'd been to talk to her, but she was so vulnerable all those weeks ago. Surely they would have come for him already? The South Africans were very clever and if he were under the vaguest suspicion he would be in the jail at Mariental already or even dead.

Just calm down and think! He knew that for some reason she was an emotional mess and she didn't want to be here. He knew too that her husband was the big boss of the war effort in his country. Maybe he'd told her something and she was merely passing it on. But one doesn't just pass on information like that. Victor deliberated as he worked. He was terrified, which made it difficult to think. At the same time elation rose up within his soul as he realised that if she were deliberately betraying her husband then he would be made. He would be the folk hero his brother had spoken of and the whole reason for him being here, working for the white racists, would be justified. It might be a trap but he had to take the risk and pass on the information and the last thing he must do was run away. If he disappeared then they would know and change their plans. No, he must be brave and pass on the information via the conduit set up years ago. What an opportunity. All these years the old Indian vegetable peddler had been waiting and now the time had finally come.

CHAPTER 23

Geoff wasted no time. He tasked Rudi to set up a communications radio room in the small study. It seemed the most logical place as the farm two-way radio was already there with the antennae in place. Whatever it took Rudi must just make it work.

He turned to leave the cramped little room and found Gabi leaning nonchalantly against the wall watching with mild amusement. Geoff tried his best not to gawk. Instead he smiled a boyish smile, stared into her eyes and took in her whole perfect frame. She wore a khaki shirt that was too big for her. It was tied at her midriff exposing a sliver of taut, well-tanned belly. Her white shorts exaggerated the deep tan of her long, shapely legs and her feet thrust into the old tennis takkies looked too small to carry her finely curved body. She was tall and her hair was tied in a thick plait. A lock of hair hung down the side of her face which somehow enhanced her looks and the blueness of her eyes.

"Are you and all your men going to move in here?" she asked innocently.

Geoff cleared his throat, blushed and looked back at Rudi who suddenly seemed intensely busy setting up his radios.

Geoff looked back at Gabi. "No, actually only Rudi and myself ...," then hastily, "I mean, we're not moving in, just manning the radio and I have to check ..."

Gabi pushed herself away from the wall, "No, please," she smiled, "you must do what you have to. You don't know how reassuring it is to have you looking after us. I feel so embarrassed about all the fuss but I would really appreciate it if you could take me with you and show me all your security arrangements."

"Of course," said Geoff quickly. "You must come with. We've been instructed to interfere as little as possible and stay out of your way, so as soon as you feel we're getting under your feet, then please let us ... or rather, let me know."

"Fine." She smiled up at him. "You're the boss." For a moment their eyes locked.

God! She's beautiful, he thought. "Okay, shall we go?" he said.

It wasn't long before Geoff found he had a little shadow, even when Gabi wasn't around. At first he noticed he was being observed from a distance, mostly from behind some cunningly disguised observation post like a wall or a tree and when he looked up the observer quickly disappeared.

Finally, when Geoff asked Gabi to accompany him on a tour of the farm's boundry in the Buffel, the observer bravely presented himself. He looked at the ground and mumbled in English. "Please may I come with, uncle."

Geoff squatted in front of the boy and stared at the angelic face with big, frightened blue eyes. He held out his hand. "Hi, my name's Geoff. What's yours?"

"I'm Sven," answered the boy quietly.

"Well, Sven, it will be a pleasure to have you come with us." The boy's face lit up and he smiled broadly at Geoff. "But you have to promise one thing," it was too good to be true and Sven's smile faded. "You have to promise not to call me uncle any more, okay?"

"Okay," he said, the relief clear on his face.

"Okay who," admonished Gabi.

"Okay Geoff," he replied and wrapped himself around his mother's leg.

Sven beamed with excitement and bounced from chair to chair as they drove. The Buffel drove along slowly and a cool breeze ruffled their hair as the sun set big and red. Geoff stole a glance at Gabi. Her chin was up, nostrils slightly flared, loose hair blew back in thin wisps behind her as the setting sun coloured her face a soft pastel orange. She looked at Geoff suddenly and the corners of her mouth lifted as she dropped her chin. She was the most perfect piece of God's work he'd ever seen.

Having set up the defence of the farm it came down to the monotony of keeping alert by day and vigilant by night. Geoff instituted ways of keeping the men stimulated. He rotated the shifts as often as possible and allowed them day passes to Tsumeb. With Gabi's permission, he organised night-time braais where, living on a cattle ranch, there was no shortage of meat. At times the men would meet at the reservoir where they would swim and lie in the hot sun until they were driven into the cold borehole water.

On one such day Geoff left Dawid in charge of the radio. Martin, Pieter, Rudi and Geoff sat naked at the reservoir, soaking up the sun as they chatted. The smoke from their cigarettes swirled lazily about in the still air and Rudi sighed deeply. "This is the life. Nothing to do and all day to do it in. How lucky did we get with this assignment, hey?"

"I dunno. This could be a double-edged sword, you know," said Martin seriously.

Geoff looked up. "How so, Marty old boy?"

"Well, we got sent here to get us out of the way because of that shit with the old people Dawid shot. I'm worried about that. Pushing beat on some farm is a smoke screen."

"Now that's just what I don't need to hear, Marty. We never killed old Grootvoet, remember, and he seems bent on killing these people. If we forget that, he could easily take us by surprise. No, the reason for us being here is no smoke screen."

"Ja. Maybe you're right. But what do you think of this lot, hey?"

"What lot?" Rudi opened one eye and peered at Martin.

"Well, these chicks are both fucking drop-dead gorgeous, especially the blonde."

"Gorgeous—yes, fucking—no."

"What about the cop and Valerie, hey? They look like an item."

"Nah," said Rudi. "I've heard them about the house. He's besotted and she's protected. She doesn't fancy him for anything else other than he's always around her. He's like a lovesick puppy with his tongue hanging out. I reckon she feels comforted by his presence."

"She's the one who was raped, hey?"

"And sodomised," added Pieter. He screwed up his eyes against the smoke as he exhaled.

"Shit, that must have been *kak*. I can't imagine anything worse than being raped by a bunch of kaffirs and then they give it to you up the shit chute." Martin grimaced and looked disgusted. "At least we blew the fuckers away." There was a moment's silence as they remembered the fire fight.

Martin shook his head, looked up and smiled suddenly "But you know, I think Gabi's got the eye for you Geoff."

"What!" he exclaimed. "Don't be crazy. There's no chance of that."

They were all smiling at him. "I've seen it too, Geoff," added Rudi.

Geoff blushed profusely. "Well I think you're all wrong."

"Why do you say that Corporal Kent?" inquired Pieter jovially. "I too have seen the way she looks at you and I'm just a dumb Dutchman." They laughed and Geoff's face turned a few shades darker.

"And I've seen the way you look at her," continued Martin.

Geoff spread his hands and shook his head. "Help me here, buddy!" he appealed to Rudi.

"I'm afraid I can't do that. The boys are very observant and if I were you I'd go for it with all the enthusiasm I could muster," replied Rudi. "How does the old adage go?" he asked, looking to the heavens for inspiration. "Something like 'Faint heart ne'er won fair lady'." They laughed.

After a while Geoff shook his head and smiled broadly. "I think she's the most beautiful woman I've ever set eyes upon but I don't know if it goes any further than that ..." The men hooted and Rudi slapped Geoff hard enough on his back to leave a red handprint. Geoff held up his hands in surrender. "You didn't let me finish. Yes, I do think I could fall for her but I think it's more of an infatuation ... I mean, what could I offer her ...? Some corporal chevrons and ..."

"A six-inch dick!" Martin finished for him and attempted flight but to no avail as Geoff pounced. He hauled Martin up in a fireman's lift, carried him to the reservoir wall and hurled him over the edge. Hoots of laughter followed the splash.

Geoff turned, frowned and cautioned them to silence as he went for his rifle. The others dashed for theirs and threw themselves flat on the hot sand. A horse whinnied suddenly and Geoff rose, aiming as the riders came into view. He peered over the sights but suddenly he was acutely aware of his nakedness.

He made a mad dash for his towel but lost valuable time balancing the rifle against the wall. He almost made it. Almost, but not quite. He looked up, flung the towel around his waist and tried to tuck it in. Typically the army issue was too small, only just covering his lower abdomen and he had to hold it up.

Gabi was looking down in that area as she rode up and no doubt caught a good glimpse of his ample manhood for her face was as red as the sun setting over the Namib desert. "Gosh! I'm so sorry ... I didn't know ..." She searched for the right words. "I didn't know that you have no swimming trunks ..." She blushed even more. It came out all wrong and the others laughed. Martin hung on his arms in the reservoir and laughed raucously. Even Valerie smiled and her face changed colour.

Geoff squirmed and blurted, "No, no. I'm sorry, Gabi. You must think we're having a bit of a holiday on your farm. It's not like that though." He looked about. "The guys must get some recreation and this is the best place ..."

"I don't mind," said Gabi quickly. She looked down at him. He was taller than Hein, his shoulders were broad and thick hair curled on his chest and arms. His stomach was flat and rippled with muscle and his legs were powerful and defined. But it was the steely blue eyes, short blond hair and rugged good looks that caught her attention. Despite the hard, chiselled exterior there was a gentleness behind those penetrating eyes and a compassion one could sense without even knowing him.

"Why don't we collect a load of bushveld wood and have a bonfire out here?" Gabi suggested. "We could braai some meat and I'll make a salad and Valerie is the best *koeksuster* maker in the world. She could make a trayful before sunset."

Geoff turned to the others who nodded enthusiastically. "I don't know ...," he hesitated. "We are here to do a job ..."

"But it would be like a night off. All of your men could come and we could all sleep here."

"Ja, that way even the sentries would have the night off because we'd all be here!" offered Martin excitedly.

"Anyway, I'll leave it up to you," said Gabi. "After all, you're the boss," she said with a glint in her eye and tugged gently on the reins. She placed her hand on the animal's rump and she swivelled. "Please let me know so I can cater for all of you." She smiled and blushed profusely before turning.

The men stared after the dwindling figures cantering into the distance.

"There is no doubt in my mind that the lady has a great big place in her heart for you, boyo."

"Oh nonsense Rudi, her husband died mere months ago. She couldn't be over him already," said Geoff irritably, but at the same time hoping it were true. "And by the way," Geoff changed tack and smiled mischievously, "I noticed how you gawked at Valerie." Rudi's mouth dropped but Geoff forestalled his attempted protest. "I also noticed how you jumped to her defence when Martin suggested that she and the cop were an item. So, now look who's talking."

"You're just trying to shift the spotlight from yourself," Rudi poked Geoff on the chest. "How could I possibly make eyes at her after all she's been through?"

"As I said before, I'm just a dumb Dutchman, but I noticed that too, Rudi," said Pieter and they all hooted with laughter.

The sparks flew high into the starry night sky, riding on the heat of the flames as the mopani timber hissed and popped. After Geoff's grateful acceptance of a bonfire night, Gabi put her army of labourers to work. They drove out in the four-ton truck, taking tables and chairs—as many chairs as could be found on the farmstead—and set up an excellent campsite between the tamboti trees and the reservoir. Then they collected timber from far and wide and piled it high next to the old fireplace. Geoff realised the family must have camped out here in the past. Large braai grids were placed over small cairns of rock. They placed the huge old bucksail for all to sleep on and swept the earth for metres around. Galvanised baths were strategically placed; one for rubbish, another for washing and a third for the beers. In the spirit of the moment, Geoff had sent Martin and Pieter into town for a couple of cases of beer and a few blocks of ice. Four each mind you and obviously none for the sentries. Despite the relaxing of the rules, at least two sentries were to patrol the campsite well out of the firelight.

The fire burned down. The soldiers raked off coals and placed them in the pits between the rock cairns. The cooking grids were replaced and soon the mouth-watering smell of marinated ribs and thick juicy rump steaks permeated the air.

The murmur of voices drifted in and out but for the most part the men were quiet as they ate. It made a magnificent change from the rat packs they'd been living on. Geoff tossed his rib bones into the fire, stood, stretched contentedly and wiped his mouth on a paper serviette. He turned to his chair and froze. Young Sven was fiddling with his rifle. Geoff took two large paces and picked up boy and rifle, swivelled and lowered himself onto a folding chair.

"Let me tell you about this piece of equipment." Geoff balanced Sven on one knee and placed the rifle on the other. "You see ...," he said seriously, "this weapon is specifically designed for killing people, so, if little boys play with it and it goes off, it could kill someone, even strong little boys like you. So, my advice is, if you want to know how it works or if you want to hold it, you need to ask one of the big soldiers, okay?"

Sven nodded. "Okay Geoff," he said in a soft voice and looked up with big frightened eyes.

For some reason Geoff was overcome with a powerful urge to protect the boy. He seemed so small and vulnerable. Geoff placed the butt of the rifle on the ground, unclipped the magazine and slid a shiny brass shell from it. He held it up so Sven could get a good look at the bullet. The firelight danced and flickered off the cartridge and reflected thin shards of light onto Sven's face.

"Inside here is the gunpowder," said Geoff, "and when you pull the trigger the bullet comes out of the barrel here so fast, it goes from here to your house in one second."

"Wow!" said Sven, obviously impressed.

"Yes, and this copper bullet can go right through a piece of steel, so imagine what it will do to a person, huh?" Most of the men stood about the fire now and smoked and chatted. Someone threw a piece of wood into the flames and sent a shower of sparks spiralling into the night sky.

They weren't interested in Geoff's little interaction with the boy but others were. The flames reflected off the adjacent tamboti covey, producing phantoms in the trees and a flickering silhouette of the women's faces. Valerie sat back in her chair and stared at Sven's angelic face. Gabi sat forward with arms folded in her lap and smiled.

"Can it go through a tank?"

"Nah, tanks are too tough."

"But what if that man who killed my dad and my sister comes to kill us with a tank?"

"You see Martin over there?" Geoff pointed and Sven nodded. "Well he has a special mortar ..."

"What's a mortar?"

"A bomb that shoots high into the sky..." Geoff looked around, "There!" he pointed at the Patmore leaning against the wall of the reservoir. "That's a sixty millimetre mortar." Sven nodded and Geoff continued. "So, Martin shoots the mortar up in the sky. It goes up and up and when it gets to the top of the sky, it turns around and comes down again. But when it comes down, two steel balls drop out of the front of the mortar and come down on top of the tank." Sven hung onto every word and stared at Geoff. "Those balls hit the hatch on the turret and go 'toc, toc'. Now the tank commander thinks that someone has come to visit, so he opens the hatch to see who's there. But just as he opens the hatch the bomb falls right inside and goes 'boom!' and all the baddies inside are killed."

"Wow!" Sven grinned. He thought for a while and then said, "What if he sends jets?"

"Nah, old Grootvoet hasn't got jets and anyway if he has, they're not as fast as the Mirages in our air force."

"Do 'Ragies go fast speed?"

"Mirages. Yep. They go so fast you can't even hear them coming."

"Wow!" Sven leaned back, placed his head against Geoff's chest and yawned. "Did you ever kill some bad soldiers?"

"I'll tell you a secret. All of those men there ...," Geoff pointed at his men, "and me caught those baddies that killed your dad and your gran and your grandpa and we shot them all except for one."

"They also killed my sister."

"Yes. I know. I'm sorry we didn't get here before they did, Sven." Geoff put his arm around the warm little body and gave a gentle squeeze. For the first time Geoff looked up at Gabi. She quickly sat back out of the firelight but not before Geoff noticed the flames reflect off the wetness on her cheeks. He noticed too how whenever she sat her fingers fondled a little Teddy bear with button eyes. They sat in silence for a while and Geoff felt the child in his arms become heavy. He looked down. Sven was fast asleep. Geoff smiled. It was a first for him. He had never interacted with kids before let alone had one fall asleep in his arms. He had a niece and two nephews whom he'd never met. Geoff stood slowly and carried the boy to his blankets on the bucksail where he knelt and covered Sven. He took a second to study the sleeping lad before he turned and headed to the beer bath.

Geoff took a cold Castle from the icy water, cracked the lid and walked off slowly into the darkness. Away from the fire he took a long drink, looked up into the night sky and sighed. There were so many stars in it was difficult to recognise the major constellations. He was deeply engrossed when a rash of goose flesh suddenly lifted the hairs on his forearms and sent shivers down his spine. He shuddered, spun around and dropped to his haunches. Gabi stood there.

She gasped and her hand flew to her mouth. "I ... I'm sorry," she whispered.

"No." Geoff stood. "I'm sorry, it's sort of instinctive." He felt foolish and took another sip of beer. Gabi stepped up next to him.

"What are you doing?" she asked.

Geoff turned and looked up, "You know how lucky you are to live in a place where it is difficult to find the Southern Cross?"

Gabi stepped closer. "Why? Where do you live that it looks different to here?"

For a moment Geoff was incredulous at her naïvety. He stifled a badly timed remark. She was an innocent, young, farm girl who lived in the middle of a huge, sparsely populated land where a war raged merely fifty kilometres away. She had a young boy for company, a depressed friend, a lot of cattle and some pretty lousy memories. "I live in Johannesburg," he said. "There's a lot of pollution and smoke. At night you can only see the brightest stars, like the Southern Cross."

"There it is!" Gabi shot out her arm and pointed.

"Well, no, actually," Geoff smiled, "that's the False Cross. It's easy to make that mistake."

"Oh. I thought ... well Hein showed me ..."

Geoff suddenly realised she was embarrassed. "Oh, I'm sorry," he said tenderly.

"What for?" she looked up at him.

"I sounded like a pompous ass, I'm sure."

"No you didn't. You were merely correcting. Which is it then, anyway?"

Geoff cleared his throat and pointed skywards. "There it is lying on its side. The best way to remember it is by the two pointers. In fact the pointers form an integral part of determining south."

"Show me how," she invited and moved closer to him. She was close enough that he could feel the warmth of her body as he went into the simple geometry of finding true south from the twinkling dots.

"But what if it stands up straight?"

"That's the amazing thing. No matter which way it lies, it always points south." Geoff gazed up and then looked at Gabi. She was staring at him and his heart skipped a beat.

"Thank you for being so kind to Sven. God alone knows the scars he must carry and he needs a father figure so badly."

"Please. It's my pleasure. I'm new to the game I must warn you. I haven't been around kids before."

"You were one once ..."

"Yeah. I don't remember that though."

"Did you really kill the people who ...," Gabi searched for the right words, "who did this to us?"

"Yes. Yes, we did."

"All of them?" Gabi shivered.

"All but one. He got away ..."

"And came back here to finish the job."

"That's why we're here." They were quiet for a moment.

Geoff glanced at the bear balanced in the crook of her arm, and smiled, "Sven's?"

Gabi looked down and dug the toe of her takkie into the sand. "No. It was my daughter's. It was Ermie's. It's getting cold and I need a jersey. Shall we join the others?"

"After you ma'am." He ushered her towards the fire. As they made their way Geoff lifted his arm as if to place it around her shoulder, hesitated and let it drop to his side. It was impossible to measure the depth of feeling he held for her. Approaching the fire Geoff noticed how the men standing there breathed out fine clouds of condensation. Winter had arrived.

Gabi pulled the thick, home-knitted jersey over her shoulders and Geoff shrugged on his bush jacket. "Seeing you riding the horses earlier today gave me an idea but I want you to be quite honest with me." At the mention of the horses Gabi looked down. "I was thinking, if you would allow it, we could ride patrols using the horses. It would certainly be a novelty and cut out a great deal of the boredom, for a while at least." Geoff held his breath.

Gabi thought for a while. "I think it's a great idea. The horses could use some exercise and it might give you and your men more manoeuvrability."

"Great!" exclaimed Geoff.

"There is one condition though."

"Sure. What might that be?"

"Please leave the two horses you saw earlier for Val and me. One of our therapies is to saddle up and ride for miles. We ride most days."

"Okay. That sounds fine. What are their names?"

"Pegasus and Carpathia."

"Okay, Pegasus is fairly obvious but Carpathia? What the hell is that?"

"Oh," Gabi grinned, "it's the name of the ship that came to rescue the survivors of the Titanic. It's become a sort of a family name since the day one of the horses saved Hein's grandfather when he was lost in the wilderness somewhere near here."

"That's interesting. I'd love to know the full story."

"I don't know all the details but it is written in one of the journals in the old man's own Gothic style."

"Ah yes, well I'll just have to brush up on my Gothic then."

Gabi laughed. It was a throaty and contagious sound and Geoff laughed too as he fought the urge to hold her. "Don't worry," she giggled, "I will translate it for you, if you'd like."

"I do like."

She smiled at him, completely oblivious to his real meaning.

CHAPTER 24

The days on the farm were idyllic for the soldiers and a sort of routine set in. Geoff knew it was dangerous and he did his best to keep his men on their toes. He would organise mock ambushes for the patrols by day and by night. He spent time drilling and honing the men in readiness for an attack that might come at any time and from any place.

Still, there were the idle times and Geoff found a new interest developing. An interest he would never have nurtured or cared about but for the fact that he was among them all the time. The cattle on the ranch took a lot more looking after than he'd imagined. There was always something to do, from fixing boundary fences to the mammoth task of herding all the beasts to the dip tanks. Of course one was forever watchful for disease, and special attention was afforded the pregnant cows. Geoff found himself helping wherever he could and much of this meant being with or near Gabi. This posed the question of whether he was actually growing attached to the ranching way of life or running after Gabi like a lovesick puppy. Either way it was a win-win situation for Geoff.

The sun set earlier each night and it was still dark when the men rose in the morning. Like a typical desert there were always extremes. The winter was upon them and with it the biting cold nights. Geoff knew problems were beginning to set in when Dawid sauntered up in his most arrogant attitude and called Geoff in front of the others.

"Hey! Corporal! When we going back north, hey? I need to kill some kaffirs!" Geoff ignored him at first and later, without making a big deal of it, quietly put Dawid in charge, choosing to ride patrols and be with the men, leaving Dawid to strut around checking the defences. Gabi too, felt the tension and approached Geoff late one afternoon as he was leaving the makeshift radio room.

"What's happening Geoff? That man seems to be onto you the whole time."

"He and I go back a long way. Don't worry about him. He's just getting restless."

"But he's so rude to you."

"I can handle it ..."

"You're my bodyguard aren't you—sort of, I mean?" she said and blushed.

Geoff scratched his head and looked at her. "Well, yes, I suppose I am. I don't really know. Why?"

"What if I had to go away for a while? Wouldn't someone have to protect me against that nasty old Grootvoet?"

"I suppose so ... but where are you going?"

"I feel the need to get away to the bush for a while and was thinking of going to Etosha Pan for a few days. Hein and I used to go quite often and I miss the peace and tranquillity and the wildness of the place. It's so lovely there."

"Well, um, I'm not sure ..."

"Of what?"

"A few things ..."

"A few things like what?"

Geoff hesitated, thought for a while and took a deep breath. "Like, am I allowed to leave the farm? Like, am I really your bodyguard ...?"

Gabi placed her hand on Geoff's arm and looked up at him. Her eyes were pools of soft turquoise. Her hand was cool and gentle and the physical contact sent a powerful shock wave through his body.

Geoff spluttered into silence and Gabi said, "Well, I'm going whether you come with or not. So are Valerie and Sven. But I would feel so much more at ease knowing you were near."

Geoff looked up the passage and then back at Gabi. The hand was distracting him and he found it almost impossible to think rationally. "Um ...," he tried.

"You'll love it," she said, "so wild and free."

"What about the farm? Who'll look after the farm?"

"The cattle can look after themselves for a day or two." Gabi dropped her hand.

Geoff tried a new tack. "Shouldn't one book? I bet you haven't booked ..."

"Don't need to with the war going on. Tourism is pretty lousy at the moment."

Suddenly 'wild and free' seemed very appealing and Geoff smiled. "Okay. When do we leave?"

Gabi shrieked with delight—*just like a young girl*, thought Geoff and he laughed.

"Valerie should be in her office by now so we can radio her and tell her to bring whatever she needs—no, tell her to come here at once and we'll collect whatever she needs on the way tomorrow ..." Gabi's excitement was infectious.

Geoff felt the same thrill well up from within. My God, yes. How wonderful it would be to get away from it all—the war, the relentless tension, the conflict with Dawid and the drab brown fatigues of battle. "Surely we can't all fit in one vehicle?" Geoff was genuinely bemused and he scratched his head. He had hoped, of course, that Gabi would commandeer him as driver.

She turned her head, dropped her chin on her chest, let her eyelids droop and looked at him from the corner of her eye. "We'll travel in my Land Cruiser and you and Rudi will follow in Valerie's."

Geoff blushed profusely. "Of course. I'd better go and brief the others." Geoff strode through the doorway and glanced back. Gabi was grinning.

In the faint light of dawn the two vehicles drove down the farm road past the stables, past the burnt-out old farmhouse and finally out onto the dirt road to Tsumeb. Geoff hung back and let Gabi get ahead in order to let the thick dust settle in the still, cold morning. Rudi shivered and shrugged into his tracksuit,

"Shit, it's cold. What day is it today?"

"Thursday."

"And we return on ...?"

"Sunday."

"Isn't there a heater?"

"It's on."

"Christ. You're full of beans this morning."

Geoff shook his head and glanced at Rudi. "Sorry old bean. I'm worried about leaving Dawid in charge ...," Geoff hesitated and sighed. "In fact, if I'm honest with myself, it's not that at all ..."

Rudi held up his hands, "At the first opportunity he's going to say we went gallivanting with the ladies and thus neglected our duties."

"Succinctly put friend."

"Could I perhaps ease your mind then?" Rudi smiled and his eyes sparkled with anticipation.

Geoff raised an eyebrow. "Be my guest."

"I took the liberty of radioing our intentions to Eenhana and received confirmation ... nay, orders, to stay with the ladies and protect them wherever they might wish to venture, even if the destination is Etosha."

"Jesus, Rudi! Why didn't you tell me?"

"Everything was a bit rushed," Rudi shrugged. "I did it as a matter of routine really, so I forgot about it. I told them that Corporal Gouws will be in charge and you and I were going to follow our charges."

"You're a champion, son!" exclaimed Geoff triumphantly. "Now maybe we can enjoy this little sojourn into the wild. I've never been to Etosha before; how about you?"

"I've never been to the Kruger Park let alone Etosha. In fact the closest I've been to the big five is the zoo when I was a child."

Geoff glanced at Rudi. The sun burst over the horizon and flooded the road with brilliant light. Dewdrops hanging on blades of grass twinkled like crystals as the grey winter bush shrugged off the cold night. "You're not serious are you?"

"Afraid so."

"But why? It's all there all on our doorstep. All one has to do is reach out and grab it."

"Believe me, I know. I suppose as kids living in 'Maritzburg, we just naturally went to the sea for all our holidays. You can't believe how much I'm looking forward to this trip."

Geoff cleared his throat and smiled. "Well, sit back and let ol' Uncle Geoff show you the way …"

"Actually, I think you should look at the road because ol' Auntie Gabi is turning and if you don't watch it, we won't be going anywhere other than into the back of her!"

There was a short reprieve from the dust as they drove onto the tar road outside Tsumeb, through the town and on to the little hamlet at Otavi. From there it was Gabi's knowledge of the area that took them along the myriad of dirt tracks and dusty roads to their destination at Andersson gate. At last they were at the famous Etosha National Park.

Gabi stopped the Land Cruiser, switched off the motor and conversed, at some length, with the gate warden. The warden nodded once excitedly and pointed past the fence into the thick dry bush. Gabi said something and the warden beamed, his teeth very white and his face a study of amusement. Suddenly Gabi's door flew open and a pair of slim shapely legs vaulted out. Gabi trotted over, her eyes sparkling with excitement. From five metres away she began speaking and gesticulating.

"Whoa!" said Geoff. "Start again, I didn't get a word."

"Elephant!" she said and pointed. "Passed by here just a few minutes ago. Just a small herd but …" Gabi leant on the open window, placed her chin on her hands and looked at Geoff. She was breathless with excitement. "So, what do you think hey?"

Geoff peered ahead. "Nothing. I don't see anything …."

"No you barbarian. What do you think of the Park?"

"Still nothing. We haven't even driven inside. Why don't you lead the way and we'll give you an assessment once we're at the rest camp."

"Okay. Follow me!" she said and took off in her vehicle. "Watch out for the elephants!" she bellowed over her shoulder.

"If she carries on like that any longer even Tarzan will know we're here and he lives in the rainforest," Geoff laughed and fired up the big diesel motor.

"My God, she's lovely, Geoff."

"I know. Every fibre of me wants to be with her." Geoff shook his head and stared after her.

"I have no doubt she feels the same ...," Rudi ventured.

"I wish you'd leave it alone. There's no way ... she's still mourning, dammit! All of it is from my side and is pure unadulterated lust," snapped Geoff.

"Sorry."

Geoff hesitated. "No. I'm sorry; I'm just a little uptight." The friends punched fists.

There was further commotion ahead and the door opened again. This time young Sven leapt free and dashed, his bare feet slapping on the sandy road. "I wanna come wiff you, Geoff!" he shouted and bounced up and down outside Geoff's door.

Geoff beamed and flung open the door. "Get in soldier." Sven took off. He bounded over Geoff's lap and planted himself squarely between the two men.

He stood on the seat and placed his little arms on the backrest. "Let's go!"

"So cocksure, hey?" said Rudi smiling at the handsome little boy.

"Wonderful after all the problems he's had, hey boy?" said Geoff ruffling his hair, and then, "Can you drive?"

"Yes. My daddy used to let me."

"Okay, we'll see how well you do later."

The vehicles cruised along silently and effortlessly thought the thick sand. Geoff and Rudi peered from side to side in the dry bush while Sven chatted away.

Rudi stiffened suddenly. "Stop, stop, stop," he said urgently.

Geoff stopped and Rudi screwed his eyes up and pointed. Suddenly and miraculously the whole animal appeared from the bush and jumped into focus. Geoff flashed his lights to attract the vehicle ahead. The more they searched the more elephant they saw. Gabi reversed and stopped just in front of Geoff who pointed frantically. It took a few seconds of searching before Valerie sat up and pointed. Gabi took a bit longer and then she too spotted the herd. Geoff slid through the open window and sat on the door.

This was absolutely fantastic. Here they were among a herd of massive African elephants and had it not been for Rudi's trained eye—trained mostly to see the enemy—they would have driven right past. The sun waxed midway and the bush was a cacophony of birdcalls. Geoff studied the closest elephant. It shifted its weight from one foot to the other and its eye was mostly hooded by the eyelid. The lashes were so long it was almost comical even on such a huge animal. A path of wetness cut through the dust on the thick hide just below the eye.

Suddenly the eye flared, exposing a huge orange ball and Geoff was alarmed, but the lid slid down half-mast once again. A pair of grey hornbills shrieked nearby as they bobbed and bowed to one another. Geoff jumped nervously, his mind still on edge. He watched the birds perform their dance and then they flew off.

But Gabi was right. He'd been there for ten minutes and already he felt the tension abandon the assault on his nerves. One of the younger elephants shook its head, slapping its ears and sent a small cloud of dust into the surrounding bush. Geoff scanned the bush. He looked at Gabi. Their eyes locked and Geoff smiled. She blushed, turned away and spoke to Valerie. She started the vehicle and drove on slowly. Geoff reluctantly slid back onto his seat and followed.

"Have you ever seen anything like that then, hey boyo?" asked Geoff excitedly.

Rudi shook his head. He was awed. "I'm humbled in the presence of such might and the fact that they outnumber us ten to one and as I counted twenty in that herd, I have to ask, what happens if we were to piss them off, eh?"

"No contest. We'd easily drive away from them."

"And if we didn't?"

"Flat Land Cruiser sandwich with raw meat filling."

"Gross."

"My daddy's four by four is much stronger than those silly ol' ellies," announced Sven and the men smiled.

Gabi took them around the loop and on to Okaukeujo. They stopped intermittently to view the game—small herds but excellent variety.

Geoff pointed. "Look!" he exclaimed.

"Impala," remarked Rudi nonchalantly. "Even I knew that."

"Ah, yes. But this one is different. It's the first time I've ever seen them myself…"

Rudi leant out the window and took a closer look. A flock of Guinea fowl scratched about the herd as they grazed. "Nope, you've got me. As far as I'm concerned they're impala."

"Look at the forehead. You see the black, um …blaze?"

"Yep."

"That makes it a black-faced impala and I think they're only found here in Etosha."

"Quite rare then?"

"Oh yes."

"Now I'm impressed. You're quite clued-up eh."

"Thank you."

"My dad could easily shoot them," said Sven and he sighed.

"Don't you think it's better to shoot them with a camera, Sven?" asked Rudi

"But why?"

"Well, that way you'll have a picture of that handsome buck and he's still alive to look after his children."

"That Grootvoet never took a picture of my dad. He just killed him."

Geoff shook his head and Rudi frowned. Sven had his hands on top of his head and he stared into the distance. Slowly Geoff edged his fist closer, stuck out his forefinger and wriggled it in the lad's armpit. Sven collapsed with laughter and fought desperately to free himself. Rudi had to grab the boy to prevent him from crashing headfirst into the dashboard.

"Why did you do that?" asked Sven still giggling.

"'Cause I like you."

Sven shook himself free, climbed back onto the seat but this time he stood as close to Geoff as possible and placed his little arm on Geoff's big shoulder.

"I like you too," he said quietly and Geoff beamed.

They drove into the camp at Okaukeujo and Geoff immediately noticed the limestone water tower. "Sundowners up there for sure, Rudi you old codger you."

"Yeah, great idea but I suggest we scout around for a beer-selling vendor first. I'm parched."

Gabi appeared from behind one of the sweet thorn trees and stopped at Geoff's door. "C'mon, lots of offloading to be done and I need to show you your room."

"So you *did* book this then," he raised his eyebrow and slid off the seat.

"Of course," she said innocently and pushed ineffectually at a loose lock of blond hair. "Now come and help. The sooner we finish the sooner we can go for a drive."

"I'd like to buy a few beers for Rudi and me, if that's okay with you—and something for you and Valerie as well of course."

She looked over her shoulder at Geoff and smiled. "Come and look here." Gabi pulled back the tarpaulin covering the luggage and food. "Ta-da!" she exclaimed. There, stacked in a corner on the food trammel were four cases of Castle Lager. "And in here …," she pointed to one of the Coleman cooler boxes, "is your stock of ice-cold ones to kick-start our little holiday."

"Wow!" Rudi broke into a huge grin. "You've packed for us."

"We'll reimburse you, of course," said Geoff sheepishly.

"Oh, there's no need for that. You're the ones looking after us and a little repayment in kind is in order, besides, I know how much you earn … as guests of the SADF, I mean." Gabi smiled. "After all I'm a well-off widower now. I can afford it." Her bottom lip gave a little quiver.

"Widow," said Geoff.

"What did I say?"

"Widower."

"Which is which again?"

"Well, you're a widow," explained Geoff and scratched his head. There was an uncomfortable silence. Gabi looked at him after a while and noticed his embarrassment.

"You're sweet," she said and lifted Sven's bag from the back of the bakkie. Geoff noticed how her shoulders had drooped.

The afternoon drive proved less of a success than their grand arrival but nonetheless splendid sightings of the majestic sable antelope with sweeping scimitar horns, jet-black hide and white stomach enthused them as they travelled along the dusty tracks of the park. By mid-afternoon they found themselves at the Okondeka waterhole at the edge of the massive pan itself. There was enough heat left in the day for them to see the silvery mirages, while far out on the pan walked two gemsbok. It was a strange and marvellous sight as the heat waves masked their legs and the handsome antelope appeared to be gliding along in defiance of gravity. Rudi handed Geoff the first beer of the day.

"Cheers," he said and the friends drank long on the cold, refreshing beer. Geoff parked next to the other Toyota and lifted his beer. "Cheers," he mouthed.

"Magnificent," whispered Gabi.

"Do you see the gemsbok, hey Geoff?" shouted Sven. Geoff was quick enough to notice the antelope bound away into the pan. He looked back and witnessed the scolding poor Sven was receiving from his mother. They drove off past a herd of ubiquitous springbok and made their way to the waterhole. A movement past the herd caught Geoff's eye. He scrutinised the grass and mopani shrub and exclaimed suddenly.

"Look!" he whispered. "Just past that dead mopani in the long grass there."

"Ah!" exclaimed Rudi. "A cheetah!"

"Not just one. I can see at least three of them."

Geoff flashed his lights at the vehicle ahead. It was then that Geoff noticed the cheetah's blazing eyes and its intense manner. It crouched, poised for attack, its large yellow eyes locked onto its prey. The black tear markings down its face were vivid against golden fur.

In a blur it burst from cover and accelerated out onto the open plain. Little clouds of dust puffed up around its paws as it clawed for purchase. The cheetah's body alternately concertinaed and stretched as it accelerated up to a hundred kilometres an hour.

One of the springbok snorted the alarm and the herd took off as one. The cheetah used its long, black-tipped tail as a counter-balance as it changed direction at high speed, its focus on one buck only. The buck seemed to play a deadly game with the cheetah. As it ran, it bounded and leaped high and graceful, losing valuable ground to its pursuer. The observers sat wide-eyed and riveted as the fascinating sequence of events played out before them. The springbok realised the cheetah was closing for the kill and ceased its acrobatics and began to run.

The buck was very fast—an obvious challenge for the cheetah—and it changed direction, running first one way then the other, using every tactic to draw out the chase. It ran for its very survival.

But it was not to be for the springbok. The cheetah seemed to stretch its already long graceful body a few centimetres more and tapped the buck on its hind leg, just above the hoof. That was enough to alter the balance of the buck and it fell headlong. A cloud of dust billowed around as it skidded to a halt, hooves flailing in the air as it desperately tried to regain its balance. It recovered quickly but not quickly enough. The cheetah's momentum carried it well past the fallen springbok. It flung its tail out and turned in an instant, Grabbing the struggling buck by the throat and pulled it to the ground.

By clamping its jaws onto the throat of the buck, it cut off the air supply and halted any distress calls. The other two cheetahs cantered over to the kill, all the time scanning for danger. The newcomers began the feast immediately. They ripped at the soft stomach and anus. They were slightly smaller than the first cheetah and it seemed obvious to Geoff that these two were siblings and the larger cat was mother. The youngsters were receiving a lesson in hunting and survival.

The buck gave a final shudder and lay still. The larger cheetah finally released her grip, stood and walked around the carcass to take her share of the bounty. She walked slowly, her head drooped. She was exhausted. She stopped and looked up suddenly, sniffing and testing the air. Her yellow eyes widened with fear and she gave a high-pitched squeak. She was warning her youngsters of extreme danger. Her worst fears were realised when a huge, shaggy-maned lion casually sauntered out of the tall grass and stopped at the area above the waterhole.

With wrinkled forehead, the lion gave a throaty grunt and trotted down to the kill. Its eyes sparkled with deadly menace. The cheetah issued a second squeak and trotted off after her children. But apparently she didn't vacate the kill quickly enough. His majesty broke into a gallop and sent the cheetahs sprinting. The lion stood no chance of catching them but gave a good chase just to show them who was boss anyway.

The cheetah stopped a safe distance away, gave one last longing look at her kill and glided into the grass.

The buck hung limply from the powerful jaws of the lion as he sauntered off. A flock of Namaqua sand grouse flew in and began drinking. After a while they dipped their chests into the water and splashed around, not to cool down, but to store the water for their young. As if by some silent command the flock took off in a flurry and disappeared over the mopani scrub. A gentle breeze rippled the water and silence descended upon the waterhole.

Geoff stood on top of the tower and scanned the area for more game. The sun was setting and the beers were cold. He took a long pull on his beer but otherwise the men stood in silence, taking in the beauty of an African sunset. Geoff scanned the horizon and looked heavenward. "Big sky. Africa has big sky."

"Big sky," said Rudi, "I'll drink to that." The red faded to indigo and then black.

The barbecue area was cosy with chairs placed in a neat semicircle about the glowing pit of embers. Off to one side Geoff had placed a small table with cooking utensils neatly stacked next to the condiments, then knives and forks and, at the end of the production line, the plates. The distribution of meat, salads, stiff maize meal with a spoon of rich tomato and onion gravy and a roll each was going to be a military drill, Rudi noticed.

"You've got far too much army in you Kent," he said with a wry smile. Geoff stood up from the sizzling fillet steaks and looked at Rudi. His face was red from the heat of the mopani coals.

Despite the cold night little beads of sweat on his forehead shone in the light. "Why?" he inquired. "What's wrong with it?"

Rudi placed his hand on Geoff's shoulder. "That's just it. Nothing. Even Joubert would be proud of you. This is military precision at its best, my boy."

Geoff eyed the area and shrugged, "Yeah. You're right. I'm sorry everyone."

"No need. You're so cute ..." Gabi looked at Geoff and smiled.

Sven interrupted and spoke through a mouthful of crisps. "Why you sorry, Geoff?"

"Because I'm being too much of a soldier, boy."

"When I'm big I'm going to be a soldier like you and kill Swapo people ..."

"Sven!" Gabi clamoured. "Stop talking like that," she admonished fiercely. "And especially with your mouth full!"

Sven sat riveted for a moment and absorbed the harsh words. They cut to the quick and immediately the tears welled up and his mouth opened wide to let out the first sob. Geoff became alarmed at how long the little boy took to breathe. Finally Sven took in a deep breath and let it out. In an instant Gabi's face transformed from anger to regret. She leapt up from her chair and gathered Sven up in her arms and cried with him.

"I'm so sorry, my darling," she cooed. "Mommy didn't mean it." After a fair deal of encouragement, the tears slowed and Sven quietened. He struggled out his mother's embrace and regained his seat. His eyes were swollen and his wet cheeks shone in the firelight. He sniffed, reached for the chips, hesitated and sat back miserably.

"Come and help me cook the meat please young man," said Geoff.

"I can't cook yet."

"I'm glad you said 'yet' because now is the time to learn. Let me show you."

"I can't. It's too hard."

Geoff squatted next to Sven, lowered his voice and spoke in a conspiratorial tone. "It's easy," he said. "All you do is turn the meat over until it goes brown and then it's cooked. After that you tell all the people to come and eat and they tell you what a good cook you are."

Sven sat up and listened. It appealed to him to have everyone heap praise upon him for something so simple. "Okay," he said enthusiastically and slid off his chair.

After supper the men took a couple of beers and walked over to the floodlit waterhole. Geoff placed his foot on the low stone wall and leant on his knee. A small cloud of dust hanging over an area off to one side caught their attention. Tiny heaps of sand, as if by some magic, leapt into the air. A sparkling dust cloud hung suspended in the bright light. Fascinated, the men stared at the activity before them.

"What the hell do you suppose that is?" whispered Rudi.

"Probably a warthog," suggested Geoff doubtfully and he shrugged. Suddenly the animal in question bounded out of the dust, landed and stood dead still, its massive ears focused like radar scanners. The bat-eared fox leapt forward, snapped at some prey and flung it high in the air. The scorpion cart-wheeled and in the light Geoff could see the tail had been bitten off—the dangerous sting was missing. As it landed, the fox pounced and snaffled the scorpion, taking care to avoid the nasty nippers. The fox chewed delightedly, its eyes half-closed as it finished off the tasty morsel.

Geoff felt the warmth of another body next to him and he tore his eyes away from the intriguing little fox. Gabi stood there. He had been so absorbed that he hadn't heard her approach. She stood so close that before he was fully aware of his actions his arm lifted and encircled her shoulders. She swayed slightly and leant against him. Her arm slid up under his jacket and around his waist. Geoff's heart pounded and it felt as if his throat might constrict.

He opened his mouth to breathe. "What a perfectly magical day. What magnificent sightings," he said, partly because he really meant it and partly because he was emotional and confused. He felt elated yet frightened. Would she take his action as a friendly gesture? And if so, why did she reciprocate? What would happen if he were to press his advantage? How would she react?

"You're not wrong there pal," said Rudi and he stared at the fox. "What's the P of A for tomorrow, by the way?" He looked back over his shoulder. Rudi's eyes widened for a second and he found himself gawking. He quickly regained his composure, "Hi, Gabi."

"Hi," she said quietly and smiled.

Rudi looked out over the waterhole. "That sighting at Okondeka today was unforgettable," he said and smiled broadly at the darkness.

"Where's Sven?" asked Geoff.

"Fast asleep and probably dreaming about his new hero."

Geoff smiled and blushed. "And Valerie?"

Gabi shrugged. "She said she would join us shortly."

"Where are we going tomorrow?" Geoff caressed her shoulder gently.

She hesitated. "To the rest camp at Halali for another night," she whispered after a while and squeezed his hip. Geoff's heart did its thing again.

"And then …?"

"To Namutoni …"

Rudi lifted his beer and downed it nosily. "Well, after so much excitement in one day I'm bushed. So, if no one minds, I think I'll turn in." He belched suddenly. "Sorry," he said and wiped his mouth on his sleeve, "I must be a bit pissed."

"Sure, buddy. You go ahead. I'll see you later."

Rudi smiled, gave a half-cocked salute and headed for his bungalow.

"What a lovely night. Look at all the stars," said Geoff. He was stalling. He didn't know what to do next.

"And that one's the Southern Cross, yes?" Gabi pointed to the heavens.

Geoff looked down at her and smiled. "You learn fast."

She looked up at him and the smile faded from her lips. She turned to him and Geoff pulled her closer. He lowered his head and their lips met. It was just a fleeting touch but there was much heat. Gabi lifted her arm, placed it behind his neck and gently pulled him down to her. Their lips melted together and Gabi parted hers ever so slightly, sensuously, inviting. Their tongues met and entwined. The kiss was divine and their bodies moved together, gently and lovingly but passionately. Geoff pressed his fingers into the small of her back and she pushed her thighs against him. The tension mounted as they swayed and moved together. Geoff heard her moan quietly and felt himself growing. He broke off the lingering kiss and gently pushed her away. "I … I … maybe …," he tried. She lifted her hand and placed her fingers on his lips until the futile protests faded. Then she traced the outline of his face, his nose and ears, all the time staring into his eyes. "You are beautiful," she said and pulled him to her.

❀

Tsumasa hill is too low for a spectacular view but the sheer vastness of the open land about them was breathtaking and Geoff lifted Sven from his shoulders. They stood enchanted by the beauty.

Sven looked up at Geoff and tugged on his shorts. "Are you my mom's boyfriend?" he asked seriously.

Geoff looked down at the little boy and then at Gabi and blushed. "Well, um, I am your mother's friend and I also happen to be a boy, so I guess that makes me her boyfriend, don't you think?"

"Well, not like that, I mean, like, do you smooch?"

"Sven!" exclaimed Gabi.

Geoff didn't hesitate, "We did smooch, why?"

"I dunno, just asking." A hint of a smile on his face. The adults turned to each other and grinned. Geoff moved next to Gabi and put his arm around her. She leant against him and slid her arm around his waist.

They stayed up on the outcrop for a while longer, enjoying each other's company and the tranquillity. For once Geoff wished that little Sven were elsewhere. Reluctantly Geoff lifted Sven onto his shoulders and they started back down.

Val hovered in the background and Rudi jogged towards them. "Holiday's over! We have to move." He stopped in front of Geoff and placed his hands on his hips.

"Why?"

"They called from the farm. They've been champing at the bit waiting for our call. We're to return post haste."

"Said who?" Geoff was crestfallen.

"Martin was on the radio but Dawid confirmed."

"Dawid," breathed Geoff.

CHAPTER 25

Gabi flung her arms around Geoff's neck and squeezed. "Come back to me," she breathed. Then she was running. He watched her flee towards the stables.

Like a galleon gliding into the doldrums for the first time, Geoff felt the wind sucked from his being and his shoulders slumped.

The whine of the Alouette beckoned and he forced himself to bundle his kit aboard. Geoff glanced back but the woman was gone.

A hand on his shoulder forestalled him. "You'll see her again!" said Rudi above the clamour of the helicopter. His smile was genuine and his friendship a rock.

Geoff grasped Rudi's hand and shook. "Thanks buddy, catch you later!"

The soldiers on the ground diminished in size as the helicopter lifted and the pilot guided them past the tall palms next to the cottage. A movement out on the vast land caught Geoff's attention. It was Gabi on Pegasus and how she flew.

August already, thought Geoff as he peered ahead over the pilot's shoulder through the Perspex bubble of the Alouette. Even with the doors of the helicopter closed, the early morning chill invaded every small opening in his fatigues and he hunched into his bush jacket against the cold and noise. He sat in the middle of the hard bench seat behind the pilot, his kit strewn on the floor next to him, his rifle clutched between his knees and his mind racing.

It was all so sudden. To be summoned by radio to return to the farm ASAP for no apparent reason smacked of Dawid playing one of his tasteless little games purely to feed the flames of hatred between the two men. On arriving at the farm though, an Alouette was waiting and the rest of Geoff's men had received the order from Eenhana to pack up and get back to camp forthwith.

At least they had the courtesy to wait for a final decision from me, thought Geoff. It gave him some small comfort that Dawid and Martin, along with the rest of the section counted him as their chief, or so it seemed. Despite all his misgivings they had waited for him and for his decision.

What of Gabi though? Geoff smiled broadly to himself. What a beautifully euphoric feeling. It boiled up from deep within and flowed to the surface where it manifested in the form of a wonderful ache that tingled all over. But with it came the confusion. Did she really love him? She said she thought she loved him. What did that mean? Rudi was convinced she had fallen for him … what the hell did Rudi know? Kathy. What about Kathy? Geoff felt guilty when he thought of her. They were on the verge of marriage. He shouldn't feel such elation over another woman, should he? After all the 'other woman' was spoilt goods with a baggage of bad memories. She was a widow, albeit young and agonisingly beautiful, who carried a toy bear everywhere she went. Was she just using him to heal her wounds? Was he just using her to heal his wounds?

Geoff was still trying to convince himself that his feeling for Gabi was merely powerful lust and that once he went away it would dwindle and die like the last embers of a wood fire. And suddenly the ache turned to the pain of loss—he was flying away from Gabi, probably never to return.

Geoff attempted to thrust his grief aside. He bunched his fists and clenched his teeth. "No! Damn it!" The lieutenant glanced over his shoulder, mistook Geoff's exclamation for a question and pointed ahead. The familiar signs of an army camp loomed. Drab neat lines of olive-green tents, a mess area and a bare parade ground with a flagpole proudly sporting the orange, white and blue of South Africa. In front of the flagpole, among a brave show of bedraggled Barberton daisies, a concrete shield had been cast and the bare footprint of a man had been painted on the rough surface. This left Geoff in no doubt that he was about to land at SWA Spes military base; gateway to Ovamboland and to the Border War.

The Alouette was so low that it hardly had the chance to kick up dust before it touched down and powered off. Geoff noticed the other Alouettes parked off to one side. One of the helicopters stood next to a big black fuel bladder and a petrol jockey pumped avgas into the tanks. A couple of vehicles were dotted around the parade ground. One, which caught his eye, was a Casspir. Standing around it, smoking and laughing and generally looking ill-disciplined, were members of the police counter-insurgency unit, Koevoet. Their unique camouflage uniforms and untidy demeanour seemed to be a trademark. On the ground lay a couple of body bags; the new transparent type. Geoff could clearly see the grizzly remains inside. Another successful contact for Koevoet.

Instinctively Geoff ducked beneath the spinning disc of the rotor as he gathered his rifle and kit and turned and ran to the edge of the parade ground. There, straight as an arrow next to the Land Rover, stood the, rigid, impeccable figure of Sergeant-Major Joubert. Geoff skidded to a halt in front of the man and stood to attention.

The sergeant-major's pipe gurgled and he gave his handlebars a twirl before speaking through a cloud of smoke. "Stand easy, corporal," he said. "So! The big holiday is over, eh Kent? And the next chapter begins," he smiled his humourless smile.

Geoff could never be sure whether the sergeant-major was fond of him or hated his guts. "What's this all about, sergeant-major …?"

"Shaddup and listen." Sergeant-Major Joubert was obviously in no mood for niceties. He sucked on his pipe, exhaled a huge cloud of smoke and licked his lips. It was as if he were stalling, as if embarrassed. "For some reason, someone in the upper echelons," the sergeant-major pointed skyward, "has decided that you have had a good glimpse of Grootvoet and now you are needed to identify him. You are to go with to attack his camp and wipe him out."

"But I never saw him sergeant-major …," exclaimed Geoff vehemently.

"That's the way I read your report. However, someone has decided that you did." The sergeant-major paused, hunched his shoulders, placed his pipe in his mouth and spoke around it. "You'll enjoy this part. You're going with a bunch of Parabats."

"But I don't know what he looks like. I never saw him. It's in my report. He disappeared! Like a ghost!"

"I know son, but it's a bit late for that now. I'm here to see that you board your transport and get there as soon as possible," the sergeant-major pointed with the stem of his pipe. There were two of them. They stood there, squat and deadly like giant dragonflies, but with a proboscis of death protruding from each of their camouflaged bodies—gunships with twenty-millimetre barrels protruding from their sides. "Go and show those 'Bats what we're good for."

Geoff hefted his kit, slung his rifle over his shoulder, hesitated, shook his head and turned to leave. "Oh, by the way, about your so-called ghost …" The sergeant-major's eyes narrowed. "They sent some Bushman trackers to where you last saw him." He dragged on his pipe.

Geoff was irritated by this turn of events. "Well …?" he prompted.

"From where the original spoor disappeared up against the fence, you know, where you last saw them?" Geoff nodded as the sergeant-major continued. "Well they walked along that fence for five kilometres and found where the tracks had resumed on the other side. From there the spoor wandered off into the bush where it disappeared under the hoof prints of many cattle."

Geoff stood for a minute, taking in the enormity of the extraordinary action. "Jes …!" he exclaimed but cut himself short. It was not a good idea to take the Lord's name in vain—especially in front of Sergeant-Major Joubert. "He walked barefoot on the barbed-wire fence for five clicks?"

"Ja, but not like a bleddy tightrope walker in the circus. He walked hand over hand, hanging on the fence as he walked."

"How the hell did they work that out?"

"Every so often he must have missed a step and stood on the bottom strand. The barb poked the sand and formed little holes, like small cones. Towards the end he must have been tired because they found many such cone holes close to the place where he hurdled the fence. To me that's quite a bleddy achievement." The sergeant-major dragged on his pipe, hesitated for a second as if to contemplate the whole saga and stared off into the haze. "Ja, that bleddy kaffir's got guts and determination, *jong*. He's quite a … a … how you say in English, quite an adversary." He pointed at the helicopters with his pipe. "You best get going, corporal. They're waiting for you."

Geoff shook his head in awe and gathered his kit. He turned and headed for the waiting gunships.

"Corporal Kent!" The sergeant-major called after him and Geoff turned. "Good luck," said the sergeant-major and this time his smile was genuine.

Previously Geoff had been afraid. Mostly his fears were confined to his subconscious for he believed that he had far too much living still to do than worry about dying in this crazy war. He fidgeted and he stared at the ground rushing by. They flew low, low enough for the pilot to weave among the islands of makalani palms and Geoff realised for the first time, he was afraid.

CHAPTER 26

Mohammed Pillay was quite used to derogatory names. Pillay or Coolie, Curry Muncher or Wagon Burner, it didn't matter. Whatever the members of the South African Defence Force deemed necessary to brand him was of no consequence. It was to his advantage that he could laugh along with their racist taunts and blatant hatred while he plied his trade and made good money to boot.

He drove his old blue Bedford truck around the entire Ovamboland district selling fruit in its varying degrees of freshness to whomever would fill his coffers. Of course he was searched every time he entered any of the towns and Oshakati was no exception, however the guards found him more of an irritant and a nuisance than any form of threat. They never found any excuse to detain him let alone discover any contraband and the more he was seen the less thorough became the searches.

This suited Mohammed handsomely and he smiled and took the abusive jokes, bobbed his head in submission and token respect and entered the town. No members of the SADF were allowed to buy fruit from Mohammed for various reasons ranging from the fact that it might be poisoned to the fact that the army supplied fresh and better quality fruit—which, at least, was true. This too did not worry Mohammed at all. He made enough money from the poor and starving Ovambos. The women, mostly with howling, snotty-nosed urchins strapped to their backs, queued to buy fruit. So too did the old village headmen and one or two of the younger bucks who weren't away fighting the war.

One such man was John Mulemba's brother, Victor. Wearing one of the brigadier's tatty, cast-off civilian shirts, the tall Ovambo leant nonchalantly against the side of the Bedford and patiently waited his turn. The queue dwindled and finally the last woman piled her fruit into a dilapidated straw basket, balanced it squarely on her head and ambled off.

Victor then stepped forward, smiled broadly and greeted Mohammed. "Tell me," he commanded jovially, "when I must give up my inspiring career as the white man's gardener and start selling rotten fruit, Mohammed Pillay."

"When you are all wise, Indian and can afford a battered truck such as this, my Ovambo cousin," came the instant retort. The men laughed and Victor selected the best-looking shrivelled yellow apple and took a huge bite. He might joke with the wizened little Indian but it didn't mean that he liked him. In fact Victor abhorred him. He hated the Indian for his freedom of movement and the trust John placed in him. But most of all he hated him because he was Indian.

Mohammed played an important role in the struggle for liberation and democracy. Because of this and the fact that some years ago he had gone to John to offer his services voluntarily, made him a spoke in the wheel and thus, readily accepted.

Victor chewed for a moment, his smile faded and he spoke around the fruit. "There is a new development. The brigadier's wife has more detailed information. I have no idea where she gets such information." He paused, spat out some pips and continued, "I am worried that it might just be nonsense but we have no way of testing the validity of it. We must, I suppose, simply take the information to my brother and let him do with it what he deems best."

"What harm could it do?" asked Mohammed and he held out his hand. Victor looked at his hand and then at Mohammed. "That will be five cents please."

"You rob the poor and hungry, Pillay."

"I make a living from rich gardeners."

Victor dug in the pockets of his khaki shorts and extracted a small handful of coins. "It could cause terrible harm if it is false information." He carefully selected a little silver coin and handed it over.

"In what way?" asked Mohammed, pocketing the coin.

"They give us the wrong information and set a snare to capture my brother and us along with him," Victor shrugged. "Lots of ways."

"But if you think that, they must suspect you then, not so?"

Victor shook his head, "I don't know." He paused and gathered his thoughts. "When she was so unhappy I told her to go home to her own country. She asked me if I was Swapo and why I wasn't fighting the war. That's as far as it went and that was months ago. Then out of the blue, the other day, she told me about the impending attack on my brother. You know, the message we sent last time."

"That message was vague. How could they possibly set a trap with so little?" Mohammed was becoming irritated with this pointless conversation. Even if the risk was minimal, it was still taking a chance meeting like this, literally in the middle of the engine room of the South African fighting machine. "You risk exposing our line of communication every time you send for me and you do so to tell me that you are worried about a trap with the little we know?" Mohammed's annoyance was plain.

Victor looked at the Indian and the scorn in his tone was undisguised. "Yesterday the woman told me the time, date and place of the attack." Victor paused. He disguised the triumph he felt at the look of astonishment on the Indian's face. "So, if I tell you where to go, will you go there and tell us if it is a trap or not, my brave and humble little fruitmonger."

"Why do you take so long to get to the point, noble and distinguished gardener?" Mohammed too, disliked Victor. The man was tall, well built and arrogant. His sheer presence seemed to highlight Mohammed's diminutive body.

"Take this piece of scrap-iron," Victor banged his fist on the side of the Bedford, "as fast as it will go and send this message; 'a hundred of the air troops',—Victor did not know the term for Parabats—'will be attacking the northern camp at lunchtime on the twelfth of this month'. And make sure it gets there timeously for it is the tenth today. So hurry little fruitmonger."

For a moment Mohammed was speechless. Conceding the importance of this information was difficult for him. "A thousand apologies. Your concerns are well founded. I believe we must act on this right away. It could deliver a resounding blow to the southern racist regime. I must leave at once." For various reasons Mohammed couldn't wait to get away. If it were a set-up, to his mind the only one that would get caught would be the arrogant gardener himself, and Mohammed wanted no part of it. But if the information were correct and he was the messenger, then a good deal of the glory would be his. Finally, and mostly, he needed to get away from this conceited bastard. The smell of his unwashed body was nauseating. How he hated them.

CHAPTER 27

With the palms far behind, the landscape and vegetation changed. The bush thickened and Geoff spotted a baobab tree. It was massive and its stark canopy towered above the surrounding vegetation. So much wonderful myth and legend surrounded these mighty trees. Geoff had fond memories of spending hours trying to knock the fruit from its lofty residence. A well-aimed stick and the triumph of a dusty green pod tumbling earthward brought a smile to his lips. But more than that was the prize—the taste of the tangy cream of tartar. Geoff felt the saliva lubricate his dry mouth as he remembered breaking open the hard coconut-like shell with a rock and ripping the white, powdery fruit from its sisal-cord grip.

Suddenly Geoff felt hungry. It was a good sign. Perhaps he was getting his fear under control. He dug around in his webbing and recovered a Cheesy. He cut the top off with his penknife and squeezed the processed cheese into his mouth. It tasted delicious. There must be another.

The Alouette pulled up sharply, banked and descended onto a concrete apron. A troop of 5.5-inch howitzers stood in perfect alignment off to one side, aiming at some target to the north. A group of gunners busied themselves cleaning the huge guns of Second World War vintage. The helicopters taxiied past to a black fuel bladder and shut down.

Geoff hopped out and stretched his legs. The nearby tarred road meandered down a gentle slope into a small town. Off to the right a deserted and partly destroyed petrol station displayed its product. He turned to the flight sergeant. "Where the hell are we?"

"Ongiva." The flight sergeant surreptitiously studied Geoff.

Geoff looked at the man, noticed his hooded gaze and smiled. "Is there a problem, flight?" he asked politely.

"No. Just wondered if you're the oke they're all waiting for."

"What oke are you referring to?"

"Well, you had that contact with Grootvoet, didn't you?"

"Yeah. So?"

"Well the 'Bats are gonna attack his camp and you know what he looks like, hey?"

"I've never seen the fucker in my life," said Geoff taking great pleasure in the man's consternation.

"Well, why the fuck are you here then?"

"You tell me, staff. I haven't got a goddamned clue." Geoff turned his back and looked at the little town. It was typical Portuguese architecture—practical, well built and neat. Red-tiled roofs and whitewashed, plastered walls. Flagstone pathways on the grassy sidewalks, but it was all but destroyed. Bullet holes pockmarked the buildings, some of which had huge holes in the walls from rocket and cannon fire. The 'splash' of explosions surrounding the ragged holes was quite discernable. Political graffiti adorned the undamaged walls and most of the roofs had fallen in.

Someone had stencilled a picture of Agostinho Neto on the church wall, funnily enough, one of the few intact buildings, and a badly painted Portuguese slogan followed. All of this struck Geoff as being incredibly sad. Here was proof that some community had lived and thrived in this remote part of southern Angola. Not too long ago it had all worked and probably even bustled, but now it was a depressing bloody ruin.

The flight sergeant called and Geoff felt his fear return. He snapped the seat belt home and watched the artillery pieces disappear beneath the fuselage.

The helicopters hopped over the higher banks of trees and dipped low, skirting the dry *shonas* and the land flowed below them. The Alouette suddenly banked sharply enough for him to feel his body pinned to the hard bench seat. He looked out and saw the HAG. What a sight. Eight Puma helicopters parked in neat staggered lines of two on the sandy opening next to a small stream.

The Alouettes didn't bother hovering. They seemed to hit the ground at a run and stopped almost immediately. Geoff grabbed his kit and launched himself from the machine the second it rolled to a stop. He ducked and as he ran he opened his eyes too soon. The dust stung and the tears poured down his cheeks. Geoff stopped well away from the danger of the rotors, straightened up and wiped the tears on his sleeve. He opened his eyes, blinked carefully and looked around. From the air he'd seen nothing other than the Pumas but now he saw military equipment and soldiers everywhere. Well concealed beneath the trees and camouflage netting, the Parabats busied themselves.

HAG is the Afrikaans acronym for *Helikopter Admin Gebid* meaning simply Helicopter Administrative Area and Geoff stood looking at a HAG for the first time. *Fucking meat bombs*, he thought sourly and smiled at his own witticism. Someone touched him on the shoulder. Geoff turned and saw the same rank as his own first and then the famous wings.

"Corporal Kent?" the man inquired and extended his hand.

"Why yes!" exclaimed Geoff sarcastically, "and you must be …," he craned forward and studied the man's name tag, "Corporal Naudé." Geoff straightened and took the proffered hand. His anger at being part of some administrative bungle still simmered.

The corporal's smile faded and he cleared his throat. "Ja, well … um. If you'd like to follow me I'll show you to the lieutenant."

Geoff slung his kit untidily over his shoulder and trudged after the corporal. His posture attested his anger. Not unusually when these men and other infantry units mixed, the result was a heated brawl. He could feel their eyes on him and the hostility was tangible. He was on totally unfamiliar turf—one among so many—and he was supposed to be the key to their success. Geoff cursed the military and its madness for the hundredth time.

"Are you tired, corporal?" asked the lieutenant.

"Oh." Geoff looked up surprised. He was so preoccupied with his own thoughts he hadn't noticed they'd reached their destination. Geoff issued a hasty salute and stood easy. "Sorry, lieutenant. I'm not really tired. Rather a bit overwhelmed by all of this."

"Ja, you certainly look it." The lieutenant glanced at Geoff's appearance, smiled, pushed himself away from the tree and held out his hand. "But never mind, a nutritious rat pack, a good sleep and you'll be right as rain, man." The men shook hands and Geoff was mystified—*two meat bombs, both so friendly*, he thought.

He pushed his hand up under his bush hat and scratched his head. "So, what's the P of A?" he asked and let his webbing fall to the ground.

"*Gaan saam met …,*" began the lieutenant in Afrikaans and then shook his head. "Sorry man, just go with Leon over there and he'll introduce you to the rest of your crew." Geoff looked a bit confused and the lieutenant pointed at Corporal Naudé. "Leon," he said. Geoff pursed his lips and nodded. He stopped suddenly remembering his manners and was about to salute. The lieutenant held up his hand. "We don't do that around here. It sort of makes a target of me. So unless you don't like me—you get my drift?"

Geoff grinned ruefully. "Thanks lieutenant," he said and shook his head. He liked the man.

Geoff followed the Parabat corporal to a large sparsely leafed tree. What was the man's name again? Geoff had been so caught up in the events and had not been concentrating when the lieutenant mentioned the corporal's name. Lance Naudé? Laurie? Geoff wracked his brain for a while and gave up. What did it matter? Someone would remind him. Beneath the tree the Parabats had set up their bivouacs.

Corporal Naudé stopped in the centre next to the trunk of the tree. "*Luister mense!*" he called in Afrikaans. "Listen people. We have a visitor and I'd like you to meet him." Whether it was his rank or just because they shared the camaraderie of the war Geoff would never know but one by one the Parabats greeted him.

"Hello corporal."

"Middag *korperaal*."

"Howzit corporal."

"Good to have you with us." The last soldier greeted Geoff and shook his hand. Geoff looked at him. His excellent English and polished accent belied the hard craggy face, a tough-looking soldier who'd undoubtedly survived many a skirmish. Once again Geoff was struck by their openness and friendliness. There were twelve of them including their section leader, Corporal Naudé, who waited until he had their attention before he spoke.

"This is the section leader of the men who blew away Grootvoet's little army. His name is Corporal Geoffrey Kent. He's travelling with us tomorrow, so I want you to make him feel at home, boys."

"Sure corporal."

"Okay by me," came the replies and they looked at him with new respect.

The story sure has travelled far and wide, thought Geoff.

Craggy face called out, "You should have been a 'Bat, corporal!"

"What!" exclaimed Geoff. "Not for me thank you. I always knew you meat bombs had a screw loose. I mean who the hell wants to jump out of a working aeroplane, hey?" The men burst out laughing as one.

"Carry on, *manne*," said Corporal Naudé with amusement and touched Geoff on the shoulder. "Come. Let's find you a place to doss down." A whining noise caught their attention and they looked at the HAG. The mid-afternoon sun flashed off slowly rotating blades as the Puma helicopters fired up. The tempo increased, the whine of the jet engines intensified until they reached a crescendo and the rotor blades were a disc above the graceful aircraft. Clouds of dust billowed out and in pairs the helicopters lifted off into the deep blue, late-winter sky. Carried on the light breeze, the smell of dust and avgas reached them.

Geoff was bewildered. "Where the hell are they going?"

"Oh, they leave every night," replied Corporal Naudé. "But don't worry, they'll return in the morning."

"Why do they leave?" Geoff was still uncertain.

"The threat of enemy aircraft," Corporal Naudé shrugged. "They'd be sitting ducks if a MiG-21 decided to sniff around."

It was still dark when the men around Geoff began preparations for the new day. Geoff slid out of his sleeping bag and was about to set an Esbit beneath his fire bucket to boil water when Craggy face appeared before him in the darkness of predawn.

"Coffee, corporal?"

"Sure!" said Geoff and accepted the cup gratefully. "Thank you." Shit, even his own troops wouldn't do that for him.

"I think today is going to be the big day, Corporal Kent." Geoff didn't hear Corporal Naudé walk up behind him and he started enough to spill the hot coffee down the front of his fatigues.

"Shit man! Do you guys always sneak around like that hey?" complained Geoff. He peered at the wet stain on his shirt.

"Sorry man," said Corporal Naudé. "I thought you knew I was there." He turned to craggy face, "Ag, fetch the corporal a wet cloth, boet."

They soon had him cleaned up and the wet patch on Geoff's shirt made him cold. He shrugged into his bush jacket, buttoned it up and turned to Corporal Naudé. "Why do you say today's the day?"

"Well, we're actually on a planned op and we've been hitting bases every day until two days ago ..."

"Contacts every day?" asked Geoff incredulously.

"Ja. Well, almost every day. One or two days we never found the bastards. They had bombshelled already," Corporal Naudé shook his head as if to contemplate what might have been and continued in his heavy Afrikaans accent. "But otherwise we've been flying out every day. Then suddenly we have two days break and you fly in." Corporal Naudé smiled at Geoff. "Today I reckon we gonna go find your nigger in the woodpile." He laughed volubly at his own wit.

The dawn became a thing of the past as the sun burst over the treetops, bathing them in light and Geoff screwed up his eyes against the glare. He shuddered slightly as the warmth began to extrude the chill from the marrow of his bones.

"Was your tracker a dog handler?"

Geoff raised an eyebrow. "Yes. Why do you ask?"

"Because we were actually waiting for two of you. The section leader and the dog handler. That's what we were told, so it figures that this oke should also be here." During their conversation the gunships landed, followed a short time later by the Pumas. Finally two more gunships landed. Corporal Naudé pointed over Geoff's shoulder. "Maybe that's him." Geoff whipped around and stared at the silhouetted figure. The excitement welled up within as he recognised the short powerful man with shoulders as wide as a doorway.

"Allan," he whispered and contained the urge to run down to where the figure waited.

Allan watched them saunter down the slight slope of the dry *shona* towards him. Small puffs of dust were highlighted by the sun and hovered about their boots as they made their way through the brittle winter grass. At first he only considered them with mild interest. There was something familiar about the tall, well-built corporal but his face was shaded by his bush hat and Allan surveyed the HAG while he waited for them. Someone cleared their throat behind him and Allan turned. One man stood in front of the other.

"*Aangenaam. Ek is Korperaal Naudé*," he held out his hand.

"You don't say. Well I'm Allan Hunt, Four South African Infantry, Middleburg, B-Special Forces: Dog Squad and Tracking, Pretoria, currently based at SWA Spes, Oshivelo, Legion ..."

"... of the Damned and in cahoots with Attila the Hun, thanking you for your services," Geoff finished for him and stepped out next to Corporal Naudé.

Allan's face remained expressionless and he hesitated for just a second before he spoke. "I was wondering why the heathens tore me away from my every comfort in SWA Spes, Oshivelo only to be escorted and rudely dumped in this den of iniquity. It must be because the team of Hunt and Kent has been dispatched to show these meat bombs how to eliminate Brother Swapo. How have you been you big bastard?"

Geoff exhaled. "Christ, you always manage to get me going," he said and clasped Allan's hand in a vice grip.

"I told you before, I'm not Christ but I do get you going, don't I?" The two men laughed. Geoff and Allan chatted and Corporal Naudé listened.

"... and your best buddy Dawid. Tell me how the precious little cherub is faring."

"Nothing new on that front, still borderline psychotic. Anyway, have you got a new dog yet?"

"Yep. There'll never be another Dart though." They fell silent for a while. Allan spoke quickly to salvage the joy of their meeting, "So, how's old Mike Theunissen?"

"Foot got blown off by a mine." Quiet again. "At least he's out of this shit for good though," added Geoff after a while.

Allan nodded. "I'm sorry to hear that. He was a good man."

Geoff spread his hands and shrugged. "I haven't heard other than he survived."

"You know ...," Allan paused, "I think we should change the subject to something like ...," he thought for a second, "like naming the first five thousand decimals of Pi in Hebrew. That way we can't fuck up this unbelievable coincidence any more than we have."

The Parabat lieutenant returned from the briefing. "Sit. Sit please men." A rustle of clothing and the tap of magazines in rifles followed. "This is going to be short and sweet. There are two Swapo bases west-northwest of us. We're going to skirt the bigger more southerly one and hit the smaller one to the north. They are far enough apart for us to hit them and get out before big brother to the south gets wind. But our target is well manned. It's supposed to be the headquarters of this Grootvoet character and his cronies ..." There was a murmur from the troops. The platoon commander frowned, his annoyance clearly evident. "I'm sick of this reaction every time that stupid kaffir's name is mentioned. You two have seen him, hey corporal?" The lieutenant turned to Geoff and Allan. There was much interest among the Parabats and they craned forward to listen.

"No lieutenant, we haven't, only his spoor."

"Spoor? Fuck spoor man! You're here because you've seen him, not so?"

"Yes lieutenant."

"Well have you seen him? Do you know what he looks like? Can you tell the rest of the men who to look for?"

Geoff took a deep breath and stood up. "We are here ...," Geoff inclined his head towards Allan, "to identify Grootvoet because we were in an extended fire fight with him but we've never seen him. Only his spoor, lieutenant."

"Well then, I don't know what you two poor bastards *are* doing here but I do have an idea. Come and see me after the op and we'll have a chat. For the rest of you, if you see a big kaffir, shoot him, and if you see a small kaffir, shoot him too, and shoot as many as you can or he might be inclined to kill you right back. I don't want to hear any more about glorified Swapo soldiers. There is no such thing."

Geoff noticed the lines around the lieutenant's eyes and his clenched jaw. *He's just as wound up as I am—as all of us*, thought Geoff as he examined the faces around him.

"Sit please corporal. We fly out at fourteen-hundred hours in those eight Pumas." The lieutenant nodded to the helicopters. "Are there any questions?"

"What's the flying time, lieutenant?"

"Approximately twenty-five minutes. Anything else?"

"Yeah," said one of the troops at the back. "What's Grootvoet's wife look like?" There were one or two guffaws and a few men laughed out loud.

The lieutenant smiled. "Okay, men, go get your kit. The corporals to stay behind please. I want a word." The men began to disperse and the lieutenant called after them, "Just remember you're going to be jammed into those heelios like sardines so be ready for a rough ride."

The blades of the helicopters thrashed the pale blue sky and the din of eight Puma engines was alarming. The men squatted and waited. Geoff didn't know whether his legs would carry him if the signal weren't imminent and he dug his finger into the white sand between the grass. He and Allan were at the back of Corporal Naudé's section. *LIFO, last in, first out,* thought Geoff and he shook his head. The movement attracted Allan's attention.

"What's up?" he shouted above the noise.

"Good! We'll be the first to show these 'Bats how it's done!" shouted Allan and he smiled. "Nervous?"

"Terrified!" admitted Geoff.

"Me too!"

Geoff could only think that it was an automatic reaction for they were up and running. With no hesitation they piled into the aircraft and as Geoff had correctly guessed, he and Allan sat in the open doorway with legs dangling over the edge of the fuselage, webbing securely strapped and rifle clutched in sweaty palms. Geoff placed his boots on the step bar and looked up over his shoulder to the commander. His eyes widened as he recognised the pilot. Strewth, what a bloody coincidence. It was the same pilot who had picked up the dead and wounded after the Grootvoet contact. He tapped Allan on the shoulder and pointed. Allan peered at the man and smiled.

As if he sensed they were talking about him, the captain turned and surveyed his cargo. His eyes glossed over the soldiers and came to rest on Geoff who smiled and waved gingerly lest the captain not recognise him. The pilot frowned and suddenly smiled back broadly. He aimed a gloved thumb and forefinger at Geoff and winked. The smile faded, he turned his head, pushed the mike closer to his lips and spoke. Geoff felt better. They were all nervous but they were a team—pilots, soldiers, corporals and lieutenants alike.

Oblivious to the airwaves, Geoff waited for the Puma to lift off.

CHAPTER 28

"Giants check in," crackled the nasal voice of the lead. "Alpha."

"Bravo ready."

"Charlie ready."

One by one the pilots replied to their lead. The commander of Alpha pulled up on the collective, waited for maximum revs on the rotor and eased forward on the cyclic. The machine responded and lifted. He held his breath. Although not quite spring it was a hot winter's day, twenty-eight degrees and he was laden with fifteen fully kitted troops. Added to this was the altitude of the region. At around one thousand two hundred metres, the air was extremely thin. He had to maintain power and lift after the ground cushion had cleared them of the trees. His concerns were short-lived as the Puma 330L model had not only the suped-up motor, but also the widened rotor blades making it a helicopter of immense power and durability.

Alpha and Bravo took off together, lifted clear of the trees and sped off to the west. Charlie waited. He had to avoid the down draft of the two aircraft ahead of him. Seconds ticked by and Charlie and Delta took to the sky. This was not so for Echo. His was a a C-model. With fourteen soldiers and three crew members he was dangerously overloaded. The helicopter gyrated and lifted, but the wheels never quite left the ground.

Captain Williams of Golf noticed the dilemma and radioed his colleague. "You're too heavy Echo. Send us two men."

"Roger Golf. What about Foxtrot?"

"He's full too. Send them to us."

"Roger. Out," said Echo commander and he turned and peered into the cargo bay. Whether it was because they had just greeted each other or because they sat in the door and therefore it was easier for them to disembark, Geoff would never know, but the captain flipped the toggle to 'intercom' and spoke briefly to his flight sergeant. The flight nodded, pulled the mouthpiece out of his way and shouted to the platoon commander. The lieutenant nodded and turned to Geoff, cupped his hands and shouted.

"Get out! We're too heavy! Get out!"

Geoff nodded and mouthed the words "Where to?"

"Golf!" shouted the lieutenant. "Go to Golf!"

Geoff gave thumbs-up, stretched across and patted Corporal Naudé on the back. The two men shook hands and smiled in mutual friendship born out of the extraordinary circumstances of war. Geoff leapt from the helicopter, followed closely by Allan. Instinctively they crouched and ran. Echo and Foxtrot were both airborne as the two corporals launched themselves into the door of Golf Puma. They settled themselves and seconds later Golf wobbled as she powered up and lifted free of the earth. Geoff smiled. What an exhilarating feeling. He looked out at Hotel as they skimmed above the treetops. They were on their way and there was no turning back. Suddenly the knot in his stomach tightened and he felt the acid rise in his throat, so strong was his fear.

The helicopter banked hard. From flying almost due west they turned north and Geoff marvelled at how he stuck to the chopper as if glued there. The Puma straightened and Geoff looked ahead. He tapped Allan on the shoulder and pointed. In staggered pairs the Pumas stretched away, ahead of them. Allan smiled and nodded. Further ahead was a very slight, flat valley with a grassy *shona* in the low area and the flight path took them directly over it.

Alpha and Bravo were well ahead of the pack and Charlie and Delta were just over the far edge of the *shona* when the world abruptly stood still and with it, the smile on Geoff's face froze. Suddenly, hideously, Echo pitched up violently, forcing the disc of the rotor vertical into the air. It was as if the pilot were trying to climb an invisible mountain in front of him. He then changed his mind and the helicopter bunted sharply forward. Like plastic, the tail rotor snapped off and fell silently to the ground. A shower of aircraft debris followed. Without the tail rotor, the fuselage began to spin as her anti-torque was rudely ripped from her. She spun all the way around and for a second Geoff could see into the cockpit. It was as if all were normal. The pilot and his co-pilot sat squarely in their seats with the flight sergeant between them. For Geoff the whole scene was like watching a movie in slow motion. The machine continued to spin until she'd turned through two hundred and seventy degrees and then exploded with such ferocity that Geoff felt the suck and push of the shockwave as it washed over them. A blaze engulfed the Puma and then a huge ball of flame burned dazzling white for a second, turned bright orange with a hint of blue and expanded to fill their vision as greasy, thick black smoke billowed outwards forming a chilling frame to the fiery wreck.

Flying along at one hundred and thirty-five knots, Foxtrot banked away to avoid the mushroom of devastation and received an intense buffeting. She clung precariously to her hold in the sky as her rotors cut through the air, biting hard to keep herself and her cargo aloft. Geoff watched in horror as Foxtrot dropped out of the sky and followed Echo down to where she lay in a million burning pieces on the open *shona*. She disappeared into the black smoke, but, as if rejected by the very earth itself, suddenly burst through the smoke, blasting it in all directions as she climbed up over the treetops.

It was then that Geoff noticed the tracers. They seemed to rocket up at them from both sides of the *shona*. He spun around as a massive commotion behind him almost knocked him from the aircraft. He teetered on the edge of the load bay, desperately trying to regain his balance. At the same moment the helicopter turned hard to starboard and Allan was thrown against him. Geoff felt his foot slip and was pitched over the edge and out of the helicopter. He grabbed desperately for any purchase and his arm hooked through the footplate just below the entrance to the load bay as his body swung over. Geoff cried out as his full body weight threatened to wrench his arm from the socket and he hung there grimacing, the wind thrashing him mercilessly. Geoff quickly slid his good arm around the plate and hung on for dear life. He looked down at the trees and shrubs rushing by far beneath him and felt dizzy. *Look up, look up, damnit!* he thought and looked at Allan who was shouting something at him.

"I'm gonna grab your webbing belt and haul you in!" Allan stretched past Geoff who felt one or two almost ineffectual tugs at his belt. Geoff weighed close to ninety-five kilos, a big man in anyone's mind. He wondered how Allan was going to manage. As if tied to a winch, Geoff felt himself hauled steadily upwards. Allan drew in a deep breath, braced himself and heaved with all his might. The muscles in his forearms writhed beneath the brown skin and his features contorted with the effort as the others in the helicopter pulled on his legs. Geoff's head came level with the floor of the load bay and anxious hands reached for him and dragged him back in. He rolled onto his back and took in the scene.

Allan's hands were on his hips and he knelt on the aluminium floor. His face was red from exertion and his chest heaved as he sucked in precious air. To his right lay two bloodied Parabats with colleagues holding saline drips as the medic tended them. The rest of the soldiers sat staring out over the canopy of trees to the distant horizon. Some of them had a haunted look about them as the realisation of what had happened really sank in. One of the most elite bush-fighting units had been dealt a devastating blow. One irreplaceable Puma, twelve Parabats and three crew killed in one miserable minute.

Captain Neville Williams of Golf watched the horrific demise of Echo and heard the desperate call from Foxtrot. "I'm hit! I'm hit! We're taking a pounding!" He watched with dismay as his colleague dropped out of the sky towards the burning wreck. His relief left him feeling nauseous as the Puma righted itself and burst through the pall of black smoke.

The voice of his formation leader served to steady him. "Starboard! Starboard! Turn right and get the hell out of here!" But straight away, Captain Williams felt the blood drain from his face as Delta called in and he listened to the words, "Golf, you've got a man overboard! He's hanging on the step rail."

"Roger. I can't land yet. We're still too close." The radio tone belied the anguish he felt.

Delta answered with the same ethereal tone that typified the Puma radio system but they were sweet words to the captain. "Stand by. It seems the others are managing to reel him in. Just keep her steady," There was silence for a second before Delta continued, "He's safe. Let's go. We're pulling out.'"

The pilots flew back to the HAG listening, always listening to the nightmarish sounds of war as the air attack continued. The Alouette gunships flew straight into the pall of smoke trying to flush out the enemy. One would pitch up and draw fire, giving the other a target, but this time the tracer fire proved so intense that it would have been foolhardy to continue in this vein.

The Mirages had been airborne for a while and so time was of the essence. Their mission was to arrive at the target as the Parabats landed in order to strafe the area and soften up the enemy. They attacked sans Parabats anyway, with their focus even more fervent after hearing of the Puma tragedy. However, their effort was met with equal ferocity and Captain Williams held his breath as he listened to the radio. "… SAM-7 and a second! Christ! Here comes a third! … Turning hard! Ahhh! It missed! Thank God it missed! I'm going in again …!"

The helicopters banked over the small stream, flared and hovered before sinking onto the sandy area of the HAG. The wounded were quickly moved to the briefing tent. Geoff climbed out and walked to the tree, the same tree where he had met the troops of Echo and he squatted for a moment. His arm ached and he winced as he sat.

Allan walked over and looked down at Geoff. "How's your arm feeling, old boy?"

"Leon," said Geoff miserably.

"What?" Allan was mystified.

"His name was Corporal Leon Naudé."

"I see." Allan looked around and then looked back at Geoff. "So?"

"Well, I'd forgotten. I wasn't listening when we were introduced and I'd forgotten his name and now he's dead." Geoff's voice shook a little as he spoke.

"Yeah," said Allan and he grunted as he sat. "His name was Leon and he doesn't care if you remember or not anymore. None of them do. Not even that pilot. We were nearly with them ..." Allan peered up at the sky and nodded, "There is a God."

"I guess so," said Geoff after a while and suddenly a picture filled his mind. It was the picture of a beautiful face, so serene and loving. A face he felt he'd known his whole life. He felt his pain ease a little as the thought of Gabi filled his being. God! How he missed her. How he longed for her—especially now. What chance though? He was clutching at straws.

Geoff's thoughts were interrupted by the approach of an air force officer. The man was of medium height and build with jet-black hair, a thick black moustache and dark features. He wore a standard flying overall with the sleeves rolled up. But most striking were his eyes with his dark black eyebrows emphasising their colour. They were deep green with golden flecks and they seemed to sparkle. Geoff and Allan heaved themselves to their feet and the officer seemed embarrassed.

"Please, gentlemen, relax. I'm Captain Neville Williams." He held out his hand.

Geoff was about to offer his hand, winced and held out his left hand. "Sorry captain. My arm is a bit sore."

The captain shook hands and turned to Allan. "Hi."

"How do you do, sir. Allan Hunt's the name and, in case you were wondering, the acrobat here is Geoffrey Parachuteless Kent."

The captain laughed gently and looked at Geoff. "Actually, that's why I'm here. I believe you tried to disembark without my permission *and* from a hundred feet."

Geoff smiled sheepishly at the captain. "Well ... not really. It's just that Isaac over here tried to knock me out ..."

"Isaac?" The captain looked at Allan. "Is your name Isaac?"

Geoff smiled again. "Isaachunt. You figure it out, sir."

The captain packed up laughing as Allan retained a poker face. "That's all the gratitude I get for saving your life? Right! That's the last time!"

"What the hell happened?" asked the captain. Allan gave a recital of the events that had them in stitches. A small group of soldiers gathered around and soon the stories were flowing.

"You should have seen his face ..."

"Remember when ol' Blackie Swart shot that rifle grenade straight up and the fucking loot asked, 'Where the hell did that go?' but there was no one left to ask. They were already half a mile away."

The laughter ebbed and flowed. A few of the troops smoked. Someone took out a chocolate bar and passed it around. Geoff looked at them. Human nature was amazing. In the face of a momentous tragedy these men of war and killing and death reached for the lighter side of life. It was all they could do. There was no place for the alternative.

With the events of Echo so fresh in their minds they managed to marvel at Geoff's brush with certain death and then to laugh at it when Allan was asked to recount the sequence of events once more. Neville Williams leant against the tree and still managed a guffaw at the end of Allan's tale despite having heard it three times. Someone called the captain's name and Geoff looked up as most of the others turned to the man striding towards them.

"Captain Williams!" he called. "Neville …!" Nobody knew who he was but most of them knew immediately what he was. He didn't need any badges or special uniform to distinguish himself. His hard face, intense eyes and the dangerous aura about him convinced most that they were looking at one of the best fighting soldiers in the world—a Reconnaissance commando. "I need to talk to you urgently!"

Neville looked alarmed and excused himself from the gathering. The two men certainly didn't move far enough to be out of earshot, as the Recce was far too agitated to wait. "What the hell happened?"

"Hello to you too, Jakes." Neville was somewhat irritated by the abruptness of the commando.

"We don't have time for that, Neville."

Jakes placed his hands on his hips, thrust his head forward, clenched his jaw and spoke through his teeth, "What the fuck happened out there today?"

Neville was taken aback by the ferocity of the commando's demeanour and although he outranked him he answered as if explaining a broken window to his father. "I don't know. What do you want to know? We followed the flight plan given to us from the colonel at the briefing. As instructed we changed heading to north at the mouth of a shallow valley …"

"What?" exclaimed Jakes. "Here. Show me on this!" he demanded and he unfolded a flimsy, dirt-stained map he had recovered from his leg pocket.

"Well …," said Neville. He studied the map for a second and rotated it to orient the north pointer. "We headed west from the HAG and turned north … here …" He stabbed at the map, barely concealing his annoyance. "Right over this little valley …"

"Jesus! Which rear echelon motherfucker told you to go there?"

"Weren't you at the briefing …?"

"No. I was having a picnic north of here. Just tell me!"

"It was the colonel … and that woman lieutenant." Neville stared at Jakes. He was completely taken aback as a single tear squeezed out the corner of the commando's eye, cut a path through the grime and come to a halt on the hair of his beard.

Jakes gritted his teeth. "I'll just have to go and tell the good colonel and the woman lieutenant how badly they fucked up then, won't I?"

Neville grabbed at Jakes' sleeve as the Recce turned to leave. "What's going on, Jakes? What's this all about?"

"Men from my stick died when we did a reconnaissance of this area. A reconnaissance we did so that you boys could have a successful hit today. And that reconnaissance revealed three camps … two we knew about and one we didn't. We walked right into it." Jakes paused, his frustration and utter helplessness evident as he took a deep breath. "My report clearly stated that the area you flew over was to be given a wide berth. You were not supposed to go anywhere near that little valley, let alone fly right over the middle of that *shona*!"

Captain Neville Williams paled. He felt a cold sweat break out on his face. "Jesus," he breathed, "it's as if they were waiting for us."

CHAPTER 29

It was neither revenge nor retaliation, merely the same operation carried out with more guts and determination than before. It would be a folly to take it any other way and the men knew it. Their adversary—the fabled Grootvoet—seemed more determined than any other Swapo unit the men had encountered in the past. However, on reaching the Echo crash site the remnants told a story that lifted the men's determination to vengeance.

Nothing much was recognisable in and around the actual burned-out wreck, but by some dint of misfortune under those horrific circumstances, three soldiers must have been flung from the doomed helicopter before it exploded. Their bodies had been badly broken, but somehow all three had survived the hundred-miles-an-hour fall from one hundred and fifty feet. The signs showed that at first they tried to drag themselves towards the shelter of nearby bushes but they never made it. They had obviously been discovered and were pulled to the nearest trees. They had been too mutilated to fight back and so no ropes were necessary—they were simply hefted up against a tree and shot through the head.

John Mulemba along with the middle camp and his own northern camp had fled. Hundreds of Swapo cadres had moved west leaving a spoor that was not only easily followed but its direction fairly accurately anticipated.

It had taken the rest of that day and the following day to gather the names of the dead and bring in a Puma full of replacement troops.

Geoff and Allan were swept along with the tide of events and found themselves part of one of the stopper groups. In fact, in his haste, the platoon commander placed Geoff in charge of a stopper group as he failed to notice the absence of wings on Geoff's sweat-stained brown shirt. The whole flight of Pumas took a totally new route as they followed the progress of the gunships that, by now, had the enemy in full flight. This time 'Giant Charlie' broke away early and headed west-northwest, flared briefly and landed in a small clearing. The last of the troops had hardly leapt free of the helicopter when she blew them a kiss of dust and disappeared over the treetops.

Geoff wasted no time. As the noise of the Puma diminished the ominous hammering of heavy 20mm cannons filled the sky. The gunships were close. So close that Geoff had hardly set the stopper group position when the first rifle shots cracked out from his own men. The shouts and rifle fire served as ample warning and Geoff took cover behind the trunk of a massive tree. He fell to one knee and peered cautiously around the edge of the rough bark. The mid-afternoon sun angled streaks of dusty light through the verdant canopy, creating wraiths of the shadows. Geoff lifted his rifle as his eyes darted from one ghostly apparition to the next. One of the phantoms burst into a blazing beam of sunlight. The adrenaline pulsed through Geoff's body like heroin in an addict's veins, and with it came a sweet relief—it had finally begun.

Geoff fired and the khaki figure disappeared. The first few seconds saw Swapo soldiers trickle through in their ones and twos, running blindly to escape the scything 20mm cannons and Geoff's men cut them down, but as time passed they came through in their hordes. From all sides the men fired at running khaki, disciplined firing. There were so many that Geoff found it increasingly difficult to restrain himself from firing on automatic. He knew it would only waste ammunition and his kill rate would probably reduce to zero. It became a matter of utmost discipline to select a target, aim and fire without jerking back on the trigger. Aim, fire; man goes down—aim, fire, miss, fire again and again; man goes down—click—magazine empty, snap in full, haul back on cocking lever, aim, fire; man goes down, tries to get up, fire again; top of his head explodes and a fine red mist follows the falling body into the undergrowth.

Geoff took a second to snap in a full magazine, wipe the sweat from his eyes and lift his rifle to his shoulder before he realised that the staccato of gunfire had faltered and diminished and finally it became quiet. He sat dead still peering over the sights of his rifle as an eerie silence came over the field of death. Nothing moved and Geoff shifted behind his tree. He stood slowly and slid his back up against the rough bark. Standing at full stretch he inched his way around the trunk until he could see more clearly. What he saw sickened him. The undergrowth, meagre grassed, open sandy areas were littered with bodies. They were everywhere; some looked as if they were lying peacefully taking an afternoon siesta while others lay twisted, mouths agape in the rictus of an undignified death, soundlessly shouting for mercy as their blood drained into the earth.

Far away someone called his name and Geoff looked up and slowly focused. Allan was standing next to him, tugging on his greasy sleeve. "Hey! Buddy! Are you okay?"

"What? Oh, yes. I'm okay."

"Fuck! That's what I call a contact hey," said Allan as he surveyed the area. "Hey you!" he shouted at the nearest trooper. "Yes! I'm talking to you!" Allan pointed at him. "Come here!" The soldier hauled himself out of the bush and walked over.

"What's up, corporal?" he asked, smiling.

"Well, not my winkie. It hasn't been up since my last tug, but have you got a smoke for me?"

The man's smile broadened. "Of course, corporal." He dug in his pocket and pulled out a crumpled pack of Gunston plain.

"Christ!" said Allan in mock agitation. "Don't you Dutchmen smoke anything else? Oh well beggars can't be choosers, hey?"

"This smoking is becoming a bit of a habit," Geoff remarked. One or two of the Parabats came out of their cover. Some walked among the dead while others joined the corporals.

"Nah. I told you, I only smoke when I kill people …"

"That's what I mean," said Geoff dryly. "By the way, have you got a smoke for me …" Geoff glanced at the soldier's name tag, "Zeelie?"

"Sure, corporal."

"You too, huh?"

"Yeah. Why the fuck not, I ask you?" said Geoff. "Got a light, Zeelie?"

"Right here, corporal. You guys are okay, hey," said the soldier. He hopped from one foot to the other and smiled again as he produced his Bic lighter, which he passed to Geoff.

"What on earth are you going on about, Zeelie?" asked Geoff. He lit the cigarette and blew out a cloud of blue smoke.

"Yeah. Spit it out, Zeelie," said Allan in a jocular tone, "and stand still man, you're making me nervous.

"Well, for regular infantry …," he began and leant forward to accept a light when suddenly he dived sideways as if heavily rugby-tackled.

Zeelie lay on the ground. Geoff stared down at him in consternation. For a second, a gaping wound showed the contents of Zeelie's head and then thick, dark-red arterial blood welled up and filled the hole. The blood flowed copiously, spilling over the jagged edges of the skull and pouring down thick and sticky through his short black hair onto the sand. Still Geoff stared uncomprehendingly at the horrific sight and then he was lying on his back with Allan's arm over his chest.

"One o'clock! Swapo at one o'clock!" shouted Allan.

"And three o'clock!" shouted another and the crackle of rifle fire brought Geoff to his senses. He leapt to his feet and ran for his tree. He and Allan fired from either side of the trunk as the attack came from two directions but this time there was not much to shoot at. The khaki-clad figures ran at them while their comrades gave covering fire. An RPG-7 whined overhead and burst beyond them. A second followed closely which slammed into Geoff's tree forcing the men to dive for cover. It exploded with a deafening roar, raining a shower of leaves and dust onto the men below. Geoff looked up and aimed at a running figure. He fired twice quickly and could hardly miss as the man was almost at their position. The enemy had closed in with alarming speed and Geoff knew they had to move or be killed where they stood.

"Allan!" he shouted. "Take those men back and cover the left flank! Start fire and movement! I'll do the same from here! Just watch who the fuck you shoot at!"

"See you in the middle!" bellowed Allan and took off. It was a slick action and the unorthodox pincer move soon had the alarmingly enthusiastic enemy attack under some sort of reverse.

Geoff dared a glance from his new position and took in the scene. He knew he was down to his last two magazines. Surely the others must be low too. He looked over to his left and saw Allan shouting as the soldiers exercised a form of leapfrog to the centre of the attack, cutting down the unusually fierce resistance from the Swapo cadres. It was a chaotic affair and Geoff was about to engage the right flank when he suddenly noticed Allan dive for cover, whip around and start firing to his rear. Geoff looked back. The undergrowth was full of khaki figures running towards them.

Having split their section and fighting on two flanks with another coming in from their rear meant, in effect, that they were surrounded and Geoff felt the first twinges of panic. They would have to finish what they were doing and then turn to the rear but if they were not quick enough they would certainly be surrounded.

In no time Geoff and the paratroopers were crawling through the undergrowth in pairs a few metres at a time. They stood back to back and shot anything khaki, dropping into the undergrowth only to repeat the process. The problem was that their personal supply of ammunition was becoming critically low. Geoff's mind raced as he stood and watched another Swapo terrorist die from the muzzle of his rifle. Whoever had been the architect of this counter-attack had to be pretty bloody smart. Even though there was very little time, the man had engineered a plan that was about to surround a section of Parabats. And he knew that no quarter would be given should they be captured.

Geoff stood and fired again. Bullets whipped and whined past his head like a hundred bullwhips cracking next to his ears and without warning his last magazine was finished. All the time the signaller had been intermittently shouting into the mouthpiece of the handset and firing at the enemy. Like the answer to the proverbial prayer, the angel of death swooped down. The 20mm blasted out its tune of destruction and in seconds the enemy were either shredded remnants of humanity or fleeing for their lives—all but one man. A man in camouflage fatigues. He was very tall, slim and finely muscled, his shoulders broad and straight, his skin, a deep, shiny, alluring ebony. But it was his eyes that caught Geoff's attention.

Even over the distance Geoff could see black pits where his eyes should have been. Black with hatred. A hatred he could almost feel. For a second the two men stared at one another across the killing field and suddenly Geoff had no doubt who he was looking at. Despite the afternoon heat Geoff felt the hairs on his arms and the back of his neck bristle as a rash of goose flesh covered his body. He lifted his rifle and aimed but the man was gone. Even if he had had some rounds left Geoff doubted that he would have been quick enough, for the man disappeared into the bush like a whisp of smoke in a gale.

While they waited for the Pumas, the men of Geoff's section searched the dead, looking for any information that might be of use to the intelligence people and soon enough an angry shout alerted them. One of the Parabats stood with a shiny object in his hands. Men crowded around to see what he held.

"Corporal! Corporal, come and look at this!"

Alarmed, Geoff and Allan jogged over to the soldier who by now, was surrounded by inquisitive colleagues. The soldier handed the chain to Geoff who read the lettering stamped in the soft metal. "J. J. H. Janse van Vuuren it says." Geoff looked up and shrugged. "Dog tags. So what? They could have got these anywhere."

"No, corporal," answered the Parabat in a shaky voice. "This was Jannie, my best friend. He was one of the men from Echo."

Geoff stared at the tags for a second and shook his head. "Jesus. I'm sorry, man," he said softly. Geoff handed back the tags, turned and walked over to a shady tree where he flopped down and took out his water bottle.

Allan joined him. "They've found the other two dog tags," he said grunting with the effort of lowering his exhausted body.

"Great," said Geoff softly. "Just look at what they're doing now." He pointed with the mouth of his water bottle and let his head flop back against the rough bark. They watched as the tearful Parabat stooped next to the body of the dead terrorist. He took a small knife from his pocket, opened the blade, lifted the dead man's hand and struggled a bit as he sliced off the little finger.

He held the dog tags and the bloody black digit to the heavens and made an oath. "I shall never forget you, my friend, I shall never forget you my enemy," he sobbed and wrapped the grizzly little trophy in a piece of two-by-four cleaning cloth, placing it carefully in his breast pocket along with the dog tags.

Geoff looked away in disgust. "Got a cigarette?" he asked.

"Yep. Still got Zeelie's."

"And I've still got his lighter."

"Let's smoke then."

"Okay," said Geoff and took a long drink before lighting up. "Only when you kill people, huh?" he inquired as he exhaled and inspected the glowing tip.

"Only when I smoke," confirmed Allan.

Geoff exhaled and stifled a cough. He looked about at the insanity of war. He looked at the dead soldiers on both sides. He looked at the boys-turned-killers who desecrated their dead enemy and wondered if he too bordered on insanity.

CHAPTER 30

Brigadier Schalk Lombard paced the operations room with his hands behind his back. His shirt was uncharacteristically creased and it seemed as if his hair had thinned even more, despite being closely cropped. He hesitated at the far end of the room, turned on his heel and paced back slowly, his footfalls muffled by the thick pile of the carpet. He stopped in front of the map of southern Angola, placed his hands on his hips, looked up and sighed deeply. "So," he said quietly as if with remorse, "we still have no iron-clad reason why the communications broke down resulting in the sacrifice of fifteen South Africans and a Puma."

The colonel shifted uncomfortably in his seat. He was incensed by the brigadier's choice of words. "They weren't sacrificed …," he began.

"Don't prescribe to me the choice of word I use to describe this blunder." The brigadier's voice was soft. He turned suddenly and smashed his fist onto the table so hard that the ashtrays lifted clear of the mahogany top. "Of course they were sacrificed! They were murdered because someone fucked up!" He paused and surveyed their shocked faces. No one had ever heard him swear before, let alone see him lose his temper. "It was someone on our fucking side!" He leaned forward over the table on clenched fists, his knuckles white, and looked at each of them in turn. First the colonel, then the two commandants and the adjutant and finally Lieutenant Botha. His face was so terrible that Elsa Botha had to look away.

"Now somewhere between the countdown and H-hour a report or portion of a report seems to have gone missing, a report which you have had under your wing from the beginning." Schalk pointed a damning finger at Elsa. "It was as if they were waiting for us!" His accusing finger pointed to the rest of them in turn. He straightened, placed his hands on his hips and looked down at the floor. "The general is arriving tomorrow. He wants to know what to tell the mothers of our dead boys. He also wants to know where the hell we're supposed to conjure up another Puma." Schalk let his words hang for a moment before continuing, his tone softer now, "*Toe maar*. The damage is done. By all accounts and according to your reports the follow-up was a great success, which lends some credence to the initial phase. So, let us begin preparations for the assault on the south camp at Mulemba and annihilate the bastards." Schalk looked at his watch. "It is late now and you all probably need a shower and some rest. We reconvene here at seven hundred hours tomorrow. Before you go, I want you to be under no illusion as to the magnitude of this operation." He paused. "This is going to be the biggest operation carried out by the SADF since the Second World War. You may go. Lieutenant Botha, stay behind please." The rest of them gathered their clipboards and folders and left the room. All but the adjutant.

Captain Jannie Groenewalt hesitated and took his time about gathering his possessions. How many times had he heard those words 'Lieutenant Botha remain behind'. At first when it had happened he was relieved; relieved to escape the tedium of clerical work, dictation and mundane filing. But as time went on he found himself becoming more and more redundant—reduced to his fundamental role, overseeing discipline. She was first choice for literally every job the brigadier needed doing and he confided much of the strategies of the war with her, mostly after the order groups. They seemed to spend an awful amount of time together, especially after hours. Although there were no set hours in wartime, their time spent alone seemed excessive.

Jannie Groenewalt made a bit of a show of leaving, much to the annoyance of the brigadier.

"*Is daar iets fout, Jannie*? Is there a problem?"

"No. No problem, brigadier," answered Jannie, his nostrils flaring white at the edges. He too, was annoyed. That bitch was stealing his thunder and despite his best attentions she had ignored him from day one. Jannie was building an unhealthy dislike for the attractive lieutenant. He turned and stormed from the room and slammed the door like a belligerent child. The double-leafed meranti door shook on its hinges, causing the latch to slip and it remained slightly ajar.

An uneasy silence pervaded the room, adding to Elsa's anxiety. Surely there was no way he could possibly know anything, she thought, and flinched as the room was plunged into semi-darkness. The brigadier switched off the harsh neon light above the map and turned and stared at her for a few seconds. He frowned, unnerving her and she shifted in her seat.

"How have you been?" he asked softly, taking her by surprise.

"Oh!" she exclaimed and sat up a little. "F … fine. Just fine thank you, " she stammered.

"I should never have let you go. You seemed stressed."

"No. No please don't worry about me. I'm supposed to be a soldier too …"

"That was not something a lady should have to endure …"

"Please Schalk …," she began.

He held up his hand to forestall her. "We have to resolve the issue of the file though," he said suddenly. He pulled up a chair and sat in front of her. Her shoulders seemed to slump and she exhaled slowly. "Jakes Jacobs is adamant that one of the issues he stressed and on more than one occasion was the existence and locality of a new camp," continued the brigadier. "Now, even I remember reading about it in his report."

Elsa sat forward and pulled the file marked 'TOP SECRET' across the table and onto her lap. She opened the file and began paging through the sheaves of papers. She hesitated at one point while she read and then continued her search. All the time Schalk sat dead still and stared at her. At one point he used the instep of his left shoe to remove the right and wriggled his toes. He then removed his left shoe and sat still.

The faint smell of hot leather sparked a memory of her father. As a child she would wait until he had sat down after returning from work. When he had settled into his chair and stretched his legs out she would remove his shoes and take them through to his bedroom. It was a fond childhood memory and Elsa felt a sudden pang of such incredible regret that it threatened to swamp her. She thrust the emotion aside and grunted with anger.

"Yes?" enquired Schalk.

"Here," she snapped and thrust the report towards him. Schalk's eyes narrowed as he took the sheaf of papers and he began to read. Most of the papers in the file were dog-eared with use but somehow one wad of papers seemed neat and square. Schalk did not notice. He was somewhat annoyed with Elsa's abruptness. Bloody women were always moody and they could get away with it because of the very reason they were women. *They should not be allowed in the army*, he thought and continued reading.

"This is exactly as I remember it," said Schalk after a few minutes. He looked up and spoke to Elsa. "Surely this report formed the basis of the method of attack? What did the colonel say at the briefing? What were his words to the leader group?" Schalk's questions seemed rhetorical and he began reading once more.

Elsa remained quiet. She slid forward in her chair slightly and pulled her shoulders back a little. When Schalk looked up again his eyes were immediately drawn to her slightly parted legs. The crotch of her combat pants had rucked up hard and the middle bulged gently on either side of the join. Her breasts thrust hard against the material of the shirt and her erect nipples were visible, even through the stiff pockets. A dark lock of shiny hair had come loose from her usually perfectly groomed hair and hung in her face. A smudge of dirt across her forehead completed the picture. Elsa had discovered Schalk's weakness and she knew how to exploit it to the full. The next question froze on his lips and he looked down at the report. As if it were completely natural he lifted his socked foot and placed it squarely between her legs.

He was no longer reading. In fact he could not even see the words on the pages such was his obsession with her. Elsa thrust her thighs forward gently to meet his foot. Slowly and ever so slightly she began to gyrate. When he looked up again she had unbuttoned her shirt and exposed her beasts. They were shockingly white against the brown uniform. In the gloom of the ops room they seemed iridescent. Her eyes were closed and her lips slightly parted. She slid her hands slowly up her stomach to her breasts and began to massage her own nipples. Schalk uttered a sound as if he were in pain and launched himself across the distance, at the same time sending the report skidding across the polished table, off the edge and onto the floor on the far side, where it lay in an untidy heap.

※

A shaft of dull light fell across the contours of the adjutant's face as he stared in horror through the gap in the door at the back of the man he admired most. Jannie's emotions ran amok. Firstly he was enormously aroused by the sight of the marble-white, shapely lieutenant, naked, legs wide astride and head thrown back. Intense passion twisted her pretty features into a grimace. But he was shocked at the man performing such intimate sexual acts with another woman. Captain Groenewalt's lip lifted in a snarl when he thought of the brigadier's doting wife waiting patiently for him at home. Finally he felt some sort of elation. He had something so damning on the lieutenant that he could ruin her—even *him* if the need arose. Jannie tiptoed down the corridor. *My God,* he thought, as he stood alone in the dimly lit street outside. How quickly could admiration evaporate and manifest itself as disrespect. Jannie shook his head as if to clear it.

※

The gauze door slammed behind Schalk as he walked through the front door and he clenched his teeth in anger. How many times had he asked Ansie to get the bloody gardener to adjust the door? Must he do it himself for God's sake! The house was in total darkness, which added to his irritation. He strode through to the study, flipped the light switch, deposited his briefcase, picked up the pile of mail and shuffled through it. He was loath to enter the lounge, as he knew what he would find there, but he did so anyway. He drew a deep breath and turned on the light. Ansie sat in the high-backed chair with her feet up on the little yellowwood stool. Her hair was dishevelled and greasy, her eyes red and inflamed and the tears slid down her face as she looked up at her husband. He stood for a moment before reluctantly going to her. He stood in front of her and held out his hand.

"Get up, my love," he implored her gently. "Get up so I can hold you and you can tell me what's troubling you. I am here for you." Schalk felt the strength of his love for her well to the surface and he dearly wanted to confess all and beg her forgiveness but the guilt and betrayal and his lust for Elsa drowned his courage and he stood there weak and swamped with guilt. For a brief second he wavered and almost relented. She lifted a trembling hand to meet his, let her feet thud to the floor and Schalk bent and lifted her gently. Her arms remained at her side as he held her and the sobs wracked her body. Schalk had known she was not happy here in Oshakati, but this was excessive.

"You have to tell me what the problem is. I can only help you if you tell me, my love," he paused as the sobs subsided and then pressed his advantage. "I cannot concentrate at work. There is a war going on out there and I am running it. I need you to be strong for me." The mention of the war caused a fresh outburst of sobbing and Schalk paused again. He was uncertain how to continue. "I love you," he whispered at last with such feeling that Ansie lifted her head and looked into his eyes.

"Do you?" she sobbed. "I need to know that. I need to know that you love me with all your heart and nobody else ..." The sobs subsided into an almost inaudible whisper.

"I do. I do, my love. I love you and only you and I want to help you," Schalk was not lying. He did love her. He certainly had no love for Elsa, plenty of uncontrollable lust but no love. Schalk squeezed Ansie closer and lowered his head onto her shoulder and he felt her arms slide up his back. They stood like that for a full minute. Her breath was warm on his neck and she craned forward suddenly and took his earlobe gently between her teeth. Her hands slid down his back, reached his buttocks and she pulled him to her. She pushed her pelvis against him. Incredibly he felt the stirrings of passion flow into his loins. Their lips touched, parted. Schalk was a little incredulous. How often had he come straight from a wild sexual encounter with Elsa only to have Ansie attack him and perform some of the most desperate and lewd sex he'd ever encountered from her? It must be that hormone or pheromone or whatever the boys had spoken about, he decided vaguely. The hand that had found its way into his trousers and slid gently up and down his stiff member disturbed his thoughts. For the first time in many years Schalk lifted his wife and effortlessly carried her through to the bedroom.

Once again their lovemaking was desperate and intense and afterwards they lay apart in the darkness. Schalk lay on his back and listened to Ansie as her heavy breathing subsided. To his dismay she sighed deeply and began sobbing once more. He rolled over, switched on his bedside lamp, rolled back to her and caressed her hair. She had curled up in the foetal position and the tears ran down her face onto the pillow. He leant forward, pulled the sheet over her, gently brushed the hair away from her ear and whispered to her, "Now you have to tell me. We can't go on like this. You seem to be bearing some terrible burden …"

She whipped her head around and stared at him. "I am! I am!" she cried. "It's those poor boys …," and she dissolved into a fit of tears.

"What boys?" inquired Schalk as he lifted himself onto his elbow. His concern for her was all-consuming and he slid up as close as he could, trying to comfort her with his bulk.

"All those young men killed in that Puma …"

"Oh! My darling!" Schalk felt relief surge through his being. Was that all it was? Good Lord! He could cope with that. "My darling, darling wife. You can't hold yourself responsible for that in any way whatsoever. Shall I tell you …?"

"No!" she rasped and then quietly, "No." She hesitated and in a shaky voice said, "Maybe—I—did—have—something—to do—with it …"

Schalk stiffened. "How … I mean, what could you possibly do …?" He launched himself from the bed and strode through to the bathroom where he wrapped a towel around his midriff. He heard her call after him.

"Don't leave me! Please come back, Schalk! I can't bear it!"

"I'm here," he said and he strolled back into the bedroom. The bed dipped under his weight. "You had better explain."

"I might have said something to … to Victor, I … I'm not sure."

"Victor?" said Schalk uncomprehendingly, then frowned. "Victor, the gardener?" Ansie nodded slowly. "What about Victor?" he asked, his voice betraying his growing concern.

"I might have told him what you told me."

"About what?" demanded Schalk. He was becoming nervous and his patience waned.

Ansie breathed in deeply. "About the attack …"

"You might have or you did?" asked Schalk. He felt the blood drain from his face and his ears burned.

Ansie sat up, leant back on her arms and glared at Schalk. "I told him exactly what you told me. The time and place of the attack. I told him in a sort of roundabout way but he would have had to have been retarded not to have understood what I was going on about." Her voice had taken on a sort of dull monotone as she continued, "He and I have become quite good friends you know. We speak of many things." She sighed and stared at the wall. "He recognised when I was so depressed and he comforted me. He said we shouldn't be in his country ...," she hesitated. "He's not wrong you know. We don't belong here and ... maybe none of this would have happened if we never came here in the first place ..." Ansie looked back at Schalk. His mouth was open and there were beads of sweat on his brow. There was a long silence and Schalk dropped his eyes and shook his head.

He looked at her. "Why?" he whispered. "Just tell me why."

"Oh," she shrugged and continued in the same flat voice, "I needed to get back at you for fucking that whore of yours ..."

Schalk jerked upright. He was shocked to the very core. Firstly he was shocked at her intuitiveness and secondly he was shocked at her language. She was a devout Christian, a faithful, dutiful wife. Schalk had no idea that she even knew such language. "You don't believe ...," he began.

Ansie carried on in the same tone, interrupting him for the first time ever. It was as if she had not heard him. "It's quite ironic you know. It might even serve to heighten your libido in some sick way to know there's some of her in me now. You came straight from her, her juices all over you and you plunged them into me. I don't really care though. I've obviously failed you so you can fuck whoever you want, I suppose."

Schalk was horrified "Ansie ...," he tried.

She shook her head and stared at the wall, her bottom lip quivering. Her owl-eyed, flat expression remained unaltered and the tears welled up, before sliding down her face once more. "I was just trying to get back at you, you know. I wanted you to fail and perhaps we would be sent back to Potchefstroom and everything would be alright again." Ansie paused for a minute as if to control herself before continuing. "Instead, because of me, all those men were killed ..." She slid down, lowered her head on the pillow and let her misery flow. "I don't know if I can live with that on my conscience. I don't know if I can live with myself ... any more."

Schalk rose slowly from the bed and stood for a moment with his head in his hands. He turned away from his wife and, like the living dead, went through to the bathroom. There he showered for a long time before changing into a freshly ironed and starched short-sleeved uniform. He went through to the study and spent the rest of the night contemplating his crumbling life. As the first shapes of the outside world loomed through the darkness in the pre-dawn, Schalk telephoned his adjutant.

"Ja," answered a sleepy, irritable voice.

"Captain Groenewalt?"

"Yes brigadier." His tone changed dramatically as the captain recognised the voice.

"Jannie. Listen, sorry to call so early but this a matter of national security."

"Not at all brigadier. How can I help?" The adjutant was eager. Very eager. The brigadier hardly ever asked anything of him. He always asked *her*.

"You know that gardener who works for all and sundry around Oshakati?"

"The one called Victor, brigadier?"

"Ja, that's him."

"What about him, brigadier?"

"Have the man arrested as soon as he enters the gate this morning. He's a bloody spy!"

"Of course brigadier. I'll go there and oversee it myself."

"Good! That's what I like to hear."

"Excuse me brigadier, would it be remiss of me to ask how you acquired this intelligence?"

"Of course not. I'm rather proud to tell you that my wife has suspected him for some time. She presented herself as a sympathiser and the other day she pretended to conspire with him." Schalk's voice seemed to gloat. "Well, he spoke himself into a corner and mentioned things …" Schalk suddenly realised that if he said any more it could point fingers at his very office. "Look, we'll discuss the details later. Just arrest him and bring him in for questioning."

"Of course, brigadier."

By the time Schalk arrived at the holding cells Victor was an unrecognisable, pulpy mess. He lay naked on the floor, his genitals swollen from the shock treatment, his eyes swollen and closed. Thick welts ran like corrugations along his back, his lips were cut and teeth were missing. A deep gash in his head bled profusely as he lay there, defiantly silent. His interrogators stood to one side, their fatigues bathed in sweat. The captain stood in the opposite corner. He nodded at the sergeant as the brigadier entered while he and his colleague left the room.

"Okay, what does he say, Jannie?"

"Well … actually nothing so far brigadier …"

Victor groaned and hefted himself into a sitting position against the wall and the two men looked at him.

"This is the brigadier, kaffir. You had better tell him all you know." The adjutant kicked Victor on the foot. With concerted effort, Victor opened one of his grossly swollen eyes and peered at the brigadier.

Since his capture, Victor had guessed the inevitable and had endured the brutal torture for this moment. "I know the brigadier," he began. He spat a lump of saliva and blood from his grossly swollen lips. "The brigadier knows me. I'm not the traitor; I'm merely a messenger. I carry information to Swapo." Victor straightened painfully and licked his lips. "But I receive the information from his wife, Ansie," Victor pointed an accusing finger at the brigadier.

The fact that he had used her first name seemed to lend massive credibility to his story and the adjutant stared at his commanding officer. Schalk stood for a moment. Suddenly and deliberately he removed the issue 9mm parabellum from its canvas holster. Victor smiled up at him defiantly as Schalk shot him twice in the chest.

The shots rang loudly in the confined space and Schalk looked at his shocked adjutant. "He was working for us and giving information to the enemy. By law and by definition that makes him a traitor. The penalty for that is death. I have merely short-circuited the lengthy process of prosecution and saved the taxpayers some money. Please see to the removal of the body." Schalk holstered his pistol and strode from the room.

Jannie Groenewalt stared at the door long after the brigadier had left. *First an adulterer and now a murderer*, he thought. *The man is full of surprises.* He sighed and shook his head. He looked down at the awkwardly twisted body lying in the pool of blood on the concrete floor. Jannie felt nothing for Victor but he did feel cheated. Cheated by his very role model. His feeling of disrespect seemed to crystallise into something far stronger—loathing perhaps?

As for Victor, he had finally realised his dream. He had died for the cause and had thus become a hero. A martyr. He had risen in status, probably even above his brother.

CHAPTER 31

Geoff sat up in anticipation as they entered Tsumeb and the convoy slowed. He looked ahead, saw the road he wanted and pointed it out to the driver. They slowed to a walking pace and Geoff jumped from the vehicle. He waited as the convoy swept past then crossed and trotted to the police station, all the time smiling to himself.

"Hi, I'm looking for Sergeant Brits please."

"Wait sir," said the desk constable. "I will see if he's here."

Geoff was delighted with his ingenuity. Instead of hoping to catch a lift down the road to Gabi's farm where there was maybe one car per hour perhaps, he need only ask Carel Brits for a lift. After all the man was besotted with Valerie and surely he would grab any excuse to see her.

"Ja!" A voice boomed and the big sergeant breezed into the charge office. *"Wie soek my?"* He looked at Geoff and his eyes widened in recognition. "Shit! It's you! Hello man, how are you?"

"Hello sarge. I'm fine thanks," Geoff beamed at such a warm welcome.

"Wait, don't tell me," the sergeant squeezed his eyes tightly shut, then looked up and smiled, "Kent. Corporal Geoff, hey?"

"That's it."

"So! What brings you to this Godforsaken hole, hey?"

"When I last saw you, you loved this town. What happened in half a season?"

"Long bleddy story ..."

"Tell you what," said Geoff. "Let me take you for a beer and you can tell me about it. After that maybe you could give me a lift to Gabi's place?"

"Ah! So that's it hey," said Carel grinning. "Ja, she talked about you a lot, but she never heard from you," his grin fading. "That made her sad I think, but she's been seeing someone. I cannot be sure though because I too have not been there for a time. I only see them in town sometimes." Geoff froze as the information penetrated his euphoria. He was speechless. His world was falling apart around him and he felt drained. He leant against the counter and put his head in his hands. Carel peered at him with some concern. "Are you alright, boet?" Geoff looked at Carel, opened his mouth and closed it again, shook his head and allowed it to sink back into his hands. "What is it, *kêrel*?"

Geoff remained like that for some time until he felt Carel's big hand on his shoulder. He looked up. "We were in the bush for a long stint," he croaked and cleared his throat, "I never had a chance to write …"

"Oh! So you do like her then?"

"Yes! No, its more than 'like'—I … I think I love her."

"That's too bad hey."

"Are you sure …?" Geoff hesitated, "are you sure you saw her with someone?"

"Ja, but …"

"I'm such a bloody fool to think a goddess like her would even give someone like me the time of day. God! I actually feel embarrassed now."

"Let's go for that beer …" began Carel.

Geoff interrupted, "I don't feel like it anymore …"

"Yes you do. Come with me." He turned and strode out into the bright sunlight. Geoff gathered his kitbag, slung his rifle over his shoulder and followed, reluctantly.

It was a typically South African men's bar. No women allowed. The rule was only broken when ladies of ill repute were admitted—for obvious reasons. A well-used dartboard hung in the corner with the last set of figures for the game of 501 still chalked up. A badly framed photograph of André Stoop scoring a try for South West Africa against Transvaal hung behind the counter and the bar stools reminded Geoff of his school science lab. The smell of stale beer and cigarette smoke invaded Geoff's nostrils as he sat. The late afternoon sun streamed through the cheap opaque glass set in thick rustic timber. There were only two other men in the bar and the smoke from their cigarettes drifted up lazily through the sunlight—it was still too early for the regulars. The other men were obviously farmers and Carel smiled, greeted them and sat. "Two Castles," he ordered without asking Geoff his preference. Everyone drank Castle.

"Aren't you on duty?"

"Why do you ask?"

"You're still wearing your uniform."

"So are you."

"Yeah, but I'm off duty."

"In that case, then so am I. Cheers!" said Carel and drank half the glass of beer in three gulps.

"Cheers," said Geoff flatly and followed suit.

"I know exactly how you feel," said Carel.

"Oh," said Geoff cynically, "how's that?"

"Well, Valerie is seeing someone else too. Just recently some bloke with a haircut like yours moved in—a big bloke, about like you, maybe bigger. I went to see her a couple of days ago and there was this bloke, obviously army, familiar face too. I wanted to take his head off. I tell you he wasn't scared. He had murderous eyes. The type of bloke, who goes to the border, gets into one fire fight too many and loses respect for life and a bit of his mind. Anyway, that's when Val told me, 'But you and I are good friends, just good friends,' is what she said." Carel shook his head and downed his beer. The two men were quiet now, wallowing in their misery.

"Two beers please barman … in fact make it four," said Geoff.

"Ah! So! You feel like getting drunk?" asked Carel and he smiled without humour.

"Yeah, I might as well stay here tonight, hit the road back to Ondangwa tomorrow and see if I can still get a flight. After all I've still got six days' leave left," he said sarcastically.

"Barman! Just bring the two, don't open four."

"Don't you want to get drunk?" asked Geoff and he placed a bank note on the counter.

"I do, but later. We must finish these and then I must take you to see Gabi. You don't want to reek of booze when you arrive," said Carel with renewed vigour.

"But you said she was seeing someone and …"

"Ja, but maybe he is just a friend like I was to Valerie. Everyone thought we were seeing each other; meantime we were 'just friends'. You have to find out for yourself. You have to be sure. You can't take my word …"

"Do you really think so?" Maybe there was a bit of hope after all. His spirits soared and Carel smiled.

"Ja. You have to find out. You can't just let it alone. But …!" he said sternly, "you must also get ready for the worst. If, like Valerie, she does not want you, you must walk away like a man."

Even though they chatted above the noise of the Land Rover, with every kilometre Geoff's hope began to wane. Then he thought of Gabi's beautiful face and he decided that he wanted to see her. He had to see her one last time even if it was just a goodbye. They turned through the gate, the tyres hammered across the cattle grid and they drove up towards the old farmhouse. Geoff saw the ruins had all but been razed and a gang of sweaty workers, bare to the waist, toiled with pick and shovel to clear the last of it. They drove past the workers and the island with its palm tree. Then past the old carports.

They were almost past the cowshed at the back when Geoff grabbed Carel's arm. "Stop! Stop! Stop!" Carel hit the brakes and the Land Rover ground to a halt.

"What is it?" he asked alarmed.

"That horse," Geoff pointed to a magnificent animal tethered to a ring at the corner of the shed. "It's Pegasus. It's hers. She must be here."

"Okay, go and see," said Carel. "Must I wait for you?"

Geoff spun around and glared at Carel. "Of course! If she tells me to beat it, I need a lift, don't I?"

"Only joking," said Carel and smiled broadly. He was as anxious as Geoff. He wanted this to work more than ever. Maybe their success would make up for his disappointing failure with Valerie. "Go to her, man!"

Geoff held up his hands and grimaced. "Stop shouting, man," he said softly.

"Why? Don't you want her to hear?" he said vociferously and laughed. Geoff shook his head and turned back to the barn. He had to watch his step as he walked over the rough ground towards the entrance and looked up as he neared the dilapidated doors.

Gabi stood there riveted, her face an absolute study of surprise. Geoff gaped at her. Instead of her usual takkies she wore a pair of hiking boots with thick red socks rolled down over her neat, slim ankles. Her long legs disappeared up into a pair of high khaki shorts. She wore a dark blue shirt, which was tied in a knot at her belly. It was far too big for her and looked very much like navy issue. Her blond hair was tied back in her usual ponytail and a loose lock floated across her face. She held her arms wide of her body, fingers spread, as they were filthy. Slowly she lifted her arm and attempted to push the loose hair behind her ear with the back of her hand and succeeded only in leaving a brown smear across her cheek.

"Hello," said Geoff shyly, as he pulled the bush hat off his head. He looked back at Carel who beamed at him from the driver's seat. He waved Geoff forward. Geoff turned back to her. "I hope you don't mind me pitching up like this, I …"

She lifted her arms slowly. They were bronze and finely muscled. Geoff began to walk towards her and she flew at him. They collided with a thump and she squeezed hard. "What—took—you—so—long?" she asked with her cheek pressed hard against the muscle of his chest. Her voice was a throaty whisper. "God, how I've missed you. Where have you been?" She looked up at him and began to cry. He lowered his head to hers and their lips met. He tasted the salt of her tears and the hot sweetness of her tongue and they clung to each other. Gabi pulled away at last and looked up at him. "You are so beautiful. God, how I love you," she said with such sincerity and conviction that Geoff felt a bolt go through his body, followed by the sting of tears.

Tenderly he held her face in his hands and gazed into the depths of her eyes. "I thought I'd lost you," he whispered. Gabi lifted her hands and hung them on his forearms and suddenly she noticed the filth on her fingers.

"Oh no!" she exclaimed. "Look at my hands! Oh shit! Look how dirty they are!" She backed away from him and wiped them on the back of her khaki shorts.

"I don't care about that! Come back to me!" exclaimed Geoff grinning. He could not stop himself. Once again they collided. She threw her arm around his neck and he let his hands slide down her back and their lips met again. At last they broke away, breathless.

"Come up to the cottage and have a beer. You must be thirsty—and hungry."

"Can Carel come too?" asked Geoff pointing his thumb over his shoulder.

"Carel?" asked Gabi, "Carel Brits?" She frowned in confusion.

"Yes," said Geoff and he turned to point at the Land Rover. His rifle leant against the tree and his kitbag lay next to it but there was no sign of the Land Rover. Geoff began to laugh.

"What's so funny? What's Carel got to do with this?"

"Didn't you see? He dropped me here."

"No! ... that's spooky. I never heard anyone. I walked out of the shed and saw you." She dropped her head and blushed. "I thought you were a ghost," she mumbled.

"I beg you pardon?" said Geoff, "what did you say?"

She looked up at him. "I thought you were a ghost. You were gone for so long I thought ...," she said and then she was crying again. They embraced and Geoff held her body to his. It felt so right.

"Where's Sven?" asked Geoff after a while.

She looked up at him and smiled. "He's at the cottage."

"Let's go and see him."

Geoff gathered his rifle and kitbag and vaulted onto Pegasus's bare back while Gabi loosed the rein. The mare danced sideways and shied a little at the sudden unfamiliar weight and smell as Gabi spoke gently to her. Gabi stroked the mare's face and edged closer to Geoff, stood on his boot and he lifted her easily. They walked Pegasus sedately to the cottage while Geoff held her tightly to him. She leant back against him and gazed into his face as they chatted easily.

"Geoff! Geoff!" Sven rushed from the side of the cottage. His face shone with delight. Geoff flipped his leg over the horse's rump and slid to the ground on the wrong side, sat on his haunches, arms outstretched and prepared to meet the avalanche. Sven's hair flowed back with the speed of his run; his eyes were his mother's—big blue sapphires. His little legs pumped as hard as they could. As the avalanche neared its destination, it began to falter and slow until it came to a full stop a few paces away from Geoff. Sven held out the toy motorcar. "How do you like my Batman car?" he said shyly.

"I think it's wonderful. The best I've ever seen."

"You can have it if you like," said Sven and stared at Geoff with big blue eyes.

"Thank you," said Geoff and took the car. Sven stood with his hands behind his back and looked at the ground. Geoff scrutinised the car, turned it over, shook his head and handed it back to Sven. "It's far too good for a soldier like me. I think it takes a special boy who loves Batmobiles to look after it, so maybe you should have it."

"Okay," said Sven softly and took the car back. "Did you come to visit my mom?"

"Yes … and you."

"Are you going to stay with us?"

Geoff turned and looked up at Gabi, "Only if your mommy says yes."

"Can he, mommy?" Sven jumped up and down, his face pleading.

Gabi nodded, "Of course he can."

"Oh goody!" shouted Sven as he flew into Geoff's arms. Geoff stood up quickly and hoisted the boy into the sky. Sven squealed with delight and Geoff caught him and hugged him.

"Are you going to stay forever?"

"No, my boy, only for a few days."

"But why?"

"I have to go back to the army."

"But why?"

"Because there are still some baddies out there," Geoff pointed to the far horizons.

"Is that man who killed my daddy and my sister out there?"

Geoff hesitated. What did he tell the boy? "He's not coming back, Sven."

Sven looked at Geoff and then at Geoff's rifle. "Can I carry your gun?"

"I tell you what, let's go inside and when we're sitting down I'll show it to you. How's that?"

"No. I want to carry it," he said petulantly.

"That's enough, Sven. Come, let's go get you into a bath. While I run it, will you get Geoff a beer, please?" The boy darted inside and Gabi handed Pegasus over to the groom who had politely waited out of earshot. Arm in arm they followed Sven into the cottage. Geoff placed his rifle in the corner behind the door and dropped his kitbag next to the wall.

"The first thing I have to do is wash my hands," said Gabi blushing.

"Are you embarrassed?"

"Well, I've been cleaning out the milking pens and digging among the mushrooms—you know, mud and dung and now you've got some on you."

"That's okay."

"But it's also in your hair …"

Geoff felt the back of his head. "Fine, so I'll just have a quick shower, if that's okay with you?"

"Of course! Bring your bag and let's go," she said and lead the way down the short passage. Geoff grabbed his kitbag and followed Gabi, his eyes watching intently the sway of her hips, the way she walked and the way her ponytail bounced from side to side with each stride. She suddenly stopped at the entrance to the spare room and stood aside to let him in. He looked up guiltily. She'd caught him red-handed, gaping at her. They both blushed.

"I'm sorry," said Geoff sheepishly. "I can't help it though. You are the most beautiful being I have ever seen."

"Come here," she commanded. She grabbed the lapels of his shirt and pulled him to her. They kissed with controlled passion. The shyness between them slowly evaporated and the kiss became more urgent. Their lips pushed tightly together and their tongues explored. Arms slid around and hands drew their bodies closer still.

"Geoff!" The shout reverberated off the passage walls. "Here's your beer!" Sven charged down the passage with the bottle held tightly in both hands. Geoff and Gabi broke away quickly, both of them panting as if they had run a marathon.

"Thanks little buddy," Geoff could see the liquid in the bottle had been well and truly shaken. "Put it in the lounge and after I've finished my shower I will really enjoy it." Sven bolted back down the passage.

"I hope that beer doesn't explode when you open it," laughed Gabi. "You'll find a towel in the cupboard. I'll see you in a mo."

Geoff tossed his kitbag onto the bed and held out his hand. His fingers trembled as if he had a fever. For a moment he wasn't sure if it was the passion or the horror of the past few weeks. *My God*, he thought, *she is perfect*. Geoff stripped down, wrapped the towel around his waist and walked through to the bathroom.

Although summer was fast approaching, the nights were cool and the mornings cold. Geoff donned a tracksuit, combed his short hair through with his fingers and strode to the lounge. The room was cosy and a fire crackled in the steel grid of the fireplace, encouraging figures of orange light to dance about the room. The rich, earthy smell of bushveld wood filled his nostrils. It was a familiar, comforting smell, a smell of Africa.

The fireplace was surrounded by a meranti architrave, supporting a wide mantelpiece of the same beautiful timber. He automatically moved over to the fire and to the pictures on the mantelpiece. He lifted the heavy, ornate silver frame and studied the group of smiling people. He recognised Gabi straight away. Her hands rested gently on the heads of the twins. Geoff studied the girl—so pretty, a typical little girl. She was a miniature replica of her mother but with her hair tightly curled and held off her face with an Alice band. Her dress was smocked in a clever and intricate design, obviously made with love. A hairy hand supported Gabi and a tall, dark-haired man stood behind them. His eyes were piercing blue. Geoff did not realise that those eyes were almost his, but the black hair, dark complexion and sulky mouth made up the man that must have been her husband.

Next to him stood two elderly people who smiled so happily that Geoff grinned. The old man was bandy—*he could never have caught a pig with those legs*, thought Geoff. The old man wore a traditional set of German lederhosen. The old lady next to him was short and stocky and held him as if they were newlyweds. Geoff stared at the picture a moment longer and suddenly he was aware of someone standing close by. He had not heard Gabi approach on the thick pile of the carpet. She stood off to one side, smiling bravely. Had it not been for her sad expression, Geoff might not have been able to stop his jaw from dropping open. She wore a white towel tucked in up under her armpits, and that was all. The towel was not too wide either and only just covered her upper thighs.

"That was my family," she said softly. "It was taken on their third birthday. We all got dressed up …"

"How long ago was this?" Despite the delicate moment he still needed a distraction. Never before had he been so physically attracted to a woman and he turned to the fire.

"Only a year ago … that picture was here when you last stayed …"

"I remember seeing it but I never took any notice …," said Geoff as he picked up the oddly shaped clay ox next to it and held it up. "Sven?" he asked and she nodded. Geoff replaced it carefully and glanced at the other trinkets on the mantelpiece. A large, wooden-framed clock took centre stage and ticked loudly enough to be heard above the low drum of the flames. Geoff turned to Gabi. The stark whiteness of the towel against her golden skin enhanced her legs and slender frame, her head supported on such a graceful neck, which flowed into square, defined shoulders. Geoff saw that she too was studying him intently. Their eyes met and seemed to burn through the surface and bare their very souls. The fire crackled gently and the clock ticked four times before Gabi spoke.

"I … um, would you please look after Sven while I shower?"

"Sure."

She smiled at him. "After that we'll grill some steaks. I thought of a braai but it may be too cold so we'll just cook inside."

"Sounds great. Um, where is Sven."

"In his room. I'll send him through." Gabi turned and strode down the passage. Halfway she turned quickly and called, "How about baked potatoes?" The towel began to slip and she squealed, caught it with her arm at breast level and darted around the corner. Her head reappeared, "So …?"

"Perfect!" Geoff wasn't quite sure what she meant by that but found the saliva pouring into his mouth and realised that he had not eaten all day. Suddenly the thought of food checked his emotions and he managed to quell his burning desires. As the smiling face disappeared, Geoff took two big steps and grabbed the bottle of beer. It had left a ring of moisture on the coffee table and he wiped it with his sleeve. He looked about for a bottle opener and found none in the immediate vicinity, so he lifted the bottle to his mouth and cracked the top off with his teeth. He spat the mangled top into his hand, tilted the bottle back and downed the contents. Tears filled his eyes as the beer bubbled down his throat. He tore the bottle from his lips, looked down and Sven stood in front of him staring up in awe.

"You opened that with your teeth!" he exclaimed. "I saw!"

"If you take this to the kitchen and bring me another, I'll show you again," said Geoff offering Sven the empty bottle.

"Okay!" shouted the little boy. He grabbed the empty but Geoff held on.

"Whoa! No one runs with glass bottles, full or empty. Walk through to the kitchen and throw this away, then walk back with a full one, okay," admonished Geoff. Sven returned with a full, icy cold Castle as Geoff slumped in the corner of the large couch.

The boy watched in wonder as Geoff popped the top off once more. "Wow! You must be the strongest man in the world."

"Maybe, but you must not try this. It'll break your teeth, see."

"Okay Geoff," he said with a serious little frown on his brow. "Can we look at your gun?"

"Alright, I'll get it." Geoff hefted himself out of the deep couch and took a big mouthful of beer—the picture of Gabi standing there half-naked still dominated his thoughts, although hunger and Sven had done their share to distract him. He recovered the rifle from the corner at the front door, pulled off the magazine, cocked the rifle twice and scrutinised the breech. It shone back empty.

Geoff sat down. "Right, this is the cocking handle and when you pull it back like this …," Geoff went through the drills of the rifle. Man and boy sat side by side immersed in their study of rifle and bullet when Gabi walked in. She wore a pair of jeans, her white takkies and a huge woollen jersey, the V of which exposed a little cleavage. Her face was different somehow, more strikingly beautiful than usual and Geoff realised that for the first time she wore make-up.

She wore very little but enough to enhance her features. Eyeliner with mascara on her lashes was probably the most obvious but the hint of blue eyeshadow and the rouge on her cheeks exaggerated the blueness of her eyes. She wore a pink lipstick that hardly changed the colour of her lips but they seemed fuller. Her hair was still damp and hung loosely on her shoulders and down her back. Her nostrils flared as she noticed the topic of conversation. She was about to comment and Geoff shook his head. Gabi strode through to the kitchen without saying a word.

"Can I hold it now Geoff?"

"Yep, but stand here like this and I'll hand it to you. That's it!"

"Wow! It's so heavy!"

"When you grow up a bit and become stronger you'll find it easy to carry," Geoff smiled down at the wide-eyed lad who searched desperately for more questions as he sensed that the attention so lavishly dealt was about to refocus.

"But … but …"

"Come on big fella. Let's go and help your mom." Sven's face crumbled with disappointment, but he bravely clambered off Geoff's lap and strolled through to the kitchen.

Gabi had the steaks laid out on the breadboard and she pulled open the oven to check the potatoes. The steaks were massively thick with a rind of white fat and covered the area of two dinner plates. Well marbled, rich red and bloody, Geoff swallowed at the sight.

"I've made a salad too. Will that be enough or should I open a can of baked beans?" asked Gabi, her face slightly flushed from the oven.

"I could eat a horse between two mattresses but judging by the size of those rumps, I think there's enough for an army."

Sven cackled like a woodhoopoe. "A horse between two mattresses," he echoed, and they all laughed, more at the boy's contagious cheer than the witticism.

"How about a bottle of wine?" asked Gabi and Geoff nodded eagerly. "You know where it is, would you mind selecting a bottle?"

"Come on Sven; let's see what's on offer."

"Do you even grow the mushrooms?" asked Geoff and stuffed another forkful of salad into his mouth

She laughed contentedly. "That's what I was doing when you arrived this afternoon."

Sven managed the last mouthful of meat and was still chewing when his eyelids slid closed and he began to slump sideways in his chair. Gabi caught him and lifted him.

"Excuse me," she whispered and left the room. When she returned Geoff had refilled the glasses and was busy wiping up the last of the blood on his plate with a forkful of potato.

"That's the best steak I've ever eaten," he said as he wiped the corners of his mouth with his serviette.

Gabi blushed and giggled. "Would you like some dessert?"

"No thanks. Let's take the wine and enjoy your wonderful fire."

Geoff stretched out on the thick carpet, propped himself on his elbow while the flames danced behind him. He held up his glass.

"To friendship, happy days and big skies," he said theatrically and Gabi laughed. They drank and the firelight burned crimson and blood red in their wine.

"How long can you stay?" she asked suddenly.

"About six days ... if you'll have me."

"Of course, I can do with some cheap labour around here." They looked at each other, smiled and simultaneously dropped their eyes. Alone at last and the shyness was upon them. "How were things ... I mean what did you ... what happened between ...? I'm not sure what questions to ask a soldier ..."

"Three against a thousand! We certainly took those three out," said Geoff and Gabi smiled. Geoff's smile faded and slowly became a frown.

"Was it bad?"

Geoff didn't know what to say. One did not talk about these things in polite company. He tried a new tack. "You shouldn't get too fussed about Sven handling rifles," he said politely. "I know he's far too young now and all it might be is a boyhood fascination but if his father were alive, I'll bet Sven would grow up with dozens of rifles ..." Geoff smiled and Gabi's cheeks transformed to an angry sanguine.

"Those things ...," she pointed at Geoff's rifle leaning against the wall, "blew my family to pieces and are precisely the reason Sven has no father today."

"The cowards who pulled the trigger blew your family away, not the weapons," said Geoff defensively.

"I hate them and wish you would put yours in the safe."

"It's the tool of my trade. I feel naked without it."

"I hate the tool of your trade," she whispered fiercely.

"I never asked for the trade in the first place. I was obliged to do so by the powers that be in my country. That does not necessarily mean that I enjoy it, but that weapon has saved my life on so many occasions that the cat with nine lives has long been extinguished. These days I live by the grace of God."

Gabi saw the look on his face and was at once remorseful. He looked so utterly sad that she supposed if the circumstances had been any different he might have wept. Geoff turned his glass by the stem, stared down into the wine and shook his head once.

Gabi's eyes grew large, her face drained and she covered her mouth with her hand. "My God, Geoff," she whispered softly through her fingers, "I'm so, so sorry."

"No, no, it's my fault. I never seem to say the right thing. There's a friend of mine, Allan. You've heard me speak of Allan?" said Geoff quickly, smiling fondly at the thought of his friend. "Well he always knows what to say in any …"

Gabi's fingers pressed gently against his lips, stopping him in mid-sentence. He turned and looked at her. He had been so engrossed in his attempt to correct his blunder that he hadn't noticed her deliberately place her wine on the table and slide across the carpet to him. She took his wine glass, placed it next to hers, and gently pushed him onto his back. "I suppose we should …," he began but she covered his mouth with hers. Her hands caressed his face and her tongue probed deeply. Geoff was taken by surprise and took a moment to recover.

They kissed like that for a while and slowly Gabi moved her hand away from his face and unzipped his tracksuit top. Her fingers rasped through the thick hairs and searched the mounds of rubbery muscle. They found their mark and stroked his nipple. It hardened immediately and Gabi rolled the hard pip between her thumb and forefinger. She broke away from the kiss and drew her tongue down his neck into the crisp curls of his chest, found the other nipple and nibbled gently. Geoff slid his hand up under her jersey and along the plane of her back. The muscles were hard and taut and he found a deep valley between them. He ran his fingers along her spine up to her neck and realised that she wore no bra. His breathing deepened as she slid her leg over his body. With a strong, gentle arm, Geoff helped her the rest of the way and she lay fully clothed on top of him. He placed his hand below the curve of her bottom and pulled her up until they stared into each other's eyes again. Gabi lifted herself free of his chest and with one arm pulled the jersey over her head. Her hair stood up and crackled with static. The fire highlighted the extremities of her fine hair and formed a halo of gold about her head. Geoff gazed at her beauty and found her breasts close to his face. They were full and proud and very white against her honey-brown skin as he pulled her higher and took a nipple in his mouth. He caressed the other with his calloused fingers. Gabi closed her eyes, her lips parted slightly and her breathing deepened as his other hand explored her naked back.

Geoff's manhood had powerfully and uncontrollably flared up, forcing its way between their clothed bodies. It was too late to do anything about it and if Gabi were going to be offended, well, she would have left already. Instead, he felt her legs part slowly and slide off his thighs. She slid down over him again until their mouths met, moving her hips in small circles about the hardness in his loins. In seconds the tension was unbearable and Geoff sat up suddenly, taking her with him. He stripped off his top and they knelt before each other, naked to the waist. He stooped towards her and they kissed again. Deliberately he slid his hands down her waist, around her hips and unbuttoned her jeans. He slid his hand inside and into her. She was hot and slippery. Their kiss broke and she gasped and pulled him closer. Gabi buried her head in the coarse curls of his chest. Moments later she pulled back slightly, looked up at him and slid her hand into his pants. She gasped again as her hand measured his girth. So thick and hard. She leant against him and they caressed each other. Geoff held her tightly and lowered her to the carpet. She lifted her hips and he gently removed her jeans.

Gabi lay naked in the light of the fire and it was Geoff's turn to exclaim in wonder for she was perfect. She looked up, stretched out her arms and spread herself open to meet him.

She flung her arms around him and cried out as he slid into her. Geoff lay still, concerned that he may have hurt her, but she began to move and gyrate beneath him, her finely muscled legs urging him on. The warmth from the fire and of their bodies caused a fine, oily layer of sweat to appear on Gabi's writhing form. Her wet body glistened in the firelight and Geoff stroked and licked her heaving breasts. The tension built and with it the last vestiges of their reservations withered and died. They reached the limit of their resistance and cried out, locked together. They stayed like that as wave after wave of passion washed over them. Slowly their bodies relaxed and Geoff held her with his arms and knees as they kissed and nuzzled.

"Goodness, Mr Kent," she panted, "where on earth did I find you?" He smiled adoringly at her and began to unwind himself from her. With the speed of an octopus engulfing its prey she wrapped her arms and legs around him, thrust her pelvis against him and held him with her thighs. "Where do you think you're going?" she asked breathlessly. "I've only just found you and you want to leave. Well, you'll just have to wait until I'm good and ready."

Geoff was surprised at her strength and determination and before he had time to subside, he felt the next surge of arousal creep back into his loins. Gabi still held him tightly, deeply within her and she slid her hand into the short hair on the back of his head and pulled him to her. They kissed gently and passionately once again and the tension built until their lips were crushed together and tongues probed deeply, desperately. Geoff moved slightly within her and she uttered a deep throaty sound. She broke away, her breathing erratic and shallow. "Yes," she breathed, "like that." And Geoff obliged with equal determination. A second time they reached the pinnacle of ecstasy together and clung on until it could no longer support them and gradually they floundered back to normality. This time Gabi let him go and they lay close together, somewhat dazed by the intensity and beauty of their love-making. The fire had burned down to glowing embers. Lambent lights flitted about the room and played on their faces as they stared at one another in the silence and contentment of newfound love. Gabi stroked his cheek and Geoff closed his eyes.

He woke with a start. He lifted himself onto his elbow and looked around frantically trying to remember where he was. The room was dark and the light of the last dying embers was restricted to the confines of the fireplace. Geoff looked down at the sleeping form next to him and sweet memory came flooding back. He smiled, gently pushed the blond hair from her face and stroked her smooth skin. Her eyes flickered open and she looked up.

"Hello lover," she whispered, smiled sleepily and stretched. Gabi turned onto her side and curled up closer to the fire. A rash of goose flesh covered her body and Geoff nudged her softly.

"Come," he said quietly, "the fire is dead and it's getting colder."

"Where to?" she complained.

"Nice warm bed."

Gabi looked over her shoulder, "With you, any time."

Geoff helped her up and they made their way to the master bedroom. At the entrance to the spare room, Geoff peeled off and Gabi stopped.

"Where are you going?" she was alarmed.

"This is where you said I must put my kitbag."

"That was this afternoon. This is now." She held out her hand and Geoff took it and smiled to himself in the darkness. Gabi led him to the big bed where she stooped and turned on one of the reading lights. "I'm going to the bathroom."

"I'm with you," he said and followed. Geoff had only been in this part of the cottage once before and then only fleetingly to check the security. He'd been brought up to know that it was impolite to enter the master bedroom uninvited and now he looked around quickly. He felt uncomfortable being there and he washed up and cleaned his teeth in record time. He dashed to the bed and slid under the duvet. He was cold now and unhappy about sleeping in the room where Gabi and Hein had slept before him. This was their sacred territory. What's worse was that the little bear lay on the middle of Gabi's pillow and stared blindly up at the ceiling with its eerie button eyes. He lay curled up, slowly thawing and it suddenly dawned on him that this was not their bedroom. It had been the old folk's room and now all her very own. He must be the first to have shared it with her and he smiled; it was suddenly very important.

Geoff awoke to an incredibly pleasurable feeling and attempted to sit up. Gabi pushed him back and in the blackness of the room, with curtains tightly drawn, he was momentarily bewildered. It took mere seconds for him to realise that she was sliding her hand gently up and down his manhood. Fully awake now Geoff felt himself transform from semi-flaccid to expectant hardness.

"Ah! You're awake," she announced with delight and without letting go, stretched across and flipped on the dim sidelight. Gabi slid back over his body, straddled him and guided him into her. She drew in a deep breath as she took his whole length to the hilt and groaned throatily as she breathed out. She sat like that for a while and smiled down at him. Geoff was so aroused by this unexpected manoeuvre that he had to desperately control the urge to hold her aloft and thrust up and down beneath her. Instead he concentrated on the wonderful feeling and left the work to her. At last Gabi began to move, sliding slowly up and down on him, her hands spread on his chest. Her hair hung in her face and she flipped it out of the way. She gazed at Geoff with that same glazed, mysterious expression he had seen earlier. It aroused him beyond the limit of his control and he groaned and reached for her breasts. They made fast, noisy, passionate love and, soon spent, slumped together, breathing hard.

After the most exciting sleep interruption of his life, Geoff quickly slipped out of bed and began to tiptoe back to his room.

"Where are you going?" asked Gabi, her eyes wide.

"Back to my bed," whispered Geoff conspiratorially. "You know—before Sven walks in and finds us together in your bed …"

Gabi smiled. "There are two things wrong with that … if I may?"

Geoff shrugged, "Sure."

"One," Gabi counted off on her fingers, "its time to get up …" Geoff frowned with surprise, "and two, Sven might as well get used to it because as far as I'm concerned, my bed is your bed."

Geoff stood and stared at her for a few seconds and he broke into a huge grin. "One," he said counting off on his fingers, "I am hugely honoured." He bowed. "And two," he said rising and placing his hands on his hips, "what the hell's the time?"

Gabi laughed delightedly. It was a contagious sound and Geoff smiled. "It's four thirty …"

"Four thirty!" exclaimed Geoff. "This is worse than the army!"

"We have to be out there by first light …"

"First light is at six! It's still winter you know?"

"It's spring now and first light is at five thirty, so move. We've got work to do."

"Oh boy," muttered Geoff, "you get away on holiday and …"

"Hey!" countered Gabi. "You're not on holiday. From now on you earn your keep."

"Oh yes? And how much do you intend paying me?"

"Let's see how hard you work." Gabi said with a wink.

Geoff grinned, raising an eyebrow.

Gabi blushed, startled by her audacity.

Geoff dashed to the shower. "Show me what to do!" he shouted over his shoulder.

The day began with a steaming mug of coffee to counter the last of the winter cold. It soon warmed up though and they started to peel off the layers they had started off with. Soon enough they were down to shorts, takkies and T-shirts. Gabi wore her usual large shirt tied in a knot at her belly. There was such an incredible amount of work to be done and the mounting list of tasks surprised Geoff. He had always wondered why his grandfather rose at such ungodly hours. What the hell did they do all day, he wondered? There was only so much work to be done on a farm and then what? Long ago, Geoff had decided that most farmers were pretty misinformed on time/management studies and spent the whole day working very hard at doing very little. He was learning to the contrary.

The fence needed repairing, in dozens of places—all miles apart from each other. The water troughs needed leak-proofing and most of the valves and cisterns were obsolete, needing constant attention or replacement. Then there was the maintenance of the wind pumps, and all this above constant vigilance of the cattle. The care of the cattle was the most demanding task of all. There were the dip tanks, the feed and the small maize crop, the dairy herd, the vegetable garden, a household to run, labour to pay and feed. Mounds of paperwork piled up in the study and then there was the stress of the final product—selling the cattle. The list seemed endless.

Geoff and Gabi drove out in the Land Cruiser to attend to some of the tasks, taking a few labourers, the fencing gang, the farm mechanic and Jacob, the foreman with them. Hein had previously undertaken all the mechanical repairs himself and now his assistant, hardly more than a tool handler, was the chief mechanic. They dropped the fencing workers at the furthest point of repair, where they off-loaded tools and rolls of thick *bloudraad* and continued on to the dry water trough. It took Geoff minutes to realise that the mechanic was out of his depth. Geoff said nothing and they left him there with his assistant. Lastly they dropped the herders off at the greatest concentration of cattle. Geoff followed Gabi like a shadow as she drove about the farm delegating tasks and making notes of cattle numbers and scrutinising them and discussing their condition with Jacob. Then between eight and nine o'clock they drove back to the cottage for breakfast. By this time Geoff had built up a healthy appetite and was delighted with the aromas emanating from the kitchen. Bacon, eggs, pork sausages, mushrooms, tomato, onions and devilled kidneys.

"Do you always eat like this?" asked Geoff.

"No," smiled Gabi. "I'm paying you in kind."

"Watch out!" he warned. "You may never get rid of me."

"Oh, I hope not," she said and blushed.

The maid had roused Sven, washed him and fed him and he danced around excitedly as they returned. Now he could join his mother—and Geoff!

Driving took up the most time, as the extent of the farm was incredible. Huge tracts of land were necessary to sustain the cattle as the veld was semi-arid and lacked the richness of typical cattle grazing. At times like these Geoff and Gabi chatted amiably and time raced by. Sven stood happily between them to begin with, then on Geoff's lap, then he steered, then he climbed in the back with Jacob and the workers (he knew all their names) and finally he was back between them.

Every now and again the vehicle would startle a steenbok. At the last minute it would dart out of the seemingly flat, open veld and bound away. There were other animals; tiny grey duiker—smallest of all the buck, a few scattered springbok, the nocturnal honey badger, which Gabi pointed out that they were lucky to see, the cute and comical ground squirrels shading themselves with their feathery tails, and finally the prince of all antelope, the magnificent kudu. They startled a pair of males at the covey of tamboti trees near the reservoir. The buck stood riveted for a second, their massive horns reached up three spirals each. They stared, poised on the edge of flight, unsure whether to freeze or escape. As if by silent command they tilted their horns along their backs and cantered off gracefully into the bush.

Geoff was amazed at how much game there was and said so to Gabi. "You know," he began, "if you banned all shooting, at least for a while, they would slowly come back and you could build up quite a reserve. In fact, seeing the size of this farm it could be more like a nature reserve or even a game reserve. What do you think?"

"With Etosha just up the road, I never really thought about it," Gabi replied. "But come to think of it I was quite excited when I saw a couple of eland down in the southeast corner of the farm about three weeks ago."

"Eland too!" exclaimed Geoff. "There, you see it's starting already."

Gabi smiled at his enthusiasm.

The sun reached its zenith and began to wane before Gabi stopped at the crest of a small hill topped by a large flat rock. It was obviously a favourite picnic spot. Sven dashed off down the side to the large bush.

"Please be careful, darling. You know the snake lives there!" his mother shouted.

"I know!" came the muffled response, "I want to see if it's here to show Geoff."

"Okay, but lunch is ready!"

Geoff retrieved the small basket from the Land Cruiser and brought it to where Gabi sat on the rock. Loose locks of hair floated about her face and she smiled up at Geoff. He smiled down at her and his eyes shifted to the tiny figure on her left. The little bear also had its place on the rock and Geoff frowned.

Seeing his expression, Gabi implored, "Please don't." Her smile faded and her bottom lip quivered at his reaction. "It's all I have left of her." Her speech faded to a whisper.

Geoff scratched his temple and looked about. He placed his hands on his hips and stared down at her. "I'm the gormless idiot. I … I'm…," he began and let his head droop. He looked up once more and Gabi held out her hand. Tears brimmed and shone in the sunlight, but her smile was radiant.

"Come to me. You're as wounded as me."

"What? What do you mean …?"

"I can see it in your eyes, you know."

"I … nonsense …"

"Hold out your hand," she said.

Geoff reluctantly obeyed. He spread his fingers and his hand shook. He clenched his fist and placed his hand behind his back. "So? It's your fault, you know. I shake in the presence of such beauty …," he began.

"Now it's my turn to say nonsense."

Geoff knelt and took her in is arms. He held her for a long while and said, "What are we going to do? If you reckon we're so wounded, then what are we going to do?"

Gabi held his face and smiled at him. "This. Just this."

After a few minutes Geoff plunged his hand into the basket and produced a parcel wrapped in greaseproof paper. He opened the fold and peeked in. "Ah!" he exclaimed. "Roast beef and mustard, my favourite." He handed a sandwich to Gabi and called Sven.

The boy darted up the rock, slapped his hands on his pants and eagerly took the bread. He took a huge bite and spoke around the mouthful. "I didn't see it, but …," Gabi pointed at her mouth and shook her head.

Sven nodded and swallowed hard. "I didn't see it but there's a huge …," Sven held out his arms to their full width, "brown house snake that lives there." His eyes were wide and sparkled with excitement. He frowned suddenly, "Hey! There's burny stuff on my bread!"

"Its only mustard, the type you like," said Gabi.

"Have you got some, Geoff?"

"Oh yes. It's my best," he nodded.

Sven took another bite. There were juicy apples, a Coke each and a stick of fresh beef biltong for afterwards. "But you know what Geoff …," began Sven. He looked at his mother, swallowed hard and continued, "The old brown house snake isn't poisonous, so you don't need to worry."

"Well, I'm certainly relieved about that," said Geoff frowning seriously. "Thank goodness you're here!"

They drove back in the mid-afternoon after moving the fencing team and Gabi parked the Land Cruiser.

She called to the maid, "Please ask the groom to bring Pegasus and Carpathia and then take Sven." Even though this was a norm, Sven knew he was to be remanded to the custody of the maid and threw a spectacular tantrum. In a flash Gabi bore him up by his arm and landed a flat hand on his behind, which brought on a flood of tears. She picked him up and looked sternly into his tearful face. "We don't behave like that, do we, especially in front of guests?"

"But I wanna come with," he sobbed pitifully. "I wanna come with you and Geoff."

"You know you can't come yet my angel. You're still too young, but soon," said Gabi. She hugged him and then handed him over to the maid.

"But I always ride with you," he tried.

"Only when we go slowly. Geoff and I are going to gallop—now please stop making such a fuss." The groom brought the horses and they mounted up.

Geoff held his thumb up and winked at Sven. "See you soon little buddy." Sven seemed so small in the maid's arms with his mouth turned down and big tears rolling down his face but he nodded and smiled bravely at Geoff. "That's it, my boy."

They turned and cantered down the drive, trotted and finally walked. "Shame man," said Geoff. "It's hard growing up isn't it?"

"I know, I feel awful."

"Then why not bring him along?"

"Because I want to be alone with you for a while," she said huskily, leaned across and touched his arm. "And because we're going to race!" She shouted and bolted off the drive onto the path opposite the old house. The builders looked up quickly at the sound of her shriek and a few of them commented and smiled at the graceful frontrunner and the large man straggling awkwardly behind. Pegasus accelerated to full gallop and Geoff held on for dear life as Carpathia bolted after them. In no time the wind drew tears that streamed down his face as he leaned forward and urged the horse on. Gabi had taken him by surprise. She had a good lead and partially disappeared over the small ridge ahead, leaving a trail of dust along the path. Her mare was agile and quick but the stallion was a large and powerful animal. Surefooted Carpathia eagerly rose to the challenge and slowly began to haul them in. Geoff waited until he could clearly see Gabi's long blond ponytail flowing out behind her before he shouted.

"If I catch you I'm going to have my wicked way with you!" Gabi looked under her arm and squealed with terror and delight as she saw how close they were. Her feelings were transmitted to Pegasus who began to pull ahead. The horses belted down the path and their hooves drummed on the ground to where it opened onto a wide sandy area. Having space to move, Carpathia relentlessly chased Pegasus and came up on her shiny, sweat-darkened flank. They stayed like that for a while and finally Pegasus began to tire. Carpathia drew level and the horses' heads pumped together as they swept past the reservoir. Geoff urged the stallion on but he began to slow to a canter and finally a trot. Without Geoff using the rein, Carpathia turned and walked back to the reservoir of his own accord. Gabi slid from Pegasus, took the rein and beamed up at Geoff.

"A dead heat I'd say." Her face was flushed with the excitement, her loose hair swept back over her head.

"Oh no, I was just about to pass you when you stopped."

"This is the finish line."

"How was I supposed to know that?"

"You didn't need to; Carpathia knows."

Geoff looked around for another excuse. "You had all the advantages of one, a false start, two, knowledge of the route and, three, the finish. In short, you cheated."

Gabi's mouth dropped open in animated shock. "Geoffrey Kent!" she exclaimed. "You're a bad loser ... anyway, your horse is much faster than mine."

Geoff laughed. "But your horse is Pegasus, he's supposed to fly."

"It is a she and she doesn't fly."

"Pegasus was a he."

"I know," said Gabi modestly, "but when she was born she just looked like a Pegasus.

"Your horse," Geoff shrugged, "you can call her whatever you want." He stretched. "Anyway, that was magic!" he shouted and the smile faded from his lips. "But did you hear what I said to you?" he said menacingly. His face grew hard, his eyes became slits and the muscles in his jaw worked. He walked slowly towards her, his shoulders squared and the muscles in his arms bunched. His bare legs were well defined and taut and he looked massive, powerful and indestructible.

Gabi knew he was superbly fit and her legs grew weak as he closed in on her. She was no match for him in any way and suddenly she was afraid. He was a killer of men. "Geoff?" she said in a weak voice and suddenly realised that they were alone in the middle of nowhere and she hardly knew him. Gabi looked around for means of escape. Both horses drank from the puddle below the reservoir and Geoff was between her and them.

"I said that if I catch you I was going to have my evil way with you." Geoff grabbed her suddenly and began kissing her all over; on her neck and face, her shoulders and arms, down her stomach, over her thigh, firstly down one leg then the other and finally he kissed her ankles. He rocked back on his haunches, looked up at her and took her hands gently in his. Her face was pale, her eyes huge and she panted as if she'd run a mile.

"I think I'm falling in love with you, if I wasn't already in love with you the first time I set eyes upon you," said Geoff with all the tenderness he could muster. Gabi was still speechless and all she could do was pull his head onto her stomach while she struggled with her emotions. She ran her fingers through his hair and held him there. Gabi had passed from extreme fear to surprise and ecstasy and finally an overwhelming love in seconds and now the way he held her and caressed her bare, smooth legs, she felt the heat build up from deep within and she held him tighter.

Gabi was astounded at her arousal. She wanted to step back and slap Geoff as hard as she could. How dare he arouse such fear in her, confess to love her and seconds later induce such feelings of reckless passion? Instead she closed her eyes and held him. They stayed like that and the only sound was the tearing of dry grass as the horses grazed nearby and a light, sibilant wind, which played the tassels of hair across her face.

After a while Geoff lifted his head, looked up at her and smiled. He saw that same mysterious expression on her face that drove him wild and the smile faded. Her eyes were fixed on his and she swallowed and breathed through her mouth. Deliberately he unfastened the knot of her khaki shirt and slid his hands up her flat, hard stomach. She wore a sports bra, which held her breasts firmly. His hands engulfed her breasts and he squeezed gently. He felt the nipples harden under the thick fabric and he took them between his fingers. He kissed her belly and moved down to the slight mound and further still to the softness between her legs. He breathed his hot breath onto her and she moved against him and parted her legs slightly to give him better access. He swirled his tongue around her hardening pea, and sucked gently. He slid two fingers around her eager wetness. She stood like that with her head thrown back, eyes tightly closed, mouth open, legs astride and she held him to her. Gently Geoff drew her shorts down, taking with them her lace panties. He pulled them over her ankles and she removed her takkies. He reached up and slid the shirt off her shoulders and unfastened her bra. Gabi stood naked in the bright sunlight and Geoff stripped off slowly. She watched his every move with the eyes of a predator. Naked and fully aroused he picked her up gently and carried her over to the brick platform below the reservoir. It was waist-height to him and he lowered her. He parted her legs and moved forward, sliding his large manhood into her. She cried out, wrapped her legs around him and held him. Pegasus looked up and whickered at the strange noises, snorted and continued to graze.

Afterwards they lay naked in the hot sun with sweat running in rivulets off them as they caught their breath.

"Shit it's hot, shall we swim?" asked Geoff suddenly.

"What the hell did you just do to me?" asked Gabi. Once again she felt her emotions run. She was not quite sure if she was angry or in heaven. Gabi felt a little vulnerable. She had never felt so wildly aroused before. She wondered how she was going to beat the uncontrollable passion he seemed to allure from her very soul. Right now it made her angry as she felt Geoff could use her as he pleased.

"What we've been doing a lot of lately," he said with uncertainty and smiled. "Why?"

"Because you scared the shit out of me and when I'm well and truly terrified you take advantage and screw me on the bricks." Her cheeks were dark and her face thunderous. She lifted her legs up under her chin, crossed them at the ankle, hiding her womanhood and folded her arms protectively over her knees, hiding her breasts. Geoff was astounded; he had never heard her speak like that before and he stared at her with his mouth slightly agape.

"I'm sorry if I offended you …"

"Well you did you big oaf!" she shouted.

The comment stung and Geoff felt his skin prickle with anger. He jumped off the platform and stood naked in front of her. "You weren't too bloody fussy a few minutes ago," he said softly through his teeth.

"Because I was scared of you!"

"We've been making love as often as we can since last night and it's been the best time of my life and you tell me you are scared of me!" he raised his voice an octave.

"Well, you … you scared me," she whispered and suddenly she was crying.

Geoff stood for a moment, shook his head, stepped forward and held her protectively in his arms. He rocked back and forward until he felt her sobs subside. Then he bent, lifted her chin gently and looked into her red, swollen eyes. "I'm so sorry," he whispered. "I had no idea I was being such an ogre. You see, sometimes I am such a clumsy oaf and you said 'big' so that makes me a big clumsy oaf. Please forgive me."

Gabi closed her eyes tight, squeezed the tears on to her cheeks and nodded.

"I want you to know that I would never hurt a hair on your head," he said as sincerely as he could.

Gabi looked into his eyes and saw the concern and knew he meant it.

"I love you," he whispered.

She sobbed one last time and flung her arm around him. "I'm so confused," she said into his shoulder. "I feel like you came for a platonic visit and I threw myself at you like a … like a *whore*," she whispered the last word. She was quiet for a while as Geoff held her. "It seems every time we touch we make love."

Geoff smiled. "Isn't it great? I feel I could make love to you all day." Gabi looked up at him and frowned. She saw he was serious and flopped her head against his shoulder.

"How about that swim, eh?" he asked cheerfully. "Last one in has to make love to the other."

"Geoffrey!" she exclaimed and laughed. "Do you know how cold that water is? Winter is still hanging about and just because the days are hot …"

With Gabi in his arms Geoff launched himself onto the platform, turned his back to the wall and flipped into the water in one fluid movement. Together they plunged to the depths where the water was coldest and Geoff let her go. He surfaced first and grabbed Gabi as her head burst into the air. Her eyes were wide and loose hair plastered her face.

She gasped breathlessly. "You devil! It's freezing!"

He held her in his arms and the water was up to his neck when he stood on his toes. "Just be still and you'll feel how nice it is," said Geoff. He held her tighter as she struggled in vain to escape.

"Shit, you're incorrigible," she said but felt the first of the warm currents drift past and she stopped struggling. It felt like a warm bath on a winter's evening. "That's wonderful," she said in surprise. The current passed and she snuggled closer to Geoff trying to absorb more of his body heat. "Where's another one?" she asked and shivered.

"Just keep still and the thin layer of water around your body will rise to ambient temperature. It's sort of how the wetsuits work."

"Can't I have a wetsuit now?" asked Gabi and Geoff laughed. Another current drifted past and she relaxed a little. "Ah, that's better." After a while the water felt tolerable around their naked bodies, even pleasant. Gabi hung on Geoff's neck and the rest of their flesh was pushed tightly together, right down to where the instep of her feet pushed against his shins. "I'm beginning to enjoy this, you rogue," she said. They smiled at each other and she wrinkled her nose and rubbed it against his. Their lips met, warm, wet and full and Geoff parted his slightly. Gabi followed and their tongues intertwined. Geoff felt himself flare up again. Gabi's legs melted open and anchored behind him. He slid into her and she gasped and whispered in his ear, "My God, here we go again. I can't get enough of you," she cried, "Oh Geoff, yes, like that!"

Their bodies tingled from the sun, the cold water and the passion as they rode back together. The sun was setting ahead of them and they squinted against the brightness. Soon the colour darkened from dazzling white to burnt orange and finally to ochre red as it melted onto the irregular mass of hills near Tsumeb. They rode into the yard and Sven darted out to meet them.

"Where did you ride to? What took you so long? Mommy, can I have some ice-cream?"

Gabi stared down lovingly at her son. "Of course you can my love ..." Suddenly her hand flew to her mouth, "Oh my ...! The fencing crew and Jacob! I forgot!"

"I have sent the bakkie ma'am."

"And the diesel for the pump?" she quizzed.

"It is full ma'am."

"And ... and the water for the vegetable garden?" She had to think hard of the most important tasks she had intended for the day.

"All done ma'am."

"You're a lifesaver, Elias." Gabi breathed a sigh of relief. "You see what our debauchment has done to my farm," she said to Geoff and slid off the horse.

"It seems to me that all the most pressing issues have been taken care of and the word is debauchery," he said and handed the reins to Elias.

"Huh? Oh, debauchery," she corrected herself. "It's just not good enough." Gabi was angry again.

"But it's great fun, though, don't you think?"

"What?"

"This new way of toiling on the farm. Just think, we fix a drinking trough and make love, install a new cistern and make love, repair the wind pump ..."

"Okay, okay," she laughed. "Do to me as you please, I'll just have to settle for being your harlot."

"I'm your man. But you can't be my harlot because I don't pay you, so I'll have to be your gigolo," he said and beamed at her.

Gabi shook her head and lifted Sven onto her hip. "Let's go and shower."

They trooped through the kitchen and Geoff swallowed as the smell of roast chicken permeated his nostrils. After a relaxing shower and a game of cars with Sven, Geoff carved the crispy bird and the adults ate in silence as the boy held the floor. Later when Gabi returned from reading *The Cat in the Hat* and singing her son a lullaby, they relaxed around the fire with a glass of wine.

"So that chicken is from the farm?" he asked seriously.

"Yes, free-range. I can show you the run tomorrow if you'd like?"

"I would, yes. It's so much bigger than the chickens we get at home," observed Geoff as he sipped his wine. "And all the veggies are homegrown, the potatoes too?"

"Yes. Hein …," she hesitated and her eyes dropped from Geoff's. "Hein wanted us to be self-sufficient. All he needed to buy was the diesel and cattle dip. He'd even started to grow our own feed. We are so lucky with the water here. All the boreholes give us plenty of water. It's all a bit brackish but …"

Geoff slid down in his chair, crossed his legs, put his arm behind his head and sipped his wine. "That's why there's so much to do around here. I'm only just beginning to appreciate it. I so want to help you but I've got some unfinished business I need to attend to first."

"What's that?" she asked doubtfully.

"I have to finish the army. I still have a hundred days to go."

Gabi was silent for a while and she stared into her wine. "Have you seen him or is he really dead?"

Geoff frowned and shook his head. "Hey, I'm only a big oaf. You'll have to help me here."

Gabi stroked his leg and her slender fingers rasped through the thick blond hairs. "Oh stop taking it so personally. We nullified that stupid argument in the freezing water or have you forgotten?"

Geoff smiled at her. "I'll never forget that. In fact I'll never forget today," he said sincerely and he looked at her with naked adoration.

"Thank you," she said, "I won't either." Gabi was quiet again.

"Well …?" Geoff prompted.

"Grootvoet." She only managed the words as a whisper.

"Who said he's dead?"

"Carel."

Geoff sat up, took her hands and squeezed them. "He's not dead. I think I saw him on this last trip."

Her hand flew to her mouth. "Oh God, Geoff! Tell me it's not true!"

"No I won't and Carel shouldn't either. You have to be on your toes until it can be confirmed."

Gabi looked around, her eyes wild. "We can't live with this threat," she lamented in a tremulous voice.

"No wait," he squeezed her hand again. "One thing I can tell you is that the threat is almost negligible. We shot them to pieces in Angola recently and if he was not killed," Geoff stressed the words, "then he's going to be very busy trying to regroup. He won't risk coming here. You have to believe me." Gabi relaxed a little. "More wine?" he asked and she nodded. They chatted around the subject a little longer and lapsed into silence at last.

"Well, I'll just clear up," said Gabi as she stood.

"Hang on; I'll give you a hand."

"No please Geoff, warm up the bed, I won't be long," she said and winked at him. Geoff smiled back and headed for the room. Gabi followed at last and went straight to the bathroom.

She walked into the bedroom and stood next to the bed. Geoff lay on his side breathing deeply and regularly. *Thank goodness,* thought Gabi and smiled. She experienced such an overwhelming feeling of love that she almost woke him. Sanity prevailed and she stared at him for a long while. She slid quietly into bed, snuggled up to him as carefully as possible without disturbing him, turned out the light and fell into an exhausted sleep.

The days were filled with early mornings, laborious toil and aching muscles but there was an ethereal aura between Geoff and Gabi as they engaged the daily tasks and routines. Intermittently, Sven joined them and it was evident for all to see how his love for Geoff had grown. He followed Geoff everywhere and Gabi smiled as she watched the small imitate the big in practically every way. As far as possible Geoff included Sven in all they did about the farm but there were times when Sven needed to go to bed or be left behind, especially when Geoff recognised Gabi's mysterious look. Apart from the mere pleasure of being in each other's company, they needed to touch and hold, hug and kiss—with alarming regularity, just in case one or the other disappeared in a puff of smoke.

Then there was the sex. Geoff's appetite seemed insatiable and incredibly she matched him, often pre-empting him and initiating intense, powerful love-making herself. It worried her at first, as nothing like this had ever happened before, not that she'd had many lovers. In fact that could have been the problem. The only two others had never awoken her passion like Geoff had. Now, a touch, a kiss or even a look would have them throw themselves at each another in a passionate embrace. Gabi contented herself with the fact that it was Geoff's influence over her and therefore she could not be held responsible. With that she ceased to worry about it.

With each day their love drew them closer together and the time passed swiftly, too swiftly for Geoff. On a slightly warmer evening with the promise of summer in the air they sat out on the small veranda, Geoff with beer in hand and Gabi sipping a glass of white wine. Sven rode his bicycle round the vast lawns below the cottage, falling precariously from side to side, saved only by the presence of the training wheels. Each time he did so, Gabi's heart skipped a beat and Geoff pointed with his bottle. "He's coming on in leaps and bounds," he said and laughed. Sven tore down, turned hard around the big tree at the bottom of the lawn next to the security fence and made it by the grace of Lord Penny Farthing or whoever the patron saint of bicycle riders might be. The dogs were an added hazard as they bounded after their personal plaything.

"I can't stand it anymore," said Gabi with her head buried in her hands. She stood and shouted to Sven. "Come on my boy, it's bath time!"

"Chicken," said Geoff.

"I don't want to bath, mama!" shouted Sven.

"Come here right now, Sven!" she shouted and then to Geoff, "I'll deal with you later." Sven arrived reluctantly and she marched him off to a hot bath, which, once there, he could not wait to get into. The dogs sat in front of Geoff with large frowns wrinkling their broad heads as if to ask why he had taken away their very source of entertainment.

"Another beer, love?" Gabi called from somewhere in the cottage.

Geoff held his up and downed the last mouthful. "Please, I'd love one!"

Gabi placed the beer next to him and sat down. "You just want to see him fall off," she accused.

"Nonsense. I love seeing how gutsy he is and how fast he goes. If he falls, he's hardly going to injure himself on this manicured turf, watered by three of your servants."

"Two actually. And what if he hits the tree?"

"Then I promise you he won't hit it again," Geoff laughed.

"Oh you," she said and sipped her wine. They sat for a while, content in each other's company and suddenly Geoff sat up.

"What the hell happened to Valerie, I nearly forgot all about her?" Geoff shook his head. "How could I forget her, she was such a sour puss."

"Oh Geoff, don't judge her. You can't begin to know what she went through."

"I suppose not," said Geoff grudgingly.

"Actually she's changed a whole lot. She has a new boyfriend and they are madly in love …"

"More than us?" asked Geoff with raised eyebrow.

"No, never!" Gabi laughed. "But she's changed for the good."

"Yeah. Carel mentioned something like that." Geoff nodded and took a sip of beer. "Oh well, good for her."

"It's funny that you ask though. I think you call it mental telepath or something …," she blushed and looked at Geoff.

"Mental telepathy."

"Yes. Anyway she's coming for supper" said Gabi, her eyes sparkling with excitement.

"With her boyfriend?"

"Yes, and you know him," she said.

"I do?" exclaimed Geoff, slamming his hand onto his chest with surprise.

"Yes. He is, or was, one of your soldiers. Taller than you, I think. They met while you were here looking after us." Gabi hesitated when she saw his face. "Are you alright?"

Geoff was momentarily speechless. He stared at Gabi, dropped his head and shook it vehemently. He looked up, his face dark. "Is it Dawid?" he croaked.

"Yes. That's it, Dawid Gouws. We escaped from him to Etosha. Why what's wrong?"

"That's exactly it for … for …," Geoff searched for an expletive that carried no foul language, "… for crying in a bucket! We escaped from him says it all! He's a diabolical pain in the butt, he's dangerous and he hates my guts is what's wrong!" Geoff ranted.

"Please calm down my love," Gabi whispered, astonished by his reaction. She knelt before him. "He was here once before and he was so charming."

"Of course he was!" shouted Geoff. He held up his hands and closed his eyes in resignation. "I'm sorry. I'm sorry I shouted. He's a—he's such a prick. Just you wait and see when they get here."

"Oh Geoff darling, I'm the one who's sorry. I didn't even think. But he did seem to have changed when I saw him last."

"When was that?"

"Umm … two or three days before you arrived."

"When I got back from Angola I heard he was away on leave and was relieved. You see, I didn't want to start another round of psychological warfare with him, but I had no way of knowing he was right on your doorstep. Why the hell didn't you tell me?"

"It wasn't important. Nothing else was when you arrived," Gabi caressed his face.

"Well, there's nothing we can do about it now, so let's try not let it spoil our evening. At least I know he's coming and forewarned is forearmed. He's going to get a shock when he sees me," Geoff shook his head. "I still can't believe you forgot to tell me."

❈

"*Genade Engelsman*! Valerie told me you were going to be here but I had to come and see your ugly mug for myself."

Geoff's eyes narrowed. He was about to offer his hand until he noticed the direction of Dawid's gaze. The insult may have been in jest and Geoff gave him the benefit of the doubt, but it was the way he ogled Gabi.

Geoff clenched his jaw and turned to Valerie, "How lovely to see you. You look um, so well, you know—healthy."

"Thank you, you're kind," she said and smiled. She was beautiful when she smiled. Her cheeks had their colour back, her hair shone and she wore make-up for the first time but she was still too thin.

"Come in. Let's have a drink before supper," said Gabi quickly. The atmosphere already felt treacle-thick.

"Here *Engelsman*." Dawid held out a bottle of South African sparkling wine. He had not shaved in days. His thick moustache with spiky black hairs gave him the look of a deranged villain. "Get us some glasses. We have something to celebrate."

A fire warmed the room and made for a pleasant ambience despite the undercurrents.

"I propose a toast." Dawid lifted his glass, "To my wife to be—Valerie."

Geoff nearly dropped his glass.

Gabi jumped to her feet and embraced Valerie. "Congratulations! I knew it would all work out." The two hugged and laughed joyously. Geoff stood and offered his hand.

Dawid looked at the proffered hand and then at Geoff. "You are not my friend. We do not have to shake."

"Perhaps I really want to congratulate you."

"I don't want you to."

Geoff pursed his lips, nodded and walked towards the kitchen. "Does anyone want a drink, other than sparkling wine, while I'm here?" he called over his shoulder.

"Please bring the wine. darling. I feel like a glass of that too," called Gabi.

"Ja, bring me a beer, *corporal*," Dawid emphasised the word. "It's about time you did something for me."

"Let's be seated." Gabi ushered them to the table and disappeared into the kitchen. Servants carrying roast topside and vegetables paraded in. Gabi smiled. "Will you be so kind and carve for us, darling?"

"That's a man's job—perhaps I should …," began Dawid and he smiled at Geoff's glare.

The evening progressed in an uneasy tension. Gabi smiled and chatted gaily in an effort to ease the situation. Underneath she felt for Geoff. He was trying his best and Dawid blocked him at every turn. After supper the men maintained a sulky silence and Geoff drank beer after beer. Gabi was powerless to stop it. She felt guilty for having initiated the evening without telling Geoff.

After an eternity Valerie stood. "We must go. Thank you for such a lovely meal Gabi." She turned to Geoff, "I was sincerely hoping that you and Dawid might …"

Geoff held up his hand to forestall her, "Don't worry about it. He needs someone like you. Perhaps, with time and a bit of luck, you can turn him into a human being some day. I tried and failed …"

"Geoffrey!" Gabi said softly. "Please my love, I can't stand it."

Gabi walked Valerie out to the car and Dawid turned to Geoff when the women were out of earshot. "I can't wait to see you back in camp. I'll make you swallow those words."

"What words?" asked Geoff.

You speak to Valerie about being human; well I'll show you inhuman."

"Bye bye Dawid, do try keeping your knuckles off the ground on your way out." Dawid stared at Geoff for a long time, his penetrating eyes black and murderous. For a minute Geoff thought that he would start something but he turned at last and strode away. Geoff was relieved. He knew he was drunk and would be no match for Dawid in his current state.

The headlight beams disappeared and Gabi skipped back inside, her arms folded against the late evening chill. "How about a hot cup of coffee my love?" Geoff looked at her, bleary eyed. He swayed a bit and nodded. Gabi returned with the steaming mugs, placed them on the table and collapsed into the big couch. Geoff sat in the adjacent chair and stared at her. He reached for his cup and burped loudly.

He smiled at her and held up his hand, "Excuse me. I've had an awful night."

"I know." Gabi reached forward and placed her hand on his knee. "I'm so sorry …," she hesitated. "I don't know how I thought we could …," she tailed off. They sat in silence for a long while and Geoff stared into the dying fire. He looked up at her at last and what she saw there frightened her.

Geoff's eyes were still red but instead of the hooded lids and dulled expression, they were sharp and shone with menace. His mouth turned up in a lopsided grin that smacked of cynicism and had Gabi known him a little better or even read the signs she might have gone straight to bed and left him to stew on his own. Instead she read the smile as a sort of acceptance of the situation and an offer of constructive discussion. Gabi couldn't stand seeing him so miserable and she wanted to fix it for him.

"So you made out that all of this a complete coincidence and then you apologise for it when your carefully laid plans didn't work?" His voice was low and inquiring.

Gabi sipped at her coffee and looked over the mug at him. "It wasn't actually 'carefully planned'. We knew you and Dawid didn't see eye to eye and in light of the coincidence of you being here …"

"So you did plan it?"

"Well, yes, but very innocently. We didn't try to …"

"Then you must have known he was there all the time?"

"Yes but …"

"And you never told me?"

"Okay. I accept that …"

"You must have made some sort of clandestine call to organise tonight's delightful evening then?"

Gabi looked at Geoff. "What is this? A bloody inquisition?" she raised her voice.

"Your anger is all the confirmation I need. So, now my question is—what else have you lied to me about if you can lie so easily about trivia?" Geoff's tone never changed but the muscles in his jaw worked.

"Good Lord, Geoffrey! You've just said it, 'trivia'. It's trivia that you are making such a bloody fuss about and no bloody lies have been told! What the hell's the matter with you?"

"If I can't get a straight answer out of you on that one then I probably won't get a straight answer on the one that counts, but I'm going to try anyway."

"What are you talking about? Gabi whispered. Tears filled her eyes.

"Who is the other man you've been seeing while I was away protecting you and your farm?"

"I don't know what you are talking about …," she said softly the first tear sliding down her cheek. "What other man?"

"That's what I'm asking you. Carel told me about it. At first I didn't believe him and in fact it went out of my mind completely until you used lies and deceit to force Dawid and me together." Geoff took a sip of coffee. "Well …?"

Gabi hesitated, put her head in her hands and began to sob. She stayed like that for a long time and looked up at Geoff at last. She reached out her hands and he looked at her contemptuously.

"Did you fuck him?"

Gabi shuddered at the question, shook her head slowly as the tears began to flow and she lowered her arms. His rebuttal of her hurt the most and the sudden vulgarity added to her dejection. "No. He was wooing me but I was waiting for you, so no, I didn't *fuck* him. I was lonely and he was good company—that's all."

"Who is he then?" asked Geoff. He kept the same unrelenting exterior, but the ache in his heart grappled with his compassion. He thrust the emotions aside and hardened his resolve.

"Tim van Dyk, a good friend of Hein's, but you wouldn't know about friendship like that would you? You don't have it in your heart. I can see that now." Gabi sniffed. She looked at him one last time hoping he would relent and grab her and hold her and tell her how much he loved her. Geoff didn't move as Gabi ran from the room. She never looked back.

It was mid-morning when Geoff finally woke. He was horrified when he looked at the time. He hadn't slept that late since he was a child. He leapt out of bed. *Jesus*! He had to be back in camp by curfew today. He'd have to move. It took him that long to realise that he was in the spare room. His kitbag lay against the wall and his rifle next to it. The magazine was on the dresser with his toiletries and his browns lay neatly ironed and folded on the chair. His boots were on the floor next to the chair, expertly polished. He shook his head. *What happened last night?* He dashed through to the shower all the time wracking his brain for the outcome of the previous evening. Did she say she had slept with that other guy? Did that really matter? She had lied to him—but only to try and reconcile the irreconcilable between him and Dawid. She did that with him in mind. She was only trying to help him! Why had she kept ... what the hell was his name ...? Tim! Why had she kept him such a secret? What had he said about Tim last night? She had cried but was it okay or was the situation irretrievable? The soapsuds slid over his skin as the steaming water cascaded down his body and his mind raced. Slowly, as he dried himself, the reality of the events of the previous evening began to sink in. He dashed through to the room, threw the towel on the bed and grabbed his brown combat shirt. A piece of paper floated to the ground and Geoff stared at it for a second before picking it up. It was a single sheet of writing paper with a pretty, ornate pattern of woven flowers around the border. He opened it and read.

"I'm so sorry I've let you down. Goodbye, my love. G." Geoff stared at Gabi's neat sloping handwriting. He felt the sting of tears and the letters blurred and ran before his eyes. Maybe she was right. Maybe they weren't compatible, what with all their differences. Perhaps it was better this way. She had a farm to run— a hard living to make and she had a son to bring up—another man's boy. He had been a bloody fool last night and he was beginning to realise just how big, but the circumstances ...? Geoff looked at the note a while longer and shook his head. He had to see her! He had to see there was no hope before he gave up for he was certain he loved her. He finished dressing, dashed outside. The Land Cruiser was gone. He recognised the foreman sitting in the sun at the corner of the stable. His eyes were shut and he dozed in the mid-morning heat. Geoff took several big strides towards him and shook the man awake. "Jacob! Jacob! Where is the madam?" he shouted.

The foreman turned a sickly grey as his eyes flew open. He looked into the eyes of the huge, angry white South African soldier. "She is gone," he squeaked fearfully.

"I know that! Where to man?"

"She did not tell me, master."

"When did she leave? What time?" Geoff tapped at his watch.

"This morning when it was still fully dark, master."

"Did she give you any instructions?"

"No sir, only that she is going away for a while."

Geoff felt his shoulders sag as he thought of his next move. "Go and fetch the big tractor and meet me at the front yard," he said and dashed inside to fetch his kit.

Jacob drove and Geoff sat on the large wheel arch with kitbag over shoulder and rifle in hand, searching the lands. They hurtled down the drive past the builders who dashed for cover at the sudden appearance of a speeding tractor with an armed soldier perched on the side. Jacob swung out onto the main road, changed to fifth gear and let the tractor go. Even though the tractor drove at full speed, their progress was still slow. At last they drove up the entrance of the neighbouring farm. They drove up to the back door as Geoff spotted the maid in the ironing room. She too was terrified when she saw him.

"Where is the madam?" he demanded and she stood there, frozen. Jacob appeared at Geoff's side and said something. The maid broke into a huge relieved grin and answered.

Jacob translated, "They went shopping in the town, sir."

"Ask her if the madam from nextdoor was with them." Jacob spoke again and the maid shook her head.

"She says …"

"I know," said Geoff. He felt as if his heart was breaking. God, how it hurt! He breathed in deeply, closed his eyes and held his breath. He exhaled and rubbed his eyes. Gabi could be anywhere and he had run out of time. It was no use even trying to look. He had no idea where to begin. There was nothing more to do but go back to war, try and see out the rest of his days and go home. "Could you give me a lift to town, Jacob?"

Jacob looked at Geoff, opened his mouth as if to decline and glanced at his rifle. "Yes master, " he said and smiled.

CHAPTER 32

'Princess Grace is dead!' exclaimed he headlines. Splashed on the front page of the local press in both official languages and newspapers around the world, the terrible news was unveiled. To most South Africans the news was horrifying enough but they could turn their back, shudder at the thought and walk away. The death of a princess had taken place so far away that for most citizens it was the tragic end to a sad fairy tale.

However, the news was of particular intrigue to a large, stooped man with a fine black moustache supporting a beaky but regal nose. The Foreign Minister wore an indelible but cynical smile, and for good reason—he was tasked to field the attack from every quarter regarding South Africa's policy of apartheid, among other lesser issues. Now he lifted the handset of one of his telephones and spoke to his personal assistant. His brow furrowed as he replaced the receiver and he hesitated for a moment before retrieving his newspaper.

A black military staff car wound its way up the sinuous road to the magnificent building perched on top of the hill overlooking the jacaranda-tree-lined streets of Pretoria. The Union Buildings, signature of Sir Herbert Baker's most famous work, housed the most powerful men in Africa and the general took the stairs two at a time in his eagerness to see the minister. The minister smiled warmly as the short, dapper general entered his plush office.

"*Kom binne generaal*," he said enthusiastically. "Come in, isn't the sky the most beautiful blue today?" he asked. Even the most steadfast of world leaders held the minister in high regard as, apart from his fearsome expression, he was a brilliant master of political tactics. After all, he was one of the few politicians in the world who had labelled the Soviets as tyrants.

The minister ushered the general out onto the veranda and they stood silently for a moment as they took in the view of the capital. The day was warm, the sky indigo and the jacarandas were just coming into bloom, painting the wide streets with splashes of purple. The general was from farming stock, himself a farmer, a practical man but a man of few words and although he was impressed with the vista before him he turned to the minister and frowned. "Would it be remiss of me to assume that the death of such a beautiful princess has given us the opportunity to determine H-hour?"

"Exactly general, exactly!" exclaimed the minister with undisguised delight. He was immensely pleased that he never had to actually give the order. His general was astute enough to read the meeting for what it was and to act on it accordingly and for this the minister admired the man. "I think that this, coupled with the ripples of world shock emanating from the Falklands War, is enough. The world also has its eyes fastened on Andropov since the death of Brezhnev," he frowned. "What a glorious day it is."

"My aide tells me we are ready to go, so if you'll excuse me, I best be on my way ..."

"Is it the attractive one—your aide?" interrupted the minister.

"Yes, I'll send her immediately ..."

"Is she here?" he interrupted again.

"Well, yes, she's waiting for me at DHQ."

The minister knew the ladies found him attractive—his sheer presence, the aura of power, his humour, all added to his personality. Some found him irresistable, but the minister had a soft spot for the general's aide.

"Send her my kindest regards and tell her to keep her head down."

"She won't actually be involved in the fighting, minister, but I'll convey your message nonetheless."

"Yes, do that. *Dankie generaal, en geluk hoor.*" The minister made to return to his desk and hesitated. "What's the op called? What can I tell them when they ask?" he pointed to the prime minister's office and smiled.

"Operation Brolly Tree, minister."

CHAPTER 33

Lieutenant Mark Scott wondered if anyone had accurately envisaged the state of the road. From the destroyed office on the Angolan border past the deserted hamlet of Ongiva the road had been comfortable. From there northwards it deteriorated into a sandy track that sucked at the tyres of the overloaded gun tractors.

Mark pondered the border post at Oshikango. Perhaps it once housed an official who wore a white uniform with black epaulettes and gold braid. A serious man who took pride in his work as he welcomed visitors to Angola. Now the ruin gave testament to the ravages of war. The once proud concrete letters announcing 'Angola' gave way to bullet holes.

During the laborious hours of training in Oshivelo and, as insufferable as the daily routine of driving for seven hours in anticipation of this very trip may have been, the time passed too quickly for Mark for as suddenly as an African sunrise, they had arrived. He recognised the kink in the corner of the *shona*. It was as obvious as he'd seen it on the aerial photograph.

"Fire the guns in anger." The words of Mark's commandant echoed in his mind. Hardly. It is merely an expression he reminded himself. No one seemed angry and the only difference between this and a shooting exercise on the range in Potchefstroom was the fact that people were going to die at the sharp end. Mark raised his eyebrows as the enormity of the situation hit him. People were going to die today.

A Troop Post Officer ran out ahead of the guns and, on the trot, retrieved a prismatic compass from its leather case. He ground to a halt and aimed the instrument. Satisfied with the direction for the guns, he gestured wildly to the men he'd briefed previously. One a TA, the other a signaller and two drivers made up the human gun poles. One by one he placed them in the correct positions and gave the arc of fire. These pre-determined positions had been worked out in the wee hours of the morning back in the planning tent at Oshivelo. How long ago that all seemed to Mark as he observed the deployment unfolding.

"Action rear!" bellowed the number ones. In the middle of the battery of two troops, stood a lone Buffel. In it, stood the Gun Position Officer, one Second Lieutenant Mark Scott and with him two TAs, the radio operator and the driver who doubled as the other radio operator. Mark squinted down at his clipboard and then up to where the TA sergeant had been. The theodolite was unmanned and Mark found himself becoming a little irritated. If for some reason that theodolite was moved or knocked over, the lines would have to be recalculated. It was then that Mark remembered that it was the TA sergeant's responsibility to find the alternative deployment position. Mark's brow furrowed and he shook his head. *Surely that's a waste of time*, he thought irritably. *Who the hell knows we're here?* To Mark the time wasted searching for the alternate position would more profitably be spent looking after the theodolite. He sighed, retrieved his clipboard and his mood lightened as he began working out the projectile flight times.

Activity ceased and gunners stared at one another. They stood with ears cocked and eyes narrowed. Off to one side a Transvaal Horse Artillery citizen force bombardier paled and tried to shout. His throat was dry and he croaked, coughed and then bellowed as he ran for cover.

"Red Eye! Red Eye!" he shouted hysterically and dived into his foxhole. The bombardier was a veteran of the 1978 attack on the Caprivi capital at Katima Mulilo. Ten SADF soldiers had died and ten more were wounded when a 122mm rocket from a BM-21 scored a direct hit on the barracks. He had never forgotten that hideous whine. The bombardier squirmed into his foxhole in an effort to make himself as small as possible. He gritted his teeth and groaned in anticipation as the first salvo ploughed into the *shona* in front of the gun position. The rockets exploded with ground-shaking force, sending columns of sand skyward.

It took Mark that long to react. He leapt from the Buffel and rolled into his foxhole beneath it. Suddenly his foxhole felt extremely shallow and inadequate. The missiles rained down with surprising inaccuracy and irregularity.

The rest of the convoy had to be informed. Mark had to get to a radio and his nearest signaller was some distance away huddled in his own foxhole. Mark peeped over the edge of his own precarious position and scanned the area. He ducked instinctively as two more rockets exploded behind him. Carefully he looked up again and searched the area. His eyes came to rest on the reed-like antenna protruding from what seemed like flat ground. Mark took a deep breath as his body tensed. He waited for a brief moment of silence and when it did he leapt from his hole and galloped across the open space. Suddenly his legs felt weak and rubbery. Disappointment surged through his body as he realised that he'd misjudged the incoming missiles. The dreadful howl assaulted his ears and magnified with each stride. Mark pumped as hard as he could but the antenna remained stubbornly out of reach. The ground around him erupted in a cloud of dust, dirt, flying clods of earth and shrieking fragments. He felt as if some giant ogre had tossed him carelessly to the ground. He lay there for some time wondering why he felt no pain. Surely his body was torn to ribbons. He shook his head and looked around. Amazingly he seemed intact. He was covered in dust and his shirt was in tatters from the force of the blast but other than the hissing in his ears he seemed fine.

Mark lay like that for a few seconds and then achingly slowly lifted his head. He stood up and sprinted the last few metres, executing a baseball slide into the signaller's foxhole.

"Two Five Bravo! Two Five Bravo! This is Two Zero! We are under rocket attack and are moving to the alternative gun position as soon as we get respite!" Mark did not pay too much heed to radio etiquette as he called his Observation Post Officer. Neither did he wait for an answer as he huddled down half on top of his terrified signaller.

"Bit cramped for two, eh Erasmus?" he enquired with an air of joviality he did not feel. "Don't worry; I'll be out of here in a second …"

"No! Please lieutenant, feel free to stay! They might want to talk to you!" shouted Erasmus with an edge of hysteria in his voice.

"Nope. You can take a message. We have to start moving the vehicles out of here," said Mark. "Carlos! Carlos!" he shouted to his driver. "Carlos! Answer me you deaf fuck!" No response. Mark felt a flash of anger. This was no time to clam up. Mark felt another emotion. It dawned on him like a warm bath on a winter evening. He had survived death twice in as many minutes and he was in control of his fear. He grinned to himself as he leapt from the tenuous sanctuary of his foxhole and sprinted the short distance to his driver's position. He jolted to a halt and peered into the foxhole.

The trail of thick dark blood told the story for it led from a nearby crater and ended in the hole. Rocket shrapnel must have caught Carlos as he sprinted. The little Portuguese had made it but had then bled to death. It was as if he'd run and dived into his own grave. Mark wasted precious seconds as he stared in horror at the mess that used to be his driver. There was so much blood. *No! This will not be your grave buddy*, he thought, reaching into the hole. He hauled the limp, blood-stained body out onto the ground. His muscles strained as he heaved Carlos over his shoulder and ran awkwardly to the Buffel where he lifted the body up and over the side. Softly, as if to prevent hurting him, he lowered Carlos onto the seats. Then he scrambled over the thick armour plate and dropped into the mine-proofed driving compartment. He was far too tall to fit comfortably. He folded his legs beneath the steering wheel, found the pedals and peered over the top of the thick armour glass frame as he drove the vehicle to the guns.

"Get in!" he shouted at the bewildered gunners. *"Klim julle!"* They took no more encouraging and sprinted from their foxholes. Mark drove past the Samil 100s and bellowed at the drivers. "Bring your …," he began but his words were cut off as the noise of an exploding rocket drummed about them. He waited for the shower of earth and the deafening noise to abate before continuing, "Bring your tractors out of the killing ground!" he shouted and drove away from the *shona* to the sparsely forested area out of range of the rockets. He waited anxiously as the first Samil blew a column of blue smoke and began to move towards them. Only when the fourth vehicle moved did he breathe properly. He looked over to his left and breathed a sigh of relief as he saw that Alpha Troop had followed suit. With all the gun tractors and most of the men well out of range of the rockets, Mark felt he'd won a small victory but still the guns remained obliterated by the dust and smoke. The worst part was that not all the men were accounted for and Mark called the number ones. "I want you to take a roll call and report any missing men," he paused and looked at their faces. Pale skin and haunted eyes peered back. He grabbed the nearest man by the epaulette and shook him. "Snap out of it, bombardier. This is only the beginning for, Christ's sake!"

The man shook his head. "I—I'm sorry lieutenant. I'll be okay."

"Good, because the minute that bombardment stops we're going to fetch the wounded and the guns," Mark pointed to the pall of smoke lifting into the still sky. "Do you understand me?" he asked with menace in his voice. The men nodded and Mark dismissed them. He summoned the signaller. "Give them this sitrep …," he began but his jaw dropped. A figure was sprinting from the cataclysm. Even from that distance Mark could see it was the TA sergeant and how he ran! As the man neared, Mark waved frantically and caught his attention. He changed direction and jogged over to Mark.

"Howzit lieutenant," puffed the sergeant and he smiled. He was sweating profusely and blood soaked through a crude bandage on his forearm. "I had to go back for the theodolite."

"You went back into *that*, to fetch the theodolite?" Mark was incredulous.

"Had to lieutenant. We need this baby for the alternative deployment," he said seriously. "By the way, I need some gun posts again …"

"Sure," said Mark gesturing towards the gunners. "Help yourself."

"Thanks lieutenant." He turned to leave and Mark frowned and scratched his chin.

"Oh, sarge," he called suddenly.

The sergeant swivelled. "Yes sir?"

"What's the likelihood of them hitting the alternative?"

The sergeant looked surprised and then a little bewildered. He cocked his head to one side and thought for a second. "Only if they had the co-ordinates; otherwise none. Why sir?"

Mark pointed at the mêlée. "What the hell do you call that?"

The sergeant shook his head. "A fucking fluke lieutenant, a fucking fluke," he said and walked away. He stopped suddenly, turned and frowned, "Or they had the co-ordinates."

Mark turned to his signaller and looked up as raucous yells of triumph echoed through the trees. He felt the hairs on his neck and forearms stand up as the Mirages thundered overhead. The gunners shouted and leapt into the air with a mixture of relief and anger. Long before the deep booming sound of the bombs reached them, the howl and thump of the rockets suddenly abated. A few of the men began to celebrate and Mark shouted for the first time.

"Shut up damn it! We've got work to do, so shut the fuck up!" he glared at them for a second before shouting his next order. "Let's go fetch the guns!"

Mark walked away and suddenly it became very clear—he was angry, very angry.

A desperate re-deployment commenced. The pressure came from call sign Two Five Bravo. He had no qualms about informing Two Zero that the air force was engaged in extended bombing and strafing in order to buy time for the artillery.

Mark felt himself relax after the trauma of the unexpected attack. He surveyed his gunners from the Buffel and allowed himself a little pat on the back. They had made a remarkable recovery from such a disastrous start.

The radio crackled to life. Two Five Bravo was calling. Mark listened and shouted the order. "Fire mission battery!" The gunners scrambled to their positions and the number one stood poised, anxious and ready. It was about to begin.

❇

Captain Jannie Groenewalt literally sat at the edge of his seat as he listened to the cries of battle over the radio. He found himself chewing on his thumbnail and he made a conscious effort to sit back and fold his arms. There were some heroes in the making, the artillery lieutenant for one. Through the jumble of thoughts that pummelled his mind as the radio regurgitated the horrors of battle, one struck him as if it were a physical entity—this was a disaster, a blunder of historic proportions. It jolted him to his feet and he glared at the brigadier. *Too many goddamned coincidences, just too many*, he thought striding from the ops room.

Back in his own quarters he sat in front of the typewriter, drew in a deep breath and fed a blank sheet into the machine. The adjutant sat for a full minute and contemplated the harvest of doomed careers this letter would reap, perhaps worst of all his own.

'Dear General …,' he typed and the words began to flow as if he were purging himself of a cancer. '… in summary and notwithstanding my previous detailed and undoubtedly linked accounts of the Puma disaster, the Mirage catastrophe and the simultaneous attacks on the Brolly Tree echelon and the artillery primary gun position, I have two sergeants who will bear witness to the murder of a detainee by the brigadier's own hand. Further, the brigadier's wife and I will bear testament to an adulterous affair the brigadier is engaged in with your own liaison officer, the aforementioned Lieutenant Elsa Botha.

'As an officer serving in the South African Defence Force I find the correct channels to your office blocked by the very man whose conduct is beyond mere question and believe it to be my duty to bypass him and deliver this missive directly to your office.

'I remain yours sincerely …'

Captain Groenewalt sat back, raked his fingers through his hair and reread the text for the third time. He scrawled his signature next to his rank and name, folded the pages neatly and slid them into an official envelope. He wrote the general's rank and name on the front, stood abruptly, glanced at his watch and trotted out into the heat. He entered the headquarters and made directly for the post room. The provost officer was in the process of locking the 'Eyes Only' bag.

"Hold on major," the captain smiled and held aloft his envelope. "There's one more for the general." The major smiled condescendingly and dropped the envelope into the bag, slipped the toggles through the steel eyes and locked the bag. "What time's your …"

"I'm already late for the Flossie, so if you'll excuse me …," the major smiled that smile.

"I'm at a loose end, how about I drive you to Ondangwa in the Toyota and you can skip the discomfort of a Buffel, that's if you don't mind the risk of attack on a soft-skinned vehicle?"

The major's attitude took on an amazing transformation. "That will be damned good of you captain. The general is expecting me and I'm sure you know how he frowns upon tardy timing."

"So you'll see him today still?"

"Well, tonight, but yes he said I must bring the correspondence whatever time I get in."

"Okay, then let's go," said the captain and then under his breath. 'My career is fucked now, so the sooner we get it over with the better."

"Hey?"

"The sooner we get going the better," replied Captain Jannie Groenewalt and he strode from the room, his shoulders slumped in resignation.

CHAPTER 34

Geoff was tired and it was obvious in the way he carried himself. After eight days in the bush even he had to admit to himself that he was not as alert as he should be. Eight days on patrol—too long. He slung his webbing down, propped his rifle against the bole of the acacia and sank down next to it. He pulled a water bottle from its worn, faded pouch, lifted it to his cracked lips and drank deeply. He closed his eyes in anticipation as the water poured down the back of his throat in an attempt to slake his burning thirst. He spat the last mouthful out in disgust. The water was hot and made him thirstier. Summer was back with a vengeance. He poured the rest of the contents over his head and shuddered slightly. The gentle breeze cooled his body as the water cut through the layer of dust and grime and soaked into his grease-blackened combat fatigues. He shook his head and the water flew off his hair in a halo of silver droplets. Geoff looked up at Rudi. The man was a sight. Rudi had long ago discarded his shirt. Instead he wore a T-shirt, which, after this patrol, would only be good for cleaning mud off floors. He had attached some foam rubber under the straps of his webbing and the magazine and water bottle pouches were blackened with the grease of days of sweat. Eight days of beard was no longer stubble and the moustache he was cultivating was in desperate need of a trim should he not want to be mistaken for a walrus. A length of two-by-four wound around his head doubled as a sweatband and the radio hooked to the front of his webbing seemed to smother him.

"Call them and tell them we're at the RV," commanded Geoff.

"Done," replied Rudi. "You're still like a bear with sore tits, I see." Rudi had long ago stopped feeling sorry for Geoff over the miserable outcome of his split with Gabi. At first Rudi could see the hurt his friend was enduring and he tried to lessen the pain by talking to Geoff about it as much as possible. When this did not work he tried to talk about it as little as possible, choosing rather humorous topics of their colourful friendship. The success was short-lived and soon Geoff withdrew into his shell of unpropitious misery. Eventually Rudi gave up and chose sarcasm as his weapon in an attempt to jolt Geoff from his pedestal of pain. This had begun to have limited success but only when Geoff was occupied. Now that they were about to be choppered back to their base at Eenhana, Geoff was reminded of his loss and with that came the uncharacteristically withdrawn personality.

Rudi dropped his kit next to Geoff's, pulled a water bottle from his webbing and finished the contents in three large gulps. He wiped his mouth with the back of his hand and looked down at his friend and leader. "You've got to snap out of it, Geoff, if not for yourself then for us," Rudi swung his arm in an arc, indicating Geoff's exhausted and bedraggled troops. "They're not too chuffed with you at the moment and believe me, neither am I." He paused, waiting for a reaction. There was none so he ploughed on, "We get back, looking forward to a bit of a rest and then you volunteer us for another patrol. So we clean up and off we go again. We can't constantly be alert for the enemy when we're all tired and it's all because of your self-inflicted, selfish state of mind." Rudi looked around. Even Allan was slumped at the far side of the all-round defence. Rudi knew he was going to touch a nerve when he mentioned the contact, but he had to get through to Geoff and perhaps this was the way. "I mean look what happened back at the cut line." Geoff quickly looked up and there was fire in his eyes. Rudi went on regardless, "We nearly shot the shit out of our own troops. Can you imagine the repercussions of that?"

"What the fuck are you trying to tell me—that it was my fault?" Geoff sat forward and glared up at Rudi.

Geoff and his men had gone out on three patrols—one after the other with only a day's rest between. When Geoff had volunteered for the third, they had argued the wisdom of his decision

"Well, I'm not taking my dog on this one," announced Allan angrily. "He needs a rest too. Another patrol so soon will kill him."

"Fine. Leave your bloody dog but get your arse into gear and let's go!" answered Geoff belligerently.

"I hope to hell I'm not going to regret my detached duty to your section," lamented Allan. "It seemed like a good idea at the time, but now …"

On the first patrol Allan's dog picked up a spoor and the men followed eagerly. Everyone was alert as they closed in on their quarry but the terrorists must have got wind of them and headed into a small village where they promptly disappeared. The men meticulously searched the village and even the efforts and skill of Allan's dog were to no avail. The terrorists seemed to have vanished into thin air.

"The bastards are here," complained Geoff. "They're probably among that crowd at the carcass," he pointed with his rifle at the Ovambo cow hanging from a tree in what could be described as the village square. A tall Ovambo hacked a lump of meat from the carcass and handed it to a wizened, bent old woman. She wore a filthy cast-off skirt and her chest was bare—her wrinkled breasts hung down to her navel. Geoff looked at her in disgust. He was frustrated but that did not deter him from salivating at the sight of the meat. *How could the sight of stringy, fly-infested, probably diseased cow make me hungry? Too many damned rat packs!* he thought bitterly. The soldiers walked among the people, gathered around the Ovambo butcher and scrutinised each person in turn. For Geoff and his men it was standard practice. This intimidating method could prove too much for a nervous terrorist and he, or she, would break and run but this time their faces were deadpan—African style.

"Damn it! Damn it to hell!" Geoff cursed through his teeth. "They're probably watching us and laughing." With belts of shiny cartridges slung around his shoulders, a cigarette hanging from his lips, Dawid's menacing and terrifying presence had no effect either. Finally Geoff had to admit that the birds had flown and they should leave. They did so reluctantly and that was the last action they'd had in weeks.

Much later and with three days left to reach the RV, the minds of the men were inundated with thoughts of a cooked meal, a beer, a shower, and a rest from all the tension when Geoff glimpsed hostile movement a fair distance off in the thicker bush on their left flank.

"Swapo! Ten o'clock! Go, go, go!" he shouted as the men were jolted from their apathy into the reality of a contact. A fire fight ensued. The enemy were alert and quickly returned fire. They spread out and made excellent use of the cover as they advanced. Geoff was astounded. Usually a contact was over in seconds with the enemy either dead or on the run. These men knew what they were doing and suddenly Geoff recognised their pattern. He felt the blood drain from his face.

Everything seemed to happen in slow motion as he looked around and he heard Rudi shout hysterically. "Cease fire! Stop shooting for fuck's sake!" The crackle of rifle fire subsided and then abated. An intense silence followed.

Geoff slowly edged around the tree. He peered across the open ground to the thicker bush. Nothing moved. Geoff waved his hand and shouted, "We're South African. Not Swapo!"

"Then stop fucking shooting at us!" came the strongly accented reply.

"Okay, I'm coming out! Don't shoot!" shouted Geoff. He took a deep breath and stepped into the open. On the far side of the open ground and as if by magic, South African soldiers rose out of the bush like Phoenix from the ashes. A lieutenant stepped into the open and waved. Geoff heaved a sigh of relief and turned to his men. "Anyone hurt or wounded?" he asked anxiously. Singly and in pairs his men stood and Geoff sighed thankfully as all were accounted for. He turned at the sound and was in time to witness a very irate officer striding with determination towards him.

"What the bloody hell do you think you are doing, you idiot?" demanded the lieutenant. "You could have killed us!"

"I'm terribly sorry, lieutenant. From that distance I couldn't see …," said Geoff defensively.

"Bullshit!" the lieutenant pushed his finger right up under Geoff's nose. "Let me tell you …," he began.

The man's entire attitude engendered a burgeoning anger within Geoff. It had been a mistake for God's sake. Did the lieutenant think that Geoff was going to purposely open fire on fellow South Africans? It was also clear to Geoff that this was one of those bullies—an insignificant schoolboy who came to the army and by some dint of magic became an officer, using his rank to crush those in his way.

"With all due respect, lieutenant, if you don't take your finger out of my face, I'll break it off and ram it right up you stinking arse," said Geoff quietly. That was one of the traits Geoff's men loved about him. He always seemed to assess the situation and deal with it accordingly, and his comment delivered a few guffaws. The lieutenant looked at Geoff and saw a filthy, big soldier with a face of chiselled granite before him. Geoff's eyes had reduced to slits and the muscles in his jaw rippled with anger. That, coupled with the humour following Geoff's comment, caused the lieutenant to back off and look around. His men had not followed and he stood alone in front of Geoff. After weeks in the bush, they were a rather intimidating sight.

"You can't speak to me like that," whispered the lieutenant tremulously, his anger and indignation clearly evident. "I'm going to have to report you. What's your name, rank and number?" he asked in a stilted voice and pulled a notebook and pen from his pants pocket.

"Exactly what are you going to report me for?" asked Geoff.

"You swore at an officer," the lieutenant shot back.

"No I didn't. Ask my witnesses," said Geoff pointing to his men.

The lieutenant looked around once more and suddenly felt very alone.

"You'll hear more of this, corporal," said the lieutenant and he turned and strode off.

Rudi walked up and looked on as the lieutenant joined his men. "Jesus! That was close. Didn't you see they were ours?" he asked incredulously.

"I suppose you did?" barked Geoff.

"Well, yes, I did actually. I thought you were joking when you called us to fire." Rudi stared at Geoff. "Some of the others did too. Even Dawid didn't fire."

"Neither did I," added Martin.

Geoff pushed his bush hat to the back of his head and scratched his temple. "I thought ... why didn't you stop me?" Geoff looked bewildered. "It all happened so quickly ..."

"It happened because we're all tired and in need of a few days off." Allan said as he glared at Geoff.

Rudi took a deep breath. "We all need a rest and when we get back I want you to sit down and write a letter to Gabi and tell her you're sorry. Perhaps that will set your mind at rest and we won't have to go out on so many of your bloody death-wish patrols."

Geoff closed his eyes, dropped his head and waited for his anger to subside. He knew Rudi was right and the mere thought of writing to Gabi filled him with hope. He shook his head, his expression pathetic. "Do you think I should? I mean, do you think she'd even read it?"

Rudi shrugged. "You can only try ...," he began and then volubly, "and stop being such a pig-headed oaf. You love the woman, that is plain to see, and she loves you, so get on with it man!"

"Shit Rudi, I've been such a fool. I lose my lover as a result of petty emotions and I make strangers of my friends and men. Maybe that lieutenant was right. Maybe I am an idiot."

"Now now, don't look for sympathy here. Just write that bloody letter and let's get the old Geoff back," said Rudi as he flopped down next to his friend. The distant but familiar sound of a Puma alerted them. "Let's go home," said Rudi. Geoff nodded and smiled for the first time in weeks.

The flight back to Eenhana was exhilarating after the drudgery of patrol. Geoff sat in the door with his legs hanging over the edge, the wind buffeting his trousers. He looked out over the vast flat land. It was beautiful and he sighed in anticipation. *Maybe, just maybe*, he thought. A massive black thundercloud boiled up as a backdrop and the waning sun enhanced the colour of the palms. It was quite beautiful and Geoff looked at the top of the cloud. It rose up and expanded dramatically. He wished it would rain. He wanted torrents to soak into the dry parched earth.

The shower was as wonderful as anticipated and Geoff stood under the cascading water long after he had finished scrubbing off the layers of filth.

Rudi interrupted the bliss. "You gotta hurry. Joubert wants to see you." Geoff nodded without looking up as Rudi continued. "Now don't go and volunteer for anything bloody stupid." He gave Geoff an austere look and Geoff smiled.

"Another smile," said Rudi in mock alarm. "Mind your face doesn't crack," he added. "Have you written your letter?"

"Yep," said Geoff and he smiled again.

"And you've posted it?"

"No. I've done better. I've had it hand-delivered."

"Jeez, how'd you manage that?"

"A convoy left for Oshivelo and two policemen in the convoy are headed for Tsumeb, so I asked them to give the letter to that sarge buddy of mine, you know," said Geoff as he turned off the water, "Carel Brits."

"All this before even showering," said Rudi. "Now that's what I call commitment."

The spring in Geoff's step was doused by the news the RSM so gleefully expounded. They were going cross-border. They were going into Angola.

CHAPTER 35

"Two Five Bravo, fire plan Brolly Tree; Quebec 1001. At my command adjust fire!" came the message. Just fleetingly as Fire Control Officer or Gun Position Officer, Lieutenant Mark Scott wondered how many times he had heard that from the OP. This time it sent shivers down his spine as he issued his command.

"Number three; ammunition HE 117. Charge three. Load! Bearing 124 degrees three seven minutes! Range nine thousand eight hundred yards!" Frantic activity followed. The barrel dropped level and the numbers four and five hefted the projectile cradle into position and slid it forward as number two stood behind with the rammer.

"*Almal geluik—stoot!*" They rammed the projectile home with a dull thud. Number two withdrew and number six stepped forward with the charge bags. He placed them behind the massive projectile. Number two closed the breech and retrieved a percussion tube from his pocket. He slid it home, lever across, hooked his lanyard on the firing ring, stepped over trail arm and waited.

The number three frantically wound the handles for elevation and line and called out his checks on the sights. With every rotation of the handles the huge barrel moved with ominous precision until the mouth stood ready to spit its deadly cargo at the enemy ten kilometres away.

"E!—L!—X!—L!—E!" he shouted while peering at his level bubble and elevation slide. Satisfied, he slapped the barrel and shouted "Up!" He too was ready. The number one glanced around his gun position. "Number three ready!" he shouted to Mark who nodded to his signaller

"Two Five Bravo, this is Two Zero, ready on Quebec 1001. Time of flight three five seconds. Over."

Mark listened and they waited. The command came. "Fire," said the voice, devoid of emotion. Mark knew the Transvaal Horse Artillery lieutenant well by now. They had worked together from the beginning and he respected the two-pip lieutenant's vast knowledge of gunnery. He was a professional.

Mark shouted with not a little excitement, "Fire!"

"Fire!" shouted the number one while the number two ducked as he yanked the lanyard. The ground shook as the 140mm howitzer kicked back against the spades in reaction to sending fifty kilograms of high explosive hurtling through the air.

Instantly Mark's signaller barked into the mouthpiece. "Shot over."

Mark looked at his watch and waited. Thirty seconds. Thirty-five seconds. Forty seconds. Forty-five seconds. "Damn. He's lost it," said Mark under his breath and the signaller nodded in agreement. They should have heard by now. Mark could imagine what it must be like though. So much smoke from the aerial bombardment and finding a projectile flash and smoke among the Eland 60 and 90 fire must be nigh on impossible. Mark knew that he was firing over the OP's left shoulder as he sat in his Eland 60. A correction was imminent.

The radio crackled, "Two Zero, this is Two Five Bravo. Drop one thousand, right five hundred. Adjust fire."

Mark called out the adjustment. Frantic activity followed as all the guns complied and number three gun reloaded. "Number three ready!" came the call.

"Fire," said Mark.

"Fire!" shouted the number one.

"Two Five Bravo, Two Zero. Shot over." Time oozed slowly by. Mark was anxious to get rounds on the ground. The quicker the OP guided them onto the target the more devastation they could wreak.

"Two Zero, Two Five Bravo. Drop two hundred. Three rounds fire for effect. Out."

There it was. "Load!" shouted Mark. "Range nine thousand six hundred. Three rounds fire for effect. Fire!" The massive boom of the guns and the hysterical shouting from the number ones calling the shots heightened Mark's euphoria. He was elated. In seconds, twenty-four HE shells would rain down on Quebec 1001.

At planning stage back in Oshivelo they'd originally spotted what looked like a Red Eye or Stalin Organ on the aerial photograph, and next to it, what looked like a couple of tanks and a 23mm AA position. Curiously they were pretty much in a straight line. Target reference Quebec 1001 was allocated to all of these.

"Number seven rounds fired!" *Shit, that was quick!* thought Mark and then like sprinters crossing the finish line, all of them had fired their rounds.

"Shots fired," said Mark to his signaller.

"Two Five Bravo this is Two Zero. Rounds fired, shots complete, over."

Mark waited and his ears buzzed after the voluble howitzers had delivered their opening chorus. His pulse quickened as the command came.

"Two Zero. Two Five Bravo. Repeat."

"Load!" shouted Mark again. "Three rounds, repeat!" And once again the gunners vociferously served the guns. Despite the first salvo unleashing its fury upon Quebec 1001 some enemy elements must have survived and reared their ugly heads. The OP had called the repeat, sending twenty-four more shells onto the same target. *Eat that, you bastards!* thought Mark as the dishevelled and blood-drained corpse of his driver filled his mind. Although Mark knew it was wrong, he couldn't help the feeling of elation surge through his body as he imagined the shells raining down on the enemy at the sharp end. By some dint of pure luck, the enemy had fired first and had hit the target, killing his men. The retaliation had been swift and precise.

They were firing the guns in anger.

"Two Zero, Two Five Bravo. Left two hundred, add four hundred. One round fire for effect," came the next command and Mark smiled. The bastards were probably running and the OP was cutting them off. The ground shook and his ears buzzed.

"Shots fired."

With the projectiles still in flight, the radio came to life. "Two Zero, Two Five Bravo, Quebec 1002 at my command, two rounds fire for effect."

There was no more time for reflection.

"HE 117, charge three. Load! Bearing!" Mark looked down at his clipboard as his command was being carried out. He looked up and shouted to his number ones, "Bearing one hundred and twenty-five degrees two nine minutes! Range eleven thousand five hundred and fifty yards! At my command, two rounds fire for effect!" Gut-wrenching activity and all were ready. To his signaller, "Two Five Bravo this is Two Zero ready on Quebec 1002. Time of flight four two seconds. Over." There was a pause and Mark held his breath.

"Fire," said the radio.

"Fire!" echoed Mark.

"Fire!" shouted the number ones. The ground shook and Mark counted the seconds. Quebec 1002 was history.

CHAPTER 36

Geoff's section along with two others made up a platoon. They formed part of Alpha Company who forged ahead through the objective with Bravo Company and with Charlie Company in reserve. Ahead, the artillery scythed a path of destruction. The armoured cars picked their way through the objective. The infantry, backed up by the Ratels, followed.

It seemed as if the attack was infallible and the infantry superfluous due to the strategy. Geoff began to feel overly relaxed. He knew he had to thrust the feeling of ease aside as it could be fatal. He noticed the artillery was bombing selected targets, as there were huge spaces within the objective untouched by projectile craters. It was in one of these open spaces that the infantry role became patently clear.

From two flanks 23mm AA opened fire at the Ratels who had no option but to charge at the anti-aircraft batteries in order to shut them down as quickly as possible or face destruction. With the Ratels temporarily out of the equation, AK fire flailed the infantry. The South Africans hit the dirt. Surprised and somewhat taken aback someone cried out painfully. Then followed shouts "Medic! Medic! Over here for God's sake!"

Geoff scanned the area and immediately took in the situation. To his left a line of intermittent flashes indicated concealed trenches.

"Swapo! Trenches, eleven o'clock!"

"Martin! Get that fucking Patmore going!"

"Pieter, Garth, Francois, rifle grenades!"

"Dawid, hit them!"

Frantic, anxious Geoff watched. Their first mortar burst on the lip of the trench. *Lucky bloody shooting*, he thought and he fired. He ventured a look and his eyes widened. The second mortar burst in the trench.

"Go Martin! You bastard!" The accuracy of the mortar gave Geoff the boost he needed and he vaulted to his feet. "Fire and movement!" he bellowed and ran forward, firing. The section followed, sending a constant hail of bullets at the target. Dawid remained where he was and hammered away at the trench, raking its entire length with deadly accuracy.

Close enough, thought Geoff. "Grenades!" he demanded and crashed to the sand. He followed the arc of one of the dark green bombs. The det handle flicked away. The hand grenade bounced once and skidded over the lip of the trench.

Wump! Wump! The noise of the explosions was dampened in the trench. That was the cue. Geoff leapt to his feet and galloped to the edge of the excavation. He fired up and down its length. To his left a figure leapt from cover. Panic-stricken, a man sprinted towards the trees at the far end of the clearing. Before Geoff could lift his rifle, a trail of bullets kicked up columns of sand and sought the fleeing man. Inevitably the bullets caught up and thumped into his back. He pitched forward and lay still. Geoff glanced over his shoulder.

Dawid was on his feet punching the air with delight. "Some more!" he shouted, "I want some more!" He all but disappeared behind large columns of sand as the 23mm opened up on him.

Geoff snapped his head around and his heart sank. Smoke poured from one of the Ratels. The crew had evacuated. They lay in the vicinity of the burning troop-carrier, returning fire. For a moment Geoff was confused as the enemy gunner searched for a target. On finding one, he would fire away for a few seconds but then change his aim and hammer away at the already knocked-out Ratel, effectively pinning the crew where they lay. It was a mystery. Why didn't he cull the Ratel crew? Suddenly it dawned on him. It was an anti-aircraft gun. He couldn't depress the barrel any lower; he couldn't fire down—only up or level. Geoff looked around frantically and caught Rudi's eye. He tapped his head with his fingers—"Come here," was the signal. Rudi sprinted a few metres, launched himself to the ground and skidded to a halt next to Geoff.

"What's up?" asked Rudi in conversational tone.

"Well, not that barrel." Geoff nodded towards the 23mm. "But it's also not down, so let's go and do some damage.

Rudi hesitated for a moment and grinned. "The bastard can't shoot down."

"Exactly," said Geoff. "Follow me." There was only one small problem. Merely minutes ago the trench had been in the hands of the enemy and not too many had fled, so it was still occupied.

It was probably because his bush hat hung from the cord attached to his epaulette exposing his short blond hair that the South Africans recognised him as one of their own and refrained from shooting at him, despite his blackened face. He and Rudi also passed at least half a dozen intact and very able-bodied enemy who froze in astonishment as the two big men raced by.

They came within fifty metres of the gun position before the gunner saw them. Geoff felt his legs turn to rubber. The gunner desperately brought the

23mm to bear. *Perhaps the fucking gun can depress*, thought Geoff and at the last moment his courage failed him. He glimpsed the gaping maw that was the flash hider. The basilisk. He dived forward as the mouth of the gun vomited more destruction. The bullets passed overhead. Geoff struggled to his feet. He aimed up at the gunner and fired. The bullet took the man in the shoulder and ripped him out of the seat. He landed awkwardly and rolled over. The gunner sat up in time to see the shot that killed him.

Geoff sank to the ground, rested his head on his knees for a second and looked up at Rudi. His face was lined with anxiety, relief. He smiled at his friend and the 23mm barked again. Both men fell to the bottom of the trench. Had the bastard survived? Rudi fired instinctively. The new gunner slid to the ground.

At last the rumour was dispelled. The gunners served their gun to the death. It was true. There had to be a bunker nearby. Enemy gunners ready to take over from their dead comrades. Geoff hauled his fatigued frame from the trench. A khaki-clad figure emerged from nowhere. Sworn foes gawked at each other. They fought desperately to bring their arms to bear. Geoff was perched precariously on the edge of the trench. The AK barrel swung towards him.

Geoff launched himself backwards and called out, "Take him Rudi!"

Rudi responded. Vague aim and pull the trigger. The familiar kick of the R1? Nothing happened. Out of ammunition for the second time that day. Rudi stared death in the face. No expression on the Swapo cadre's face. Cadre aimed at Rudi from point-blank range. Rudi knew it was over. He felt desperate. Sad that it should end this way. He turned his back in anticipation. Bullets would thump into his body. A machine gun fired. Rudi fell to the ground. He looked into Geoff's eyes. Confusion. Geoff grinned at him. "Not too amusing looking down the wrong end, eh old cock?" said Geoff. He picked himself up from the trench floor, dusted himself off and held out a hand to Rudi.

"What the fuck ...?"

Geoff shrugged. "Someone got him," he said and eyed the bullet-riddled body of the terrorist.

Rudi stood and shook his head. "I thought it was all over ..."

A shadow fell across the trench and both men turned. Dawid stood there. His eyes were slits as he peered down at them. His MAG hung from its canvas strap at a careless angle across his midriff. He smiled, retrieved a Texan plain from its crumpled pack and lit up. He blew a wobbly smoke ring, turned and walked away.

Geoff gaped at Rudi and smiled. "Christ, that's a first. The bastard saves our lives and says nothing."

Rudi gawked at the bodies littering the 23mm anti-aircraft position and turned to Geoff. "He will though. Wait and see."

"Come on," said Geoff, "this can't be over." They scrambled out of the trench and began searching for the entrance to the bunker. It was a masterful disguise with the narrow opening behind a broken, abandoned anthill. A clump of dead grass covered the opening. A deep frown creased Geoff's brow and he signalled for silence. He pointed at Martin. Martin nodded and tossed a grenade into the small opening. A dull thud shook the earth and smoke billowed out the hole. The tension mounted and they waited.

Towards the opposite end of the trench, rifle fire echoed across the open ground. Bravo Company and the surviving Swapo guerrillas engaged. Geoff found the sand. He ventured a glance. The Swapo soldiers threw their hands in the air in desperate surrender.

They waited as the corporal yelled at the prisoners to get out of the trench. Immobilised, the guerrillas froze. The corporal bellowed incoherently and shot them where they stood.

Martin opened his mouth. Geoff gesticulated wildly. "Shut up!" he urged.

A sudden flurry of movement alerted them and a black, dusty arm emerged from the smoking hole. A man hefted himself out of the opening. He placed his hands on his knees and coughed hoarsely. A second man followed and a third. They reached back into the opening and hauled out a fourth man who was bleeding from multiple wounds in his body and head. He was as good as dead. Geoff stepped forward and spoke in Afrikaans and then English. "*Is dit almal?* Is that all of you?" The man nodded and licked his lips.

"*Ek soek water*," he rasped, "I want water." Geoff hesitated and then reached for his water bottle. A single shot rang out and the man fell as if bludgeoned with a lead pipe. Geoff whipped around, his face a study of surprise and anger. Dawid stood side on. The barrel of his MAG still pointed at the dead man.

"How the fuck can you …?" he shouted. Geoff flinched and ducked. Dawid fired a short burst. Geoff stumbled backwards. He tripped and sat down hard. The other two guerrillas lay dead in the sparse dry grass.

"Like that," said Dawid calmly and drew on his cigarette. As if spring-loaded, Geoff bounded up and strode towards Dawid his face murderous his intention clear. As he drew level with his friend, Rudi stuck out his arm and restrained him.

"Don't," he said quietly, "the terrorist had a knife. He would have slit your throat."

Geoff grimaced. "What?" he croaked and struggled to break out of Rudi's iron grip.

Rudi clenched his jaw and held on. "He had a knife," he said again in a calming tone. "He would have killed you." Rudi nodded towards the corpse. "Take a look." Geoff turned and Rudi let go. The terrorist lay face down with his arm twisted up behind his back. His fist still grasped a long-bladed Ovambo knife, rusty and evil-looking. For a moment Geoff stared at the corpse and then looked up at his men. They stood quietly, giving him time.

He shook his head and looked at Dawid. "I think I owe you an …"

Dawid held up his hand. He dragged on the last of his cigarette, spat out a piece of tobacco and exhaled slowly. He let the smoke drift up past his face. "That's twice today, Kent," he said evenly. "Fortunately I don't keep score," he paused. "Surely you gotta realise that if these bastards can serve a gun to the death then when captured they might as well die trying to take you with."

Geoff nodded slowly and looked around. "Okay team, let's hit the road. We've got work to do." He was angry and embarrassed. He should know that a show of compassion to the enemy was a show of weakness to his troops. Above all, it had nearly cost him his life.

Geoff sat back and let his weary muscles relax. He allowed himself a little congratulation. Earlier the captain had informed them that they had advanced five kilometres through the objective on that first day. Geoff closed his eyes. *Thank you Lord,* he prayed. Immediately he felt embarrassed. There was no God. Not with all this sort of misery surrounding them.

"Hey Martin!" he called suddenly. "Give me a smoke, buddy."

"You don't …," he began and smiled. "Kill a few today, hey corporal?" he asked and lit a cigarette for Geoff. He tossed it over and Geoff caught it as a small shower of sparks erupted about his hand.

Geoff inhaled and grimaced. He hated the taste and wondered why he tortured himself with this silly ritual. *Curse you Allan Hunt!* he thought, wondering how he was faring with the most dreaded of tasks—walking patrol around the Ondangwa Air force Base. Nevertheless Geoff persevered with the cigarette and peered around at his exhausted men. Some ate from their rations; others tried sleep while others took their turn standing guard. Geoff turned to Rudi. He was trying hard not to cough as he dragged on a cigarette.

"Oh, not you too," groaned Geoff.

"This is a load of shit," croaked Rudi. He held up the cigarette in disgust. Geoff nodded and together they flicked away the half-smoked stubs.

"So this is what Joubert wanted you for, " Rudi pointed out to the killing field, "our part in Operation Brolly Tree."

"Yep, " Geoff nodded slowly, "but that wasn't all."

"Oh? What else?"

"Some staff sergeant …," Geoff paused. "Benade, I think, has been tasked with an investigation into the kraal killings. They're onto us …"

"Us?"

"Yeah, well Dawid, I suppose."

"For what? Killing collaborators?"

"Nope. For murdering them."

CHAPTER 37

Rudi Barker peered up the barrel of his R1. In the gloom of pre-dawn it was hard to tell if it shone although that hardly mattered; he knew that he had cleaned it well. He slid the dustcover home, snapped the rifle closed and clipped the magazine in place. Satisfied, he laid the rifle across his webbing and inspected the water in his fire bucket. The metal mug was battered and blackened with use. Balanced precariously above the burning tablet Rudi waited for the water to boil.

Geoff stared at the little flame and sipped noisily. He always seemed to be ready first. He sat with his legs astride, elbows rested on his knees and blew the steam off the top of his coffee.

Rudi glanced at Geoff. "What's got you so deep in thought?"

Geoff shrugged and the corners of his mouth hinted at a smile.

Rudi knew his friend so well. He retrieved his fire bucket, emptied the contents of the sachet into the boiling water, squeezed in a dollop of condensed milk and stirred. "It's her again isn't it?" he asked.

Geoff looked up and smiled. "What makes you say that?"

"It's the letter you received just before we left Eenhana and it's written all over your face."

"Nonsense."

"Then pray sir, why are you smiling?"

Geoff shook his head and smiled. He slipped his hand into his top pocket and carefully retrieved the page. He turned it over as if it were a piece of fragile china and stared at the neat cursive writing on the front. 'Geoff' it said and he shuddered. The memory of the last letter with the same neat writing and floral pattern had sent him into the depths of despair. He smiled nervously and tapped the letter on the palm of his hand. He opened the page, peered at the message in the strengthening light and read aloud.

"If you've got anything to say, stand before me and say it. You know where I live. G."

Geoff read the note again and again, slowly. He was trying to read between the lines, to fathom if she were being sarcastic or hurtful or if the whole meaning were derogatory or hopeful.

"That's the proverbial olive leaf, boyo," offered Rudi and sipped noisily on his coffee.

Geoff was embarrassed. "Can it, old cock," he admonished. "We've got work to do today."

Geoff threw the dregs of coffee on the ground and packed his fire bucket away. He stood, slung his webbing over his shoulders and lifted his rifle by the strap.

"Come on, Dawid, you'll make us late," he urged.

"Ja, ja. I'm coming."

"Pieter have you filled your magazines?"

"Sure corporal."

"Martin, did you manage to organise a few more mortar bombs for the Patmore?"

"Ja, corporal, but only four."

"Okay, that'll have to do. How about grenades?"

"Plenty."

"Francois, is that your water bottle lying there?"

"Ja, sorry man, corporal."

"No problem, just don't leave it there."

"Rudi, have you got spare batteries for that?" Geoff pointed at the radio.

"Yep. We're all juiced up and ready to go."

"Shit, I'd love to be juiced up right now," said Martin. No one laughed. The tension was a physical thing that shrouded them like a thick blanket.

Once again the waiting began. Geoff felt his old and familiar friend tighten its grip in his guts. He held out his hand and spread his fingers. They shook so. Geoff quickly clenched his fist. Perhaps Gabi was right, perhaps he was wounded. "God I wish it would begin," he whispered. Rudi pursed his lips and nodded. He was staring at Geoff's clenched fist.

God answered. The first artillery shell crackled overhead and burst north of them. That was the signal and the vehicles—armoured cars, Buffels and Ratels—began moving through no man's land to the objective. A second shell ripped into the earth and threw up a column of sand and smoke. It was followed by a third and a fourth and finally the barrage came down—the OP had found his target. The death acre was an eruption of dust, smoke and living hell as the Eland 60s and 90s added their projectiles to the cataclysm. Alpha and Charlie Company closed in on their quarry, leaving a litter of bodies behind them.

The pursuit slackened and Rudi shouted to his corporal. "Geoff, stop! Stop for fuck's sake! We're running onto the stopper groups!" He held up the handset of his radio. Finally the entire infantry, mechanised and foot soldiers, ground to a reluctant halt and watched from a distance as the fleeing enemy thrashed themselves to death against the waiting ambuscade of Parabats. It was awful. So much death and so much destruction and so many bodies and so much indignity in death. Geoff had seen this before, but probably not in such profusion and he felt sick to his stomach. They littered the dry veld as far as the eye could see. Some of them still lived and thrashed around in agony. Geoff looked about expectantly. The adrenaline coursed through his veins as he searched the area for any threat or counter-attack.

"What's the buzz on the radio, Rudi?" asked Geoff. He held his rifle at the ready.

Rudi shrugged, "I dunno. Nothing's come through yet."

"Okay, let's stick together. Perhaps it's all over …"

"Don't speak too soon!" admonished Rudi and he crossed his fingers. "Let's not spoil it by speaking too soon."

Geoff smiled at his friend. Rudi had a thick stubble covering his blackened face and his eyes were bloodshot and sunken. "Okay buddy, I'll shut up."

"Good. Wanna sip?" Rudi offered his water bottle.

"Nah. I'll use mine, thanks."

"Jeez, look at that!" exclaimed Martin and all heads followed his gaze. Bravo Company had been busy cleaning up and a string of Swapo cadres stood in a line with their hands on their heads, but that was not too unexpected. What was unexpected though was the group of white men in camouflage uniform standing off to one side with an eager and attentive section of South African soldiers hovering menacingly about them.

"Ruskies, I'll bet."

Geoff shook his head incredulously. He pushed his bush hat back and scratched his forehead. "Let's go take a closer look," he said with a glint in his eye. They passed a Ratel where a team of combat medics tended to the wounded. A soldier lay on the ground and moaned. An aide stood by and held up a drip. The medic worked frantically on the wounded man. It was a stomach wound and Geoff knew that he wouldn't make it. There was so much blood. "Poor bastard," he said and Martin nodded.

"Yeah. He's a goner for sure."

They moved on and halted in front of the sorry band of Soviet soldiers.

"So you bastards *are* involved," said Geoff and he gestured towards the many dead. "Supporting the wrong side, wouldn't you say, hey Boris Kutyurkokov?" Laughter rippled. "So what's it like now that you're stripped down to the bear necessities, eh Vladimir Punchyerfacein?" More laughter. "You shouldn't go Russian in where angels fear to tread." This time the laughter caught on and became contagious. Geoff stood directly in front of one of the larger Russian soldiers. "You see that man busy dying back there, Gregori Haventlostmydickyet …?" He jerked his thumb over his shoulder. "He's going to die because you dicks support these useless fuckers," They stood eye to eye and Geoff poised to strike. Like lava welling up to the lip of the volcano, Geoff felt an uncontrollable hatred brew and fizzle in his veins.

"Hey you! Corporal!" Geoff turned. The captain's face was vaguely familiar.

"Captain?"

"Get the hell away from those prisoners."

"But …!"

"Get away!" The captain shook his finger aggressively and closed in on Geoff. He had read the situation well. There was bound to be reaction especially after the adrenaline high of combat. The prisoners were worth their weight in gold. The world had to know that the Soviet threat in southern Africa was real.

Geoff spun around and lifted his hand as if to strike. The Russian flinched, lost his balance and nearly fell. A chorus of laughter followed and Geoff stepped away sneering, "God, that felt good."

CHAPTER 38

The BM-21 multiple rocket launcher is an incredibly impressive weapon. Ten pipes horizontally and four vertically—a pod of forty rockets per launcher screamed over to the South African gun positions. John had supplied the co-ordinates. Although they seemed unimpressed, the Cubans would definitely be inquisitive about his intelligence network. John had supplied enough information to stop the South Africans in their tracks. The gun positions, the position of the helicopter administrative area and the echelon position.

But for now John held his hands to his ears as another salvo of rockets streaked into the heavens. The noise from the rocket blast was tumultuous, leaving a corduroy of smoke trails in the sky. The second salvo took to the heavens and John smiled. He felt the jubilation; it effervesced in his veins. At last they were fighting back with force. They were inflicting losses!

Then, as if by some ancient sorcery, the jets were there. They came in so fast that John hardly had time to escape the terrible bombardment. The first bomb exploded, sending a shock wave rippling across the earth that slapped his fatigues against his skin like a blast of wind. And he moved. He and those around him never stopped moving. For the next nine or was it ten days, John had lost count, they ran.

John's hatred manifested itself like a cancer. It grew fast, spreading its tentacles throughout his body and the pain that it caused him was debilitating. There was nothing he could do to stop the southern racist regime's war machine as it inexorably moved through the meticulously constructed military base. Even worse was the deliberate turn to the north as if they knew exactly where the headquarters were.

Despite intermittent incoming artillery, John had learned that the cover of darkness was a time to recover from the brutal pruning he and his troops were suffering. John sat with his lieutenants and smoked. Their eyes betrayed the horrors they'd witnessed.

The captain pondered. He needed to somehow pacify their anguish. "What of Enoch Shongwe?" he asked and smiled.

"He has conjured up an intelligence source. He guards it with his life."

John lifted his hands, his fingers curled into claws. Even in the darkness the captain witnessed the menace in his eyes. "As long as he supplies information of such value he lives."

"Why would you want to destroy a source so vital?"

John exhaled and spat. "He was in the Mariental gaol. There you either die or they force you to work for them." John searched the heavens as if to find the answers. "No one just walks out of that, that Gehenna," he shook his head, "but Enoch did."

"You think they bait him to get us?"

"Yes."

"Why not kill him now? Find him and rid yourself of this burden."

John shook his head. "Because of the information we received from Victor before they killed him."

The captain hesitated. He was confused. "Victor said the information came from the woman, the brigadier's woman?"

"Oh, it did alright. But the same information also came from Enoch."

The captain shrugged. "So they spoke."

"Enoch never met Victor. He never met the woman. He was never allowed to enter Oshakati."

A silence followed. Then the captain gave a discerning nod. "Ah, so he received this same information from a completely different source."

John sat forward. "Not only that. It was Enoch who gave me the co-ordinates of the South African gun position!"

"Have you asked him about this source?"

"Oh yes," John nodded. "I asked and he rambles on about two people—a white man, a police lieutenant he has met and a white woman, an army lieutenant he has not. A brother and a sister."

"But you struck their artillery position and inflicted losses …"

"And ever since then we have been running," John spat. "Have you ever seen what one of their projectiles does when it penetrates the ground even metres away from a bunker?" He leant forward and peered into the captain's eyes. "The shock waves alone rupture a man's spleen. It bursts his eardrums and it sucks the living breath from his lungs without the shrapnel even touching him!"

The captain held up his hand, "Don't shout …"

"Have you seen what happens to a man standing within fifty metres of a projectile explosion? He is vaporised! You never even find the body! And further away men are blasted into a pulpy mess of blood, splintered bones and sinew that my men have to bury." John sat back. He was breathing heavily. He closed his eyes. His breathing normalised and he whispered, "We've buried a lot of them lately."

※

For once John was at a loss. Reluctantly he climbed down from his place of concealment and made his way back to where his men waited in a shallow ravine. The bush in the immediate vicinity was relatively lush and fairly thick. Apart from the cover that it offered, it concealed a string of shallow hollows beneath a low overhang. Bushes grew in front of the overhang and the cave-like hollows were difficult to see even if one peered through the bush. John and his men had stumbled across this natural little hideout quite by accident. He rubbed his jaw thoughtfully and called his men.

"We have a few options," he told them gravely. "We can walk away from here and never come back." There were a few gasps. John had been the only one who, without doubt, had remained so incredibly steadfast in his commitment to the war. "And I say that because we must continue the struggle from within our own country. Here we are getting mixed up with the Angolan struggle and the issues are becoming blurred." He was then silent.

"You said there are options," inquired one of his lieutenants. "What else can we do?"

"Harvest a little revenge and then head south, back to the unfinished business in Tsumeb," John said with the gleam of hatred in his eye. "That way the Boere will see that the war is as far south as it is north here in Angola. And that farm is the key; it lies on the border between what is south and what is north."

There were smiles now. They liked the sound of John's second option. "What is your plan?" asked the lieutenant.

"There is a platoon of South Africans sitting off to one side near to us. We should attack them with everything we have and run like the wind to this place." John pointed to the overhang with his chin. "We attack at last light and hide here until they leave."

The lieutenant looked uncomfortable. "What if they find us?"

"Look around you," commanded John venomously. "Look how they destroyed everything. I will welcome it if they do find us. Then we fight to the death. But if they don't, we live to fight another day. Now who is with me?" he asked menacingly.

They took a long time to get close to the South African section. Once a soldier walked away from his colleagues, unbuttoned his fly and began to urinate. In the twilight he did not notice how close he was to dying. Achingly slowly John lifted his head and surveyed the scene and then he saw Geoff. Even through the dirt and camouflage paint John recognised him. Wherever and whenever John was on the rampage the South Africans had this big white-haired man waiting for him. He was now convinced that this man was after him as ordered by higher authority.

John thought for a moment. Everyone knew of Grootvoet and even the South African Government was afraid of him. That was it then—this man was probably Special Forces and was specifically tasked with the destruction of Grootvoet. This would be small compensation and a fitting end to the South African invasion. John lifted his AK and took careful aim. He squeezed off a shot and two men went down. The tall blond one was gone. Another stood riveted with shock and John fired again. Once again the Swapo officer was surprised by the reaction of the South Africans for he never heard a single shot from any of his own men before the soldier with the MAG opened fire. In the dying light John ran with all the adrenaline of a hunted man. He ran far away from their little hideout to an agreed point whereupon he began the tedious task of anti-tracking. He knew he had to do it properly for if there were any of the ghostly ones with the war machine they would pick up the ruse immediately.

For hours John lay dead-still in his little hollow and listened to the night sounds. At one stage there were voices close by and some distant shouts but later it was only the sound of the crickets. John relied on the crickets for they ceased their incessant chirping only if disturbed.

It would take a normal man a great deal of self-control to avoid a constant vigil on the time, but John had his thoughts and they were evil. As he waited, his mind drifted back over the years and more vividly through the past few months. At every turn he was beaten. Beaten by an enemy so vile that the thought of them and their successes against him brought bitter bile flooding out from under his tongue. He clenched his fists so hard he heard his fingers crack. He resisted the temptation to scream his frustrations and woes to his ancestors and his dead father. He bit his lip and grimaced as the coppery blood ran down the back of his throat. It was then that he felt it happen. Almost as physical as a pulled muscle he felt the fabric of his mind stretch and tear. All emotions drained from his being, leaving only one. He never felt the blood drip from his chin, only the narcotic of hatred that coursed along every fibre of his being and it gave him strength. That night, John stepped across the border that separates the irrational from the monstrous—and he took the step willingly.

He retrieved his watch from his pocket and squinted at it in the darkness. The night sky gave just enough light for him to see that it was three o'clock—time to move.

He stood up cautiously and looked around. He couldn't see much in the blackness but that could not be helped; they simply had to move. John lifted his hands to his mouth and contrived the call of a nightjar. Like wraiths his men appeared at his side and squatted. John looked at his band of warriors. Their number had been sorely depleted, especially by the white monster with the MAG.

"We must go," he said simply. "We meet at the 'Mississ' in a week." Mississippi Satisfaction, a brothel outside Oshakati that all of them knew, some too well. The men wandered off into the darkness. No man followed the same path. They had bombshelled.

CHAPTER 39

The HQ was built entirely underground and although slightly cramped it housed the nerve centre of the combined forces against South Africa and the rebel forces of Jonas Savimbi's Unita. Even the generator supplying electricity was below ground with only the exhaust visible, cleverly camouflaged to look like the central stem of a thick bush. Maps covered the walls and a bank of Soviet-built radios filled the one corner. A suite of eight chairs and a table filled the middle of the shelter and boxes of food supplies took up the remainder of the space. Throughout the network of trenches were many smaller shelters and bunkers, most empty but a few housing copious quantities of small arms and ammunition.

The others contained food supplies. When finally hauled to the surface, there were hundreds of food crates. On closer inspection it became evident that they were supplied from the most unlikely sources. Geoff wondered if countries like Denmark and Holland and organisations like UNICEF were aware that their supplies fed a long, nefarious war.

"Damn their self-righteous ignorance," said Geoff bitterly. "They should come and take a look at this mess before they say their evening prayers." The bodies were beginning to swell in the midday heat. The flies were busy too. Clouds of them hovered and buzzed greedily around the bodies not yet zipped into bags and Geoff shook his head. "I've had enough of this shit," he said. "I want to go back to Eenhana. It's far more comfortable there."

Rudi smiled, "Yeah it seems ludicrous that we want to go back to the border. It may even seem tame after this."

"Damn right!" exclaimed Geoff.

The cleaning-up continued and convoys of captured vehicles headed south. It was almost twilight when Rudi trotted over and joined the rest of his section. He could hardly contain himself as the others waited patiently for the news.

"You boys been waiting for me …?"

Geoff grabbed a fistful of sleeve and pulled him closer. "Do you value your genitals old friend?"

"Of course and watch out, they're full."

Geoff laughed. "Yeah? Now out with it," he ordered.

"Well," began Rudi, "it seems we've managed to piss off old Perez de Cuellar. He's decided that we are now no longer defending but invading and we have been ordered to get the fuck out—immediately!" A cheer rang out and Geoff leant forward to quieten his men. He didn't need attention. They were standing off to one side avoiding the tedious and revolting work of stuffing dead terrorists into body bags. Geoff leant forward enough to grab Martin as he was making the most noise. He didn't even hear the shot. The men stumbled back and fell to the ground in a heap.

"Get off me!" Geoff pushed Martin. "What the fuck do you think you're doing ...?" Then he saw the blood. Confused, he looked up at Rudi. His eyes widened in horror as Rudi's head snapped back. His bush hat spiralled away and he slumped to the ground.

"No!" he shouted. "Oh God, no!" Geoff jerked his head around and saw the flash as the third shot rang out. The shooter wasn't far away. Time stood still. Geoff stared at the terrorist. He froze. At the sound of the MAG he snapped back to reality. He rolled Martin away, grabbed his rifle and came to a sprint in one fluid movement. He dived to the ground, aimed and fired. He pulled the trigger until the rifle clicked empty. When Geoff next looked over his sights the man had vanished and it was then that he realised that he'd seen the man before. The fact that he recognised the terrorist was a certainty.

Dawid continued the pursuit. Geoff ran back to Rudi, knelt next to him and eased his body up against his leg. Rudi's head lolled to the side and Geoff saw the wound. The blood was thick and black and poured out of a gaping hole.

"Medic!" screamed Geoff. "Medic, for God's sake!" He pulled Rudi's head to his chest and held him hard as if to staunch the flow of blood and prevent his soul from leaving. "Rudi ...," he moaned. "Don't leave me, buddy. Please don't leave me." The blood was sticky on his hands as he cradled his friend. "Medic ...!"

"I'm here corporal, I'm here. Let me take a look. Let go of him and let me take a look." Reluctantly Geoff lowered Rudi's head. Immediately the medic took over. He wiped around the wound and poured some water over it to get a better look. The blood welled up immediately and Geoff's eyes widened in horror as the medic suddenly plunged his finger into the wound and began digging around in there. His horror turned to confusion as the medic's finger emerged from a second hole just inside Rudi's hairline. "He's bloody lucky your mate. Got a head like a fucking cannon ball."

"What do you mean? Is he okay?" Geoff hesitated. He couldn't dare hope.

The medic breathed in deeply, "Well he's going to have one mother of a headache but yeah, he'll live."

"Jesus Christ, that's unbelievable man! What, I mean how …?"

"Flesh wound. The bullet hit his head at a very small tangent and instead of smashing into the skull it travelled around it beneath the flesh and came out here." The medic pointed to the exit wound. "He's one lucky guy. Now help me with this drip."

"Wait," said Geoff, "what about the other one?" He nodded towards Martin.

The medic shook his head and pursed his lips, "No point; he was dead when I got here. Now just hold the drip up like this."

Geoff gaped at Martin. He shook his head slowly. The enormity of death suddenly struck him. Minutes ago Martin had been so alive—so much so that Geoff was becoming irritated with his vociferous behaviour and now he was dead. Just like that. The lump in Geoff's throat was so intense that it hurt.

"Sorry Martin," he whispered. "I'm so sorry buddy." Martin's dirt-stained face blurred before him and a single tear escaped and slid down his face. Geoff wiped it away quickly, looked up at the evening sky and whispered, "Gabi, I need you."

CHAPTER 40

"*Baie dankie, meneer.* Thank you very much for the lift," said Geoff as he hauled his legs out of the cramped space of the van and gathered his rifle and kit. Geoff stood in a cloud of dust, contemplating the wisdom of his decision to see Gabi. It was the note that did it, he reminded himself, and Rudi's complete confidence in the final outcome in their relationship. Gabi had left it up to him, but at least she'd shown him that the way forward was not barred. Geoff looked up the drive, sighed and began to walk towards the cottage.

Even though the summer rains had not yet brought relief to the hot, dry land, the new shoots were everywhere and the farm was transformed from dull brown to hopeful green. In places there were splashes of colour—red poinsettia at the corner of the old farmhouse and the turning island at the back with the strelitzia beneath the palm and the bougainvillea creeping towards the fronds. He noticed too how the restoration of the old house had advanced at a snail's pace. The corner stones had been delivered and the brickwork was up to sill height but Geoff could see the builders were way behind on the programme that Gabi had shown him. She didn't seem to be in any sort of rush though and it wasn't his place to interfere anyway. Strewth! What the hell was he thinking—she might not even take him back, let alone ask for his opinion. God! What a bloody fool he'd been. Geoff hefted his rifle higher up his shoulder and watched the labourers as he pondered her reaction to his arrival.

Something was making him feel uncomfortable. It gnawed at his subconscious. Was it something he forgot to do before leaving camp, some duty left undone or perhaps something he was going to say to Gabi? Something was wrong—very wrong and he couldn't put his finger on it. He continued to watch the builders without seeing them. Geoff couldn't be sure what it was or even if it mattered but all too often in the past he'd relied on his instinct for his very survival and now the warning bells were chiming so loudly that he rubbed his eyes and looked up again.

The builders sweated as they toiled, all of them heads down and aggressively engaged in their specific tasks, but they were doing nothing. A labourer pushed a wheelbarrow full of bricks to his bricklayer who helped offload them onto the scaffold planks tied to the trestles. All over bricks were being moved about and the bricklayers busied themselves with stacking. No profiles had been fixed and even more confusing was the fact that no mortar had been mixed. Geoff smiled at one of the workers. The man looked away quickly and carried on with his task. Geoff looked over at the cement shed. Through the open door he could see brown pockets of South African cement stacked to the roof. He looked past the shed and noticed that the pile of building sand was at least waist high. Surely the only reason for not mixing the mortar was water, or a lack of it. Perhaps the borehole was dry. He shrugged and was about to walk away when one of the builders walked over to the tap, squatted, placed his mouth over the tap and drank deeply. The man stood and rubbed his hands under the gushing water. As he walked he wiped his mouth on the sleeve of his shirt and Geoff noticed something else. All of them were wearing khaki shirts and short khaki pants. The last time he remembered they wore overalls, all blue and in varying degrees of disrepair, but overalls nonetheless. Still, their manager could have bought them new clothes in the interim. Strange though, how many of these men could do with a needle and cotton on their khakis. And thinking of managers, Geoff wondered where the old gang boss was.

Previously, whenever he or Gabi rode past, the old man would drop whatever he was doing and wave frantically. Geoff looked past the building to the big tree on the front lawn. The grass was unkempt. A tall man stood beneath the tree supporting himself on one of the lower branches, his face partially hidden by the shade. Geoff peered at the man for a second, smiled suddenly and waved. Reluctantly the man dropped his arm to return the wave and in so doing, moved fractionally. As he did so a ray of sunlight fell across his face, lighting it for a second. It certainly wasn't the old gang boss but Geoff did recognise him—from somewhere. Geoff turned and carried on up the drive to the cottage. All the time Geoff's mind raced as he tried to fathom the situation.

He stopped and shook his head. How incredibly stupid he was being; the solution was simple. Gabi had most likely fired the previous builder and hired another. Geoff continued on his way, feeling as if a huge weight had been lifted from his shoulders and he quickened his step in anticipation of seeing Gabi again. But a little niggle stubbornly lingered and refused to give way to his lighter mood. What the hell was the matter with him? It could only be the anticipation of the meeting … no. It was the face. The fleeting glimpse of the gang boss. He'd seen that face before and the last time he looked into those eyes he had stared into the depths of a monstrous hell. Geoff was certain now. It was the terrorist he had seen on the follow-up after the Puma disaster, when they had come so close to being surrounded by the well-trained gang led by a madman. Geoff could still remember the depth of horror he felt as the man's eyes bored into him before he disappeared into the bush. It was the same man who had deliberately aimed at him and killed Martin. The very same man who had shot Rudi. Sweat broke out on Geoff's forehead and began to run trickle his face. He felt the itch of it as it ran down his back and soaked into his shirt. He dare not look back for fear of arousing suspicion and if he ran, the game was over. He forced himself to take a single step at a time, his back cringing in anticipation of knife or bullet.

At the top of the gentle rise by the bend, Geoff knew he was no longer in sight and he ran. He ran with all the power he could muster, pumping arms and legs with single-minded determination. He grimaced with the effort, increasing his speed as the cottage came into view. He ran past the security fence, along the side of the cottage and into the back yard. No one was in sight but the Land Cruiser was there and Geoff suddenly wished it wasn't.

"Gabi!" he called, knowing his hysterical bellow would carry to the men at the old house. He was out of time though and he knew that they were on their way already. "Gabi! Gabi, where are you?" he called frantically. "Gabi …!"

"I'm here." Gabi emerged from the vegetable patch with a basket of freshly harvested tomatoes. She stopped at the gate and looked at Geoff with such a damning expression that had the circumstances been different, he might have lost his nerve and walked away. Despite the situation, Geoff paused for a fraction of a second, for he suddenly knew that he wanted her more than anything else in the world. But he might lose her if he didn't act now.

"Get the Cruiser and pick me up …"

"Just a minute …," she began and placed her hands on her hips.

"There's no time to argue!" he bellowed.

"Geoff!" A shout from behind her and Sven raced past Gabi and flew at him. Geoff gathered the child as the first shot rang out. It kicked up a column of sand in front of them.

"Take him and bring the bloody Cruiser!" shouted Geoff. He wore a dreadful expression. He spun to face the men running up at them. He picked the man he wanted, dived to the ground and squeezed off a shot. Too quick. His target was better than that. Without a second thought, Geoff turned the rifle a fraction and fired at the next man. He went down. Geoff fired again and again, aiming each shot. The attack abated. How many were there? Geoff had to know! Five lay on the ground, four of them still. One dragged himself towards the cover of the mopani scrub. Geoff fired again and the man lay still. This was the perfect time to move—where the hell was Gabi? Geoff grabbed his kitbag and rolled into the drainage ditch next to the vegetable garden. He dug around for an extra magazine. He looked back for Gabi and his heart sank. The farm foreman … the bloody foreman was aiming a pistol to Gabi's head and held Sven up in front of his face. The man was grey with fear and unpredictable and the longer Geoff waited the worse the situation became.

"Please put down your gun Mister Geoff," said Jacob, "I don't want to hurt Miss Gabi or Master Sven."

All the time Geoff had known him, he'd only ever spoken Afrikaans and now he spoke clear, piping English. *The bastard must have been involved in the original farm massacre*, thought Geoff. *A bloody two-faced traitor.* He felt anger displace his numbing fear. He looked for a gap and was astounded to see none. Jacob must have had some sort of training. He held Sven high up covering his body, with Gabi in front of him. Geoff stared at Gabi as if to will her to do something. Her face was white with terror but suddenly, perhaps due to the expression on his face or because her son was being threatened, Gabi spun, snatched at Sven with one hand and went for Jacob with the other. Jacob was taken by surprise and stepped back to avoid Gabi's raking nails. Geoff lifted the rifle, took vague aim and fired. Jacob never felt the pain as the 7.62mm bullet smashed through his shinbone, blowing it to smithereens. The momentum jerked his leg out from under him. He dropped Sven in order to break his fall. The shock slowed his reactions and before he could recover, Geoff fired twice into the foreman's torso.

"Bring the Cruiser, Gabi!" shouted Geoff hoping to snap her out of the shock that riveted her. Sven began to cry and Gabi moved. She gathered him up and dashed to the bakkie. Seconds later Geoff heard the big engine roar to life. The wheels spun, hauling the vehicle out of its parking. The gears grated as she slammed the LDV into first. She tore down the drive and Geoff judged it finely. He dived into the back with his rifle as the vehicle roared past. The back window shattered followed by the front and glass showered down over him. He closed his eyes instinctively and covered his face with his arm. He lifted his head and his eyes widened in disbelief as ragged holes quickly appeared in the side of the body. He ducked down, flattening his body on the corrugated steel of the bakkie load bay, cringing as the sound of automatic fire engulfed him. The Land Cruiser skidded from side to side and a jolting crash concluded the tumult. With it ended Geoff's last memory of their desperate flight.

The blackness faded. Geoff shook his head and struggled to sit up. Something crashed against his head and bright lights flashed before him, blinding him with immense pain. Instinctively he rolled over, lifted his legs to his chest and covered his head with his arms. He could feel the blood flowing down his face. A brutal blow to his exposed ribs sent another wave of agony through his body. He rolled from side to side in an effort to alleviate the pain. A sonorous voice issued some sort of an order and Geoff was dragged roughly to the workbench and slung against the wooden leg. His body ached everywhere as he shook his head, waiting for his sight to focus. He felt the icy grip of despair as he took in the situation. A gang of khaki-clad black men stood around, all of them armed with AK-47s. A man stood on either side of him. The one on his left looked down at Geoff and smiled. The smile faded suddenly as he made the motion as if to strike. Geoff lifted his arms and cringed in anticipation of another wicked blow. The terrorist pulled his punch and the men laughed volubly at his reaction.

In an effort to thwart the blow, Geoff retracted his head below the workbench. He emerged and peered up warily, ready to defend himself. The butt of an AK protruded from the edge of the work top. He felt a glimmer of hope, a tenuous flicker of light in a vast ocean of darkness, but the risk was great. It had taken this long for him to realise that he was in the shed at the back of the cottage. The workbench was close to the entrance and the double-leafed, wooden-slatted door stood wide open allowing the bright afternoon sun to beat down. It reflected off the white sand, blinding him so much that the interior of the shed was impenetrable blackness.

He heard a sound in the darkness at the back of the shed and he held his breath. A distraction! A bit of inattention from these bastards and the game was on. There was no way they were going to let him live and there was no way they were going to let him die easily. Geoff resigned himself to his fate but if he were going to die, he might as well die trying to escape. Snatch the AK on top of the workbench! Was the rifle's selector on safe or automatic? He must remember that the selector is on the opposite side to the R1 and the first notch sets it to automatic. Who should he shoot at first? The men stood around him and he was certain that there was someone standing in the darkness at the back of the shed. Perhaps he should shoot randomly into the darkness first then hit the others. The more Geoff's mind raced the more he grew in confidence. He tensed up and took a deep breath—he needed another distraction and he was ready to explode into action. His best bet was to grab the AK and hit the floor, offering as small a target as possible, fire into the dark, roll over, take the group next to the work bench, roll again and hit the others at the door. *God, please help me*, he prayed. *Please be on my side*.

Funny how desperately one needed God in these situations and suddenly Geoff thought of Gabi and Sven. Where were they? Had they been injured in the crash—or even killed? Perhaps the terrorists had done their dirty work already. As if in answer, Geoff heard a muted whimper emanate from the darkness at the back of the shed. There was no mistaking the voice. It was Sven. Geoff looked around. The terrorists were peering into the shed. The time was now! Go! Go!

Sanity prevailed. If he fired into the darkness he could hit the boy, perhaps even kill him. He couldn't live with himself if that happened. The squeak of steel wheel on rusty axle caught his attention and then the horror. The sunlight bathed the rusty engine gantry and tied to it was Gabi. Her face and arms were bloodied from flying through the windscreen of the Land Cruiser and her clothes were torn and filthy. They had tied her wrists to the opposite corners of the cross-member. Her feet were tied to the support struts at either side of the gantry. Gabi hung, spread-eagled like a star. She was completely vulnerable. The blood had run down her arms and seeped into her shirt, making the spectacle look worse than it was. Tears ran down her face, cutting paths through the blood and dirt. She shook her head slowly, hopelessly, as she looked at Geoff.

A man appeared at her side and Geoff recognised him immediately. He had a presence about him that sent shivers down Geoff's spine. He was taller than Geoff and easily as athletic. His features were typically those of an Ovambo headman or chief. Somehow he was handsome, but it was his eyes—they were darker than his skin and exuded a deep evil. Sven started to crawl desperately towards Geoff. The big terrorist grabbed a handful of his hair and yanked the boy back.

"Geoff," he whimpered. Big oily tears streamed down his face and the terrorist shook Sven's head vigorously.

Be still, brat," he said in the sonorous voice Geoff had heard earlier.

"Don't cry Sven, just look into my eyes and bite hard boy," urged Geoff and his personal sentry punched him in the mouth. Geoff tasted blood, shook his head and stared at Sven. His look was intense, even fierce, as willed the boy to be brave.

"I'm so sorry Geoff. They said they'd kill us if we said a word …," began Gabi in a tremulous voice. The big terrorist let go of Sven, turned and slapped Gabi such a blow that her legs buckled and she hung from her arms. Her hair whipped around her head, covering her face and Sven took the opportunity to run. From two metres away he leapt into Geoff's arms, buried his head and sobbed. Geoff's arms engulfed the boy and squeezed. Two of the terrorists lifted their weapons and aimed. Geoff lifted his hand in a pathetic gesture to stop the bullets and hugged the boy to his body.

"Please don't shoot. Please don't kill the boy," he begged. Incredibly they acceded to his pleas.

Geoff looked at the big terrorist. He stood with arms folded and legs astride. "It seems rather ludicrous to save your miserable life only to kill you later, but I think you might appreciate why in a short while." He spoke very well, with only the slightest accent. Geoff blinked and stared at the man. "You seem surprised at my command of the English language," he smiled. It was an evil grimace. "I have travelled the world in order to learn how to kill young white South Africans …," he paused and aimed an open hand at Geoff, "… like you and coincidently I picked up an education. I had to learn English. It will be our official language when we take our country back. You see I'm going to outlaw Afrikaans and German. They have done a lot of damage here as you well know."

"I'm English …," began Geoff. The big terrorist nodded. This time the blow knocked Geoff to his side and he nearly lost Sven. He sat up slowly, holding the distraught boy to his chest and he rubbed his aching head.

"Never interrupt me. I thought your army prided itself on its discipline. I outrank you so shut up and listen." The big terrorist looked at Gabi and back at Geoff. "I used to hate the name because it is Afrikaans but then I realised that it struck fear and uncertainty into the hearts of my enemies and it started to work for me." He shook his head and smiled. "Grootvoet," he rolled the name around his tongue. "I suppose you think I should be insulted too, but for us Ovambos it is a sign of virility. I have the biggest feet in the whole of Ovamboland and you people fear me."

"You're Grootvoet?" asked Geoff in amazement.

John Mulemba frowned and looked at Geoff suspiciously. "You seem like you did not know that." John smiled again. "Well then, I have succeeded better than anticipated, but I do find that difficult to believe. After all it is you who has been chasing me for months now, is it not?"

"I was carrying out my orders, the orders issued to me by the South African government." To argue was pointless; Geoff was merely playing for time. His plan of attack might still work. It had to work, they were going to die anyway—all of them, so there was nothing to lose. The problem was Sven. The boy clung desperately to Geoff and so he needed a bit more time. "We have no option in my country, we are compelled to do national service and some of us land up here."

"It seems to me that you carry out your orders with extreme prejudice and even enjoy killing my men, so you being English does you no good." John stared out at the yard and looked at Geoff with that evil stare. "You foiled my efforts with the new drive south." John paused. "You may as well know the whole story; it will do you no good now anyway. Your army is quite happy to believe that the war for independence is contained in your so-called danger zone, north of Oshivelo. I am taking this war south and it begins with this farm," John gestured towards Gabi, "and coincidentally I have not finished, as you can see." He stroked the hair from Gabi's face. "Yes, we are going to finish the job today—finish it well."

John stood in front of Gabi and slowly, deliberately unbuttoned her oversized shirt. He untied the knot and let the shirt hang open. Gabi wore her sports bra, her breasts standing firm and in her fear her nipples were erect and very obvious. John drew his hunting knife from its sheath. Gabi's eyes widened at the sight of the huge blade and she struggled frantically. John neared and held the blade in front of her face. She whimpered as he slid it between her breasts and cut the material. He went on to cut the straps, jerked the severed bra from beneath her shirt and threw it on the ground in front of Geoff.

Gabi sobbed as she hung helplessly from the gantry with her breasts exposed, her legs bare—her very being naked to these vicious men. Geoff noticed how they began to fidget as they stared at her. John lifted his hands and fondled Gabi's breasts. He took her nipples between his thumb and forefinger and squeezed hard. Gabi cried out with pain and humiliation and Geoff's heart screamed. He realised that this stripping of her dignity was only the beginning. As terrible and hopeless as it was he decided that should his planned rescue attempt fail, he must try and put Gabi out of her misery and, for that matter, Sven too. They would suffer terribly at the hands of these savages, for Geoff was convinced that John was a madman. Should there be enough time, he must rob them of the satisfaction of torture and take his own life as well. It was during this thought process that he noticed that John held no rifle; instead he had a Tokarev pistol strapped in a holster at his side. It would take a few seconds to bring that weapon onto target. *He must die first*, Geoff decided; the others would not be as vigilant as John.

"Operation Brolly Tree—two thousand of my countrymen killed and our headquarters destroyed!" John pointed down the driveway. "And there are another five comrades—dead. Killed by your bullets and now you will pay!" he shouted as bubbles of spittle flew from his lips. "You can watch as we take your woman—all of us. When we have finished we will put a stake in her and then one in you and one in the brat. After that you can watch and listen to each other die." Geoff followed John's gaze. Near the door and supported between two fencing standards were a pile of wooden stakes with sharpened points used for supporting newly planted saplings. Geoff shuddered.

This was it. Time was running out. Where was the opportunity? Where was the gap he was waiting for? There was only one more chance. When John turned to Gabi then was the time to act. Geoff glanced up at the butt of the AK and waited for John to turn.

A loud crack rang out. One of the terrorists standing opposite Geoff crashed back through the slats. Two more cracks. The whip of bullets filled the air. They rocketed through the sides and back of the shed allowing shafts of sunlight to penetrate. The second man lifted his weapon and his head burst. A pink cloud hung in the still air as the terrorist disappeared behind the wall of the shed.

Geoff had been poised for any distraction. He ripped Sven from his chest and bundled the boy unceremoniously under the workbench. He stood and grabbed the assault rifle, spinning around and smashing the raised front sight of the AK into the face of the man who had hit him so brutally. It caught him in his eye, sinking deep as Geoff ripped it out in a desperate attempt to bring the AK to bear on the other sentry. The eyeball burst and blood and liquid pumped from the hole in the terrorist's head as he hit the ground screaming. Half-turned and off balance, Geoff ducked instinctively. He knew he'd taken too long and the terrorist attacked with his knife. Geoff had his rifle. It was the fall that saved Geoff and the blade thumped into the wood of the workbench. Geoff lay on his back, hauled up the barrel and fired from his waist. There had been no time to check. The selector was set on automatic and a fusillade of bullets tore through the terrorist's torso. It lifted him clear off the ground and flung him on his back at the foot of the gantry. There were still two more enemy—and John.

John was gone! Geoff rolled over, fearful of the two remaining terrorists. There was no need. One lay on the sand in the middle of the yard, his body twisted at an impossible angle. The second terrorist fired his AK frantically. Suddenly he dropped his weapon and ran backwards as crack after crack sent bullets thumping into his body. The smell of cordite hung in the hot afternoon air and an uneasy silence followed. Geoff edged around the workbench to the opening of the shed. He hesitated at the door and slid to the ground. He glanced and withdrew his head. He frowned. It couldn't be. A tall man carrying an R1 appeared at the entrance. The man busied himself with lighting a cigarette.

He lifted his head, exhaled a cloud of smoke and smiled at Geoff. "Having yourself a grand old time, hey Engelsman?" asked Dawid casually. "I loved the part when that kaffir started taking Gabi's clothes off." He walked past Geoff and Gabi, into the gloom of the shed and aimed his rifle suddenly. "Don't try it! I'd love to blow your balls off, you black bastard!" Slowly, painfully John lifted himself from behind the old tractor block. "Come here Mister fucken Grootvoet. I've wanted this for a long bleddy time." John hobbled over to the gantry, his pain evident. His face was grey and he bled profusely.

Geoff's mouth hung open. It had all happened so quickly. "Gabi," he said and turned to her. He pulled at the strips of rag that bound her to the gantry. Gabi called a warning but too late Geoff felt his head explode. He flew from the gantry and crashed into the picks and shovels stacked against the wall. He felt fresh blood pour down his forehead and over his eyebrow. He lifted his arm and wiped it away. "What the hell did you do that for? What the fuck are you trying to do?" yelled Geoff. He was sick of being beaten and of being afraid. He was sick of the killing and the hurt and the insanity. Adrenaline coursed through his veins. Murderous anger threatened to swamp him.

"Humour me and stand on this side of the gantry, please corporal. You don't mind if I call you corporal, do you hey?" asked Dawid. Geoff looked around frantically. Dawid shook his head and smiled. "Is this what you're looking for?" He held up the AK that Geoff had used. Geoff hung his head and Dawid laughed raucously. He threw the AK to one side.

"What the hell do you want, Gouws?" asked Geoff and a new fear spread through his body. Dawid's eyes were the same as John's. His usual green eyes were dark pits. Was Dawid also mad?

"Just do as I say and move over to the gantry." Dawid used the barrel of his rifle as a pointer. Geoff moved next to Gabi. Dawid stood back and surveyed them with a stilted look. "Ah," he said, "what a sight. I can't decide what to do next," he paused theatrically and pointed the barrel at Geoff, "kill you or the kaffir first." He walked around to John and looked into his face. "I'll get a medal and promotion for your scalp." Dawid stood back and rubbed his chin thoughtfully. "On second thoughts, your woman looks like someone I'd like to fuck, hey Geoff?" Dawid walked closer and rubbed the barrel of his rifle between Gabi's legs. "Lovely tits too, hey." He looked at Geoff and smiled without humour. "Is she a good fuck, hey corporal?" Dawid stood back again and looked at them. Geoff parted his legs, came up onto the balls of his feet and bunched his fists. Dawid noticed the movement and swung the barrel to cover Geoff. He smiled. "So, she must be good if I managed to get you so pissed off, hey?" Dawid snarled suddenly, "If you come at me I won't even get my hands sore; I'll shoot you like a dog, Kent." He glared at Geoff until he saw the fight go out of him. "I think I've solved half the problem; I'll shoot you two first and then because she's all trussed up and ready for me, I'll screw Gabi. What do you think of that, hey corporal?" Dawid shook his head. "The only problem I have is who to kill first."

A quiet, timid voice interrupted them. "Perhaps you'd let me choose." They looked up and Dawid spun around as Valerie stepped up to the threshold of the shed. She looked awkward with the huge double-barrelled shotgun held at the level. It looked too big for her small frame. Valerie looked at John and then looked at Dawid and with horror she saw their eyes were the same.

"Darling ... I ... wait ...," began Dawid as he lifted his hand towards her. A shot rang out. It was deafening in the confines of the shed. It was followed by a second and a third, fourth, fifth and a sixth. Each time the shots rang out Dawid took a step forward. John held the Tokarev pistol in his hand and smoke drifted up from the barrel. He frowned and his eyes grew wide in amazement. Geoff too stared incredulously as Dawid turned, his body awash with blood from the heavy bullets. "You shouldn't have done that, kaffir. Now I'm going to kill you first." Dawid spoke almost conversationally. Valerie lifted the shotgun, aimed the long, smooth barrel and fired. A massive boom dwarfed the Tokarev shots and every ball of large game shot smashed into John's stomach. It ripped his innards and dragged them through his body. They burst through the muscles and sprayed them out of the flesh of his back. One of the heavy balls hit his spine and crushed the bone to splinters. Having the muscles of his lower abdomen ripped away, John's body bent over before he collapsed to the ground. He was all but cut in half as he looked up at Gabi. His mouth opened and closed like a fish at the edge of a polluted stream. He glared at her with such hatred and malice. In his madness he still managed to lift the Tokarev. A second shot boomed out and the upper torso rolled away from the legs. Valerie lowered the shotgun slowly and sank to the ground below Gabi. She stared at the body for a while. Then she began to rock back and forwards on her haunches, her hands clutched to her bosom, her eyes devoid of emotion.

Quickly Geoff walked over to Dawid and grabbed the rifle. Still he couldn't believe it as he stared into Dawid's eyes. He looked slightly disoriented but he remained standing and Geoff looked down. Already a pool of blood was forming at his feet.

He turned his head and looked at Geoff. "I was never going to shoot you or harm Gabi, " he said quite clearly and sank to the ground.

Geoff grabbed him and helped him down. He propped Dawid up against the wall, looked him in the eye and placed a tremulous hand on his shoulder. "Stay with us Dawid, I must rescue Gabi."

Dawid looked up, his eyes were sunken and he smiled. "Go save her Geoff," he slurred.

Geoff stood, yanked the hunting knife from the workbench and hurried over to Gabi. He reached up and sawed through the rags. Gabi collapsed forward onto Geoff and he steadied her as he cut the rags from her ankles. He carried her to the workbench, lowered her onto it, squatted and peered underneath. Sven sat there owl-eyed and unmoving, his cheeks wet. Geoff held out his hand and Sven ignored him. He sat motionless, staring, his eyes glazed.

Geoff smiled. "You are the bravest boy in the world. It must be because you ride your bike faster than anyone I know." Sven's eyes seemed to clear and focus on Geoff.

"I want my mama," he whispered, prompting a fresh bout of sobs.

"She's right here," said Geoff softly.

"Where?" came the small voice.

Geoff pointed up. "Right above me. Take my hand."

Sven looked around slowly. "Where are the baddies?"

"All gone, boy. All dead." Geoff nodded towards his hand. Sven lifted his arm and reached towards Geoff. "That's it. Come on. Mommy wants to see you." Sven clambered over the strut and grabbed Geoff who held him and hugged him fiercely. He extracted himself from below the workbench and stood up with Sven holding on tight. Sven saw his mother and launched himself at her. Geoff had to hold on lest the child fall to the ground. Gabi grabbed her boy and sobbed.

"Oh my boy! Oh my brave little boy! I love you more than all the world. Thank you! Thank you for being mine!" She sobbed and smiled up past him at Geoff. He smiled back at her and suddenly her smile evaporated. "Look at you! My God, look at you!"

"Yeah, I can imagine." Geoff leant on the bench and looked down at the two people he loved most. "You don't look so bad yourself. You're going to have to look after those lovely hands too," he said as he helped her button up her shirt.

Gabi lifted her hands and rotated them. They were blue and swollen. "Oh no Geoff, what am I going to do?"

"They'll heal."

She shook her head. "Please help me up," she said and Geoff put his arm around her and lifted her into a sitting position. She swung her legs over the edge of the bench and looked around. "My God," she whispered in horror. "What a massacre." She looked around a little longer and then looked at Geoff.

Valerie had moved to Dawid's side. She leant against him and caressed his face. He was deathly pale. He wouldn't last much longer. Geoff suddenly felt an overwhelming guilt.

"I should get an ambulance …"

"What!" said Gabi explosively. "For that … that monster!"

"He needs help Gabi. He's very confused but he told me he would never have harmed us. We have to take that and hold onto it because he saved our lives." Geoff swallowed and looked at them and then at Gabi. "He saved my life more than once. I owe him," said Geoff simply. He pushed himself away from the bench and ran out to the cottage. He skidded to a halt in the yard as a Land Rover followed by a Buffel drove up past the cottage and ground to a dusty halt in front of him. The passenger door swung open and a hard-faced army staff sergeant stepped out. He wore a red band on his arm with white lettering emblazoned on it. MP it said. The staff sergeant stood, placed his police cap with the red band onto his head, tilted it low over his eyes and looked up. He started visibly as he saw Geoff's bloody face and the litter of bodies.

"*Wat!* he exclaimed. *"Wat het hier gebeur?"* The staff shook his head as if to clear it and looked around. "What the hell happened here?"

"We were attacked and we fought back. What the hell are you doing here?"

Benade pushed his cap to the back of his head, exhaled loudly and looked about. "I … um … I am looking for Lance-Corporal Dawid Gouws. He's supposed to be on the nextdoor farm but the workers said he'd come here for a visit."

"Well, he certainly did come here for a visit. He shot the shit out of Grootvoet and his men and saved our lives," said Geoff. "Why are you looking for him?"

"Well … um, he's been charged with murder. You know …," Benade was embarrassed now. "Those old folk. Um, the kraal chief … shit, you know the story."

"Yep, a bunch of useless terrorist harbourers were killed and a hero is going to take the fall," said Geoff with intended sarcasm. He nodded his head over his shoulder. "He's in there. Have you got a radio? We need to call in a casevac. We've got wounded here."

"Yes, yes of course. Please speak to the corporal in the Buffel."

"You bring a whole section to escort one man? Shit, you must be terrified of him." Geoff put his hands on his hips and shrugged, "Mind you he *is* a real soldier." Geoff turned to the Buffel, "Corporal! Corporal!" he shouted. The man looked over at Geoff. "Call up a Puma for casevac immediately, please."

"Sure," the section leader turned to his radioman and nodded. "You heard the man."

Together Geoff and Staff Sergeant Benade walked into the shed. Benade stopped and looked around, his eyes widening as they became accustomed to the gloom. Geoff motioned for the staff to follow. He stopped next to Dawid and Valerie. She continued to caress his face, speaking softly to him. His breathing was shallow, his eyes closed and his forehead was covered in tiny beads of sweat. Valerie lifted her head, whispered something and he managed a smile. Geoff squatted next to him and placed his hand gently on Dawid's shoulder.

"I've called in a Giant."

Dawid opened his eyes at the new voice and looked at Geoff. His green eyes were glazed and he frowned. "Is that you Geoff?"

"Sure is buddy. There's someone here to see you though God knows I should tell him to piss off. It's an MP."

Dawid managed a smile, followed by a weak cough. Blood trickled down the corner of his mouth. "So, they want me after all. They're going to call it murder?"

"What's this all about Geoff? Can't you all go away? I want to be with him—alone," said Valerie in a tone devoid of expression.

"This man just wants to ask Dawid something and then I'll personally see him off the farm," said Geoff. She nodded and remained next to Dawid, holding him. Valerie took a embroidered handkerchief from her jeans pocket and dabbed at his forehead.

Benade got to his knees and leant close to Dawid. "The old folk in the kraal …," he began softly as Dawid closed his eyes and nodded. "Did you kill them?" Dawid nodded almost imperceptibly. Benade looked up at Geoff and then back at Dawid. "Did you murder them?" he asked. Dawid shook his head. He opened his eyes and tried to answer. He looked at Geoff and lifted one finger, summoning him. Geoff leant close to Dawid and placed his ear next to the dying man's lips. After a long while Geoff nodded and sat up. He cleared his throat and took a deep breath.

"They were harbouring terrorists and he killed them. He never murdered anyone." He looked at Benade. "You should go now and tell your authorities that this man deserves a bloody Honoris Crux. In fact he needs one for every time he's saved our section."

Staff Sergeant Benade stood, looked down at Dawid and sighed. "I'm sorry," he whispered, "I'm so sorry."

Geoff nodded and felt a presence at his side. Gabi stood there holding Sven on her arm. She looked at him and saw the misery in his face and slid her free arm around his waist. Geoff hugged her to him and Valerie continued whispering soothingly to Dawid. No one moved for a while and Staff Sergeant Benade made to leave. He was about to turn away when Dawid sighed deeply and died. Valerie wiped Dawid's brow and gently closed his eyes. Her expression was unchanged but for the tears that slid down her cheeks.

Geoff turned away quickly and strode outside. The sunset was beautiful as the first thunderclouds boiled up into the atmosphere, giving life to the horizon. The setting sun played with the colours of red and purple, reflecting them onto the great clouds. The familiar silhouette of a Puma helicopter passed across the transient canvas.

Benade stood next to Geoff and looked up at the helicopter. "My corporal will shoot some flares. We'll stay and help with the clean-up … if that's okay with you?" Geoff nodded and turned to look for Gabi.

"I'm right here, my love. I'm right here with you," she said. Geoff engulfed her in his arms and dropped his head onto her shoulder.

"He told me he loved me, you know. He said he was sorry … he really meant it," said Geoff and fell silent. After a while he cleared his throat and continued. "He wished us both God's speed and asked that we look after Valerie. He never said anything about the old folk." Geoff stood back at last and held Gabi at arms' length.

Her face was wet as Geoff succumbed finally, venting his grief with tears.

Gabi reached up and placed her free arm around his neck. Geoff shook his head and whispered in her ear. "I don't know what to do next. For the first time in my life I don't know what to do …"

"You will just stay here with us. We need you. I need you." Gabi squeezed hard. "I love you with all my heart Geoff."

He nodded. "I needed to hear that more than anything else … I need you too. Both of you," he whispered and they turned their backs as the Puma churned up the dust.